BENVENUTI·

THEIR LIVES WERE THREADS IN THE GOLDEN WEB OF KARMA

JEBU—The valiant Zinja. It was his destiny to ride beneath the White Dragon banner of the fierce Muratomo family . . . to kill the slayer of his father . . . and, against all odds, to love the woman who could never be truly his.

LADY TANIKO—Fate had given her to a cruel husband—but would lead her to the gilded gates of worldly power . . . and even to the Shogun himself.

HORIGAWA—A prince of the Takashi camp, he abandoned Taniko to the barbarians' mercy.

YUKIO—The Muratomo heir who is marked for death by the triumphant Takashi clan. Exiled in China, he and Jebu battle the Mongol fury of the Great Khan, Emperor of the World.

KUBLAI KHAN—Wondrous ruler, warrior, and lover, he would decide the outcome of Jebu and Taniko's love.

**SHIKE
BOOK 1: TIME OF THE DRAGONS**

By Robert Shea
from Jove

SHIKE

SHIKE

BOOK 1
TIME OF THE DRAGONS

A NOVEL BY
ROBERT SHEA

A JOVE BOOK

Requests for permission to make copies of any part
of the work should be mailed to: Permissions,
Jove Publications, Inc., 200 Madison Avenue,
New York, NY 10016

The author gratefully acknowledges quotations from the following:
    Excerpts from *China's Imperial Past* by Charles O. Hucker, with the
permission of the publishers, Stanford University Press. © 1975 by
the Board of Trustees of the Leland Stanford Junior University. These
excerpts include four lines from the poem "Thinking of My Brothers
on a Moonlit Night" and an adaptation of three lines from page 103
of the book, appearing on pages 125 and 126 respectively of *Shike: Time
of the Dragons*.
    Excerpts from *The Pillow Book of Sei Shonagon*, translated by
Ivan Morris, with the permission of the publisher, Columbia University
Press. © 1967 by Ivan Morris. Excerpts include lines from the
poem "The Song of the Lute" by Po Chu-I, appearing on page 70 of
Shike: Time of the Dragons.

First Jove edition published June 1981

First printing

Printed in the United States of America

Jove books are published by Jove Publications, Inc.,
200 Madison Avenue, New York, NY 10016

To Ruth D. Shea,
my mother,
who taught me to admire
all the peoples of the world

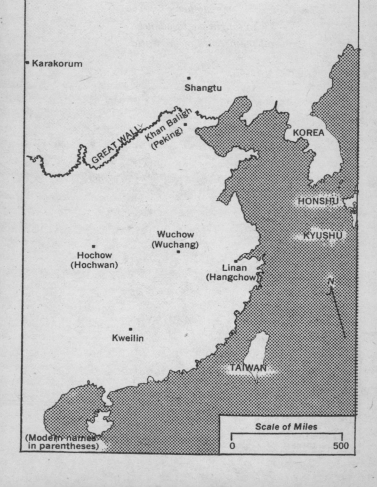

CHINA

Karakorum

Shangtu

GREAT WALL

Khan Baligh
(Peking)

KOREA

HONSHU

KYUSHU

Wuchow
(Wuchang)

Hochow
(Hochwan)

Linan
(Hangchow)

N

Kweilin

TAIWAN

(Modern names
in parentheses)

Scale of Miles

0   500

JAPAN

HOKKAIDO

LAND OF OSHU

Hiraizumi (Maezawa)

KOREA

HONSHU

Tsushima

Shimonoseki Strait

Iki

Heian Kyo (Kyoto)

Tokaido Road

Kamakura

Hakata Bay (Fukuoka)

Nara

Inland Sea

SHIKOKU

KYUSHU

Ichinotani

N

(Modern names in parentheses)

Scale of Miles
0   150

PART ONE

THE BOOK OF JEBU

The Zinja does not find happiness in the
things of this world, because they do
not last. He does not find happiness in
eternal things, for there are no eternal
things. He finds his happiness in
nothing at all.

—*The Zinja Manual*

1

They stripped Jebu naked. They threw his yellow aspirant's tunic into the fire bowl on the right side of the altar.

"You will not need that again. Tomorrow morning you will put on the gray robe of an initiate. Or you will be dead, and we will burn your body." Sitting on an unpainted wooden stool before the altar, Taitaro, abbot of the Waterfowl Temple, looked steadily at Jebu. Around his neck Taitaro wore the plain white rope that symbolized his office. He was Jebu's stepfather, but tonight his eyes said, I know you not. He would burn Jebu's body and throw the ashes in the rubbish pit if his son failed, and he would never look back.

The flimsy tunic flared up with a hiss, throwing sparks into the air. As it crisped and blackened, a rope of smoke coiled up to the dark cypress beams of the ceiling.

"As that tunic is reduced to ashes, so will your entire life be consumed this night. Know this, aspirant Jebu: whatever comes to pass, whether you live or die, tomorrow morning you will be nothing." Taitaro's mouth was set in a straight line behind his short black beard, and his weary, deep-set eyes burned into Jebu's.

A monk on the left side of the altar struck a wooden club against a hollow log that hung suspended from the temple ceiling. A deep, musical boom resounded through the hall.

3

"Take the aspirant to the crypt," said Taitaro in his quiet voice.

Two gray-robed monks carrying blazing pine-knot torches stepped to either side of Jebu. The tops of their heads did not reach his shoulders. He stood straight, fighting the urge to stoop over and try to make himself shorter. It was so painful to be different from others. Had Taitaro deliberately picked the two shortest men in the monastery to stand beside Jebu, just to humiliate him?

The two monks took a step forward in unison, their wooden sandal soles clacking on the stone floor. Jebu stepped forward with them, starting off on the left foot as he had been instructed, his bare sole shrinking from the cold floor. He had better get used to pain. There would be much more of it before morning came. He walked with the monks around the black stone block that served the Zinja temple as an altar. In the dark wall behind the altar was the simple outline of a waterfowl, incised by a sculptor when the temple was built.

The monks said the Waterfowl Temple was so old it had been here when the sun goddess Amaterasu appointed her great-great-grandson, Jimmu, the first Emperor of these islands. It was a wooden framework with paper walls, standing on a platform of stone. The platform had been carved out of the rock of the mountainside. The Zinja kept no records, and no one knew exactly when the temple had been built. Pits, chambers and tunnels had been dug into the mountain beneath the temple, and with the passing centuries had grown deeper and more tangled, like the roots of an ancient tree.

Directly behind the altar was a square opening in the floor. Stone steps led down into darkness. Jebu had only been in the crypt three times before, when monks of the Order had died and their ashes had been carried there in procession.

One of Jebu's escorts gestured, and Jebu started down the steps of the crypt, feeling a strange, tremulous sensation near his heart. The torchlight did not reach to the bottom of the steps, and he seemed to be descending into total blackness. It frightened him, frightened him all the more because he didn't know what was going to happen to him. He had never been permitted to see an initiation, and there had been very few such ceremonies during the whole time he had lived at the temple.

The two monks followed him down the stairs. In the light of their torches Jebu could see the ninety-nine black stone jars standing on nine steps carved in the wall of the crypt. Every crypt in every Zinja temple contained nine times eleven urns. Each time a monk died, the leftmost urn on the bottom step was carried up out of the crypt, and the ashes in it were scattered on the ocean wind that beat against the temple all year round. Then the jar, refilled with the ashes of the monk who had just died, was put on the right side of the top step, while all the other urns were moved one space to the left. Over the years, death by death, the urn would travel along the steps until it reached the bottom of the crypt, and the ashes of a monk whose name by then had been forgotten would be thrown away.

"These are the relics of the brothers of our Order," said one of the monks with Jebu. "You have seen them before. You may not know that almost half of these jars are empty. The bodies of these brothers were lost. We put the empty urns here in their memory."

The other monk said, "Almost all the monks whose funeral urns are here were killed by men. They died in combat, or they were murdered, or they were executed. This is what a Zinja can expect—you are asking to be killed. And yet you want to be a Zinja. You are a fool."

Jebu guessed that the words were part of the ritual. He saw no need to reply.

The first monk said, "Now take that ring there in the floor, and lift it."

The ring, made of black iron, gleamed in the torchlight, having been polished by the grip of many hands. Jebu tugged at it. The Zinja were trained for strength, and Jebu, being bigger than most of the monks, was the strongest young man in the Waterfowl Temple. Even so, he could only slightly raise the great stone slab to which the ring was attached; then he had to let it fall back. One of the monks handed his torch to the other and helped Jebu. Together they slid away the stone. The monks gestured silently to him, indicating that he was to climb down into the chamber below the slab. It was a stone box with just enough room for him to lie down. The cold of the stone shocked his naked body; the little chamber was damp and smelled of mold.

"You will lie in this chamber and we will put the slab back into place. No matter what happens, you must not try to get out. If you do, you will die. It may *seem* that you are going to die if you do not escape, but you will die if you try to escape. Believe that, and believe nothing else that you hear from this moment on, until the Father Abbot himself comes to release you, at his pleasure."

Jebu lay in the stone box, staring up at the two monks. He had thought them short before; now they towered above him, their faces strange masks in the flickering torchlight. Together the monks pushed the slab into place. The darkness was total. He brought his hand up over his face and moved it from side to side, but he could see nothing. He was buried alive in a stone chamber the size of a coffin. It was made for people smaller than himself; the top of his head and the soles of his feet pressed hard against the ends when he lay at full length. There was barely room to move his hands away from his sides. And when he lifted his head he struck his forehead against the top of the chamber.

He was afraid, but not panic-stricken. He had begun his Zinja training at the age of four, learning to balance on wooden railings, to hang by his hands for hours, to run, to dive, to swim and to climb; but the first thing he had learned was mastery of fear in any threatening situation. "The purpose of fear is to drive us to preserve our lives," said Taitaro, "just as the purpose of hunger is to drive us to eat. But a Zinja is not interested in preserving his life. His aim is to lose the craving for life. Only those who have lost this craving are truly free." So, little children not yet able to read or write were subjected to sword thrusts, mock hangings, the bites of supposedly poisonous insects and snakes, and dozens of other frightening experiences. As the children dedicated to the Order grew older and harder and became proficient in the use of weapons, these encounters with terror, at first only simulated, became more realistic. The year before, one of Jebu's friends had died at the age of sixteen when he panicked and fell from a plank no wider than a man's foot which bridged a mountain gorge.

Jebu lay on his back in the dark in the stone coffin and wondered, not for the first time, whether the Order consisted of madmen and fools and whether he himself was the biggest fool of all. Why was he doing this? Because they got him when he was young. Because his father was killed and Taitaro married his mother and adopted him and put him through the training as a matter of course.

Though no light penetrated the stone above him, sound did, and Jebu heard approaching footsteps, and then a voice saying, "My son."

"Is that you, Taitaro-sensei?"

"Yes," said the abbot, his voice muffled but unmistakable. "We come now to the center of your initiation, to the truth which is to be revealed to you as a Zinja. This truth will sustain you through this trial and through all the ordeals of life to come. We call it the Saying of Supreme Power. Swear now before all the kami of this place, all the kami of the Order and all the great kami of these Sacred Islands that you will reveal to no one what I tell you now."

"I swear."

"Even if other brothers of the Order tell you they already know the Saying of Supreme Power and are only testing you to learn whether you know it, you must not repeat it to them. You must not even admit that you know it. On pain of expulsion from the Order, and even death, Jebu."

"I understand," said Jebu quickly, eager to learn what final truth lay locked at the heart of the Zinja mysteries.

"Then hear the Saying of Supreme Power." There was a silence in the absolute blackness. Then: "The Zinja are devils."

"What?"

"The Zinja are devils."

"Taitaro-sensei, I don't understand."

"Say it back to me. I want to be sure you heard me correctly."

Jebu hesitated. "I may not."

"Good. You have understood that much."

Jebu shook his head. He wanted to climb out of this stone box and seize his stepfather by the shoulders and shake him. "But, sensei, that is contrary to everything I've ever been taught. Is it a true saying, or is it just the kind of spell conjurers use to call up spirits? I don't see how it can be true. The Zinja are not—we are not—that."

"You do not know. You are not yet a Zinja. Farewell now, Jebu. I hope I shall see you in the morning."

Jebu was acutely conscious of the enormous weight of the stone suspended over him. It seemed suddenly as if there were no air to breathe. What could it mean: *the Zinja are devils?* He had been taught to believe that the highest calling a man might hope for—unless he were born to the robes of the Emperor—was to be a Zinja. Anyone, no matter how lowborn, could be a Zinja, if he could endure the training. Even an untouchable, a slave, a hairy Ainu from the north, even a barbarian foreigner. Yes, that was why he was a Zinja, because they would take anyone, even the strange-looking red-haired son of a man from across the western sea. But perhaps the Zinja would take anyone *because* they were devils. Devils would take anyone.

Something icy touched his shoulder blades. He wriggled to try to escape it, and his heart started pounding harder than ever. Was it the touch of a devil? The cold feeling spread to the small of his back, to his buttocks. He put his hand flat on the floor of the stone coffin in which he lay. Water. Water was trickling into the chamber from outside. The temple was at the edge of the sea; perhaps when the tide rose the water entered this box. No, unlikely. This chamber was high above the level of the sea. It was more probable that this was part of the ordeal. The water continued to rise. His back was submerged, the cold trickling into his armpits and freezing his groin, and his teeth began to chatter. He lifted his head as the water soaked into his hair and bumped his forehead painfully against the stone slab that imprisoned him. The water rose around the sides of his head and he grimaced and shook his head from side to side as it crept into his ears. He put his fingers into his ears to keep it out.

The water seemed cold enough to freeze his blood. He began automatically to twitch the muscles all over his body, in a regular rhythm he had been taught, to raise his body heat. The Zinja training enabled a man to endure freezing cold for hours. But how high would the water go? Another inch and it would drown him. Or else he would have to try to push that stone slab out of the way, even though he probably could not manage it and even though, if he succeeded in climbing out of the crypt, he would be killed. This was what they had warned him about: it may *seem* that you are going to die if you do not escape, but you *will* die if you try to escape. The water stopped rising when only the front of his face was still clear of it. He lay immersed, buried in the total blackness, shivering. How long would he have to stay like this? How long before he died of the cold?

There was a grinding noise above his head. The stone slab was moving.

"Jebu. It's Weicho and Fudo. Come out of there before you drown." A torch was waved over his head, its light blinding him after the hours—or was it only moments?—he had spent in the darkness. Gradually he made out the shadowed faces of the monks Weicho and Fudo looking down at him. They were a few years older than he, an inseparable pair, known for the slackness of their discipline, which had led Taitaro on one occasion to threaten to cast them out of the Order. Fudo was lazy and Weicho was cruel. It was rumored among the aspirants that they were lovers. Jebu had always disliked them.

"No."

"It's all right. The Father Abbot has given permission."

"I'll come out when he himself tells me to."

There was a silence, then Fudo, the taller and thinner of the two, laughed.

"You're a fool, Jebu. You'll drown in there. The purpose of the initiation is to test whether you think for yourself or follow orders blindly. If you follow orders blindly, you die."

Jebu said nothing. He was not following orders blindly. He was choosing to follow a particular order. He was making a judgment about which orders to follow and which not to.

Short, stout Weicho whispered to Fudo, giggled and said, "Jebu, you are the stepson of the Father Abbot and his favorite."

"I am the stepson of the abbot, but he has no favorite."

"You lie, Jebu. Listen. We know that the Father Abbot has shown you special favor. He has given you the Saying of Supreme Power."

Jebu did not answer. So this was what Taitaro meant when he warned against revealing the Saying to anyone.

"We want the power the Father Abbot has through the Saying. All of us were promised the magic Saying. Otherwise, do you think any of us would submit to this hell on earth of being a Zinja? We know now that only a favored few actually get it. The rest of us grub out our lives in poverty and misery, living on false hope until we are killed serving the Order. We are not among the favored, Fudo and I, because we have been caught disobeying some silly little rules of the Order.''

Fudo said, ''We intend to be miserable no longer. We know you have been given the Saying of Supreme Power, Jebu. You must give it to us.''

''I don't know any magic Saying. The abbot has been as a father to me only on the days when everyone spends time with his family. Otherwise, he is as distant from me as he is from anyone. He has given me no secret. What you are doing is wrong. You sow dissension in the Order.''

Fudo laughed. ''You think there is harmony in the Order, Jebu? The Order is riddled with hatred and treachery, just as you are lying to us now.''

The Zinja are devils. Was this what it meant?

Weicho said, ''Enough of this.'' He stepped away from the edge of the crypt and reappeared holding a naginata by its long pole, the polished steel blade glowing red in the torchlight. He thrust the weapon down into the pit. ''Feel this, Jebu.'' The sharp point pressed against Jebu's breastbone. He shrank away from it, and it scratched him. Weicho probed at him, pricking his chest in different places till the point of the naginata came to rest on the upper part of his belly, just below the rib cage.

''Tell us the Saying, Jebu, or I'll slice your belly open.''

'' 'A Zinja who kills a brother of the Order will die a thousand deaths.' '' Jebu quoted *The Zinja Manual*, the Order's book of wisdom.

Fudo snorted. ''That book is a collection of old women's tales. You are wrong, Jebu. The Father Abbot foolishly appointed us to guard you. We have only to say we killed you because you were trying to escape from the crypt.''

''I don't know any Saying.''

''Kill the dog and be done with it, Weicho.''

The instant Jebu felt the point of the naginata press harder against his skin, he swung his hand over and struck the weapon aside. With a quick chop of his other hand he broke the long staff into which the blade was set. The curved steel blade splashed into the water, and Jebu felt around for it. He grabbed the broken wooden end and held the naginata blade like a sword. But he still dared not climb out of the crypt.

"Come and get me," he said.

"Come and get us," said Weicho.

"He won't," said Fudo. "He still thinks he'll die if he comes out of that grave."

"Jebu," said Weicho softly, "we can make the water rise all the way to the top of your chamber. Tell us the Saying, or we'll drown you like a kitten."

"I don't know any Saying."

"Fare you well then, Jebu. May you be wiser in your next life." Jebu heard the grinding of the stone, then a heavy thud as it fell into place. Was the water higher? It might be.

He had learned, as had all aspiring Zinja, to slow his breathing so that he would need hardly any air. He could do that now, but he could not breathe under water. The water was now tickling the edges of his nostrils. He lifted his head and wriggled backward in the tiny space so that the back of his head was wedged in an upper rear corner of the stone box. It was an uncomfortable position, but no more so than hanging by his hands for hours in the course of Zinja training, and it was a position he could hold without conscious effort. He began counting his exhalations—one, two, three, four. . . . He went into a light trance.

He was riding on the back of a white dragon whose wings beat only once a minute, so powerful was each stroke. Far below he could see the four great islands of the Sunrise Land, Hokkaido, Honshu, Shikoku and Kyushu and the four thousand lesser ones. Then they were over the blue western sea. They sailed through a sky that was clear overhead, though he could see masses of gray-green thunderclouds to the south as if a terrible storm were rising there.

They passed over land. Below were enormous walled cities and palaces with red-tiled roofs along the banks of gigantic, winding rivers. He saw a stone wall fortified by guard towers that stretched on and on, like an endless, twisted bamboo pole, over grasslands and mountains and valleys.

A mighty army of men on horseback swept down toward the wall. All moved as one man, flowing in wavelike patterns over the land below. They breasted the wall like a flood cresting over a dam.

He saw a great battle being fought. The men on horseback met another army of men in horse-drawn chariots and scattered it, leaving the land littered with the dead.

Then the white dragon was drifting over a desert painted gold by the late afternoon sun. He saw the hide tents of savage people and their herds of cattle. The herders, dressed in furs, sat around smoky fires. The animals munched gray-green vegetation. He sensed that the dragon was carrying him backward through time as well as through space, and that the herders below would later become the terrible army on horseback he had seen in the land of huge cities.

Then he was flying toward a giant.

The giant was taller than the mountains around him, and he stood with one fur-booted foot planted on each side of a broad lake. His head was covered with a fur-trimmed steel helmet. He was dressed in furs, and there was a necklace of jewels around his neck. One great white jewel, larger than all the others, blazed on his chest. His face was hard and seemed like wind-worn rock. His green eyes glittered, and he laughed and stretched out his arms, sweeping clouds aside as the white dragon, with slow, stately wingbeat, flew toward him.

In a voice that shook the earth he said, "Welcome, little cousin, to your homeland."

2

Jebu felt himself being lifted by many hands. They stood him on his feet and rubbed him with warm blankets. Shivering still, he tried to fight off those who helped him. He must get back into the water-filled stone coffin until the Father Abbot called him.

"Jebu, awake." It was the voice of Taitaro. Jebu was

standing in the crypt, facing Taitaro. Behind Taitaro were the ninety-nine stone urns, and on either side of him stood Weicho and Fudo and the two monks who had brought Jebu into the crypt. Would he ever stop shivering?

"Come upstairs, Jebu," said Taitaro. "You can stand beside a brazier until you are warm again."

Wrapped in a heavy robe, Jebu stumbled up the stone steps on legs that almost refused to move, a monk supporting him on either side. Taitaro led the way. They bundled Jebu back into the main hall of the temple and led him to a pile of cushions beside a charcoal brazier. He sat facing Taitaro in front of the altar. All the monks of the chapter sat cross-legged on the floor, in rows, their gray hoods pulled over their heads. The temple was still lit by candles set in bronze lamps suspended from the ceiling. The sun had not yet risen.

"Tell me everything that happened during the night," said Taitaro.

Jebu began his account, not with his visit from Taitaro, but with what happened between himself and Weicho and Fudo. The two sat grinning at him with infuriating audacity when he looked accusingly at them. Jebu went on to tell of his journey on the back of the white dragon and his encounter with the giant.

Taitaro said, "If you see an animal or bird in your initiation vision, it means that animal or bird has adopted you as its own. There is no kami more wise and powerful and fortunate than the kami of dragons. That you rode a white dragon suggests that your future may be bound up with that of the Muratomo clan, whose crest is the White Dragon."

"But what of the giant?" said Jebu.

"As you describe him, he could be either your father or your father's slayer, but there is nothing in the vision to suggest that he is either one. He is most certainly one of your father's countrymen. He must be a powerful spirit. That is why you saw him as a giant." Taitaro smiled. "It may require the rest of your life for you to unravel fully the meanings of what you have heard and seen this night. You have experienced an authentic vision and, I believe, achieved authentic insight. I welcome you into the ranks of the Zinja. Bring him the robe of a brother of the Order."

Joy flooded through Jebu like the golden sunlight that had

bathed the desert in his vision. The wings of the dragon he
had seen in that vision suddenly seemed to be his. Still seated
on the cushions, his eyes fixed on Taitaro, he soared inwardly. He had passed the testing, and he had at last the prize he
had worked for since early childhood.

A monk stepped forward with a gray robe draped over his
outstretched arms. Jebu looked beyond him and saw the
sapphire light of morning through the open doorway of the
temple. The monk helped Jebu pull the gray robe on over his
head. The Zinja robe was really more of a tunic, stopping just
below the knees. The sleeves came halfway down the forearms. On the left side of the robe was sewn a circular patch of
white silk on which a willow tree was embroidered in blue
thread. It seemed a simple garment, but it was lined with
hidden pockets to accommodate a variety of Zinja weapons
and tools. A strip of gray cloth belted the robe. Jebu tied the
ends of the belt in the intricate world-serpent knot that the
Zinja always used for this purpose. He pulled the hood of the
robe over his head.

"Beyond this robe, you need possess nothing," said Taitaro.

In unison the monks chanted, "The gray is all colors. The
cloth is all matter. The Willow Tree is all time."

Taitaro said, "Bring him the bow and arrow of the Zinja."
Another monk stepped forward with the short, powerful,
double-curved compound bow which the Order had been
using for centuries, and a cloth quiver containing twenty-three
arrows with various heads—willow leaf, turnip head, frog
crotch, armor piercer and bowel raker. The monk slung the
bow and quiver over Jebu's left shoulder. Glancing at the
temple door, Jebu saw that the light in the sky was almost
white.

"You are warrior as well as monk, monk as well as
warrior," said Taitaro. "Take the bow and arrow with reluctance. Use the bow with dread. Grieve for those who fall to
your arrows. But make every arrow count."

The monks chanted, "The arrows kill desire and point the
way to insight."

Taitaro said, "Bring him the sword of the Zinja."

A third monk stepped forward with a sword in a plain
wooden scabbard and belted it around Jebu's waist. Unbid-
den, Jebu drew the sword and held it out to look at it. The

Zinja sword was broader and about half the length of the swords most samurai used, but it was heavy and sharp and hard enough to cut through solid rock. The handle was longer and wider at the end than most samurai swords. Zinja swords were forged by the Order, using a secret process centuries old. As Jebu gazed at the sword, its polished steel surface suddenly reflected a blazing light that dazzled him. He looked at the temple doorway. The sun was rising. Its crimson edge appeared over the mountainside, silhouetting the pines that grew outside the temple.

Taitaro said, "Take the sword with reluctance. Draw it with dread. Grieve for those who fall to it. But make every blow count."

The monks chanted, "The sword is the Self, cutting through matter and time and penetrating to true insight."

Taitaro stood and raised his arms. "Welcome the new brother into the Order of Zinja!"

Suddenly, the temple, always so solemn and quiet, was pandemonium. The gray-robed monks threw back their hoods, baring their heads, and shouted for Jebu. They broke ranks and crowded around him, touching him, squeezing his hand, slapping his shoulder, hugging him. Many were openly weeping. Pride and joy buoyed him up like winds lifting a kite. He was a Zinja. Over the tops of the monks' heads he could see the full red disk of the sun framed in the temple doorway.

Then he remembered. Weicho and Fudo were on the edge of the crowd around him, smiling at him like the others.

Jebu broke free from the crowd of well-wishers and held up his hand. "Wait. Father Abbot, I have denounced these two before you. I demand that you pass judgment."

Taitaro laughed. "I judge them to be consummate actors. The testing by brothers of the Order is the climax of the ordeal an aspirant must undergo to become a Zinja."

"Ours is a hard task," said Fudo. "Our obedience to the Order lies in seeming to be disobedient."

"And our success is failure," said Weicho with pain in his eyes. "If we are clever enough to deceive the aspirant, it is we who must kill him."

Jebu wanted to ask if they had ever killed. He tried to remember whether any of the initiations that had taken place in his time had been followed by the mysterious disappear-

ance of the aspirant. He could remember only five initiations
and in all five cases he had not seen the aspirant afterward.

Taitaro said, as if guessing his question, "After an initiation
the newly ordained monk is immediately sent from the temple. The aspirants do not know what has become of him. That
way they cannot be sure whether any initiation ended in the
creation of a new brother or the death of an aspirant."

"I will be sent away now?"

"Yes. We'll go to my cell now, and I'll tell you where you
will be sent." Taitaro smiled. "Then you will have time to
say good-bye."

The house of the monks was built of cypress beams, roofed
over with bark shingles and screened with paper and bamboo.
It was somewhat sheltered from the seaside cliff on which the
temple itself perched. Beyond the house was the stable.

Jebu climbed the steps and entered the one-story building.
It was empty, the futons on which the monks slept rolled up
against the walls. The shoji screens around the abbot's cell at
the northeast corner of the hall were closed. Taitaro was
waiting for him there, drawing a screen aside and beckoning
him to enter.

Taitaro's cell was empty except for a simple dark brown
vase of irregular shape that stood on a low unpainted table in
one corner. In the vase was a deep red peony blossom flanked
by two willow branches. The screen on the east side of the
room was open, giving a view of the pine forest that grew on
the mountainside.

Taitaro was still wearing the white rope of office around
his neck. Slowly he took it off and placed it carefully on the
table before the vase. His dark, tired eyes burned into Jebu's,
and Jebu realized that Taitaro must not have slept the night
before. Taitaro opened his arms to Jebu, and they embraced
and stood silently together. It was Jebu who drew away first,
his mind full of the unspoken question, What does my father
think of me now?

It was Taitaro, though, who asked the first question. "Tell
me, Jebu, do you think I should have done anything to make
the ordeal easier for you?"

Jebu was shocked. "I would be shamed forever if I thought
you had done anything like that."

Taitaro smiled. It seemed to Jebu that he looked relieved. "Your ordeal was as painful as it has ever been for any Zinja. But we can't make the initiation as severe as life itself will be. For you, as for all of us, the worst is still to come."

Jebu remembered the words his stepfather had spoken to him as he lay in the stone coffin: *The Zinja are devils.* "May we speak of the Saying of Supreme Power?" he asked.

"Nothing can be gained by talking about it, and much could be lost that way. You must think it through—live it through—for yourself, in silence."

"Then tell me, Father. What has the Order in mind for me? Is there a task for me to perform?"

Taitaro chuckled. "There are more tasks than there are Zinja to perform them. You will go to Kamakura, a small city on the northeast coast of Honshu. You will serve the Shima, a very wealthy family which holds first rank in Kamakura. They are a branch of the Takashi clan."

"The Takashi," Jebu said. "The house of the Red Dragon."

"Yes. Even though your vision was of the White Dragon of Muratomo, your first task will be in the service of the archrivals of the Muratomo, the Takashi."

During his training Jebu had learned about the wars of the two great samurai clans, but now that he had passed through the death and rebirth of initiation, all that seemed rather remote to him. "Tell me again, sensei, why the Takashi and the Muratomo are such great enemies."

Taitaro recounted the story. The Emperors of long ago had had many wives and many sons. The Imperial family had grown so large that its support became an intolerable burden on the national treasury. It was decided to lop off some of the branches, give them new names and some land, and let them fend for themselves. The descendants of Emperor Kammu—he who built the capital at Heian Kyo—were called the Takashi. They took as their symbol the Red Dragon. The descendants of Emperor Seiwa were known as the Muratomo, and their crest was the White Dragon.

No longer dependent on the throne, the newly created families lost the gentle, refined ways of the Imperial Court and became tough and self-reliant. They took up arms to defend their lands against frontier barbarians and against other landowners who coveted their holdings. They armed their servants, who became known as samurai.

Meanwhile the Imperial army had dwindled to a few troops of exquisitely caparisoned courtiers who had neither the will nor the ability to wage war. And so, when there was hard fighting to be done, when great landowners rebelled against the throne, when the hairy Ainu attacked in the north, when pirates made the Inland Sea impassable, the Son of Heaven would call for help from his cousins, the Takashi and the Muratomo. The armed clans became known as the teeth and claws of the crown, and their samurai armies grew larger. Inevitably the two families became rivals, trying to outdo each other in feats of glory and conquest.

Inevitably, too, they became involved in the intrigues around the Emperor. There had always been factions jockeying for power around the throne, and those who failed at political maneuvering sometimes sought to win through force, with the help of the samurai. As a matter of course, whichever side the Muratomo took, the Takashi would support the opposing faction.

The competition between the Takashi and the Muratomo had turned into a blood feud four years earlier, when the Emperor's brother had raised a rebellion, claiming the throne for himself. The chieftain of the Muratomo clan came out in support of the pretender, setting up a stronghold in a palace in Heian Kyo and sending out a call for reinforcements.

One prominent member of the Muratomo family remained loyal to the incumbent Son of Heaven. This was Domei, captain of the palace guard. He had taken an oath to protect the Emperor, and he believed the rebel brother's claim to be false. Domei was the son of the Muratomo clan chieftain, so his decision put him in the agonizing position of fighting against his own father.

The Takashi also sided with the Emperor. The chieftain of the Takashi was Sogamori, a wily, bloodthirsty and ambitious warrior. Seeing that most of the Muratomo were backing the pretender, Sogamori saw his chance to ruin the rival clan by making war on them. Thus, the unhappy Captain Domei found himself fighting alongside the enemies of his clan.

Domei was a renowned and audacious fighter. In spite of his difficult situation he led the palace guard and his temporary Takashi allies in a night attack on the rebel stronghold. He burned it to the ground and captured his father.

The victorious Emperor now had to decide what to do with the leaders of the uprising. Since the coming of the Buddha's gentle way to the Sacred Islands, centuries ago, there had been very few executions. Those rebels who had survived the perils of battle might expect, in the normal course of events, no worse punishment than exile. The death penalty was meted out only to commoners, and then only when they were found guilty of murder or major theft. Sogamori now shocked the capital by calling for the execution of all the captured rebel leaders.

Sogamori had an ally close to the throne, Prince Sasaki no Horigawa, an Imperial adviser. Prince Horigawa pressed the demand for the death penalty in the Emperor's council. Finally the Son of Heaven decreed over seventy executions. Going beyond that, he commanded Domei to behead his own father, the Muratomo clan chieftain.

Ultimately, another Muratomo relative volunteered to perform the execution, then killed himself by cutting his stomach open.

"What a painful death that must have been," Jebu said. "Why would anyone deliberately do that to himself?"

"It is a new practice among the samurai," said Taitaro. "They kill themselves to expunge stains on their honor. But they don't want it to be said that they committed suicide from want of courage, so they inflict on themselves the most excruciating death imaginable."

Instead of rewarding Domei for his loyalty to him, the Son of Heaven had ignored him ever since, resenting Domei's failure to execute his father. The Takashi, on the other hand, enjoyed the Emperor's favor and were raised to new heights. Sogamori, the Takashi leader, became Minister of the Left, one of the Emperor's chief councillors.

Domei, still captain of the palace guard, was now chieftain of the Muratomo clan. He seethed with hatred for those who had engineered his father's death and his own disappointment. And all over the country small battles between supporters of the Takashi and the Muratomo would break out at the slightest provocation.

"It is into this cauldron that I am about to toss you," Taitaro chuckled, "to serve the Shima family of Kamakura."

"What will I do?"

"Lord Shima no Bokuden, chieftain of the house of Shima, is sending his daughter, Taniko, to Heian Kyo to be married to a prominent person there. You will escort Shima no Taniko to Heian Kyo for her wedding. Your party will journey down the Tokaido Road from Kamakura to the capital."

Jebu grinned delightedly. "Heian Kyo. I have been hearing about it since I was a child. The most wonderful city in the land. And soon I shall see it. And the famous Tokaido Road as well."

Taitaro shrugged. "I hope you won't be disappointed. Had we lived in earlier times, then you would have seen Heian Kyo in its glory. Now the city is tumbling down and overrun with brawling samurai. As for the Tokaido, much of the territory it passes through is controlled by the Muratomo. And the girl Taniko is a kinswoman of the Takashi. What's more, her husband-to-be is Prince Sasaki no Horigawa."

"The one who pressed for the executions of the Muratomo?"

"Yes. The Muratomo hate him even more than they do their Takashi foes." Taitaro stood. "Prince Horigawa comes of a Heian Kyo family that has an ancient name but little wealth. The Shima have an inferior name but great wealth and great ambition. Both sides look on the match as useful."

Together Jebu and Taitaro walked out of the monks' quarters. Taitaro went on. "But Lord Bokuden, Taniko's father, is one of the most tightfisted men in the Sacred Islands. Witness the fact that he is only willing to pay for one Zinja initiate to escort his daughter all that way through enemy territory. As for Horigawa, he is bloody-minded and treacherous, and has worn two wives to death already. And the Lady Taniko is a willful girl of thirteen. She has never met Horigawa, and my informants tell me she rebels fiercely against the match. She would rebel even more if she had met him.

"You are going to be in the midst of a very interesting situation."

Then Jebu found himself alone, standing at the edge of the cliff with the temple behind him, its peaked roof spreading low over the rock like the drooping wings of a huge bird. The sea wind blew against his face; the rising sun warmed his back. Below, the white-capped waves rolled in as regularly as the beating of a heart, carrying unreadable messages from the land of his father.

The women's quarters of the Waterfowl Temple were set back from the cliff, to the east and north of the main temple and a respectable distance from the monks' building. It was a distance that made little difference, because there was nothing in the Zinja rule to stop the men from visiting the women's quarters whenever they wished. In the past few years Jebu had been among those unattached monks who slipped into the women's quarters at night. There was great pretense of secrecy about such visits, but actually they were condoned by the Order.

As befit the wife of the Father Abbot, Jebu's mother, Nyosan, had the largest bedchamber on the eastern side of the women's quarters, with a view of the morning sun and the monastery garden. Amazingly, there were no other women in the building, or so it seemed when Jebu entered. Nyosan was sitting with her back to him, watching the red ball of the sun float above the small, wind-twisted pine trees. A singing board, placed so as to warn the abbot and his wife of intruders, squeaked under Jebu's foot as he entered the room. Nyosan's back stiffened.

"Mother."

Nyosan turned, looking at him with anguish and joy, and scrambled to her feet. "I have been waiting. I have been waiting oh, so long. This has been one of the two longest nights of my life." She did not have to tell Jebu what the other one was.

They held each other, and she wept in his arms. "My son, my only son. I died a thousand deaths for you. All last night and the weeks before that, when your father told me the time had come for your initiation."

They sat facing each other. Jebu's mother was not yet forty, but her face was lined and tired, though her eyes were serene now that she knew her son had lived through the Zinja ordeal. She wore a plain commoner's robe, as did all the women connected with the temple. Beside her there was a pot of hot rice gruel, a bowl of pickled vegetables and a basket of cakes. She handed him a cake. Smiling at her, he took it and devoured it in two bites. It was juicy and still warm. She handed him another and filled a small bowl with rice gruel. Except for the cakes, it was an ordinary Zinja breakfast.

"Was it truly dangerous? Might you have died?"

Jebu thought of protecting her from the truth, but instead said, "Yes." When tears came to her eyes he added, "Mother, I am a Zinja. The Zinja are dedicated to death. You must remember that I may die at any moment. Perhaps you should think of me as one already dead."

Nyosan wiped her eyes with her sleeve and shook her head. "Strange. Your father spoke that way to me, many times. When I told him I feared to lose him, he said, 'Think of me as one already dead. I have been condemned, and I await my executioner.' "

"Taitaro-sensei says they are going to send me away at once, Mother."

"He told me. And I may never see you again. But I am thankful for the years I have had with you, even though I know you are doomed, just as your father was doomed."

"To be alive is to be doomed," Jebu said.

Nyosan laughed. "Oh! Ordination in the Zinja has made my son a wise man. He is full of sayings that boom like the hollow log in the temple."

Jebu joined in her laughter. "You're right, Mother. My sayings are hollow. I know nothing."

"How could you be expected to know anything, a boy of seventeen years? You will know something of life if you live as long as I have. I have been the daughter of a peasant, and I became, barely out of childhood, the bride of a splendid foreign giant, rich with jewels. And your stepfather, Abbot Taitaro, he, too, is a strange and wonderful man. He has loved me fully, and I have been very happy. Not that I'm so old. I may be twice your age, but I'm still young enough to have babies. Only, what the monks call karma has decreed that Taitaro-sensei beget no babies. So you will always be my only son. My magnificent, red-haired, gray-eyed giant of a son. Live long, Jebu." She took his hands and held them. "Live long, long, long. Love. Marry. Be a father. Don't let the Zinja destroy you when you are still little more than a child. You are not just a Zinja, to be used and thrown away like a gray robe. You are Jebu. A man."

3

Above the gatehouse of the Shima mansion the Red Dragon banner of the Takashi snapped and sparkled in the clear autumn air. Two retainers armed with long naginatas lounged on either side of the entrance. When Jebu showed them the letter from Taitaro to Lord Bokuden they called inside, and the great wooden gate, reinforced with spike-studden strips of steel, swung open.

Jebu strode across the courtyard, his wooden-soled sandals crunching on the white gravel. Solid ground still felt strange under his feet after so many days on a deck. He was delighted to be off the trading vessel that had carried him through the Inland Sea and up the east coast of Honshu to Kamakura. Trained though he was to remain calm and meditative, he found the journey extremely boring.

He kept the hood of his gray robe pulled up over his head. He hated to see strangers staring at his red hair. His second robe was folded and tied at his cloth belt. His short Zinja sword swung at his side in its wooden scabbard, and his small bow and quiver were slung over his shoulder. He touched the Willow Tree patch sewn on the breast of the robe for reassurance as he approached the main house of the Shima compound.

A steward wearing a gray silk kimono met Jebu and conducted him into the main building of the compound, down a series of screened, shadowy passageways. Finally the servant slid back a shoji screen, announced Jebu and gestured for him to enter.

Lord Bokuden, chieftain of the Shima clan, was a small, bald man with a deeply lined face and a thin moustache.

23

Wearing a gold-embroidered green kimono, he sat before a
carved ebony table which Jebu recognized as a costly import
from China. On a scroll, he added up accounts with brush and
ink. One side of the small chamber was partly open to let
sunlight in.

Jebu felt himself disliking Shima no Bokuden at once. He
had heard that the Shima were grasping, cold and treacherous, and Bokuden looked as if he epitomized all those
qualities. The Shima were a branch of the great Takashi
family, but declining fortunes had reduced them to earn their
way through fishing, trading and, some hinted, piracy. Having fallen far, the family was rising again. They used their
profits as merchants to buy and develop tax-free rice land in
the Kanto Plain north of Kamakura. As wealthy landowners
they produced samurai sons, and hired bands of warriors.
Now they were the first family of Kamakura and were marrying
into the nobility of Heian Kyo.

Jebu bowed and said, "Initiate Jebu of the Order of Zinja,
here at the invitation of Lord Bokuden." He handed over the
letter from Taitaro, which Bokuden unrolled and read with a
suspicious frown.

"I suppose that as an ordained Zinja you should be considered a shike. However, since you are not even wellborn
enough to have a family name, I shall address you merely as
'monk.' Has your abbot explained this mission to you?"

As Jebu repeated what Taitaro had told him, Bokuden drew
a scroll out of a drawer in his chinese table and unrolled it,
revealing a map of Honshu. "This is the season of storms,
and the fishermen are turning to piracy. The season's catch
was poor. Therefore you will take the Tokaido Road to Heian
Kyo." His fingernail traced the thread of black on the map
between Kamakura and Kyo.

Jebu reflected that the trading vessel that had brought him
here had not encountered any pirates. But Bokuden undoubtedly knew more about piracy than he did.

"From here to Miya you will pass through country controlled by the Muratomo. The less attention you attract, the
safer my daughter will be. Surrounded as we are by Muratomo,
we would need an army to protect her if she were to travel in
the state appropriate to her family's station. My hope is that
you will slip out of Kamakura and get as far as Miya unno-

ticed. The whole journey down the Tokaido should take you from ten days to a month."

"I will need a horse."

"You have no horse? Are we expected to supply you with a horse?"

"I bring with me no more than what you see, my lord."

"I will supply the horse, then, and whatever else you need. But if you fail, monk, if anything happens to my daughter, you will die and I will seize all the wealth of your temple."

Jebu pressed his lips together to hold back an angry answer. Like all boors, Bokuden imagined that the Zinja hoarded vast wealth in the dozen temples they had scattered over the islands. But Bokuden was undoubtedly too cowardly to make any move against the Zinja. Surely he knew that those who offended the Order never lived long. In a casual-seeming gesture Jebu touched the Willow Tree patch on his chest. Bokuden looked into his eyes and swallowed.

"Armed monks are a plague on the country," he muttered.

"But they can make themselves useful, my lord," said Jebu. "If anything happens to your daughter, I shall certainly die. Because whoever would harm her must kill me first."

"I hope you live up to your brave words, monk. You will spend twenty days on the road with my daughter, who will have only two maidservants with her. Even if you are rather odd-looking, you are young, and subject to a young man's passions. What guarantee do I have that my Taniko will arrive in Heian Kyo—" Bokuden hesitated "—intact?"

"You are your own best guarantee of that, Lord Bokuden."

Bokuden frowned and pulled nervously at his moustache. "What do you mean?"

"Lord Bokuden would hardly raise a daughter so foolish as to give her virginity to a poor monk on the eve of her wedding to a prince of the Imperial Court."

"You are, perhaps, too clever, monk. Go now. My servant will show you where you may eat and sleep."

Jebu laughed to himself as he followed Bokuden's servant out of the courtyard.

Jebu was awake long before sunrise. He washed in a bucket of cold water and passed an hour in seated meditation in a corner of the yard. He made his mind blank by counting his exhalations up to ten, then starting over again. As the

edge of the sun appeared at the top of the bamboo palisade
that protected the Shima grounds, Jebu stood up and began
his calisthenics, a series of movements from position to position that looked like—and in fact, was—a vigorous, complicated dance. Next he drew his sword and performed his
sword drill.

Now he could hear the sounds of the household waking up.
An attendant in a gray cloak took him to the stable and
showed him the horse Bokuden had chosen for him. Jebu
examined it closely. It was a brown stallion with no outstand-
ingly good qualities, a little past his prime, but with no
serious defects either. He was called Hollyhock. Jebu was to
return Hollyhock to the Shima town house in Heian Kyo. The
selection of Hollyhock as his mount showed typical Shima
parsimony, Jebu thought.

Lady Taniko's party was beginning to gather. Two porters
loaded large, heavy packs on the backs of two ancient, wheezing mares. Those jades would be lucky if they survived all the
way to Heian Kyo. Servants in gray robes led three more
horses out of the stable. Jebu went and fetched Hollyhock. He
stood beside the brown stallion, holding his reins. The
maidservants, wrapped in identical peach traveling cloaks,
appeared on the porch of the women's house. They looked at
Jebu, whispered together and giggled.

Apparently the plan was for the women to travel on horseback. No self-respecting lady of Heian Kyo would ever ride in
anything but an ox-drawn carriage. Of course, no lady of
Heian Kyo would ever venture more than a few miles outside
the walls of the capital. It was a good thing the Shima ladies,
like most samurai women, were able to ride horseback. A
carriage could not negotiate the whole Tokaido Road from
Kamakura to the capital.

At last the Lady Taniko came out on the porch of the
northern building, the women's house, followed by a group
of children and a blubbering, middle-aged woman, doubtless
her mother. Lord Bokuden emerged with stately stride from
the central building and joined his family on the porch of the
women's house. All bowed low to him.

Jebu studied the girl he would be escorting halfway across
Honshu. She wore a lavender traveling cloak over a dark red
trouser skirt. She had a fine, pale complexion, a tiny, rounded

nose, a wide mouth and a pointed chin. Her gaze swung round to Jebu, and he felt as if the claws of a cat had raked his face. It was a surprisingly mature, candid look for a pretty thirteen-year-old girl. There was something ruthless, even cruel, in Taniko's eyes. Her look raised Jebu's hackles and excited him all at once. This baby chick could grow up to be a dragon.

"Is that gangling, ugly monk to be my sole escort?" Her voice was light and slightly metallic.

Bokuden said, "It is well known that one Zinja is the equal of ten samurai."

"If I know my family, it is more likely that ten Zinja are the equal in price of one samurai."

"I would not send you with this monk if I were not sure you were absolutely safe."

"It might serve your purpose better if I were raped and murdered by a gang of bandits on the way to Heian Kyo. Then you would have made the gesture of offering your daughter to the elderly and influential Prince Horigawa and be saved the expense of a wedding."

Jebu chuckled to himself, amused at the way she bore down on the words "elderly" and "influential." By the Willow Tree, the girl was shrewd. She might even be right. Perhaps the two of them were both being thrown to the sharks by this son of pirates.

Bokuden's seamed face was white with anger. "Keep up this disrespect toward your father before his household, and there will be no journey to Heian Kyo and no wedding. You will spend the rest of your life in a convent telling your troubles to the compassionate Buddha."

Taniko fell silent, her cheeks burning red. She has gone as far as she dares go in baiting her contemptible father, Jebu thought. Many times further than most daughters would have the courage to go. He liked her. She was brave. She was intelligent. She was witty. Indeed, she was destined to be a dragon, quite a beautiful one.

Servants helped Taniko and her maids to mount their geldings. The women rode sidesaddle. Jebu in the lead, the three women next, and the two porters on their baggage-laden old horses last, the party clattered out through the gateway. The

Shima gate shut on the weeping mother, the impatient father, the cheering children, the waving servants.

The Tokaido passed north of Kamakura, and they rode out of the city in that direction. From here on, five lives were in Jebu's hands. He reminded himself that a Zinja acts for the sake of action and does not concern himself with the outcome of what he does. Whether the party got to the capital or was massacred by Muratomo hirelings within the next mile should be as one to Jebu. Should be, but in fact he was nervous.

The horses' hooves thudded on the packed dirt street. The smell of fish—fresh fish, cooking fish and rotten fish—pervaded the air of Kamakura. Every so often as they rode out of the city Jebu looked back to see if they were being followed. There was no sign of it. Evidently the third daughter of Lord Shima no Bokuden was not of enough interest in Kamakura to attract even the hint of a threat.

As their road climbed into the hills, Jebu looked back at Kamakura. It was a city dominated by the sea; the heart of the city was clearly the collection of wharves and warehouses at the crescent-shaped waterfront, and its pulsebeat was the arrival and departure of its big fishing fleet. Ringing the dock area were the humble houses of the fisherfolk and those who worked on the wharves. Beyond them were the larger houses of the owners of ships and warehouses and of those who had grown wealthy trafficking in each season's catch. But at the outermost edge of the city, rising into the hills and far from the docks, were the newly built mansions of the great lords who were moving into Kamakura from the north, great land-owners like Lord Bokuden, whose estate, as befitted the first family of Kamakura, was visible from a long distance, the red Takashi banner standing out against the dark green trees growing near it.

Jebu noticed that Taniko was riding beside him. She never glanced back at her childhood home but kept her face resolutely turned forward. Perhaps the long journey ahead frightened her. Jebu turned to her with a smile and said, "Kamakura is as important in this part of the country as Heian Kyo is in the south."

Taniko's piercing black eyes glared at him. "Of what interest is the opinion of a ragged monk of an obscure order who has doubtless never poked his long nose out of the monastery before? Keep to yourself and do not speak to me again. I have troubles enough."

"In my Order we say, he who thinks himself a victim, makes himself a victim. But if you choose to consider yourself a person of many troubles, my lady, I wish you joy in your choice. And I respect your wish to brood over your sorrows in solitude." He spurred Hollyhock up the path ahead.

He felt not the least bit angry; he still liked the girl. In fact, that had been a rather neat touch, the business about his long nose. She was a keen observer; the nose was one of the things he'd inherited from his foreign father. Jebu felt pleased with himself that his Zinja training enabled him to remain calm and cheerful in the face of hostility from others. He hoped Taniko would not fret constantly about her grievances, though. That would be a heavy burden to carry all the way to Heian Kyo.

That night they stopped at the country home of one of Lord Bokuden's allies. From her baggage Taniko took the pillow she had slept on ever since she was a little girl. Its paint worn, its corners chipped, the wooden headrest gave Taniko a warm, safe feeling, just as a cherished doll or a favorite sleeping robe might give to another girl. In the pillow was a concealed drawer, its edges made to look like ornamental carving. Taniko opened the drawer and took out a notebook, its carved wood covers bound with decorative red and gold string. Also in the drawer were a brush, an ink stick and an ink stone. Using water she had brought with her to the bedchamber in a soup bowl, Taniko began to rub the stick on the stone to make ink.

From the pillow book of Shima Taniko:

People who cannot think for themselves are in the habit of saying fall is the most beautiful season of the year. I think it is too sad to be beautiful. I do not, like so many silly young girls, think sad things are beautiful. I see the lines of ducks flying overhead and think to myself that they are deserting us. They fear the coming of the cold that kills. I hear the murmuring of the insects in the woods and think to myself that soon they will all freeze to death.

And for my life, too, the summer is over. I am to become the wife of a man whom I have never seen, but who, I have heard, is old and cruel. Like winter, he will chill me through and through. But this also means I leave the rustic back-water of Kamakura to live in the city I have always longed to see, the capital, Heian Kyo. To see and walk among the exalted people who rule this Sunrise Land! It has always been my dream to move among the great ones. If I must suffer a misconceived marriage in order to climb above the clouds, I am willing to pay that price.

My father, it seems, is unwilling to pay much to insure that I travel safely, judging by the strange youth he has hired to protect me. One hears dark tales about this sinister Order of Zinja, that their warriors are aided by evil spirits and that no one is safe from them. One also hears interesting things about the goings-on between the Zinja monks and their temple women. I wonder if this one has ever been a lover. He is so huge and of such an odd color, I would be afraid to let him near me. But if he were near me, I would be afraid to refuse him whatever he wished. There is some-thing pleasurable in the thought of a man who makes one feel helpless. The Zinja monk's presence makes this journey far more interesting.

—*Seventh Month, twenty-third day*
YEAR OF THE DRAGON

4

The white cone seemed to block out half the sky. Every time Jebu looked at it, he gasped again. He had never seen a mountain of this size. No one had warned him that on this journey he would behold such a marvel.

He had seen it from a distance as they rode into the hills above Kamakura, but then it was small and far off. As they crossed the neck of the Izu Peninsula he began to grasp its size. Its simple symmetry astonished him; the way its snowy peak reflected the colors of the day, from rose to white to gold, brought tears to his eyes. But it was only today, approaching Hara, that he had a full sense of the silent volcano's immensity. Yesterday he had spoken to no one of his feelings about the mountain. Today, as it happened, the Lady Taniko was riding beside him. He overcame his hesitancy and addressed her.

"Please, my lady, what is the name of that magnificent mountain?"

She turned to him slowly, her face a mask of exaggerated surprise and contempt. "You mean you've never heard of Fuji-san? Truly, the Zinja are ignorant as well as poor and miserable."

She lowered her head so that the brim of her circular sedge hat hid her eyes. She pulled her horse's head around abruptly and trotted back down the road toward her maids. The sudden movement startled two cranes in the nearby reeds, and they flapped upward until they were two tiny silhouettes in the sky above Mount Fuji.

The journey down the coast was slow. No one spoke to Jebu. Taniko and her maids apparently considered him beneath their notice, and the porters were afraid of him. The days were punctuated only by frequent rainstorms and the necessity of passing innumerable toll barriers. Every so often the road would disappear altogether, and they would have to pick their way along boulder-strewn beaches or through pathless woods.

The baggage included a small tent, which the ladies used for sleeping outdoors and as a shelter in wet weather. Jebu and the two porters took turns standing watch when the party slept out of doors. When possible they stayed at monasteries or at the homes of Lord Bokuden's friends, several of whom had built castles overlooking the Tokaido.

One sunny afternoon, eight days after they set out, they were riding single file along a hillside that rose sheer out of the sea, when the porter leading the way suddenly threw up his hands. He fell from his horse, rolled over and over down the hill, arms and legs flailing, and disappeared with a great splash amid the brown rocks and blue-white breakers. Jebu got a glimpse, as the man fell, of the gray and white feathers of an arrow protruding from his chest.

Jebu clenched his fists and ground his teeth with rage. He had failed. Because he had chosen this particular afternoon to bring up the rear, he had let the porter ride to his death. A life that had been in his keeping was lost. He shut his eyes momentarily and reminded himself that a Zinja is aware at all times of his own perfection, regardless of circumstances. Then, shaking his head angrily, he spurred Hollyhock up the path to put himself between the rest of the party and the attacker.

Blocking the road was a big samurai in box-shaped, many-plated leather armor, mounted on a black roan horse. In one hand he held his longbow—a bow that must have required three men to bend it for stringing. Beside him stood three tsuibushi, each holding the foot soldier's favorite weapon, the long-handled naginata.

Jebu estimated that the samurai was not quite as tall as he was. Bareheaded, he wore his greasy hair pulled back tightly and tied in the round black knot of hair by which the samurai identified themselves. His beard was raggedly trimmed. He had the pink eyes and permanent flush of the heavy sake drinker. Jebu recognized the type at once: a rustic bully, too in love with fighting and drinking to settle down to farm work. Doubtless the terror of the neighborhood when young, enjoying his pick of the girls. One who might as easily have become an outlaw but who, through some accident of birth or social connection, was made a local official and could legally prey upon the peasants. Growing more cruel, more dangerous, more unpredictable as he got older and the futility and boredom of his life began to eat at him. At bottom, most samurai were like this man, though some were born to greater wealth, were more competent in the arts of fighting, traveled farther and did better for themselves than others. The samurai saw themselves as noble and redoubtable warriors. The Zinja saw them as destructive, dangerous and stupid, like small boys whose parents have foolishly permitted them to play with knives.

Jebu reined up Hollyhock a short distance from the samurai and his men and said, "You.have murdered an unarmed man. You will answer for it to the oryoshi of this district. We will demand justice."

The samurai laughed and struck his leather-armored chest with a gauntleted fist. "Then you must demand it from me. I'm the oryoshi here. I enforce the law in this place."

The words and the man's bearing made it clear: they would have to fight. Jebu began to compose himself in the Zinja manner. *Your armor is your mind. A naked man can utterly demolish a man clad in steel. Rely on nothing but the Self.* Here it was, his first combat, the moment toward which his life had pointed for the last seventeen years. The bottom of his stomach felt hollow. Yet, for a Zinja, every combat was the first, and the first was like every other. So they said in the monastery.

Now he would see. Now he would have to try to kill a man. He had been trained to do it. He knew ten thousand ways to kill. But could he really do it?

He heard hoofbeats on the stony road behind him. Taniko's metallic voice said, "That man you killed was a servant of Lord Shima no Bokuden of Kamakura. You will answer to Lord Bokuden and his allies, oryoshi."

Jebu kept his eyes on the samurai. "Get back, my lady, back behind everyone else."

"I am responsible for my father's servant."

"And I am responsible for you. Back. Now." He admired her courage. It was what he expected, having seen her confront her father.

The samurai smiled broadly. Several of his front teeth were missing; others were yellow. "Your father's name means nothing here, my lady. This is Muratomo territory, and I am their ally. We are the only true warriors in the land, living and dying by the sword. We're not effeminate courtiers like the Takashi. How typically Takashi for your father to send you this way with no more escort than a monk armed with a sewing needle. Armed monks are fit only to clean fish. I'll kick this monk into the sea where he belongs, and then I'll take charge of you, little lady."

Jebu said, "If you force me to fight, one of us will die. Perhaps both of us. Perhaps others, too."

"Either kill him or be killed yourself," Taniko said. "That's what my father hired you for. Don't sit there and argue."

"I'm obliged by the rule of my Order to warn him."

The samurai laughed, threw out his chest and squared his shoulders, his armor creaking and rattling. "Warn me? *Warn me?* I am Nakane Ikeno, son of Nakane Ikenori, who put down the Abe in the land of Oshu and slew Abe Sadato, their champion. I am the grandson of Nakane Ikezane, who fought against Takashi Masakado, captured him and sent his rebellious head back to Heian Kyo. I am the great-grandson of—"

Jebu, sitting easily in his saddle with his reins loose and his fists on his hips, interrupted. "You are an ape and the son of an ape and the grandson of an ape. As for me, I am nothing. I have no family name. My father was unknown in the Sunrise Land. I have done nothing. I come from nowhere and I go nowhere." Jebu touched the Zinja emblem on his chest. Ikeno's eyes flickered to the blue and white circle of silk and widened slightly. Jebu went on, "I want nothing and I fear nothing. If you kill me you will have accomplished nothing, and no one will care. Let us pass."

"Am I supposed to be terrified because you're a Zinja, boy? The Zinja are cowards who kill by stealth. And you're a coward, or you'd challenge me like a man. Why should I give way before someone who calls himself nothing?"

"Air is nothing. Yet a windstorm can destroy a city. Stand aside, ape." Even as he spoke, Jebu repeated to himself the sayings that quieted his mind and filled his body with the power of the Self. *Rely on nothing under heaven. You will not do the fighting. The Self will do the fighting.*

Ikeno bellowed, "You dare call me an ape and insult my ancestors? I'll see you die a shameful death. You will not be burned or buried. Your body will lie aboveground to be eaten by dogs, and your bones will be bleached in the rain and the sun."

"The lickspittles of the Muratomo can kill only unarmed porters." Now Jebu was deliberately goading Ikeno.

Ikeno's long, heavy sword flashed out of its scabbard with a hiss, and he spurred his horse. Jebu remained where he was until Ikeno was upon him. Then, as Ikeno's sword came around, he threw himself flat on Hollyhock's back, hugging the horse's neck, and the samurai sword whistled through the air above him. Jebu heard screams as Ikeno's horse hurtled on toward the remaining porter and the three women, who all turned their horses and fled from him. Ikeno was far down the narrow path, still waving his sword over his head, before he could stop his horse, turn around and come back for a second try at Jebu.

Jebu glanced at Ikeno's three tsuibushi. They stood openmouthed and staring, showing no interest in joining the fight.

With a rattle of hooves Ikeno was on him again. Jebu jerked his horse to one side and Ikeno thundered harmlessly past, the sword again slashing through empty air. I told you I was nothing, thought Jebu.

Cursing, Ikeno jumped down from his horse and threw the reins to one of the tsuibushi. He ran at Jebu, reaching with leather-gloved hand to pull him down from the saddle. Without any prompting from Jebu, Hollyhock reared back on his hind legs, and Ikeno had to halt his rush and jump back to avoid the flailing front hooves. Jebu felt waves of pleasure rising within him and radiating out to Hollyhock, to Ikeno, to the mountain, to the ocean. They were all part of one stately dance, and time seemed to slow so that he was able to turn his head and look for Taniko. As he expected she was looking at him at the same instant, just as Hollyhock had known exactly when to rear up and check Ikeno's attack. Taniko's eyes, wide with awe and fascination, looked straight into Jebu's, and he saw what Taitaro meant when he said that the eyes are more beautiful than any jewel. And he knew that the Self was looking at the Self. They both turned away at the same moment and he found himself looking into Ikeno's bloodshot eyes, full of anger and befuddlement. Jebu felt compassion for Ikeno. You do not know who you are, he thought.

He drew the short Zinja sword, which Ikeno had called a sewing needle. It was small indeed, compared to Ikeno's sword. He swung his leg over the saddle and dropped lightly to the ground. Ikeno gripped his sword with both hands, holding it before him in the samurai attack stance, and took a step toward Jebu.

"I'll slice that smile off your face and your head from your body, monk."

Ikeno lifted his great sword over his head to bring it down on Jebu. At that same moment, taking three quick steps toward Ikeno, Jebu drew his own blade back, one-handed, then whipped it around in an arc completed so quickly the sword seemed at one moment to be poised over Jebu's right shoulder and at the very next to be beside the left. Jebu relaxed, dropping his hands to his sides. He knew he had killed Ikeno.

Ikeno stood silent and motionless, the long, gleaming blade raised to shoulder height, still tightly gripped in his gloved hands. The anger in the samurai's face faded, became horror, then agony. The mouth fell open. The eyelids fluttered. The sword fell from the hands with a clang, and the hands dropped limply. The whole body began to lean forward, falling from the feet. A thin ring of bright red appeared around the dirty brown neck.

Then, suddenly, the head separated from the shoulders and fell to the dirt and stones of the path. Blood fountained up, hissing, from the stump of the neck. The body stood like a pillar for a moment longer, then collapsed with a crash of steel and leather on top of the severed head.

The three tsuibushi dropped their naginatas, screamed and ran. Unhurriedly, Jebu strode back to Hollyhock, took his small bow from its saddle mount, nocked an arrow with a willow leaf head and fired. One of Ikeno's men fell with the arrow between his shoulder blades. Jebu dropped a second man with another willow leaf arrow. The third man turned at the edge of the pine forest, fell to his knees and raised his hands in supplication.

Jebu took a coil of hempen rope from his saddlebag and strode up the hill to where the trembling man knelt.

"Please don't kill me, shike," the man quavered. He was cross-eyed, and Jebu couldn't hold either eye with his own. What would Taitaro say about these jewels?

"Come over here." Jebu motioned toward a big maple. When he stood under the tree, he cut off a length of rope with his sword and tied the man's hands behind him.

Taniko rode over to them, her horse's hooves thudding softly on the mossy hillside. "What are you going to do to him?"

"Cut his head off."

The man screamed and fell to his knees again. "Oh, no, shike, don't kill poor Moko. I have five children. I meant you no harm. Ikeno made me come with him. Moko's no soldier. He's just a poor carpenter."

"A cross-eyed carpenter?" said Taniko. "I'd like to see what sort of houses you put up."

Moko tried to grin. His two upper front teeth were missing. There was a rare beauty in his ugliness, Jebu thought. In the space of a minute he had gone from thinking of this man as just another enemy tsuibushi to seeing him as a likable person. I'd really rather not have to kill him at all, Jebu thought.

"I'd surprise you, my lady," Moko said. "I'm a good carpenter. Please ask this great shike to have mercy on me. Compassionate lady, you wouldn't want my six children to starve."

"Do spare him, Jebu. He's harmless."

"Harmless? He'll be back tonight with a gang of cutthroats." Good, she's on Moko's side, too, he thought. I'll let her talk me out of it.

"No, I won't, shike. Lord Nakane Ikeno was the only real fighter around here. That's why he was the oryoshi. He forced the rest of us to follow him. None of us men would go out to fight if he hadn't threatened to kill us. I promise you, nobody will come to avenge Lord Ikeno, may his soul inhabit a night-soil jar—begging your pardon, compassionate lady."

"Jebu, I'm going to be married. I don't want the memories of my wedding marred by an act of cruelty."

"I thought you considered your marriage to the prince a cruelty in itself," Jebu said dryly.

"You are impertinent, monk. I do not want this man's ghost haunting me."

"Why should he haunt you? You will not do him any harm."

"You are my escort. Therefore I am responsible for what you do."

"I am impressed by your sensitivity, my lady. To spare you any pain, I shall spare this man's life." He turned to the kneeling carpenter. "All right. You may live. But you must transport Lady Taniko's baggage to Heian Kyo, replacing the porter that samurai murdered. If you run away, I'll track you down and kill you."

His hands still bound, Moko threw himself flat on his face at Jebu's feet. "Thank you, shike, thank you. I'll go anywhere you say. To China, if need be."

Taniko said, "What about your five children? Or is it six? Surely they would starve if you went to China."

Moki raised his head and gave Taniko a gap-toothed, crosseyed grin. "No children, my lady. I'm so ugly no woman would have me. So, no children. A man like me, a mere carpenter of no honor, will say anything to save his life."

Jebu kept his face severe as he cut Moko's hands free with his sword. This man was going to be a blessing from the kami. A man who could be amusing in the face of death was bound to be a better traveling companion than any of the members of the Shima party had so far proved to be.

Thanking Taniko and Jebu many times over, Moko ran off to join the surviving porter and the maids.

"I hope your kindness doesn't bring trouble down on us later on," Jebu said to Taniko.

Jebu was so tall and Taniko so tiny that even though he was on foot and she on horseback, their eyes met almost on a level. She smiled at him for the first time.

"You are a remarkable fighter, Jebu. I've never seen anything like the way you killed that Muratomo lout. When you were fighting him your eyes met mine and I felt something—I cannot describe it. Perhaps some day I will be able to express it in a poem. For now, I want to apologize for my rude words to you. I didn't want you to spoil my new appreciation of you by killing that helpless man."

Jebu was pleased, but he kept up the pose of the stern warrior. "An egg is helpless, but it may hatch a deadly serpent."

"One thing the Zinja taught you well."

"What?"

"How to be a windy bore." She whirled her bay gelding and rode off, calling mockingly over her shoulder, "Shike!"

5

Sliding back down the hillside, Jebu stopped at the body of one of the tsuibushi. He rolled it over and studied the young face, tough and stupid-looking even in death. Yet this commonplace countenance had been in life a marvel of intricately coordinated parts. The most skillful artist in the world could not create a statue that could duplicate the delicate and complex movements of that mouth, now slack. And the miracle of beauty that had been this country ne'er-do-well was now ended by a single crude blow from a feathered stick with a metal point. That exquisite structure, its movements ceased, was now already beginning to turn back into slime. Jebu squatted beside the body, his hands hanging limply between his knees. I did this.

In his mind he recited the Prayer to a Fallen Enemy. I am heartily sorry for having killed you. I apologize to you a thousand times and ask your forgiveness a hundred thousand times. I declare to all the kami of this place who witnessed our encounter that I alone am to blame for your death, and I take upon myself all the karma stemming from killing you. May your spirit not be angry with me. May you find happiness in your next life and may we meet again as friends.

He said the same prayer to the other tsuibushi and then to the headless, leather- and steel-clad body of Nakane Ikeno, the first man he had ever killed.

The safest thing to do with the bodies, Jebu decided, was to dump them into the sea. If the waves cast them up on shore again, it might be days or weeks from now, by which time Taniko and he would be far away from this part of the

39

country. And with luck the bodies would be eaten by fish and never seen again.

As if reading his thoughts, Moko came to stand beside him and said, "I make bold to tell the shike, this oryoshi stood well with the Muratomo. If it became known who killed Ikeno, the shike would have powerful enemies."

"You give me a reason to kill you."

"You already have reasons, and you have decided not to kill me. My life is in your hands at all times."

Jebu led Moko and the porter in prayers over each body. Then they rolled the bodies down the hill and dropped them into the white foam.

Ikeno was the last. The porter protested. "This armor is worth a lot."

"It was worthless to him," said Jebu, even as he admired the pattern of orange silk lacings that lashed together the leather and steel strips of armor. "And it is easily recognized. If we were found carrying Ikeno's armor, it might be embarrassing for us."

"At least keep the sword, shike," said Moko. "A sword is a thing of beauty. It has a soul. The art of a master swordsmith has gone into forging it, and the Fox Spirit has presided over its creation. It would be a shame, a blasphemy, to throw it into the sea to rust."

"You are almost a poet, Moko. Very well, I'll keep the sword." Moko unbelted the scabbard and gingerly picked up the shining weapon that lay where Ikeno had dropped it. Jebu took the sword from Moko and examined it.

A shadowy temper line ran along the blade where the hard steel of the edge met the flexible steel of the core. The swordsmith had worked the temper line into a decorative pattern reminiscent of bamboo leaves. There was writing engraved on the blade as well.

"There is nothing between heaven and earth that man need fear who carries at his side this magnificent blade."

Jebu shook his head. Foolish. Such words taught the samurai to rely on his sword and throw away his life. Far wiser was the Zinja maxim: *rely on nothing under heaven*. He handed the sword to Moko. He might send it, he thought, to his mother and Taitaro.

"I'll pack it in the baggage for you and no one will see it till you want it again," said Moko.

And so Ikeno, his armor, his bow and his head, but not his sword, all went into the sea. Jebu slapped Ikeno's black roan on the rump and sent it galloping up the Tokaido Road to the northeast, away from Ikeno's village.

The three men and three women hurried down the coast, riding as rapidly as they could, avoiding houses and villages and hiding in the forest whenever there was a chance of meeting someone on the road. Still not sure whether Moko might betray them, Jebu did not give him a watch to stand, but divided the night between himself and the Shima porter.

The day after the fight with Nakane, they were riding over grassy hills when Taniko drew alongside him.

"The company of those women has become such a trial. They have been my servants all my life, and there is nothing they can say that I have not heard a hundred times before."

"You have mentioned that I, too, can be boring."

"At least you say things I haven't heard before."

Jebu smiled at her. "I sympathize. I've had no one to talk to but myself since we began this journey. And I know myself better than you know your maids. I find myself even more tiresome company." He and Taniko had warmed toward each other. It was obviously the killing of the samurai that had won her over to him. Well, what of that? Some good must come from every act that harmed someone.

He recalled that moment in the heat of battle when their eyes met. He doubted that he would ever forget it. Today she looked more beautiful than ever, and knowing her better, he now saw that the seeming ruthlessness in her eyes was simply a candid intelligence coupled with a clear certainty about how she felt and what she wanted.

She said, "You are reminding me of my rudeness to you on the first part of this journey. I'll make amends. We'll keep each other company. What bores you in yourself might intrigue me. And you might find me interesting, though I believe myself to be quite ordinary. Just as the bodies of men are of no interest to other men, but are quite fascinating to women."

How bold of her! "I am sure that you are too young and

too modest to know anything about the bodies of men, my lady.''

"Even so, I can talk to you about such things without fear of seeming foolish. You are young also, and a monk.''

"The Zinja take no vow of celibacy." Jebu looked her in the eye. *Just because I may not touch her, I need not hide from her that I am a man.*

Taniko turned pink. "Oh, I see that I am in great danger. I'd better ride back to the protection of my ladies." Her laughter tinkling in the warm air, she rode off through the high, yellowing grass. He felt such an ache of desire for her that his stomach knotted itself. *Was there, perhaps, some way he could manage to lie with her without shaming her, endangering himself and dishonoring the Order?*

Next day, after their midday meal of rice cakes, seaweed and dried fish, she was back again, riding beside him.

"How old *are* you, Jebu?''

"Seventeen. I was born in the Year of the Pig of the previous cycle.''

"And I was born in the Year of the Hare. You are four years older than I. That isn't a great difference. I am old enough to be married, it seems.''

"I didn't mean to suggest that there was anything childish about you, my lady.''

"Quite right. There is nothing childish about me." The secretive smile and the sidelong look left him in no doubt of what she meant. "And since you Zinja are such lusty men, at what age do you marry?''

"Usually not until we are over thirty. If a Zinja can stay alive until he is thirty, he is considered a safe prospect to take a wife. Monks over thirty are given the less dangerous work to do. They are inducted into one of the inner circles of the Order, the teachers or the abbots." Jebu smiled and met her eyes. "But when I said the Zinja are not celibate, I wasn't talking about the fact that we eventually marry.''

Her wide mouth, the lips carefully painted a bright red, parted momentarily, and she turned pink again under the light dusting of white face powder. *This one had a real problem with blushing. She gave herself away.* Then that hard, intelligent look was back, the look that had surprised him the first day he met her.

"In your case I should think paying for a woman's services—if she were that sort—would be the only way you'd get to lie with her."

"Why do you say that?"

"Because you are the ugliest man I've ever seen. You're not deformed, but you are strange-looking. Like a demon mask. Everything is the wrong color. For instance, your skin is like the belly of a fish."

"The very color you try to make yourself with your face powder, my lady."

"Yes, but my face powder is beautiful because my skin is not that color, do you see?" Jebu did not, but let her continue. "Your hair looks as if your head is on fire, and your eyes are the color of the sky on a rainy day. The whole effect is grotesque and frightening. I've never seen anyone who looks like you. And then, you're so big—you're huge, a monster. If you came anywhere near me, I would run away screaming."

There was a time, a few years ago, when what she said would have hurt him. But Zinja training had taken hold, and he was able to respond with amusement. "All men are the same color in the dark. And as for my size, some women have found it pleasant."

"You're vulgar, too. There is nothing more repulsive than a lecherous monk. What riffraff the Zinja must be, if you're any example. I declare, I would sooner make love to Moko the carpenter than to you." It did not escape Jebu that it was she who brought up the subject of lovemaking.

"Doubtless Moko could construct a tower tall enough to please you."

"You disgust me." She rode away.

A moment later Jebu heard Taniko telling something to the maids, and all of them broke into peals of laughter.

Riding alone and in silence, he thought about Shima Taniko. Her small face with its mobile, expressive mouth attracted him. She was not really beautiful, but then, all beautiful women looked exactly alike. Hers was the beauty of a crooked tree, of an earthenware teacup, of an oddly shaped cloud. A sudden thought flashed through his mind: might he not possess, for some beholders at least, the same sort of rough, strange beauty? He wondered if this were a genuine Zinja insight.

He thought about the look that passed through Taniko's eyes from time to time, a look that suggested something strong and sharp and flexible as a sword blade. Her position might be that of third daughter in a provincial house, but in her own right her strength and wit might rank her first in the empire. He entertained himself with visions of making love to her. His daydreams became so vivid he could feel her small hands scratching his back, her slim legs twined around his hips.

Moko, drawing up beside him, interrupted his thoughts, which somewhat relieved him because the fantasies had begun to cause distinct discomfort. Moko grinned at him, and Jebu wondered whether the cross-eyed, gap-toothed carpenter could be said to have the same beauty of the nonsymmetrical, the natural, the stark that Taniko and perhaps he himself possessed. Once again he was grateful to whatever kami supervised his destiny that he had not killed this man.

"Shike, I wanted to tell you, since we're going to Heian Kyo. I've been there before. I wondered if you have."

"No, Moko. My travels are just beginning. How did you come to visit the capital?"

"My mother's family lives there. It was the custom among her people for a pregnant woman to stay with her parents, so she went there and took me with her when my young sister was about to be born. I do not think she wanted to get pregnant again for a while, so she stayed there for three years."

"What is Heian Kyo like? I'm so anxious to know."

"Very big and very old. But you would think carpenters designed it. The streets are not winding and narrow as they are in other cities. They are straight and cut across each other to form squares, and they are very wide. Some are so wide you could put a whole village in the middle of the street and still have room left over on either side. A hundred thousand people live within the city's walls."

Moko went on to describe Heian Kyo in detail and to tell Jebu tales of life there. Jebu decided he had guessed right about Moko. The man made a more interesting traveling companion than anyone else in the party. Except, of course, for Taniko.

*　*　*

The next day Taniko was riding beside him again.

"Please don't distress yourself out of kindness to me," he said. "It must be painful to ride next to one as hideous as I am."

She shrugged. "The maids are more boring than you are hideous. Actually, I find your appearance interesting. Tell me how you come to look as you do."

"I am my father's son."

"Well, then, why does your father look like that? Come, come, don't draw things out."

"My father is dead. He was murdered a year after I was born. He was a foreigner. His eyes were green, not gray as mine are."

"Who killed him?"

"He was murdered by a tall, red-haired foreigner like himself, who came here to kill him."

Taniko stared at Jebu. "You mean that while I've gone almost mad with boredom for nearly a dozen days as we creep down the Tokaido on this unhappy journey, you could have been regaling me with the mysterious story of your life? You are too cruel!"

"I thought you would find the slaying of the samurai Ikeno entertainment enough." She was the one who was cruel; didn't she realize it was his life, the story of his murdered father, she wanted to be *regaled* with?

But a Zinja did not own his life. He owned nothing. He passed through this world without leaving a trace. If she wanted his history for her amusement, he would unfold it for her like a paper fan, and when she was through with it, she could throw it away.

"I'm not the kind of person who gets pleasure out of seeing people die," she said. "But a story, that's different. Where did your father come from? Who murdered him? How did you come to be born?" Like a little girl, she jumped up and down on her sidesaddle with eagerness. "Please! Go ahead! Start at once!"

"My father's name was Jamuga. He told my mother that his people came from a desert place far to the west."

"From China?"

"North of China. They were wandering tribesmen, like the Ainu, who live on our northern islands. They raised cattle and

fought among themselves all the time. They were so poor
they had no houses, and instead lived in tents made of animal
skins. They had no family names."

"No wonder your father came to the Sunrise Land."

"No, he came here against his will, in a way. He was
fleeing from something. He came on a trading ship from
Korea, and my mother said that he paid for his passage with a
jewel worth enough to buy a whole fleet of ships. He carried
a dozen jewels like that with him, sewn into his clothing."

"It's a wonder the Koreans didn't kill him and throw him
overboard and take the jewels. It is well known that the
Koreans have no honor and would not be above doing such
things."

"They wouldn't have dared. My father was the sort of
warrior who could easily kill a whole ship's crew. He was a
huge man, bigger than I am, but swift as the wind and master
of every kind of weapon. It was only *his* honor that required
him to pay for the voyage. For a barbarian he was an unusu-
ally *good* man, so my mother says. Anyway, he landed at
Mojigaseki and set out for the countryside nearby. There he
presented himself to one of the local landowners and bought,
with another jewel, an estate with horses. With a third jewel
he purchased my mother, and the most beautiful woman in
the area, to be his wife."

"Where did he get the jewels? You said his people were
poor."

"They made war on other, richer people and won. The
jewels were my father's share of the loot."

"It is against the law to sell land to a foreigner. And how
could any man sell his daughter to such an outlandish creature
as your father must have been?"

"The ink in which the laws are written fades rapidly, the
farther one travels from Heian Kyo. And this landowner took
the jewel my father gave him for some grazing land too poor
to grow rice on, and turned around and bought a huge tract of
rice land. That one jewel made him rich. As for my mother's
father, he was a poor farmer, and his daughter, pretty as she
was, was only another mouth to feed. Now he's the richest
rice merchant in the province. A few of the wild young men
in the area—some who had courted my mother—resented my
father's coming and he had to fight them. He was careful not to

kill any of them, which shamed them utterly and forced them to move away from the village. He was a master of the arts of war."

"But someone killed him."

"Someone who was a better fighter than he. I wish I knew who it was. And why."

"You said it was a red-haired foreigner like himself."

"Yes. There was a Zinja monastery, the Waterfowl Temple, in the neighborhood. As soon as my father moved into the area, he visited the monastery and became friendly with the abbot, Taitaro. He would go frequently to the monastery and spend many hours drinking sake and talking with Abbot Taitaro. One day he heard that a giant Buddhist monk from across the sea was coming up the road from Mojigaseki, asking about a certain Jamuga the Cunning."

"The Cunning?"

"Apparently he was called that by his people because he was more intelligent than most. When my father heard that name, he said that an old enemy had come to claim his life. He took my mother and me to the monastery and commended us to the protection of Abbot Taitaro. If he were killed that night, we and his land and the remaining jewels were to belong to the Zinja.

"Then my father went back to the farm he'd worked for the past two years. He saddled his best horse, put on a suit of samurai armor he'd had especially built for himself, and took out a bow and arrows and a sword he had brought with him from his faraway desert country. He waited. After nightfall the monk from across the sea came riding up the road. My father went out on horseback to meet him. The stranger threw off his monk's robe. Underneath was a huge warrior wearing a red surcoat over his armor. They shouted at each other in a strange tongue none of the peasants, who were watching from hiding places, understood. They fired arrow after arrow at each other, and when their arrows were all used up, they rode toward each other and slashed at each other with swords. Both were men who preferred to fight on horseback. At last the stranger got past my father's guard and drove his sword into his throat. My father fell, and his enemy cut his head off. He wrapped the head in cloth and put it in his saddlebag."

Jebu stopped speaking, seeing in his mind, as he had many times before, the scene of his father's death. It did not make him sad. It puzzled and fascinated him. He wanted to know everything about who his father really was; it was more important to him than being a Zinja. One day, he would learn everything, even if he had to travel to that desert land across the sea.

At last Taniko said, "Your father must have been a brave man and a great fighter. Did the warrior in red ride away and vanish, then?"

"No. He had asked many questions before he encountered my father, and he knew that Jamuga the Cunning had a son, and the son was at the Waterfowl Temple. He climbed the mountain to the temple that same night, stood outside the gate and demanded that I be turned over to him. He said it was his mission to execute Jamuga and all of his lineage."

"To kill a baby? How cruel!"

"He didn't know what the Zinja are, and I suspect he must have thought he was dealing with ordinary, harmless monks. Eventually Taitaro got tired of arguing with him and sent three of the brothers out to kill him. He may have been surprised by the attack, but he surprised the Order, too. He killed two of the monks and escaped. Rarely has an ordinary warrior bested a Zinja in combat, and for one warrior to defeat three Zinja is unheard of."

"My father told me one Zinja is the equal of ten samurai. After seeing what you did to Ikeno, I believe it."

"Yes, but this red warrior is not a samurai. I believe that somewhere in the world he still lives and still wants to kill me. Some day I will meet him. I will defeat him. That is one reason why I've given my life to the Zinja training. To prepare myself for him. Before I kill him, I will force him to tell me why it all happened."

Taniko looked at him, her red-painted lips parted in awe. "For a monk, you are quite an exciting person, Jebu." Then she turned pink and wheeled her horse to leave him. Her gelding brushed, seemingly by accident, against Hollyhock, and her small hand, seemingly by accident, stroked the back of Jebu's hand.

6

The next morning, when Jebu awoke, he found a pale green paper among the arrows in his quiver. The paper had been folded into a narrow strip and the strip knotted around a small sprig of pine. When he opened the paper he found inscribed on it, in beautiful brushstrokes, a poem:

> The red fire consumes the desert pine,
> But the wings of the young waterfowl
> Soar above the flames.

In the silence around him Jebu heard a redbird singing and his heart hammering. She had made this beautiful thing for him, for him alone. He rode over to her and looked at her and said nothing. As she watched, he refolded the poem carefully and put it inside his tunic, against the bare skin of his chest.

They rode side by side that day, sometimes talking casually, much of the time in silence. That night they reached Miya and stayed at the mansion of a Takashi lord. Jebu asked a servant for ink stone, brush and paper, and in his best handwriting wrote a poem the way Taitaro had taught him, going into meditation first, then writing whatever words came, without trying to think and without criticizing afterward.

> The young waterfowl tries to fly
> But a snare hidden in the lilac branch
> Holds him fast.

The paper the servant had given him was violet. He found

49

a fallen maple leaf of a shade of red that seemed to suit the paper well, and folded his poem around it.

The next morning he slipped the poem into a box of provisions their host had given Taniko for that day's journey. At Miya the Tokaido was cut off by the sea, and they spent the day traveling by boat to Kuwana, where they could resume the journey by land. From the bow of their boat Jebu watched Taniko walk to the rail, unfold the violet paper and read the poem. Their eyes met and she quickly looked away.

The days that followed felt like a slide down an ever-steepening hill. With each passing moment their party seemed to move more swiftly toward Heian Kyo. The closer they came to the capital, the better the road, the easier the journey, and the more Jebu wished they would never get there.

When he was a child his mother had told him stories of the wonderful city of the Son of Heaven and of the adventures of the lords and ladies of high lineage who lived there. For years he had dreamed of the capital as the center of all that was noble, wise, ancient, beautiful and rich. To see Heian Kyo had been a lifelong wish. Now it was the last place in the world he wanted to see, because seeing it would mean the end for him and Taniko.

At last they came to the mountains surrounding the Imperial city. That night they would leave the Tokaido and stay at the Zinja Temple of the New Moon on Mount Higashi, overlooking the capital. It was one of the largest Zinja enclaves in the Sacred Islands, housing over four hundred monks. The Imperial officials of Heian Kyo lived in mortal fear of the Zinja monks dwelling on Mount Higashi. More than once the monks had descended into the city to punish some noble who had offended them. The Imperial troops were no match for monks trained in the Zinja arts of combat. Once or twice the Zinja could even have seized control of the capital, but the rule of the Order forbade them to hold political power.

Jebu sensed something wrong as soon as he glimpsed the temple. Where there should have been stone walls and towers there was a heap of broken rocks. No rooftops were visible above the jumbled stones. Telling the others to wait, he rode on ahead.

"Earthquake," one member of a group of monks seated on the tumbled-down monastery walls told him. "Two nights ago the kami of this mountain shook us as a wild horse shakes off a man who tries to ride him. Then it took the form of a shark and opened its mouth and swallowed us by the hundreds."

"By the hundreds?"

"These brothers you see here are all who are left." The monk raised an admonitory hand. "You look shocked. Do not be. It is not our way to let disaster overwhelm us. We pass through life leaving no trace. This is as true for hundreds as for one. What happened was neither good nor evil. It simply happened. We will move on."

"Will you try to rebuild?"

"Perhaps. We will await word from the Council of Abbots on whether to rebuild or simply to join another community. I am sorry we cannot offer you and your party hospitality, but you will be more comfortable sleeping under the stars. And safer. The god of the mountain may shake us again at any time. There is a lovely shrine to the Emperor Jimmu down the road. There you will be protected by the Emperor's spirit. And there is a view of Heian Kyo. Let me direct you to it."

Their path took them out of the forest and to the edge of a cliff. Suddenly all of Heian Kyo lay spread out before them on the gently sloping plain below. The sun was low over the mountains in the west, and it bathed the city in the golden glow of late afternoon. The dark rooftops of the city and the trees from which they emerged, stretching into the distance, took on a purple color and seemed to float in a violet haze.

Jebu recognized the Nine-Fold Enclosure, the grounds of the Imperial palace, from the many descriptions of it he had heard. It was a town in itself. The gigantic Great Hall of State, with its elaborate roof of green glazed tiles, towered over the other buildings. South of the palace enclosure was a spacious park with a large lake, a hill and a thatch-roofed pavilion.

From the center gate of the palace grounds an avenue as wide as a river, paved with black stone, swept all the way to the southern wall of the city. Other streets running north and south and intersecting with avenues running east and west subdivided the city into many squares, each a park, each dotted with palaces.

The sunlight glinted on two rivers that ran on either side of the city and on canals and reflecting pools shaded by willow trees. The huge black towers of the gates rose massive, complex and ornate at intervals along the low city walls. In and out of the eastern gates flowed endless streams of people on foot and in sedan chairs, litters, ox-drawn carriages and on horseback.

There was very little traffic through the western gates. The half of the city west of the central avenue seemed deserted and overgrown with trees. Only a few buildings scattered here and there poked their rooftops above the greenery.

Moko reined up beside Jebu. "Beautiful," he said. "As always. That great street running south from the palace is Redbird Avenue. It is so wide that a hundred men could march down it abreast. And the gateway at the south end of Redbird Avenue is the Rasho Mon. That's where you find the thieves and beggars and spies. I used to slip away from my mother whenever I could, to go down to the Rasho Mon to talk to the wicked ones. It was haunted by a ghost a long time ago, you know. A hideous demon that used to make people disappear. But Muratomo no Tsuna cut her arm off with his famous sword, Higekiri, and drove her away."

"Why is the western half of the city so empty?"

"It has been that way for hundreds of years. The ground is soft and swampy and thieves haunt the area, frightening away the good citizens. Everyone prefers to live on the east side of the city. Do we go down there now, shike?"

"No. It's still a long way off. We'd never reach the gates before nightfall. And from what you tell me of demons and thieves, I'd rather not sleep outside the gates. We'll rest here and go down the mountain tomorrow." Jebu dismounted and bowed to the nearby grotto in a grove of pines where a small, worn figure carved in pale stone, Jimmu Tenno, first Emperor of the Sunrise Land and descendant of the sun goddess, stood guard over Heian Kyo. The Emperor was portrayed as a warrior in full armor, wearing a bowl-shaped helmet and a ferocious expression, and holding a short, broad sword more like a Zinja weapon than the long sword of the samurai.

The chill of autumn was in the night. Wrapped in a heavy robe borrowed from Taniko's baggage, Jebu lay near the cliff edge and watched a full moon rise like a white lantern and touch the rooftops and canals of Heian Kyo with silver light.

Poets, he knew, proclaimed the moon of the Eighth Month the most beautiful of the year, but sad and bitter feelings gathered like a dark pool in his chest. Tomorrow he would lose Taniko forever. Just because he was young and a nobody and Prince Sasaki no Horigawa was a man of rank. He was not a very good Zinja, he told himself. Those monks up the road could take with calm the loss of hundreds of their brothers and the destruction of their monastery. He should be able to forget Taniko the moment his back was turned on her.

He wondered if he would forget her.

At last he fell asleep.

He woke suddenly and instantly. In the Waterfowl Temple the boys were encouraged by rewards and punishments to steal from one another during the sleeping hours, or to try to catch one another stealing. By the time he was eight Jebu had been trained to awaken the instant he sensed an intruder, but to remain motionless and to continue breathing as if he were asleep. Now he lay, opening his eyes just a slit, all his Zinja-trained senses focused on the person stealthily moving toward him. A small, light person, scarcely disturbing the grass. A rustle of silk, shallow breathing. A flowery scent.

"Who are you?" he whispered.

"Saisho."

"Who is Saisho?"

"My lady Taniko's maid." By this time the woman had crept so close he could feel her breath on his cheek. The moon was high in the sky, but her head and face were shadowed by the hood of a traveling cloak.

"What do you want?"

"My lady Taniko talks of nothing but you. She makes you sound quite interesting, Jebu. Why should she have you all to herself?"

Jebu laughed and reached out to stroke a soft cheek.

"Tell me, Jebu, are you as valiant in the flowery combat as you are in battles with arrows and swords?"

Jebu threw back her hood. The face in the moonlight was Taniko's.

"The lilac branch," he whispered.

Sighing, he put his arm around her and they lay for a long time in silence, listening to each other's breathing and gazing down at moonlit Heian Kyo. After awhile their bodies began to move, their fingers reaching to touch each other under their garments. Jebu gasped as his fingertips grazed her smooth, warm skin. He pressed himself against her.

"No. Stop."

"What if I can't stop?"

"You must, or my life is ruined."

"Forget the future. There is only here and now."

"The Zinja are said to be magicians. Can you magically restore the gate of this castle if you batter it down?"

"What if I batter it down even though I can't restore it?"

"Then I will be forced to kill myself. And you will be executed as a rapist. And your Order will pay dearly to my father."

"I will not break through your castle gate. The Order commands me to deliver you safely to Prince Sasaki no Horigawa. The Zinja do not betray their Order."

She giggled. "Is your hair red here, too?"

"Yes."

"Then I am glad I can't see you in the dark." She giggled again and her fingers teased him.

He drew in a sharp breath. "Why do you tempt me?"

"There are other pleasures we can share without your breaking into my castle. You can picnic in the castle garden."

She continued with what she had been doing. The lightning would flash at any moment. It had been so long since he'd lain with a woman. The ground under him seemed to tremble a little. Was it the kami of the mountain, or was it his body?

The lightning flashed. They sighed together.

When he was breathing normally again he said, "You are very good to me."

"I did that for my own protection. Now your battering ram is no threat to my castle gate."

"The threat may arise again in time."

"Until it does," she arched her back and wriggled her hips against him, "you may perhaps enjoy the repast in the garden I spoke of."

The lore preserved and transmitted by the Zinja included more than the arts of combat. Through the study of books from across the sea and with the help of the women who lived with them, each young Zinja became adept in the arts of the bedchamber. The Order treated these arts with the deepest devotion, as vehicles for the achievement of illumination. Even before he was old enough to participate, Jebu had been permitted to observe others in the practice of those arts.

The flesh is holy, Taitaro said. No act of the flesh is base or trivial. To fan the flames of desire is to heighten the powers of the mind. To invoke the forces of life is to touch directly the light and wisdom of the Self. Taitaro taught Jebu a ritual and a prayer for his moments with women.

Now Jebu's lips and tongue performed the ritual while his mind recited the prayer: I enact this mystery in honor of the Self. I ask the Self to enter into me with its power. Let the Self enter my body through the body of this woman and fill both of us with light.

Taniko started to cry out, then put her hand over her mouth.

They lay holding each other under the heavy robe, his lips against her neck, looking down at the squares of the city under the full moon.

Jebu whispered to her. He felt that the words were not his, but that some powerful kami spoke through him. "I am yours for the rest of my life and the rest of your life. As I belong to the Order, so I belong to you. Wherever you are, call me, I will come. Whatever you need, command me, I will do it. All things pass, all things die, but this oath which I take on your sacred body will not die."

"Oh, Jebu, whatever words are said to bless my union with Prince Horigawa, those words will be dry and dead as autumn leaves. The lilac branch will always be waiting for the water-fowl."

Jebu felt tears come to his eyes. He pictured years and years to come, a desert of time in which he would wander, separated from Taniko.

He must have fallen asleep. When he awoke again Taniko was gone and the ground was cold. The moon had set, and he could see someone standing nearby looking over the edge of the cliff. He stood up. There was a pink glow in the east, the glow of dawn. But there was a red light nearer at hand that sent a chill down the back of his neck.

Heian Kyo was on fire.

Looking closely, he saw that banners of flame were fluttering above certain scattered palaces while others, though brightly lit, remained untouched. In the dawn's glow and the firelight Jebu could make out figures milling in the streets and around the gates. Screams and faint war cries reached his ears.

Moko came to stand beside him and turned frightened eyes up to him. "Shike, there is war in the streets of the capital. A little while ago I heard sounds that made me uneasy. I got up and looked over the cliff edge. I saw palaces burst into flames, men fighting in the streets. Shall I wake the others? What shall we do?"

"We will do nothing until we know exactly what is happening. Let the others sleep. You and I will watch." Jebu squatted down at the cliff edge. He looked over to the dark, silent shape of the tent Taniko shared with her maids.

By the time the warmth of the sun woke the others, a pall of smoke hung over Heian Kyo. Motionless figures could be seen lying in the broad streets and avenues while riders on horseback raced up and down.

Tears streamed down Taniko's face. "Oh, Jebu, it was so lovely last night, and now it is being destroyed." The sunlight sparkled in her tear-filled eyes. Perhaps the eyes are most beautiful when wet with tears, Jebu thought. He felt his own eyes grow hot and wet, and her face blurred. But he was not weeping for Heian Kyo. Her fingers touched the back of his hand.

"You were beautiful last night," he said, "and you are still beautiful in the sunrise."

She shook her head. "For me the sun is setting."

She turned and walked away to join the two maidservants, who were standing before the statue of Emperor Jimmu in the dark green grove of pines. What Jebu felt, he had no name for. A woman gave you pleasure, and you remembered her fondly. That feeling was pleasant. That feeling was no bigger than a forest pool. What he felt now was pain, a pain that almost made him forget the strange and terrible sight of Heian Kyo's agony. This feeling was an ocean. It seemed, at that moment, that life was over for him, that he was already dead. Taitaro was forever saying that we should live as if already dead. If this was what he meant, he was wrong. This was unbearable.

To ease the pain he forced himself to consider the immediate problem. "Moko, you know Heian Kyo. Go down there and try to find out what has happened. Find the house of Prince Sasaki no Horigawa and make sure all is well with him. See whether it will be safe for us to bring the Lady Taniko into the city. Then meet us here."

The cross-eyed carpenter came back after the midday meal. He shook his head sadly. "The beautiful streets of Heian Kyo have become a battleground for samurai. Such things did not occur when I was a child."

"Tell me exactly what has happened, Moko-san."

Moko waved his hands in distress. "It was all over nothing. A street-corner brawl between Takashi and Muratomo samurai. But hundreds joined in. Then bands of samurai took to attacking people's houses. The Takashi samurai burned the houses of Muratomo families and killed their servants. The Muratomo did the same thing to the Takashi."

"What of Prince Horigawa?"

"It was hard to find out anything about him, shike. If you ask too many questions, people look upon you as a suspicious person, and suspicious persons don't live long in Heian Kyo today. The Takashi have put a heavy guard around the prince's house, though. He is safe enough."

Jebu recalled that Taniko's family was a branch of the Takashi. "Is Lady Taniko's family in any danger?"

"Shike, everyone who lives in Heian Kyo is in danger today. But the Shima mansion is not among those I heard were burned."

Jebu felt a momentary panic as he realized he was uncertain what to do next. The one thing about this journey he had never questioned was its unchanging destination.

Rely on nothing under heaven.

Now he had to decide whether to take Taniko into a city torn apart by warring samurai or whether to seek uncertain refuge somewhere in these hills. Perhaps he should defy her father and the Order and flee with her in the hope that they might find a life together in hiding somewhere. Just as his father fled his people.

He looked at smoldering Heian Kyo. Whatever he decided might bring swift death to himself and Taniko.

7

Taniko joined Jebu at the edge of the cliff. Looking around quickly to make sure she was not observed, she took his hand and smiled up at him.

"If you are trying to decide what we should do, please let me help. As you know now, I prefer to make up my own mind."

Jebu squeezed her hand with such passion that she winced, but she did not pull away from him. "What is your wish?"

"That we go forward. We will all go together to the nearest gate. You will wait there with the women and me, and you will send Moko and the other porter to my Uncle Ryuichi. Moko will tell my uncle to send a carriage for me, so I can enter the capital in proper style. It is too bad that Moko has to make two trips into the city, but if you had asked me the first time you sent him, this is what I would have told you."

They descended from the mountain and returned to the Tokaido. This close to the capital, it was a broad, well-traveled highway. Here on the city's east side, buildings had spread beyond the walls. Temples, mansions and humbler dwellings encroached on the rice land surrounding the capital.

The party passed a park surrounded by a stone wall twice the height of a man. Within it stood three fortified towers, taller than any buildings Jebu had ever seen. Red banners flew just below the protective dolphin sculptures on the peaked roofs of the towers.

"That is the headquarters of the Takashi clan," said Moko. "It is called the Rokuhara. Sogamori lives there with his sons and thousands of samurai. They have added many buildings since I saw it last.''

Now they rode over a long wooden span, which Moko called the Gojo Bridge, arching over the Kamo River. The bridge and the gateway to which it led were a continuation of Gojo Avenue, one of the ten principal east–west thoroughfares of Heian Kyo.

As they approached the city's walls, Jebu saw that many of the large stones had fallen out of the pounded earth core of the ramparts which, unprotected, were eroding. He remembered what Taitaro had said about Heian Kyo's having seen better days.

Sending Moko on through the Gojo gate, Taniko and Jebu and their party settled down in a field outside the city wall. Jebu stood guard atop a large stone, his back resolutely turned to Taniko. There was nothing more that could be said between them. Anguish lay like a crushing weight on his chest.

The sun had nearly set when Moko returned leading a handsome ox-drawn carriage, its roof thatched with palm leaves. Five samurai walked beside it. Clearly her Uncle Ryuichi was not as miserly as Taniko's father.

Taniko and her two maids rode in the carriage. The samurai kept their hands on their sword hilts, their eyes darting warily from side to side.

Moko walked solemnly beside Jebu, pulling his wheezing, baggage-laden horse. He had promised Jebu and Taniko that he would remain with her as part of her household.

''I will be the link between you,'' he said.

At the Gojo gate the party identified themselves to a lieutenant of the Imperial police, a nervous, pale man carrying an ivory baton. He looked incapable of dealing with so much as a band of mischievous boys. Smiling politely at the Shima family samurai, the police officer waved the party through.

''It's a wonder that man was at his post at all,'' said Taniko's silvery voice through the orange-tinted blinds of her carriage.

To ease the pain of the imminent parting from Taniko, Jebu focused his attention on the sights and sounds of the capital. He had never seen so many people in his life; crowds filled the wide avenue like a river about to overflow its banks. People on foot dodged samurai on horseback and oxcarts piled high with bales and boxes. Every so often handsomely dressed men carrying small sticks would push through the throngs shouting, "Make way!" and then, slowly, an ox-drawn carriage, like the one Taniko was riding in or even grander, would roll through the cleared pathway. People would bow or peer curiously into the carriage, trying to see the great lord or lady within; usually the passenger's silhouette was visible through the screened sides. Frequently these passengers would let the long sleeves of their many-layered costumes trail out through the rear doorways. Jebu heard knowledgeable comments from the crowd, not only identifying the carriage riders but commenting critically on their choice and matching of colors. The people of Heian Kyo talked much and rapidly, seemed to run rather than walk, and often talked and ran at the same time.

Gojo Avenue was lined with willows, the leaves on their trailing branches turning to autumn gold. The mansions along the avenue were surrounded by low walls of white stone, a token hindrance to intruders. But, a sign of troubled times, many of the mansions had new, high bamboo palisades built around them. Others looked abandoned, as if their owners had sought safer places to live. Each estate consisted of numerous one-story buildings connected by covered corridors and surrounded by graveled courtyards and landscaped gardens.

Twice they passed mansions that had been burned during the night. The grounds of one were completely deserted. Nothing was left but smoldering ruins. Burnt trees stood like black poles.

The second burnt mansion was surrounded by samurai, who greeted Taniko's escort familiarly. Servants combed through the ashes for valuables and loaded whatever they could find in an oxcart.

"That was the home of a noble who supports the Takashi," one of the samurai with Jebu explained. "The Muratomo dogs burned it. Tonight we will burn some Muratomo mansions."

Stupid, thought Jebu. People spent years of their lives building these homes and the beautiful things that went into them. Centuries had gone into the making of this lovely city.

All to be destroyed in one night by some idiot with a torch. What prize could be worth such a loss?

Taniko's uncle, Ryuichi, stood on the veranda of the main house of the Shima family's Heian Kyo residence, waiting to greet his niece. He resembled his older brother, Bokuden, but was stouter in body and rounder in face, as if life in the capital had softened him. The look he gave Taniko as she stepped down from her carriage was kindly. His manner reassured Jebu as he prepared himself to leave her.

Covering her face modestly with her fan, Taniko said, "Uncle, this Zinja monk single-handedly killed a band of three samurai who were threatening to kidnap me. He faithfully escorted me all the way from Kamakura and brought me safe to your door. I hope you will reward him appropriately."

"How awful that my lovely niece should have been in such danger," Ryuichi exclaimed. "With respect to my elder brother, I knew the Tokaido was dangerous and I believed you should have had a large escort of samurai. But, thanks to the prowess of this monk, you are safe. I will speak to him in a moment. Taniko-san, it is not proper for you to display yourself in the open air before a group of men, even when the occasion is important. You must learn the manners of the capital, my child. Come into our house. Your aunt, Chogao-san, will make you welcome and comfortable."

Without a backward look at Jebu, Taniko was gone. Ryuichi followed her. Jebu turned toward the street. He did not dare look after Taniko. What was between them must remain secret forever. He felt a hand on his arm. It was Moko. Jebu looked into the crossed eyes and found them bright with tears.

A moment later Ryuichi returned to the veranda. "You have done well, shike. You have earned the gratitude of the Shima family. How may we reward you?"

Jebu could imagine Lord Bokuden's rage if he knew his brother was offering a reward. "The Order has been paid for my services, my lord. I may not accept a reward for myself."

"Nothing at all?"

Then Jebu remembered. "There is one thing. I took a sword from a samurai I had to kill, protecting Lady Taniko. It is in her baggage. I would like to keep it as—as a memento of the journey."

Beaming, Ryuichi clapped him on the shoulder. "Of course. And you shall have that horse as well. You may turn it over to your Order if you wish, but at least you won't leave here on foot."

Smiling to himself at the thought of Lord Bokuden's annoyance, Jebu accepted.

A row of white stones, intended to represent the Shima trading fleet, crossed the center of the pond in the mansion garden. Jebu sat cross-legged looking at the women's pavilion on the north side of the garden. The pavilion stood on pilings half the height of a man that kept it well off the slightly damp ground. Taniko was in there, probably being prepared for her first encounter with Prince Horigawa.

Silently Moko stepped down from the veranda of the women's building, bringing the sword and scabbard. They bowed to each other as Jebu took the sword, and Moko turned away, wiping his eyes.

At the eastern gateway of the mansion a servant was holding Hollyhock for Jebu. He opened his traveling case to pack the samurai sword. Under the lid of the case there was a piece of folded, red-tinted paper. Jebu's heartbeat speeded up. He opened the paper and read the poem in Taniko's hand.

> The autumn leaves fall,
> But the pine tree's green lives on.

In a spasm of anguish Jebu's hand crushed the poem. He wanted neither poems nor pine trees. He wanted the living woman behind the Shima walls.

He smoothed out the poem, folded it again and tucked it into his tunic. He mounted Hollyhock, sadness weighing down his shoulders. He waved to Moko, who had followed him to the gate.

Slowly, feeling that he was riding away from life itself, he rode out of Heian Kyo.

8

Prince Sasaki no Horigawa made his first courtship visit to Taniko the very night of her arrival in Heian Kyo. Taniko's Aunt Chogao warned her to expect him and helped her bathe and dress in her finest gown and jewels. She washed and combed the softly glowing black hair that hung to Taniko's waist. All the while Taniko protested, trying not to cry and feeling as ill from the loss of Jebu as if one of her hands had been chopped off.

"I have been traveling for twenty days. I'm worn out. Can't he give me one night to rest before he sees me?"

Aunt Chogao shrugged. "He told your uncle that he is extremely busy with matters of state. He is an Imperial adviser, don't forget. Besides, he has waited a long time to meet you. You are lucky to have such an eager lover."

Taniko made a face. Her aunt added, "Of course, he is lucky to get such a beautiful young woman. When he sees you, I'm sure he'll be even more eager."

How will I ever get through this, Taniko wondered. I was sickened before at the thought of spending the rest of my life with the old bloodsucker. But before I met Jebu, I never knew the kind of beauty that could exist between a man and a woman. Now that I do know, how can I give my life to something that is so much less?

For hours after she had dressed, Taniko, her aunt and the two maids waited for Horigawa's visit. Taniko insisted on writing in her pillow book, despite her aunt's protest that she might get ink stains on her fingers or her Chinese jacket. Taniko declared that she had never splashed ink on anything in her life. She offered to stop writing if her aunt would bring her a book to read, but the few books in the mansion, it seemed, were in Ryuichi's quarters, and her uncle was not to be disturbed. So Taniko wrote by candlelight.

At last there was a commotion in the garden. Chogao scurried to the blinds and peered out. "It's him. It's him," she whispered and waved the maids out of the room. She set a tall screen of state with flowered curtains in front of Taniko. For centuries it had been the custom at the capital for women of noble birth to remain concealed at all times from men other than their husbands or fathers. They received gentleman callers from behind portable screens of state. So significant a barrier was the screen of state that a man who got past it usually had no further difficulty in gaining his desire with the lady behind the screen.

Chogao snatched the pillow book out of Taniko's hand and shoved it into the pillow drawer, seized the ink stone, ink stick and brush, and hurried out of the room.

"Pretend to be asleep," came her voice through the sliding door.

There was a scratching outside on the veranda, and suddenly the blinds were raised and a short man with a powder-whitened face stepped into the room. His eyes stood out like two shiny black beans. He ducked his head to keep his tall black lacquered hat of office from being knocked askew.

Ignoring her aunt's advice about feigning sleep, Taniko peered through the screen of state at her future husband. Prince Horigawa's face was small and square, reminding Taniko of a grasshopper's head. A wisp of black beard decorated his bony chin. He fanned himself briskly with a black and white fan, as if climbing into the room had been a great exertion.

"Are you back there?" he said, directing his dry, rasping voice at the screen of state. Yet he spoke only slightly above a whisper. Not very gallant language for a prince come courting, Taniko thought. The sight of him made her heart sink. He was as unattractive as she had imagined. In his beady eyes there was nothing but nastiness and calculation.

"I am here, Your Highness," she said softly.

"Ah, very good, my dear. Let me join you behind your screen, where I can see you and make myself more comfortable." Without waiting for her reply, he skipped around the screen, seating himself beside her and seizing her hand. She had to restrain herself from pulling free of his clawlike grip. Had her aunt left them alone together? Taniko wondered.

The prince patted her hand. "Do not be frightened by my impetuosity, my dear," he whispered and grinned. At first it seemed to her that he was toothless, then she saw that his teeth had been dyed black in the Court manner. His grin faded as, still holding her hand tightly, he stared at her. Starting with her face and hair, his eyes traveled over her jacket and her many layers of skirts and dresses. He pursed his lips as he considered her selection of ornaments and her matching of colors.

"You appear to be as satisfactory as the matchmaker claimed," he said. He gestured at a jar of sake Taniko's aunt had left standing over a charcoal warmer, with two cups carefully placed on either side of it. Taniko poured sake, first for him, then for herself. Perhaps sake would help.

His cold fingertips scratched the nape of her neck. She could not help herself. She shuddered.

"The trapped bird trembles," he murmured. He drew a deep breath and threw himself upon her.

Taniko gave a little shriek as he clawed at her jacket, his face reddening. He seemed almost frantic as he plunged his hands under her skirts, trying to undo his gold-splashed black robe at the same time. Taniko had seen sparrows mating, and this flurried, furious assault reminded her of that.

"Your Highness," she gasped, out of breath. "This haste is inelegant." Recalling one of her mother's bedchamber books she added, "Permit me to unfold the pleasures of my body to you in more leisurely fashion, I beg you. To an inexperienced maiden, the charms of so handsome and distinguished a lord are irresistible, but do not press me so quickly."

"Your notion of the arts of the bedchamber are countrified," Horigawa panted. Inexorably he peeled away the layers of her clothing. In the flickering candlelight she caught a glimpse of his aroused body. It sickened her. She squeezed her eyes shut.

She reminded herself that she should not resist him. Custom demanded that she let the prince have his way. Keeping her eyes shut, she tried to relax. She remembered how, during their night together. Jebu had told her many things about the Zinja and the arts they practiced. He said they could take their minds out of their bodies and go on long mental journeys, leaving their physical selves behind. She made herself think of the great white mountain, Fuji-san, that she had passed with Jebu at the beginning of their journey from Kamakura. This ugly little prince had doubtless never seen Mount Fuji.

He was hurting her. He had no consideration for her feelings, no tenderness for her virginity. From his grunting and his hard, sharp movements she sensed that he was aware only of his own need for relief.

There was a searing pain. She gritted her teeth, but she could not stop herself from screaming aloud. It felt as though she had been stabbed in the bowels with a samurai dagger.

Horigawa opened his eyes and grinned at her, showing his blackened teeth again. "Your scream gives me pleasure," he whispered.

He threw back his head, the cords in his scrawny neck stood out and his body convulsed momentarily. Then panting heavily, he stopped moving. He pressed his brow, covered with cold sweat, against her cheek, then pulled away from her. She felt wet and soiled. She pulled her skirts down to cover herself. Would she have to spend the rest of the night with this man?

And there was worse. She was expected to spend the rest of her life with him. There would be countless nights like this one. Despair overwhelmed her, and she wanted to cry, but with the little man still lying beside her, duty to her family forbade any show of her real feelings.

"That was very pleasant, my dear," Horigawa said with a small, false smile. "It has been some time since I have lain with a woman. I have simply been too busy. My work at the Court, in these difficult times, has allowed me no leisure. But it is not healthy for a man to abstain for too long. It puts the forces of yin and yang out of balance in the male body. You have made it possible for me to return to my work with renewed vigor."

Taniko felt a flicker of curiosity. "I am pleased to have been of help to you, Your Highness. Your work must, indeed, be very demanding." She added what good manners required her to say. "I cannot imagine that such a vigorous man would wish to abstain for very long."

"Quite right," said Horigawa smugly. He began to draw his dark robes together. "And for that reason I came to you tonight, even though, as you say, my work is very demanding. Although it pains me not to spend the night with you, I must leave you now."

"Will the streets be safe for you tonight, Your Highness? I saw the fighting last night and the burning of houses, and I was frightened." Actually, she had not been that frightened, but she hoped Horigawa would shed some light on what was happening in the capital.

"I appreciate your concern, my dear, but I am quite safe. My friend Sogamori, the Minister of the Left, has provided me with a samurai guard, both for my house and for my person when I go abroad. These disturbances are the work of rebellious elements who refuse to yield to the will of the Emperor. But they will soon be crushed, and you will have no further need for fear."

Taniko knew how meaningless was Horigawa's accusation that his opponents were rebels against the Emperor. All sides in any major political dispute claimed to be doing the will of the Emperor and charged their enemies with treason. Actually the Emperor had no power of his own, and his will was the will of whichever faction controlled him at the moment.

"These rebels, Your Highness, are they the Muratomo?" Taniko asked. "You must forgive my country ignorance, but I do not know."

"Women are not expected to know anything, my dear," said Horigawa.

Taniko resisted an urge to throw her candle at him. Instead she said, "But I find you so fascinating, Your Highness, that I cannot help but be interested in the world in which you move." The fact was that it was only his connection with high places and great political matters that made the thought of marriage to him at all bearable.

"Very nicely put," said Horigawa, rising to his feet. "On future visits I shall explain as much of matters of state as your female intelligence seems capable of grasping. Meanwhile, be assured that we are doing everything necessary to maintain the safety of the realm. More blood will have to be shed. We

must deal mercilessly with rebels. We must be as fierce as
were our ancestors of old Yamato. Many, many heads will
fall.''

A chill went through Taniko. She sensed that this pompous
creature's feeble frame harbored a thirst for blood almost
unnatural in its intensity. As a daughter of samurai she had
known many professional fighting men, and none of them had
spoken as lovingly of mass slaughter as did this scholarly
government official.

She placed her hands on the floor and bowed. ''It is an
honor to be courted by a man of such greatness.''

Tying his tall black hat under his chin, Horigawa turned
and let Taniko raise the blinds for him so he could step out on
the veranda and thence into the Shima garden, thus preserving
the ritual secrecy of his visit.

When he was gone, Taniko turned to find her aunt was
already back in the room with towels and a pot of hot water.
Taniko sank to her knees and put her face in her hands. Her
body shook with wracking sobs. Aunt Chogao knelt beside
her and put her arms around her.

''Was it that bad for you, my dear?''

''Aunt, I can't go through with it. I can't.''

Chogao patted her shoulder. ''You have to. Your father
commands it. Your family needs this marriage.'' She stroked
Taniko's hair. ''I know it's hard. What you have to do is
harder than anything I've had to do. I was married to a man
with whom it is very easy for me to live. But you, because
you must do the more difficult thing, will be the nobler
person.''

''I can't. I don't want to.''

Chogao moved so that she was facing Taniko, her normally
cheerful features suffused by a burning seriousness. ''You are
samurai. What you feel does not matter. If you were a man,
you would go to war and die. It would not matter that you
were terrified of death, that you wanted to live. It would be
your duty to your family. Do not women have as much
courage as men? We give our lives, too, by marrying as we
are required and bearing the children that are needed. Didn't
your mother teach you these things?''

''Yes,'' said Taniko in a small voice.

''Then never forget them. If you do not live your life as a

samurai, it is not worth living. Now lie back, my dear, and let me wash you. That miserable man. He should have spent the whole night with you and left at dawn. What sort of lover does he think he is? Oh, well, I suppose, considering his age and all the work he does, that's the most you can expect. He certainly doesn't have much fire left over for women, does he?''

Closing her eyes, grateful that Horigawa had left her as quickly as he did, Taniko said, ''I want nothing more from him.''

''Good, my dear. Be content with your lot. That, too, is the way of a true samurai.''

From the pillow book of Shima Taniko:

My future husband's next-morning letter was clichéd and perfunctory, and his love poem was copied straight out of the *Kokinshu.* The prince must think we have no books in Kamakura. Even my aunt, who keeps trying to persuade me to accept this marriage, made a sour face when she read his effort. But the letter and the poem mean he intends to continue courting me, and that is what the family wants.

In the bleakness of these days my greatest pleasure is my conversations with Moko. I have convinced my aunt and uncle that Moko is an expert carpenter whom I brought with me from Kamakura at my father's suggestion. My father will never know the difference. Fortunately, there are plenty of repairs needed around this house, and every day, pretending to give Moko instructions, I learn the news he has picked up in the street.

Samurai crowd the streets of Heian Kyo, swaggering about with their long swords. They accost people and demand to know if one is a supporter of the Takashi or the Muratomo. Such encounters lead to blows and sometimes to bloodshed, though both the Takashi clan chieftain, Sogamori, and the Muratomo clan chieftain, Domei, claim to deplore all disorder. There has not been any rioting as bad as that of the night I arrived here.

It was as though the riot in my soul that night was reflected in the streets of the city.

There was a full moon, too. That may have had something to do with it.

Moko reports that Domei has been heard to repeat the old

Confucian saying, "A warrior may not remain under the same heaven with the slayer of his father." Since Prince Horigawa appears to be chief among those responsible for the execution of Domei's father, it is possible that I may find myself a widow soon after I am married.

The grounds of the Imperial palace are kept bare, but in winter certain herbs flourish in concealment under the snow.

—*Eighth Month, twenty-first day*
YEAR OF THE DRAGON

Ten days after Taniko's first night with the prince, her aunt warned her to be ready for his second-night visit.

It was all she could do to restrain herself from laughing as the spidery little man carried out the ritual pretense of slipping into her bedchamber. The blinds knocked his tall hat off his head, leaving it dangling from his neck.

But there was nothing laughable in the way he fell upon her, first blowing out the candle to thwart spying members of the Shima family. This night his lust was tainted with cruelty. Taniko discovered that there is a kind of man who is aroused by inflicting pain on others. None of the small torments to which Horigawa subjected her left any mark, but she was frightened and revolted. He must know, she thought, that my family will insist on my marrying him. Otherwise he wouldn't treat me this way.

After he had worn himself out on her body, Horigawa ordered her to relight the candle so he could dress himself. Embarrassed by the ugliness to which she had just submitted, Taniko kept her face turned away as the room filled with yellow light and flickering shadow.

Horigawa laughed and said, " 'She lifts the lute, and I can see but half her face.' " He spoke in Chinese.

Recognizing the poem, Taniko replied in the same language. " 'The music stops, but the player will not speak her name.' " The line seemed a subtle way to express the shame she felt at what she had undergone. Like the woman in Po Chu-i's poem, she felt she had known better days and had now sunk to a low status.

But Horigawa reacted, not to her line of verse, but to the language in which it was uttered. "Do you know Chinese?"

Taniko answered him in that language. "Our family is involved in trade. My father has seen to it that all his children are educated in the skills that are useful in commerce. Knowledge, he says, can be wealth."

Horigawa pulled his robe around his spindly limbs. "Who would have thought that a child-woman from the provinces would possess such a valuable skill?" He was still speaking Chinese. "Mine is a family of princes and scholars, and Chinese has been our other language for centuries. Do you read and write it as well?"

"Better than I speak it." Actually, she surprised herself by being able to carry on the conversation.

"Excellent. When you are my wife you will serve me as secretary. The trade with China is a great source of wealth for the Takashi, and with my own knowledge of things Chinese, I humbly endeavor to help them. As Lord Sogamori's authority continues to grow, we will see a reopening of closer relations with China, which our rulers have long neglected, to our cost. The communications I undertake with China are delicate and require secrecy. It is difficult to acquire servants who have the necessary education and are also trustworthy. You will be very useful to me."

"Thank you, Your Highness," said Taniko, trying not to grind her teeth.

The thought that Horigawa was already planning her future appalled her. She tried to remind herself that many of the women in the Sunrise Land had husbands as repulsive, or worse. It did no good.

As before, Horigawa excused himself from spending the night with her, citing the pressure of his work in the service of the nation. After he was gone, Taniko sat in the dark, crying softly. To refuse the marriage her family had decreed for her was unthinkable. But the prospect of a lifetime tied to Horigawa filled her with such despair and dread that she was almost ready to kill herself to avoid going through with it.

Almost, but not quite. Even in her anguish she felt a deep certainty that she wanted to go on living. And she was as strong as Horigawa; in time she could put a stop to his horrid little practices. He was more than forty years older than she; he could only grow feebler and easier to manage with the passage of time. And in the fullness of time she would be rid of him. She had only to endure, to do her duty as a samurai, as Aunt Chogao put it.

The prospect of working on Horigawa's Chinese correspondence was fascinating. The little she knew about China was information over a hundred years old that had been taught to her and her sisters by monks. How wonderful it would be to learn what was happening to China now.

Five nights later a messenger came from Prince Horigawa, and Ryuichi ordered the third-night rice cakes placed in Taniko's bedchamber. After sunset the prince's ox-drawn state carriage drew up before the western gateway of the Shima mansions without even a pretense of secrecy, and the prince, wearing his usual tall black hat and a scarlet and white cloak, more festive looking than the black and gold one he had worn previously, strode through the lamplit gate, while the Shima family peered at him through screens and blinds.

His performance with Taniko was as brief as at their first encounter. This time, though, he bit her breast at his moment of supreme pleasure. This left teeth marks, which he looked at with satisfaction afterward.

As was expected of her, Taniko paid him a pretty compliment on his manly strength. Inwardly, she was quaking. They were now committed. She was bound to him. It was this third-night visit, with the ceremonial eating of rice cakes, which actually sealed their marriage. It was all over, and now that it was done she could see no future for herself. She felt a sensation of sinking into a bottomless black pool. She had done her duty as a samurai woman, yes, but might duty not be easier for a man, who died only once and quickly, than for a woman who had to die a little bit each day for years and years?

Horigawa nodded in acceptance of her compliment. "You are fortunate to have a wellborn man of the capital as a husband. Think how miserable you would have been in the arms of some rough country man smelling of the rice paddies."

Remembering Horigawa's role in the executions of four years ago and his talk about massive bloodshed, Taniko thought, I would prefer the smell of the rice paddies to the stink of the execution ground.

Horigawa reached into the sleeve of his robe and drew out a scroll. "This is a report I received from a monk in China. I intend to present it to Lord Sogamori. You will translate it into our language and write it out in your best hand. I trust your handwriting is acceptable?"

"My handwriting has been praised," said Taniko, "but it is, of course, only the poor effort of a girl raised in a rustic fishing village."

The sarcasm escaped Horigawa. "Lord Sogamori is a man of some discernment, even though he is merely the chieftain of a samurai family. You must be sure to form your characters as beautifully as you can."

Taniko put the scroll in the drawer of her wooden pillow. She could hardly wait for some time to herself, to read the letter from China.

Horigawa ate the ritual rice cakes with her, honoring Izanami and Izanagi, progenitors of all the kami and creators of heaven and earth. She almost wished her own cake were saturated with poison. Then Horigawa removed his hat of office and lay down, resting his head on the wooden pillow she had placed beside her own. With a wave of his hand, he indicated that she was to blow out the candle.

They slept in the same clothing they had worn all day, as was usual. Side by side they lay in the dark on quilted futons. Horigawa was a restless sleeper who mumbled and moaned as if bad dreams troubled him all through the night. Bad dreams might portend future disasters for Horigawa. The possibility pleased her, because her only hope was that he might not live long. Perhaps he was haunted by the ghosts of those whose executions he'd demanded.

Taniko lay awake most of the night. As she had tried to do on her first night with Horigawa, she sent her mind on a journey—this time to Mount Higashi and the night she had spent there with Jebu.

In the morning the Shima family, led by Uncle Ryuichi, Aunt Chogao and their eldest son, five-year-old Munetoki, burst in on them with the expected cries of joy and congratulations. Having spent three nights together and partaken of the sacred rice cakes they were now officially married. However, Taniko would remain in the Shima household, as was the custom among people of their class, and Horigawa would visit her as often as he chose to bestow his princely favors. Taniko hoped lust would provoke him infrequently. She would go to his house when needed there for ceremonial and social occasions.

Taniko's uncle and aunt each picked up one of Horigawa's shoes. By taking the shoes to bed with them that night, they would try to insure that Horigawa would never leave Taniko. Each such sign that the world wanted this marriage to be permanent made Taniko's heart sink a little lower.

Horigawa imperiously handed Ryuichi a scroll. "This is a list of the guests I wish you to invite to the wedding feast. You will hold the feast on the thirteenth day of the Ninth Month, four days after the Chrysanthmum Festival. My diviners tell me that will be the last auspicious day for quite some time." He took another scroll from his sleeve. "I have also included a set of instructions on how the feast is to be conducted. It is essential that every detail be both correct and fashionable. I prefer not to rely on the judgment of a provincial family in such matters."

After Horigawa was gone, Ryuichi raged and wept. He was furious at the prince's contempt for his family, and appalled at the cost of the wedding feast, which, he claimed, would wipe out the family fortune if he followed Horigawa's instructions.

"Why did you have to marry that leech?" Ryuichi howled at Taniko.

Taniko bowed to hide her amusement. "Forgive me, Uncle. I regret that he causes you such pain. My father commanded me to marry him for reasons that seemed wise to him."

Ryuichi subsided. "We expect the marriage to do us good. But if my esteemed older brother had only let me arrange a match for you, instead of doing it by himself from such a great distance—" He smiled suddenly. "You, also, might have been happier with the result. You're a good daughter, Taniko, to put up with marriage to such a repulsive person."

"I intend to do more than put up with it, Uncle. I have always wanted to live in the capital and be part of the doings at the Court. I have never wanted the lot of an ordinary woman. If Horigawa is the price I have to pay to live here, I accept that price. Perhaps I will do well for myself despite the match my father made.''

Her little cousin Munetoki stared at her, his eyes shining with admiration.

9

On the day of the wedding feast some of the best-known names in Heian Kyo came to see the mating of a major councillor of the Fourth Rank to the daughter of an unknown, but reputedly wealthy, family of the provinces. Taniko had studied the guest list carefully. As the presiding priest, the abbot of the huge Buddhist monastery on nearby Mount Hiei intoned blessings and purifications, the guests clapped their hands ritually. Whenever she dared, Taniko glanced here and there among those present, trying to match faces and costumes with the names she knew.

Many members of the Sasaki family and their principal wives had come to sit behind Horigawa to represent the clan. And another old and powerful family was there in large numbers—the Fujiwara. While they were not Emperors themselves, the Fujiwara had held supreme power in the capital until recent times. So many Fujiwara daughters had married Emperors that, among those who dared to be irreverent, the Imperial house itself was sometimes described as a branch of the Fujiwara.

In recent times, though they still enjoyed great prestige, the real power of the Fujiwara had declined. Their strength lay in courtly intrigue rather than force. But these days, with the rise of the samurai families, force counted for more.

Among those supplanting the Fujiwara in national importance were the Takashi, also heavily represented at this wed-

ding feast. They sat in the front row of guests facing the abbot and the altar. Sogamori, chieftain of the Takashi clan and Minister of the Left, was a round-faced man whose partially shaven head was hidden under his black hat of office. He wore a red cloak embroidered with gold and lined with white satin. He looked as florid and petulant as Taniko had expected, given his reputation for bad temper.

The man in a similar scarlet robe beside Sogamori must be Kiyosi, his eldest son. Taniko's heart beat a little faster when she saw him. There was a family resemblance to Sogamori, but Kiyosi was lean, vigorous-looking, and square of jaw. Oh, to marry a young man like that, instead of a spider like Horigawa. Such a young man, she thought, might almost help me forget Jebu—for a time.

Kiyosi sat proudly upright as befit a military man of noble rank. Yet there was kindness and intelligence in his face as well. She suspected that, like Jebu, Kiyosi could be frighteningly violent, gently compassionate or overwhelmingly ardent.

She wondered, will I spend the rest of my life comparing every man I meet to Jebu?

She wondered too what might have happened if, that night on Mount Higashi, she had suggested to Jebu that they run away together instead of going on to Heian Kyo. He was dedicated to his Order, but he was young and passionate. He might well have broken his vow of obedience for her. But she had not asked, and he had not been tested. Why? Because she did not want to give up her way of life, any more than he would want to give up his.

Just as he would not want to betray his Order, she did not want to betray her family. It was as Aunt Chogao had said; she was samurai just as much as any man of the Shima, and if war was the duty of men, marriage was the duty of women. If the men of her family could face the naked swords of their enemies, she could face the bitterness of a life with Horigawa.

The wedding banquet was long, and some guests left early while others stayed late. Much sake was drunk, but many of the guests were intrigued by a beverage from China called *ch'ai*. It was not new to the Sunrise Land, but drinking it had only recently become fashionable. As a wedding gift the Takashi lord, Sogamori, had had nine large metal boxes full of *ch'ai* bricks sent from one of his ships recently landed at Hyogo.

Sogamori and his son Kiyosi, sitting beside Horigawa and Ryuichi, were among the late stayers. Each banqueter had his small, individual table for food and drink, and each had several attendants hovering behind him. Taniko sat behind her husband and served his food and kept a sake jar and a pot of water for *ch'ai* warm for him. Horigawa ate and drank little, and most of the time Taniko sat with her eyes downcast and her face hidden behind her fan, with nothing to do.

"I notice you're careful to drink mostly *ch'ai*, Horigawa," Sogamori said in his deep, hoarse voice. "That's very wise. You wouldn't want to be too drunk to enjoy the night with your new wife."

"I must keep my mind alert to converse adequately with the distinguished Minister of the Left," Horigawa said in a voice as sweet as a plum. "Ch'ai sharpens the wits."

"I'll bet the lady is dozing behind her fan," Sogamori laughed. "This banquet and all this men's talk is putting her to sleep, Horigawa. If I were you I'd take her to bed and wake her up."

"I'm sure you would, if you were I," said Horigawa. "The minister's exploits in the flowery combat are as well known as his valor in war."

Kiyosi laughed. "As well known, but not as successful, eh, Father? You may have more authority and honor than Domei, but he's bested you in the bedchamber."

"I don't know what you're talking about," Sogamori growled.

"Neither do I," said Horigawa.

Kiyosi said, "Your Highness is so conscientiously devoted to affairs of state, you pay no attention to affairs of the heart. I'm referring to my father's impetuous wooing of Lady Akimi."

"You ought to have more respect for your father than to mention such things in public," said Sogamori irritably.

"You should have more respect for your clan, Father, than to make us a laughingstock at Court." Kiyosi's tone was light, but there was a barely concealed edge in his voice.

Taniko was surprised that Kiyosi would needle his father in front of herself, Horigawa and Ryuichi. She knew quite well what they were talking about. All the Shima women were laughing over Sogamori's rude attempt to seduce Akimi, the beautiful lady-in-waiting who had been Domei's mistress for many years.

Like most of Heian Kyo's aristocrats, Sogamori had many women in his life. Besides his principal wife, Kiyosi's mother, he had a number of secondary wives, each of whom had her apartment in the Rokuhara. Gossip also attributed one or two mistresses to him at any given time. But, just as he was always reaching for more power in the realm, so he was always pursuing new women. Taking advantage of the Muratomo lord's temporary absence from the capital, Sogamori had laid siege to Lady Akimi with flute-playing, poetry, dancing and flowers, as if he had but to display his interest to win her. All this despite the fact that Akimi already had a son by Domei. Akimi adamantly ignored Sogamori's advances and he eventually had to give up. The Court, which had come to fear him, enjoyed the opportunity of ridiculing him. When Domei returned and heard about the incident, he was enraged at first, but ended up laughing along with everyone else.

"The lady showed poor taste," Ryuichi ventured. "How could she prefer a rough, ill-mannered warrior like Captain Domei to a polished gentleman like Lord Sogamori?"

Sogamori looked at him sourly, obviously unimpressed by the flattery.

"With respect, Ryuichi-san," said Kiyosi. "Warriors are not to be sneered at. We Takashi, are we not a clan of warriors?"

Taniko couldn't help but look directly at Kiyosi, drawn by the strong, pleasant voice. She knew it was shameful for a woman to look into the eyes of any man other than her husband, but her growing fascination with Kiyosi, fed by her dislike for Horigawa, drove her to stare directly at him for the briefest of moments. The large, dark eyes held hers, enchanting her. She gave a little gasp and then looked down at the charcoal warmer she was watching over.

Kiyosi held his sake cup out to her to cover the look she had given him. She quickly raised the white porcelain jar and filled the dainty cup.

"Neither gentlemen nor warriors should concern themselves with idle Court gossip," said Horigawa sententiously.

"You need not interest yourself in women of the Court," said Sogamori. "Your own wife far outshines Akimi in beauty." He raised his sake cup toward Taniko and drank. She felt a chill of fear at the undertone of lechery in his voice.

Horigawa said with faint contempt, "She is merely a young girl of provincial family, not used to the ways of the capital."

"She is of good family, related to the Takashi," Sogamori retorted. "You forget yourself at times, Horigawa. Or else you forget who I am. Your wife will learn the ways of the capital. The courtiers laughed at my father for his clumsy dancing when he visited the great temples, but I was born here in Heian Kyo and my father saw to it that I studied under the finest dancing masters. Now, when I dance before the gods, no one laughs at me."

"No one would dare," said Kiyosi wryly. "You'd have their heads."

"Is it not this little wife of yours who translated the letter from China for me?" Sogamori asked. "Her handwriting is exquisite."

Horigawa bowed as if he himself had been complimented.

He squints like an old ape, Taniko thought. She screened her face with her fan, conscious of Kiyosi smiling at her.

From the pillow book of Shima Taniko:

Old Squint-Eyes has arranged for me to be appointed a lady-in-waiting to the Empress, a unique honor for a girl born and raised so far from the capital. I am to be presented at Court on the first day of the Eleventh Month, as soon as the inauspicious Tenth Month, during which the kami are absent, is over. Uncle Ryuichi is tearing his garments over the cost of my new wardrobe, but I have promised that whenever I can I will pass on secrets of the China trade. One good investment will repay the cost of my Court robes many times over.

I have already learned a number of fascinating things about China, just from the three letters I have now translated for my husband. For one thing, there are two Chinas, a northern China, also called Cathay, which is ruled by ferocious barbarians, and a southern China, which is governed from Linan by an Emperor of the Sung dynasty.

The barbarians, known as Mongols, who rule Cathay have conquered many kingdoms to the north and west of

China. They were making war on the Sung Emperor, but they stopped three years ago, when their own Emperor, whom they call the Great Khan, died. When their Great Khan dies these Mongols immediately cease all warfare until they have chosen a new ruler. They choose their Emperors at a great council of the Mongol chieftains. A strange and frightening people.

As for me, I cannot wait to take up my duties at Court.

—*Ninth Month, twentieth day,*
    YEAR OF THE DRAGON

Used to the bustle of a provincial family devoted to war, land and trade, Taniko found life within the Nine-Fold Enclosure very different and very elegant, but frequently dull. Ladies-in-waiting lived most of the time in the Empress's residence, the Wisteria Hall. Nothing ever happened except when the diviners declared the day auspicious or when the calendar called for the performance of some age-old rite. There were endless stretches of idle time during which the ladies-in-waiting entertained one another by playing games such as go and backgammon or holding contests in poetry-writing, flower matching or incense comparing.

One afternoon in early spring a commotion in the Empress's chambers caught Taniko's ear—barks and growls, mewings and hissings, the shrieks and screams of the Empress and other women. Taniko rushed into Her Imperial Majesty's bedroom.

The Empress's favorite cat, Myobu, a beautiful creature with long orange hair, was perched atop a tall mahogany cabinet, screaming feline imprecations and batting its claws at a brown dog no bigger than itself. The dog kept up a ferocious, high-pitched bark and bounded into the air, trying to get at the Empress's cat.

Empress Sadako, normally a placid woman, was as frightened by the dog's frenzy as her cat was, and was weeping with anxiety. She and the other ladies in the room were rendered helpless by their distress.

"Oh, Taniko-san, rescue Myobu. Please, please hurry."

With a bow to the Empress, Taniko seized the dog and tucked him under her arm. He squirmed and barked furiously.

He was of a Chinese breed and looked to Taniko like a giant, furry frog. Taniko recognized the dog at once. He was called Li Po and belonged to Lady Akimi, Domei's mistress. Akimi had been away from the palace for several days. It was customary for ladies-in-waiting to retire to their homes during their unclean time of the month.

Taniko knew Akimi as well as she knew most of the Empress's attendants, but there was something that set her apart from the other women, a calm nobility of manner that made Taniko want to get to know her better. But Akimi was reserved with Taniko. After all, Taniko was married to one of the Muratomo family's worst enemies. Akimi could not know that Taniko heartily approved of Akimi's lover. She had seen the dashing, mustachioed Captain Domei riding on the grounds at the head of the palace guard. How could the bearlike Sogamori imagine that he could compete with such a man for Akimi's favors? She had heard how the previous Emperor, now retired, had ill-treated Domei, how he had repaid Domei's loyalty to him during the insurrection by ordering him to execute his own father, how Domei had been neglected while that Emperor and his successor showered favors, offices and honors on his Takashi rivals. Her heart went out to Domei.

Empress Sadako floundered over to the cabinet, her skirts and underskirts billowing around her, and held up her arms to the cat. "Come down, my precious, come to Mother." Myobu jumped into the Empress's arms.

Her Imperial Majesty turned to Taniko. "That dog has terrified my poor Myobu. Animals like that should not be permitted to run loose in the palace. Have him punished."

Taniko was about to point out that the dog belonged to one of Her Imperial Majesty's senior ladies, but she realized that the Empress probably knew that and preferred not to acknowledge it. Did Sadako want the dog destroyed? Taniko decided it would be best to get the animal out of sight and not ask any more questions.

But, she thought as she hurried out of the Wisteria Hall with Li Po in her arms, if she had Akimi's dog killed, she would make a permanent enemy of Domei's mistress, who already, regrettably, had reason to dislike her. Besides, she liked the little dog. He lay in her arms calmly and trustingly. At the foot of the Wisteria Hall's steps, she looked about her.

In the distance a group of officers of the palace guards were playing football in front of the Hall of Military Virtues.

The game was an ancient favorite with the male nobles. A circle of men tried to keep a soft leather ball in the air as long as possible, solely by kicking it. Taniko approached them. She knew a few of the guard officers slightly, and one of them might have an idea about what to do with the dog.

Once again Taniko thanked her karma that she was serving at the Court, where she was permitted to go and talk to anyone, man or woman, face-to-face. It must be maddening to spend all one's days and nights hiding behind a screen or fan as noble ladies who lived at home did.

One of the football players was Domei. That gave her an idea.

Domei must have been at least ten years older than any of the other men playing, but he had the greatest energy and enthusiasm. He played competitively, trying to keep the ball to himself, kicking it out from under the noses of the other players, aiming his kicks so close to their heads that they were forced to back off. The men playing with him laughed heartily at each new display of Domei's aggressiveness.

Taniko waited until there was a break in the game, then diffidently beckoned Domei. The captain came to her at once and bowed.

"Lady Taniko, how may I serve you?" If he felt any hostility toward her because of her husband, he didn't show it.

His breath steamed on the winter air. Muratomo no Domei was a tall, broad-shouldered man with the dark complexion of one who spent most of his time outdoors, an unfashionable color at a Court where men and women powdered their faces to make themselves even paler. His forehead was high and bulging. All his hair was shaved away except for the lock on top neatly tied in the samurai topknot. His large head gleamed with perspiration. His big moustache drew attention to his most unfortunate feature, protruding front teeth.

Taniko explained about the Empress's wish to punish the dog. She didn't bother to point out that it was Akimi's pet. She was sure Domei recognized it.

"Frightening Her Imperial Majesty's cat is a grave offense.

I will take change of the prisoner.'' He took the dog from her hands and held him, stroking his head.

"What are you going to do with him, captain-san?'' Taniko asked uncertainly.

"Well, the palace guards use stray dogs for archery practice.''

Shocked, Taniko put a hand to her mouth.

"Would you like to witness the execution, my lady?''

"No, no.''

Taniko's impression of the Muratomo was still colored by the uncouth oryoshi Jebu had killed last year on the Tokaido. But that man wasn't a member of the Muratomo family, just one of their paid supporters. Domei seemed pleasant and kindly enough, although his manners did lack the refinement one found in members of the old families of the capital. Taniko didn't believe Domei would really kill Akimi's dog.

Everyone said the Muratomo were dreadfully crude, but Domei was undoubtedly an excellent choice for the post of captain of the palace guard. He was obviously a born fighter, as different from the stout, moon-faced courtiers as a falcon is from a partridge.

When it came to military glory there were more legends about the Muratomo family than any other. They had migrated to the eastern provinces centuries before to build up their fortunes. There they spearheaded the opening up of the rich rice lands of the Kanto plain, driving the savage hairy Ainu before them. Their patron kami was Hachiman, god of war, and one Muratomo general who won dazzling victories was called Hachiman's Oldest Son.

In the last century the Muratomo had quelled two of the most dangerous rebellions ever raised against the crown, the Early Nine Years War and the Later Three Years War. Ill-mannered the Muratomo might be, but they were peerless warriors.

Lady Akimi returned to the Wisteria Hall a day later. Her eyes were red with weeping, and several times she burst into unexplained tears in the presence of the Empress.

Sadako was a kindhearted woman who couldn't stand to see any of her ladies unhappy. But try as she could, it was

almost impossible for her to persuade Akimi to tell her what
was wrong.

Only when the Empress herself began to cry did Akimi
answer her insistent questions. "Oh, Your Majesty, I've
heard that the captain of the Imperial bodyguard has shot my
little dog, Li Po."

The Empress looked away uneasily. "I had not heard
that."

"Oh yes, Your Majesty. But what really makes me weep is
that Li Po displeased you. Killing him was the only thing to
do." ·

"I didn't order your dog executed, Akimi-san," the Empress said pleadingly. She turned to Taniko. "Please send for
Captain Domei."

Domei came quickly and prostrated himself before the
Empress. She asked him what happened to the dog.

"As I told the Lady Taniko, Your Majesty, I felt that the
only proper punishment for a dog that frightened Your Imperial Majesty's cat was to let it be used as a target for mounted
archery practice."

"Barbarous," the Empress exclaimed. "You have caused
great pain to one of my most esteemed ladies. I am very
angry with you, Captain Domei."

Domei lowered his head. "I ask that Your Imperial Majesty
order me beheaded in expiation."

Sadako winced. "Please, Captain Domei. There has been
quite enough killing. Just leave us now. There is nothing
more you can do."

Domei left. But later in the day he returned and presented
the Empress with a little brown dog that looked to be Li Po.
He insisted, however, that the dog wasn't Li Po.

"I believe this to be the reincarnation of Li Po," Domei
said. "By a special blessing of the kami we have him back
among us." Akimi hugged the dog.

"How can this be the reincarnation of the other dog when
it is obviously the same age as that dog?" the Empress asked.

"I wouldn't pretend to know, Your Majesty," Domei said.
"I'm not a very religious man." Seated in a corner of the
room, Taniko hid her smile behind her fan.

The Empress said, "Might it not be simpler to say that this
is that dog and that you did not kill it?"

"But that would mean I had disobeyed Your Majesty," said Domei. "As it is, the dog has been disposed of as you ordered, but we have another dog and the Lady Akimi is happy."

"Do the two of you imagine you are tricking me?" Sadako asked sternly.

Akimi immediately fell to her knees and pressed her forehead against the floor. "No, Your Majesty, never. We regret that we have disturbed your harmony with this matter of the dog. Dogs."

The Empress dismissed them. The new dog, which Akimi called Tu Fu, was accepted as a resident of the Wisteria Hall.

The next day Akimi came to Taniko's chamber. She was about ten years older than Taniko and one of the most beautiful women Taniko had ever seen, with large eyes and a face shaped in a perfect oval.

"Domei and I want to thank you for your kindness. If you had given my little Li Po to anybody but him, I might have lost him forever. Li Po is a favorite pet of our son, Yukio, and he would have been heartbroken if anything had ever happened to him."

Taniko bowed. "I was very grateful for the opportunity to be of service to you, Lady Akimi. May I say also that you are a marvelous actress?"

Akimi laughed. She held out a package wrapped in silk. "I would like you to have this. It is a small gift, compared to the life of a beloved pet, but I hope you will enjoy it."

Taniko unfolded the silk cloth and found a book bound in red leather.

"This is the first volume of a very long story called *The Tale of the Hollow Tree*," said Akimi. "It was written about two hundred years ago by an official of the Court. This particular copy was presented to me by my mother. Both the calligraphy and the illustrations have always given me much pleasure."

"Thank you," said Taniko, opening the book and admiring a delicately tinted painting of a weeping woman. "I don't deserve this."

Akimi looked grave. "Domei and I believe that you wanted to show friendship for us. We do not have many friends in the

Court, and none among the members of your family. Forgive
me for mentioning it, but there is undying enmity between
Domei and your husband.''

''I know,'' said Taniko. ''And, of course, I have a duty of
absolute loyalty to my husband. But where duty does not
compel me, I believe I can pick my friends as I choose. I
should be deeply honored to be counted among your friends,
as far as that is possible.''

Akimi looked at her gravely. ''Karma brings many surprising turns to our lives. We will think of you as a friend.
Whatever happens.''

Later, reading the book Akimi had given her, Taniko let
her eyes wander from the page. She was happy that her
gesture of friendship had been accepted, but there was an
ominous note in Akimi's voice when she said, ''Whatever
happens.'' Domei was obviously a proud man, and he had
lived a long time with heavy grievances. Was the apparent
serenity of the Court, Taniko wondered, actually the heavy
silence that comes before an earthquake?

10

For Jebu, the world had come to seem like a desert after he
parted from Taniko. He returned to the ruins of the New
Moon Temple on Mount Higashi, overlooking Heian Kyo,
where he waited with his brother monks for a new command
from the Order. A month later a monk arrived with a message
from the Zinja Council of Abbots. The site of the New Moon
Temple was to be abandoned, and the survivors of the
earthquake were to move to the Autumn Wind Temple at
Nara, two days' journey from Heian Kyo.

Three months after Jebu took up residence at the Autumn
Wind Temple, a new abbot arrived. He sent for Jebu.

"Your father, Abbot Taitaro of the Waterfowl Temple, sends you greetings and congratulates you on the performance of your first task. You sent him a samurai sword which you took in battle. He wanted to know why you did that."

"I sent it to him as a gift, to honor him," said Jebu. "And I had some notion that treating a samurai sword as a trophy might chasten the arrogance of the warriors."

The abbot looked thoughtful. "One captured sword would not have that effect, but a large collection might. You're a big, strong lad. You might live long enough to collect a hundred samurai swords."

"I'll try."

"You'll have plenty of opportunities. You're now commanded to enter the service of the Muratomo. Your father urged the Order to be guided by your initiation vision. You will work for various members of the White Dragon clan, but your orders will ultimately be coming from the head of the family, Domei."

Jebu carried messages from Domei to the eastern provinces and to the northernmost reaches of Honshu. He traveled to the southern end of Kyushu, where the people retained some of the barbaric customs of the Kumaso, those cannibal tribesmen long ago conquered by the founders of the Imperial family.

Often there was fighting to be done. Whenever he defeated a samurai he would send the long sword to the Waterfowl Temple. The collection of swords grew to ten, then twenty. Jebu had recited the Prayer to a Fallen Enemy so many times that it required intense concentration for him to maintain awareness of its meaning.

When he was not traveling, he remained at the Autumn Wind Temple, seeking insight through the practice of swordsmanship, archery and various kinds of hand-to-hand combat. He helped to teach the few aspiring monks who lived at the temple and even participated in two initiations.

He never met Domei. The Muratomo chieftain transmitted his messages and orders through others. Jebu preferred it that way. He wanted to avoid Heian Kyo; he had no wish to see Taniko or hear anything about her. But not an hour passed that he did not think of her.

News from the capital reached the Autumn Wind Temple

often, though. Power and honors flocked to Sogamori as birds gather on a temple roof, while Domei was repeatedly slighted and passed over. Bitterness between the two clans continued to grow.

In the Twelfth Month of the Year of the Horse, two years after Jebu had escorted Taniko to Heian Kyo, the abbot of the Autumn Wind Temple handed Jebu a message signed with Domei's cipher. Jebu was to come to the Imperial Palace immediately, prepared for combat.

The abbot's eyes were alight with excitement. "This morning Domei seized control of the Nine-Fold Enclosure and placed Emperor Nijo under guard in the Serene and Cool Hall. Domei has been planning this for some time. Five days ago the Takashi clan chieftain, Sogamori, and his son, Kiyosi, left on a pilgrimage to the family shrine dedicated to the kami known as Beautiful Island Princess on Itsukushima island. With the Takashi leaders out of the capital, Domei chose this moment to strike. He remembers the many missions you've performed for him and wants your services now."

On the afternoon of the following day, Jebu rode to one of the three gates in the eastern wall of the Imperial Palace grounds and identified himself to the guards. Captain Domei, they said, was at the Hall of Military Virtues.

Over his gray robe Jebu wore the standard black-laced battle armor of a warrior monk. It might be true, as the Order taught, that a man's armor was his mind and that a naked man could utterly demolish a man clad in steel, but the Order also taught that for stopping arrows there was nothing like metal and leather. The armor of the warrior monks was lighter and closer fitting than the box-shaped armor of the samurai. Instead of a helmet Jebu wore a gray cowl tied around his head and covering the lower part of his face and the back of his neck. In addition to his sword and his bow, he carried a naginata with a long blade.

The walls of the Imperial Palace enclosed a park and a collection of buildings which constituted a city in itself. Some of the halls were huge and heavy, set on stone bases with roofs of green glazed tile supported by white walls and red lacquered pillars. Other buildings, though also large, were built in a style more familiar to Jebu, of plain wood with wattled roofs. All the halls were connected by a maze of colonnades. In the northeast corner of the enclosure was the simple wooden residence of the Imperial family, surrounding a landscaped garden. The rest of the grounds was strewn with finely raked white gravel.

On the parade ground before the Hall of Military Virtues, a tile-roofed pavilion which was headquarters for the palace guard, a hundred men, deployed in extended order to form a square, were practicing sword drill. Off to one side lines of men with tall samurai bows were waiting their turn to shoot at targets shaped like warriors. In the distance lines of horsemen galloped back and forth firing arrows at fleeing dogs released by attendants. Domei was keeping his tense fighting men busy with drill and more drill.

Domei stood in the center of a group of samurai, all wearing armor with white lacings. Jebu bowed and presented himself. Domei's men eyed his gray cowl and black-laced armor with curiosity.

"Ah, the Zinja I sent for," Domei said. "Shike, are you prepared to fight and die to rid the empire of criminals and traitors?"

Jebu was prepared to fight and die, and he didn't particularly care for what reason. His Zinja training encouraged him to view the purpose of life as action, and life and death as equally acceptable. His meeting with Taniko and his loss of her made the Zinja philosophy even more congenial.

"I do as my Order bids," he said.

"I have His Imperial Majesty in my safekeeping, I have control of the Imperial Palace, and I have most members of the Great Council of State. There are two things that must be done now. The first is to kill Prince Sasaki no Horigawa, the man who brought about my father's death."

Jebu was startled to hear the name of Taniko's husband. He should have realized, he thought, that Horigawa would be one of the first targets of any Muratomo coup. He must not involve himself in Horigawa's death. Taniko must have nothing to reproach him for.

He was relieved when Domei continued, "My son Hideyori here will lead men to hunt down Horigawa." Domei rested his hand on Hideyori's shoulder. Hideyori had the same high forehead as his father, but he was very young. "This one is

only fifteen," Domei said with a smile. "We have just cut
his hair and tied it in the samurai topknot. At first I wanted
him to stay home like his younger brother, Yukio. But all my
other sons are with me, and Hideyori insisted that he, too,
must share in restoring the glory of the Muratomo. So I
relented." Hideyori looked at Jebu without smiling. He had
the coldest eyes Jebu had ever seen.

"The other task is to take the Retired Emperor, Go-
Shirakawa, into custody. At the moment he is at his Sanjo
palace, guarded by his own men. That's what I want you
for."

Jebu's training had included a grounding in politics. He
understood that for hundreds of years the office of Emperor
had been a ceremonial one, without power. It was the Re-
gents, always members of the Fujiwara family, who were the
real rulers. But recently the Emperors had found a way to
assert themselves—by retiring. A Retired Emperor was free
of time-consuming ritual duties. He was not under the control
of the Regent. He lived in a palace of his own, away from the
Imperial Palace grounds. And he retained the prestige of
having been an Emperor. To make themselves even more
revered, many of the Retired Emperors entered the Buddhist
priesthood. The Retired Emperors were thus a new center of
power, and were even able to name their successors on the
throne.

To hold the Emperor in captivity, while valuable, was not
as useful to Domei as having the Retired Emperor in his
power. That would give him virtual mastery of the realm.

"Once we have His Retired Majesty, Go-Shirakawa," Domei
went on, "we will require the Great Council of State to meet.
They will proclaim Sogamori and Kiyosi rebels and outlaws.
They will appoint me Minister of the Left in place of Sogamori.
And they will appoint a new Regent chosen by me."

"You want me to take Go-Shirakawa for you?" Jebu
asked.

"Yes. As a Zinja you are two things a samurai is not. You
are a monk and you are capable of stealth. I want you to lead
a party of men to the Sanjo palace tonight. We could make a
frontal attack during the day, but it would take too many men
away from here, and I must hold the Imperial Palace at all
costs. And seeing us attack the Retired Emperor's palace

might stir up the people against us. I want this done quietly
and quickly, with as few men as possible. You will have the
honor of scaling the wall first and opening the gate for my
samurai. Then you will handle Go-Shirakawa. Since he is a
priest, most samurai would be reluctant to touch him. Being
an ordained monk, you will, I hope, feel no hindrance. Are
you up to all that?''

"I think I can do it, Lord Domei.'' A wave of exhilaration
swept through Jebu. What he did tonight might well determine the future of the empire. And it would allow him to use
his powers to the fullest and to risk his life. For the time
being Taniko seemed unimportant. This was what he had
been put into the world for.

Long after sundown Jebu and a small body of mounted
Muratomo samurai were on their way to Go-Shirakawa's
residence, the Sanjo palace. Behind them was an ox-drawn
carriage.

When they were close to the palace, Jebu signaled a halt
and crept toward the building on foot, taking one samurai
with him. The palace was a two-story building surrounded by
a bamboo palisade twice the height of a man, and it, in turn,
was protected by a wide moat.

Jebu handed his bow and quiver to the samurai accompanying him. Thinking of a shadow, he crept along the street to
the edge of the moat and slipped soundlessly into the water.
Swimming in armor was one of the many skills stressed in the
training of a Zinja. The water was ice-cold, almost paralyzing
him. Without hesitation he plunged his head under the surface
and, relying on his sense of direction, swimming as a frog
swims through the blackness, he touched the opposite bank of
the moat.

There was a low stone wall on this side, behind which the
bamboo palisade had been built. Clinging with his fingertips
to the wall, Jebu drew a strong, light silk cable and a grapple
out of a bag at his belt. The grapple was weighted in the
center, and its four hooks folded together for compactness in
carrying. Jebu snapped the grapple open, drew back his arm,
and threw it to the top of the palisade.

Pulling himself hand over hand, he was up the palisade in

two breaths. On the other side there was a newly built gallery
for archers; Go-Shirakawa had evidently feared an attack.

Dripping cold water and smelling of rotten weeds, Jebu
tiptoed along the gallery toward the gate where a guard armed
with a naginata stood, relaxed. Jebu drew an eight-pointed
shuriken out of his robe and scaled it at the guard. The
whirling blades bit into the man's throat, spraying blood as he
fell.

The man was making gurgling sounds, trying to give an
alarm as he died. Jebu dropped down from the gallery, picked
up the fallen guard's naginata and stabbed him in the chest,
muttering the Prayer to a Fallen Enemy under his breath. He
straightened and pushed up the bolt that fastened the wooden
gate .

He heard heavy feet rushing at him. Whirling, he swung
the naginata with all his strength and sliced the attacker's
right leg off below the knee. Even as the man's scream woke
the defenders of the Sanjo palace, Jebu finished him with a
naginata thrust into his mouth.

Repeating the Prayer to a Fallen Enemy, Jebu pushed the
gate open. The Muratomo samurai who had come with him
were through the gate and fanning out in the courtyard. A line
of Go-Shirakawa's servants formed to block the way to the
Retired Emperor. Jebu felt sorry for them. They were not true
samurai, only armed servants. Beyond the defenders, in the
main hall of the Sanjo palace, Jebu could hear the screams of
women and the cries of courtiers.

Some of the retainers fell with falcon-feathered Muratomo
arrows in their chests and bellies. Others were cut down by
slashing samurai swords. Jebu ran up the steps of the pavilion. He stabbed one of the Retired Emperor's guards with his
short Zinja sword. Another guard lunged at him, holding a
long, thin courtier's sword in both hands. Jebu darted aside
and stabbed his attacker through the forearm. The man came
at him again, one-handed, chopping. This time Jebu cut off
his sword arm, and the guard screamed and fell.

Then Jebu was in the presence of Go-Shirakawa. The
Retired Emperor sat cross-legged on a high pile of cushions
on a dais, his pendulous lower lip jutting out as he frowned
severely at Jebu.

"Truly we have entered an age when the teachings of

Buddha are forgotten, if an aged monk in his retreat can be attacked by bandits."

I can posture as well as you, Jebu thought. Glancing around quickly to make sure no one was about to attack him, Jebu fell to his knees and knocked his forehead on the cedar floor. "Oh, Holiness, this miserable monk has come at the command of the captain of the palace guards. Captain Domei believes that you are in grave danger here and respectfully urges that you take the carriage he has provided to the Imperial Palace, where he can better protect yourself and His Imperial Majesty."

Go-Shirakawa settled himself rocklike on his dais. "The Zinja are murderers masquerading as monks. Be warned: to lay hands on me is to insult the very flesh of She Who Shines in the Heavens. I will not go."

Jebu heard a cry behind him. He whirled. A courtier brandishing a dagger was leaping at him. Jebu grabbed the man's wrist, tripped him and threw him to the floor. He knelt on the courtier's back and used the man's own knife to cut his throat. He stood back, wiped the knife on the dying man's robe, and stuck the blade in his belt, stepping away from the widening pool of blood on the polished floor.

"Indeed, these are unsettled times, Holiness."

Go-Shirakawa looked thoughtful. "The red of his blood contrasts with the pale green silk of his robe. Clearly if such things as this can happen at my very feet I am not safe here. You may escort me to the Imperial Palace."

Jebu preceded Go-Shirakawa through the doorway of his palace. Outside, the pitiful courtier guards who knew next to nothing about swordplay, lay scattered on the ground, so many butchered corpses.

The helmeted samurai prostrated themselves when Go-Shirakawa in his orange Buddhist priest's robe appeared on the steps of the pavilion. Jebu snapped his fingers and the ox-drawn carriage was brought around to the steps. A samurai knelt and presented his back to the sacred feet as Go-Shirakawa climbed into the carriage. Another warrior slid the door shut, and the Retired Emperor was alone with his meditations.

"Mount up," Jebu ordered. "Form a circle around the carriage." They had not lost a single man. That pleased him.

The last person to leave the Sanjo palace was a samurai with a bloody sword in one hand and a torch in the other.

"No!" Jebu called, even as the man's arm snapped forward and the torch flew through the air. Flames leaped up to engulf the palace.

Domei had given strict orders that the taking of Go-Shirakawa be smooth and quiet. But no discipline seemed strong enough to contain the samurai lust for destruction. The samurai, thought Jebu angrily, why were they such brutes? Supposedly in arms to serve and protect the empire, they were reducing it to ruins.

Go-Shirakawa had said something about this being an age when the teachings of Buddha were forgotten. Jebu had heard other Buddhist priests speak on the same theme, calling these times the Latter Days of the Law. The Buddha, they said, had predicted that the day would come when his laws would be broken and the world sink into chaos. It did seem, thought Jebu as the bonfire of the Sanjo palace roared into the sky, that everything old, everything beautiful, everything wise was gradually vanishing. Perhaps, indeed, these were the Latter Days of the Law.

11

At sundown on the day the Muratomo seized control of the Imperial Palace, Horigawa and a small contingent of bodyguards stopped at the Shima residence. Horigawa sent for Taniko.

"I got your message. Your are a dutiful wife. But by the time it reached me I had already learned of the Muratomo coup. How did you escape from the palace?"

"I was able to slip out through the northeast gate before

Domei's men had complete control of the palace. The palace grounds and buildings are so complicated; they're hard to guard and easy to escape through if you know your way around.''

What Taniko did not add was that a frightened Akimi had awakened her before dawn. ''You are in danger. You must leave the palace now, by the northeast gate. It isn't guarded yet.''

''What's happening, Akimi-san?''

''Domei is about to seize the palace and take the Emperor and Empress prisoner.''

''Why? He must be mad. It's his duty to protect the Emperor.''

''He's been abused for too long. He wants to take control of the government and avenge himself on his enemies. His men are ready to move at sunrise. This is your last chance to get out. Hurry and dress.''

Taniko's mind was racing. ''It's my duty to stay here with the Empress.''

''No one will hurt the Empress. But you are Horigawa's wife. Even though he likes you, Domei will have to use you as a hostage to try to get Horigawa. We know that Horigawa won't put himself in Domei's hands to save you. That means Domei may have to hurt you. You must get out now.''

''I must warn the Empress.''

Akimi's beautiful face was grave. ''I won't let you do that. I'll turn you over to Domei's men.''

''Do you approve of what Domei is doing?''

''Approve? I have loved him for twelve years. I'm part of his family. My son is a Muratomo. I saw Domei's father beheaded. I watched the Takashi seize every opportunity to insult him, to grind him into the dirt. Yes, I approve. If he did not fight back he would not deserve to be chief of the clan.''

''Yes, I see.'' Taniko was dressing quickly with Akimi's help. ''Of course he must try to win back all that his family has lost. But to seize the Emperor is unheard of. What if Domei can't hold the palace? The Takashi have tens of thousands of men over at the Rokuhara. I don't trust this way of doing things. It's too simple and too violent. It makes Domei look like a rebel.''

Tears glittered in Akimi's large eyes. "I know, Taniko, I know. I'm terrified for all of us, for Domei, for my son, for Domei's other sons. He's wild—desperate. He has to do something. He isn't cunning, as the Takashi are. He thinks he can cut through the net they've woven around him with a single sword stroke." She sighed. "There's no turning back now. It's in motion. Our karma will decide what happens."

Hurriedly, wrapped in a heavy cloak, Taniko followed Akimi out of the Wisteria Hall. In the distance, before the Hall of Military Virtues, she could see dark, square masses of men gathered. The clink of weapons and armor carried clearly through the cold, still predawn air. She followed Akimi along a winding path through the twisted trees planted in the northeast corner of the palace grounds. They came to an ox-drawn carriage held by a servant. The women said good-bye and Taniko got into the carriage. The guards at the northeast gate were apparently not involved in the plot. They didn't question Taniko and let her through. Soon afterward she was at the Shima mansion.

Now Horigawa said, "As soon as Domei feels he has the palace under control he'll send men after me, and I don't intend to give him the pleasure of catching me. The Muratomo may attempt to take you as a hostage. Take your carriage and follow me to Daidoji as quickly as you can. We'll be safe there until Sogamori returns to the capital."

"There's no need for me to take a carriage," said Taniko. "I can ride as well as you. Perhaps better."

"Thank you for reminding me that I married a rustic wife," said Horigawa.

Taniko looked at him levelly. "You married a samurai wife."

Heavily cloaked against the cold of the last month of the year, Horigawa, Taniko and their party, riding without stopping, took half the night to reach Horigawa's country estate, the manor called Daidoji. The samurai and peasants on the estate had heard nothing of events in the city and were amazed to see their lord and his lady suddenly appear at the gate.

"Dig a pit deep enough to bury a man behind the guards'

quarters," Horigawa ordered the steward, "and cut a length of bamboo that will reach to the bottom. Post a lookout above the pass. I want to know at once if armed men ride this way." Without another word to Taniko or anyone else, he disappeared into his quarters. A moment later Taniko heard the steward's angry voice commanding groaning servants to take lanterns and shovels down to the guards' quarters and begin to dig.

It was the hour of the ox, the blackest part of the night. Taniko went to her chamber in the women's house, tended by sleepy maidservants she had come to know on previous visits to the manor. She had a charcoal brazier brought in to warm the room and wrapped herself in as many robes and quilts as she could find. But she could not sleep. She lit an oil lamp and settled down with *The Tale of the Hollow Tree* given her over a year ago by Akimi.

Strange, she thought, that of all the women she had met at Court her closest friend should be Akimi, Domei's mistress. It had begun with the incident of the dog, and after that, as they talked, she had found she could share thoughts with Akimi as she had never been able to do with another woman. Although Taniko would never have said so, the Empress was a rather dull person, the other women of the Court even more so. Taniko's career as a lady-in-waiting would have been unbearable without Akimi.

And now, thought Taniko, I am in flight from Domei with Akimi's help, and comforting myself with a book Akimi gave me.

It was two years since her marriage to Horigawa. She found the prince as repulsive as ever, but his conjugal visits were, happily, infrequent. He seemed to want a wife mainly because a man in his position was expected to have one or more wives. While it must be bad karma that had afflicted her with a husband like Horigawa, she had learned not to consider herself uniquely unfortunate. Many women had unappealing husbands. Perhaps most did. Rebirth as a woman was probably a punishment for misdeeds in a previous life.

Still, there was much pleasure in her life. Living in the Imperial Palace most of the time, serving the Empress, she felt close to the center of things, where she had always wanted to be. The letters she translated for Horigawa brought

her news of the fabled land of China. Horigawa's close ties
with the Takashi enabled her to watch Sogamori's rise to
power and also afforded occasional glimpses of the splendid
Kiyosi. All in all, it was an exciting life for a young woman
of fifteen.

There was, of course, the horrid possibility of her becoming pregnant by Horigawa. But she faithfully followed the
precautions her mother had taught her, and anyway, she
doubted that Horigawa's seed had any life in it. Neither of his
earlier wives, she learned, had ever conceived.

One thing was missing, though. In dreams and in waking
reveries there would often appear a very tall young man with
red hair and strange, gray eyes. In a way, the memory was
sweet. It was good to know that once in her life she had held
the strong body of such a man in her arms. But it was
unbearably sad to think that she would never know such joy
again.

If only she had fully given herself to Jebu. Horigawa had
hardly seemed to notice or care whether she was a virgin.
Now she might never know what it was like to have such a
beautiful man inside her. And Jebu had seemed to know so
much about a woman's body. What exquisite pleasures he
might have given her if she had permitted him the final
intimacy. What marvelous memories she might have now.

When she thought of what she had lost, apparently forever,
tears filled her eyes.

The river that flowed through the hills above the manor
was frozen, and she missed the sounds of the waterfall and
the mill wheel, which usually furnished a background for her
reading. Instead, from a distance rose the ringing sound of
shovels biting into hard, cold earth. She and Horigawa and
the others on the estate were simply waiting, waiting for the
Muratomo. She wondered what he meant the pit for. Was he
going to kill himself?

Reading by lamplight tired her eyes, and she blew out the
lamp and tried to sleep. She lay awake on her futon, frightened, wondering what danger was coming their way, wondering what was happening in Heian Kyo. Was Jebu involved?
Thinking of Jebu, she imagined herself in his arms. She
thought about him and talked with him in her mind. Calmed
by the fantasy, she fell asleep.

* * *

The lookout, half dead from a freezing night spent in the hills, rode into the yard shortly after sunrise. A party of armed men was on the way. Horigawa emerged from his hall wearing an old black kimono. Summoning Taniko, he headed for the guard building. Behind the building, where it could not be seen from the main houses or the gateway to the estate, two men had dug a deep, square hole. Puzzled, Taniko watched as Horigawa ordered a ladder lowered into the pit and then climbed down.

Looking up from the pit at his bewildered servants, Horigawa said, "Any of you who reveals my whereabouts will wish you had never been born." He glared up at Taniko. "Any of you." Taniko felt her face grow hot with anger. The offensive old toad.

He lay down in the pit. Taniko peered over the edge. He had the bamboo tube in his hand, holding it to his mouth. He drew a white silk cloth from his kimono sleeve and spread it over his face.

"This is madness," Taniko said.

"It is a device others have used. I am certain they will never find me. Fill the pit. Bury me."

The pit was filled in long before the Muratomo riders came to the gate. Following Taniko's directions, men spread gravel over the surface to hide the freshly turned earth. Only the tip of the breathing tube showed above the gravel, unnoticeable unless one were aware of it.

We have no way of knowing whether the other end is in his mouth or not, thought Taniko. He may be dying even now. She suppressed the thrill of hope that thought gave her. She wanted, as best she could, to do her duty to her husband.

The head of the guards came up to her. "A party of twenty-four samurai is approaching," he said. "If they are Muratomo, shall we fight them?"

"That would be an utter waste," said Taniko. "His Highness has hidden himself so that it will not be necessary for you to fight to protect him. Resistance would only tell them that he must be somewhere on the manor. Let them in, be hospitable. Send their leader to my quarters."

Going to the women's building, she ordered her maidservants to arrange the wall screens to create a spacious audience chamber. At one end of the room they set a screen of state whose curtains were decorated with a design of snow-covered mountains.

She heard horses and cries in the courtyard, and a moment later a warrior's heavy tread on the steps of the women's house. A young man's voice spoke to her maidservants.

A moment later the samurai leader strode into Taniko's chamber on stockinged feet. He made a low bow. "Am I in the presence of Lady Shima no Taniko, wife of Prince Sasaki no Horigawa?"

The blinds and screens around the room were pulled tight to keep out the winter air, and little light came into the room from outside. Taniko had arranged the lamps so that the light was on the intruder, leaving her screen and herself in the shadows. Through tiny apertures between the screen's hangings she studied the Muratomo leader. In the palace, on the Empress's business, it was occasionally permissable for her to be seen by men. In her own home, and especially meeting with an invader, she was required to shield herself behind a screen of state.

The samurai was a boy. His face was smooth. His forehead, surmounted by the samurai topknot, was high. When he was fully grown, she thought, his face would be strong. As yet it had a boy's smoothness.

"I do not know who you are," said Taniko, "but you appear by your dress and bearing to be a wellborn warrior. Your arrival is sudden and surprising to us, but we will make you welcome as best we can."

His eyes were alert, suspicious, unfriendly.

"I am Muratomo no Hideyori, son of Muratomo no Domei, captain of the palace guards and chieftain of the Muratomo clan. I have come at my father's order, seeking His Highness, your husband."

To kill him, thought Taniko. She said, "The prince would certainly wish to meet you, were he here. Alas, he left us last night. His destination, he said, was a temple on the northern shore of Lake Biwa."

"He began a journey at night?"

"So must you have, to reach Daidoji from the capital by morning. In His Highness's case, a diviner warned him that north would be an unlucky direction for him today." The nobility of Heian Kyo frequently planned their movements on the basis of lucky and unlucky directions.

"Staying at home might have been unlucky for him as well," said Hideyori. "In spite of what you tell me, I feel I must seek the prince here at Daidoji, in the hope that I may present him with my father's greetings. Do I have your permission to look for him?"

"Of course, Hideyori-san," said Taniko. "You will have every assistance from His Highness's servants."

Hideyori bowed, turned and left her. He had his father's commanding manner and good looks, she thought. A few moments later she heard his voice shouting orders. She moved two lamps closer to where she sat, settled down again with *The Tale of the Hollow Tree*, and waited, wondering what it must be like for Horigawa in his pit and how long he could live under the weight of all that earth. It did not matter that she loathed the man. He was her husband, and it was her duty to do everything in her power to preserve his life.

After a time Hideyori returned. Taniko quickly withdrew behind her screen. "You are correct, my lady. Prince Horigawa appears to be gone. If you will permit me now to search the women's house, I will accept what you've said, that Prince Horigawa is not here, and I will leave you in peace."

"Surely you would not distress my ladies by searching their quarters. Prince Horigawa is a man of noble birth. He would not hide among women."

The young Muratomo looked at her gravely through the screen. "You are of a samurai family, my lady. Do you give me your word as a samurai that Prince Horigawa is not here?"

"He is not in the women's quarters. You have my word."

"Then I will leave your ladies undisturbed if you will grant me one favor."

"What is that?"

"I have heard that the wife of Prince Horigawa is one of the most beautiful women in the capital. I would like to see for myself. Come out from behind that screen and let me look at you. Then I will go."

He was bold, for one so young. She studied him through the screen. His eyes were a fathomless black. He was staring back, trying to see past the hangings, but his expression was one of unabashed interest, with nothing corrupt, nothing cruel about it. It was not the look she had seen in Sogamori's eyes when Lady Akimi was mentioned, or for that matter when the Takashi chieftain looked at her. There was something straightforward and likable about the Muratomo men.

"Very well." Daintily, drawing her kimono, patterned with red flowers, more closely about her, and taking an ivory fan from her sleeve and opening it, she stepped out from behind the screen and stood before Hideyori. She stood partially turned away from him with her eyes downcast. She held her fan so as not to hide her face, but to shield and reveal it at the same time.

There was a very long silence. At last, Taniko could stand it no longer. She looked up and allowed her eyes to meet his. He sighed.

"Well?" she said with a touch of impatience.

Young Hideyori bowed. "They lied, those who said you were one of the most beautiful women in the capital. There is none more beautiful than you."

"Your mother is more beautiful than I am."

"My mother?"

"Yes. Lady Akimi is a good friend of mine."

Hideyori's face hardened, as if turned to stone. "Lady Akimi is not my mother."

Taniko turned away, mortified by her mistake. Hideyori must be Domei's son by one of his official wives. She knew that Akimi had a young son by Domei and had simply assumed that this must be he.

"Please forgive me. My error was stupid beyond belief. I meant no offense."

Hideyori shrugged. "No doubt I have offended you greatly by coming here. Forgive me for bringing trouble to your house. May the kami show favor to you, my lady. I take my leave of you now." He bowed again and was gone.

What a marvelous young man, she thought. When there are men in the world like him and Kiyosi and Jebu, why must I be married to Horigawa? Of course, this one is a bit young, even for me. But those black, penetrating eyes.

She lit a one-hour stick of incense. In an hour Hideyori and his party would be far away. It would be time to dig up old Squint-Eyes, if he were still alive.

12

Jebu had been placed in charge of the guard over the Retired Emperor, who was installed in the minor palace, one of the residential buildings in the northwest section of the palace grounds. Go-Shirakawa had remained in seclusion except for the previous evening, when there had been a meeting of the Great Council of State. Jebu heard the meeting had not gone well for Domei. In spite of the presence of armed Muratomo samurai, a major councillor had made a speech denouncing Domei as a rebel against the crown. Encouraged, the council had avoided approving Domei's demands. This delaying tactic could be as disastrous for Domei's cause as outright rejection.

In addition, Hideyori and his men had returned, and Jebu heard that Horigawa had eluded his pursuers. Jebu felt a pang of disappointment, and realized he had been hoping to learn that Taniko had been made a widow.

Domei's forces, the thousand samurai of the palace guard, augmented by six thousand Muratomo samurai called in from around the country, continued to drill and to stand guard over the walls surrounding the palace grounds. The White Dragon banner over the main gateway flew just as bravely in the cold winter air. But there was a feeling of tension and uncertainty among the samurai. They needed action, but there was nothing for them to do.

At noon on the third day of Domei's seizure of the palace, a young samurai came to Jebu, who was meditating on the veranda of the minor palace.

"Captain Domei wants you at the south-center gateway."

Domei and other Muratomo leaders were standing on the

parapet of the palace wall overlooking Redbird Avenue. Domei appeared tired and discouraged.

"You did well bringing in His Retired Majesty, shike."

"I should have prevented the burning of his palace."

Domei shrugged. "Just another old building. The main thing is, we got Go-Shirakawa and we didn't lose a man." He lowered his voice. "I'm speaking to you now because you're not one of us. You're not samurai, nor a member of the Muratomo clan. Perhaps you won't be as affected by the news. I've tried to keep it a secret. This morning Emperor Nijo escaped."

"How?"

"Some Takashi infiltrated the palace grounds, disguised the Emperor as a lady-in-waiting, and whisked him out one of the side gates in a carriage. What's more, Sogamori and Kiyosi have returned to the city. We expect an attack at any moment. When it comes, I want you to guard my son."

Jebu knew that Domei had five sons, but he had only met Hideyori. "I presume you mean your youngest son, Hideyori?"

Domei smiled. "I have a son younger than Hideyori. He's eleven and he's safely at his mother's house. I do mean Hideyori. He's a proud devil. He wants to prove himself better than his older brothers. But he is young to be in the thick of the fighting that will come. The greatest casualties are always among the youngest. Stay close to Hideyori. Try to protect him. But also, try not to let him know you're doing it."

Jebu was touched. He remembered Taitaro's careworn face the morning after his initiation as a Zinja. Fathers loved their sons, but had to send them into danger.

A cry of alarm came from the nearby Muratomo officers. "Here they come."

Jebu looked over the wall. The Takashi were advancing. Led by a small group of mounted samurai, the Takashi marched a hundred abreast, their ranks filling the entire breadth of Redbird Avenue. The sun glittered on their armor and the ornamental horns on their helmets. Their hundreds of red banners looked like a sea of poppies. Their war taiko thundered a relentless, triumphant rhythm.

Their leader, riding down the middle of the avenue, wore a helmet crowned with a red-lacquered dragon. His black armor was decorated with gold butterflies and orange-tinted lacings. He rode a chestnut stallion with white mane and tail, and his saddle was inlaid with mother-of-pearl in willow and cherry designs. In his hands he held a long sword curved near the base, the haft decorated with gold and silver mountings.

"That magnificent one," Domei snarled. "That's Kiyosi, Sogamori's son. Look how he's got himself up. The Takashi are all so vain. We'll spoil their looks for them today. That sword in his hand, that's Kogarasu." He drew his own sword. The winter sun glinted on its long, almost straight blade. "I, too, have my heirloom sword with me—Higekiri, the sword that sliced off the arm of the demon of the Rasho Mon. We'll see whose sword has more power today."

These samurai deceived themselves into thinking their blades had magical power. "A sword has only as much power as the man behind it," Jebu said.

Domei shook his head. "Any time a man believes he has power, he has it. This is one of the secrets of warfare, shike. Go now, and find Hideyori."

At that moment Kiyosi broke into a gallop, pointing Kogarasu at the little band of Muratomo standing atop the wall. With a roar, the Takashi warriors ran behind their mounted leader, their heavy sandals drumming on the pavement of Redbird Avenue like a stampede of wild horses. Thousands of long swords stabbed the air. The sea of poppies had become a wave of steel.

Scaling ladders sprang up from among the flashing swords, and the Takashi wave crashed against the walls of the Imperial Palace. Over the din Domei shouted orders to his men on the grounds below, and archers sprang to the walls to loose their arrows into the mass of Takashi warriors.

Forcing down his urge to join in the fight at the wall, Jebu hurried down the steps leading to the palace grounds. He ran across the white gravel to the inner wall surrounding the main buildings of the palace. A long line of defenders had formed between the two ancient trees, the Cherry Tree of the Left and the Orange Tree of the Right, which stood before the Ceremonial Hall. Jebu found Hideyori among them. The young man's fingertips nervously tapped his sword hilt.

"Have you ever drawn blood with that?"

Hideyori shrugged. "I tried it out on a slave. But you

heard what my father said. I just had my topknot ceremony.
I've never been in real combat. Why do we have to stay here?
I'd rather be on the outer wall.''

Jebu looked through the gateway leading out of the compound. He saw a Takashi banner wave briefly on the outer
wall, then fall. ''From the look of it, the Takashi will be
coming to us,'' he said. In his mind he was repeating the
Zinja sentences to compose his mind for battle. Arrows flew
through the air, but none of them fell near the Muratomo line
within the palace compound.

There came a rush of Muratomo defenders from the outer
wall to join the line between the two trees. Right behind them
the Takashi burst through and streamed into the palace compound like a long ribbon of red silk unwinding. Jebu unslung
his bow and took aim at Kiyosi, but the scion of the house of
Takashi changed direction suddenly, and the arrow flew past
him and disappeared. *Make every arrow count*, Jebu reminded
himself with chagrin. He wanted Kogarasu, which he could
see slashing like a great silver scythe, too badly. He was
infected with the lust for success. He resolved just to act and
to forget about Kiyosi's sword. The Self doesn't collect swords,
he thought.

''Stay close to me,'' Jebu said to Hideyori. The young
Muratomo had his sword out. Jebu stood to his left and
slightly in front of him, acting as a shield. Other Muratomo
samurai, seeing their leader's son in their midst, crowded
around him protectively.

Jebu wished Domei were more of a planner. The Takashi,
at least, seemed to have some sense of direction, and it was
working for them. The Muratomo fought as samurai usually
did, every man for himself, and they were being driven back.

A big Takashi samurai drove his naginata straight at
Hideyori's chest. Jebu brought his Zinja sword down in a
chopping swing and broke the naginata pole. But the broken
end of the pole struck Hideyori and threw him, stunned, to
the ground.

''We have Domei's son,'' the Takashi samurai shouted,
drawing his sword against Jebu. Jebu swung his sword at the
Takashi's legs. The Takashi brought his sword down to block
the swing. Jebu drew his sword back and struck again, but
this time as the attacker's sword came down to block him,

Jebu turned his blade and struck upward. The force of the Takashi's blocking motion brought his right forearm down on the Zinja blade. Only by quickly letting go of his sword was he able to save his arm from behind severed. As it was, Jebu's blade had cut through muscle and sinew right to the bone. The big samurai, bellowing in pain and anger, fell back among his comrades.

Jebu stood over Hideyori, his short sword cutting and thrusting this way and that. An empty circle formed around him. Slowly Hideyori got to his feet and the Muratomo samurai closed around them.

Domei, recognizable, in spite of his face plate, by the white horsehair plume on his helmet, came riding toward Jebu and the other men near the Cherry Tree of the Left. Domei leaned down and patted Jebu on his shoulder.

"I saw that. My son would not be alive now if it weren't for you. You're a marvelous swordsman. In battle, the Zinja are devils. You must train my sons."

The Zinja are devils. But Jebu did not have time to think about that now. Domei wheeled his horse and began rallying his men. In a moment the Muratomo had steadied their line between the two trees.

Domei gave the command, and the Muratomo counterattacked, those at the far right end of the line running at full tilt, spearheaded by horsemen, slashing wildly with their swords, thrusting with their naginata. Nearer the Cherry Tree the Muratomo line advanced more slowly. Jebu and Hideyori stayed at the left side of the line to hold the samurai there to a slow, inexorable walk controlling the pivot. Many white banners were waving in the air now, and the Muratomo taiko drummers pounded wildly to spur on the attack.

It now appeared that the Muratomo had the Takashi on the run. The southern half of the inner palace compound was swept clear of Takashi, and the pivoting advance of the Muratomo became a rush as the Takashi began a headlong retreat.

A flash of gleaming red caught Jebu's eye. It was the dragon on Kiyosi's helmet. Waving his sword, the Takashi leader was calling his men to fall back before the onrushing Muratomo. He was leading the retreat.

But a Takashi retreat made no sense. Kiyosi should be

rallying his warriors to make a stand. The Takashi outnumbered the Muratomo three to one. They had managed to overwhelm the outer defenses. They had only to keep on and they would grind the Muratomo down. But so rapidly did the Takashi fall back that there was no time to pin them against the Ceremonial Hall, the aim of Domei's counterattack. Instead, the fleeing Takashi and the charging Muratomo circled the Cherry Tree a second time, swirling like a whirlwind.

And now Kiyosi's red helmet and dazzling sword could be seen leading the Takashi out the gate they had broken in through. A cheer went up from the Muratomo as they rushed out of the palace grounds in pursuit of their foe.

"Stop!" Jebu called. "Stop! Close the gate and hold the palace." But the samurai flooded past Jebu as if he were just another ornamental tree on the palace grounds. The Muratomo vanguard, led by Domei's white plume, was already far down Redbird Avenue. Jebu and a handful of Muratomo samurai remained behind. In a moment the walled park was nearly empty.

A strange silence fell. The scream and shouts and clatter of battle faded in the distance. All that remained, besides Jebu and the few samurai, were hundreds of armored bodies scattered over the white gravel of the outer grounds and the inner compound. Here and there lay a severed head, arm or leg, a dark lump of leather-wrapped flesh surrounded by a puddle of blood. Blood was everywhere, in pools, splashes and streams, as if the palace grounds were white paper on which a giant calligrapher had been writing with red ink. The white of the Muratomo and the red of the Takashi, thought Jebu. Together they have inscribed their poem of war on the most sacred ground of the Sunrise Land.

The realm would never be the same again. This palace had been built four hundred years ago by Kammu, the ancestor of the Takashi. Since then it had been the center of harmony and serenity for the whole empire. Now it was splashed with blood and littered with mutilated bodies. The Emperor would undoubtedly survive these great changes that were shaking the land, but he would not govern, nor would his ministers. Whoever governed in the future would govern with the sword.

Men screamed for help, other men begged for a quick death, while some groaned in half-consciousness. The few

Muratomo samurai who had stayed behind walked about identifying their dead comrades and trying to help the wounded. Others systematically went from one wounded Takashi to the next, slitting throats, spilling more blood on the white stones. Some performed the same service as a mercy for the badly injured Muratomo. Jebu looked down at his armor, dappled with blood.

Young Hideyori came up to him, wiping his sword clean with a white cloth. "We had better get these men together, shike. The Takashi will be upon us at any moment."

"You saw that? Good, Hideyori-san. You'll make a good general."

Hideyori smiled, his eyes as remote and cold as ever. "You saw it and I saw it, but my father didn't see it. My father—" He broke off, shaking his head.

"There'll be too many of them for us to fight," said Jebu.

"We can hold the inner compound. Or at least the Ceremonial Hall."

"Yes, and the last of us to die can set fire to it."

"Why not?"

"Nonsense. I'm going to deliver you to your father alive."

"A foolish promise, impossible to keep."

At that moment the lookout on the inner wall gave a long, shrill cry of alarm, and the storm was upon them again. There was no stopping the Takashi who swarmed up their scaling ladders, planted their bloodred flags on the parapets, and dropped from the walls to the ground like a swarm of beetles falling upon a mulberry tree.

"This way," Jebu called. Followed by about fifty Muratomo samurai, he and Hideyori burst through an unguarded gateway leading to the northern part of the palace grounds. Takashi samurai raced after them.

Half the Muratomo samurai, forced to act without orders, stopped, turned and formed a defensive line to hold back the Takashi. Jebu could see Kiyosi's dragon-crowned helmet as it passed through the gateway through which they had just escaped. A mass of Takashi fell upon the Muratomo line. Then Jebu could look no more.

They ran past the Imperial residential buildings surrounding the little park in the northwest section of the grounds. A samurai beside Jebu took an arrow in the back and fell into the ornamental pool. Frightened maidservants and ladies-in-waiting peered out at them. Some were supporters of the Muratomo and called out frantic questions, which Jebu and the samurai ignored.

Beyond the residential buildings Jebu saw a stable. There was no time to saddle the horses. Panting, their breath steaming, the men threw themselves on the animals' bare backs. There were only a dozen horses. Those samurai who were left without horses turned and lined up to hold off pursuers.

They rode for the northwest gateway in the outer wall. A Takashi humming-bulb arrow shot past Jebu's head with a piercing whistle. Jebu decided that if the Takashi caught up with them he would turn and fight them at the gate, giving Hideyori time to escape.

They were through the gate and galloping wildly down the city streets. A startled ox pulling a carriage lumbered out of their way and crashed into a nearby wall. What was anyone doing on the streets on this day? Arrows splintered against the pavement behind them. Jebu jumped his horse over the low wall against which the ox had just blundered, followed by Hideyori and six other mounted samurai. They rode through the gardens of a nobleman's estate past screaming, terrified servants.

In a short time they had lost themselves among the houses of Heian Kyo aristocrats. Pursuit seemed to have been called off. For the moment the Takashi had what they wanted, the palace.

Hours later, circling cautiously through the streets, they found the main body of Muratomo warriors. Domei was sad and tired. His force had been greatly reduced, not only through casualties but because of men getting lost in the streets, wandering away or, discouraged, fleeing.

While Jebu and Hideyori had been looking for Domei, he had realized too late that the Takashi were doubling back for the palace. His men had reached the main gate only to find a much larger army than their own in possession. Then they had marched across the city in the hope of mounting an attack on the Rokuhara, but the Takashi stronghold was occupied by Sogamori with an even larger force of samurai. Domei estimated that between the men stationed at the Rokuhara and the

Takashi allies who had come in from the countryside, there were forty thousand Takashi samurai in the city.

"They hold the Imperial Palace against us. They have the Emperor and the Retired Emperor in their hands. Both Their Majesties have proclaimed the Takashi their defenders and us outlaws. Everything has turned out exactly opposite to my hopes." Suddenly he lifted his head and smiled, almost gaily. "Many times the falcon stoops and comes up with empty claws. Then he must fly away to try again."

Jebu glanced at Hideyori. The fifteen-year-old boy was staring at his father with an appraising look that was almost contemptuous.

A few hours later the Muratomo army was streaming out of Heian Kyo by one of the western gates. The weary samurai glanced over their shoulders from time to time, expecting a Takashi pursuit. Jebu rode with Domei. One of Hideyori's older brothers lay in a horse-drawn carriage, his right leg almost severed. Jebu had attended him with Zinja remedies, a powder to clean the wound and a tourniquet to stop the bleeding.

When they reached the heavy woods at the base of the mountains north of Heian Kyo, snow began to fall.

Domei said, "We must scatter. My older sons must go with me. But, hideyori, I want you far, far from Sogamori's reach. Since Jebu brought you safely through the battle, I will entrust you to him."

Domei turned to Jebu. "Lord Shima no Bokuden of Kamakura is a secret ally of mine. He is not a very good ally—he feigns friendship for both sides. But he should be able to see that Hideyori can be valuable to him, and only he is far away enough and powerful enough to protect Hideyori from the Takashi." Domei sighed heavily. "My youngest son, Yukio, is in the capital. I can't save him. Hideyori may be the last of us. He is the future of the Muratomo clan."

Jebu nodded, astonished at the revelation that the calculating Lord Bokuden, Taniko's father, was in league with the Muratomo. Perhaps that was the reason he had relied on one inexperienced Zinja to escort his daughter through Muratomo territory to Heian Kyo. And the reason their party was attacked only once. But Jebu agreed that Bokuden could not be considered a very trustworthy ally.

When Hideyori had walked away, leaving Domei and Jebu alone, Domei let his head drop.

"I have been a fool, shike. I helped the Takashi destroy my father and now I have ruined myself and my sons. I have done everything wrong. I would welcome death now."

Jebu said, "In my Order we are taught to see that all is one. Victory or defeat, life or death, it is all the same. The act is everything, the result nothing."

Domei shook his head. "It would comfort me to believe that. But I can't. Go now, Jebu."

13

Five days after the Muratomo defeat at the Imperial Palace, Moko brought Taniko the news that Domei had returned to Heian Kyo. Taniko was again at the Empress's Wisteria Hall, Horigawa having rushed back to the city as soon as he heard that the Muratomo had been driven out of it. Empress Sadako was prostrate in her chambers, still not recovered from the fright Domei's insurrection had given her. Lady Akimi was conspicuously absent.

Moko knelt on the veranda outside Taniko's room and spoke to her through the screen, shaking his head.

"It was very sad. Domei and his older sons were attacked by a party of Takashi samurai. They fought their way through, but all their escort was scattered. Domei and his three sons found themselves alone in the mountains in a blizzard, with their enemy in hot pursuit. One son was wounded and could not keep up. He begged his father to kill him, rather than allow him to fall into the hands of the Takashi. Finally Domei gave in and stabbed his son in the heart. At least the boy did not cut his belly open, as some samurai do when they want to kill themselves."

"Horrible," said Taniko. "And Domei still couldn't escape?"

"He tried, my lady. He and his two remaining sons dug a grave for the dead young man and struggled on through the falling snow. They stopped at a farmhouse to rest, not realizing how close behind them were the Takashi samurai. The peasant who offered them hospitality betrayed them. Domei was bathing when his enemies burst in upon him and captured him. The two sons were also unarmed. The Takashi took all three prisoner and brought them back by order of Sogamori, to be publicly executed here. They even dug up the body of the dead son and brought his head back to the capital. Many other Muratomo leaders are to be beheaded as well."

"How sad. What of Domei's two younger sons?"

"One of them, Yukio, is here in the capital at the home of his mother, the Lady Akimi, whom you know. They are both under house arrest. The other—this is very interesting, my lady."

Taniko leaned forward and peered through the screen. She could see that Moko was smiling, revealing all the gaps left by his missing teeth.

"What is it?"

"You might not have heard this, because you had fled the capital with your honored husband when the fighting was going on, but a huge Zinja monk with hair of a fiery color is said to have performed prodigies in the battle for the Imperial Palace."

Taniko's heart beat faster. "That can only be one person."

Moko nodded. "So I thought, my lady. I have also heard that this same monk escorted Domei's other young son, Hideyori, into the northeast."

The northeast, Taniko thought. She would have to send a secret message to her father to watch for them.

"When are the executions to take place?"

"In three days' time, in a pit beside the prison at a place called Rokujo-ga-hara, where Rokujo Avenue crosses the Kamo River. All around the execution ground poles have already been set up, and the heads of a dozen of the better-known rebels who were killed in the fighting look down on all passersby. Truly, as I heard a monk say, we must be living in the Latter Days of the Law."

"Yes," said Taniko. "Moko, I want to know so much
more about the world than I do. All I can see is what happens
within this Nine-Fold Enclosure. It is a great pity that Captain
Domei and his sons must die. I knew and liked him. But the
power of men to execute other men in the name of the
Emperor is what holds this realm together. If I want to know
the world, I must know this. Will you go to the execution and
be my eyes, Moko? Will you see them for yourself and me?"

"I've seen a good deal of killing in my life," said Moko.
"And I'll probably have to see much more before I myself
step into the Great Void—or am pushed. The last thing I want
is to go look at killings that I don't have to see. But if it will
help you, my lady, I'll go, and I'll tell you about it."

Moko went to the execution ground early to find the best
possible vantage point. The place where the condemned were
to die was a wide, circular depression, somewhat deeper than
the height of a man, beside the Kamo River. Court attendants
in shining, light green robes had already roped off the area
nearest the pit for the noble witnesses. Moko saw that if he
joined the crowd of common onlookers on the riverbank he
would be too far from the edge to see anything.

But there was a huge, old cherry tree beside the prison
which had long been used for public floggings. From its
topmost branches a man would have a fine view. Used to
working on buildings, Moko had no fear of heights. In a
moment he was securely perched on a high, but strong, limb
that would allow him a good view of the proceedings.

It was only after he was settled on his perch and could look
around a bit that he saw a pair of dead eyes staring at him. A
pole bearing the head of a rebel killed in the fighting at the
Imperial Palace had been set close to the cherry tree. A bit
shocked, Moko took a deep breath and winked at the head.

"Good morning to you, my lord, whoever you are. I trust
you are not suffering?"

Just think, this could be the head of the shike Jebu. But
they probably wouldn't bother to set a monk's head up on a
pole, any more than they would his own.

Gradually the area around the pit filled up with spectators.
Carriages brought the men of rank, who were admitted to the
best positions, close to the edge of the pit. From his cherry

tree limb Moko could see along Rokuju Avenue, which was
filled with ox-drawn carriages—wickerwork carriages, palm-
leaf carriages, and the towering, elaborate Chinese carriages
with their green-gabled roofs, whose use was restricted to the
Imperial family and the highest officials of the Court. The
carriages blocked one another's way, and Moko watched with
amusement as three fights broke out among forerunners of
rival noblemen.

The confusion was rendered worse when a mounted troop
of Takashi samurai, their gold ornaments gleaming in the
morning sun, forced their way down the center of the avenue,
carriage attendants scurrying out of the way of their horses'
clattering hooves. In the distance Moko saw a blaze of gold,
and as it came closer he recognized the gold roof of the
Emperor's palanquin, an enormous, magnificently decorated
portable building carried by dozens of men and surmounted
by a golden phoenix. The Takashi horsemen must be substi-
tuting for the palace guard, destroyed in Domei's insurrection.
People fell to their knees as the Emperor passed. Moko was
awestruck as he watched the palanquin pass near his cherry
tree and settle on a commanding spot on the riverbank.

Sudden horror froze Moko. In his excitement at these
splendid sights he had forgotten the age-old rule that no one's
head may be higher than the Emperor's. If anyone saw him
up here now, he would be dragged down, and the Emperor's
guards would chop him to bits. It was too late to climb down.
The sacrilege had been committed. He must remain absolutely still. His only hope was that no one had seen him climb
up here and that no one would see him during the executions.
He might, he realized with increasing dread, have to remain
in this tree until nightfall, and even then he would be in
terrible danger when he tried to climb down.

The curtains of the Emperor's palanquin were opened. In
spite of his terror, Moko studied the Emperor curiously. Nijo
wore a high, jeweled headdress and a massive diamond necklace. His silk gowns, worn one over the other, were so
voluminous that he seemed like a bodiless head resting on
piles of magnificent fabrics. His cloak was of plum red lined
with scarlet, chosen, Moko suspected, because the color
matched the mood of this occasion. The young Emperor's
face was powdered white and was without expression—

almost without features. It was perfectly round, with a tiny mouth, nose and eyes, and a wisp of a beard on the point of the chin.

Smiling triumphantly, Prince Horigawa, Lady Taniko's repulsive husband, sat on a bench below the palanquin along with a number of other nobles in violet Court cloaks. Beside Horigawa sat a heavyset, balding man whom Moko had also seen before—the Takashi clan chieftain, Sogamori. His broad face was alight with relish, as if he were about to sit down to a fine banquet. He and Horigawa were like a pair of swollen toads, on the verge of bursting with pleasure over their victory.

Now the condemned men, wearing only fundoshi, loincloths, were marched out of the prison and down a ramp into the pit. There were twenty of them. The famous Muratomo chieftain, Domei, was the first to enter the pit. Moko had seen him before, riding through the city on horseback. How sad, Moko thought, that this splendid man's life must be cut short, while the ugly and poisonous Horigawa lived on and on.

Five executioners stood across the pit, facing their victims. One of them was Kiyosi, scion of the house of Takashi, dressed in red-laced armor decorated with black lacquer and gold ornaments, and an underrobe of red brocade. He held a long, deeply curved sword.

The first to die would be five of Domei's lieutenants. They stepped forward. A courtier in a light green robe read off the list of their crimes, concluding with the treasonous uprising against the Emperor. The Emperor's face remained blank. The five turned and bowed, first dutifully to the Emperor, then loyally to Domei, finally politely to their executioners. They knelt.

Moko wondered, are they thinking about what is going to happen to them? Are they fully aware of it? Or are they trying not to think about it? Moko remembered how he had felt when Jebu said he was going to behead him. His whole body had gone ice-cold and he had thought he was going to lose control of his bowels. It was the worst feeling in the world. And these men had endured that feeling for days, ever since they had learned they were going to be executed.

The five executioners, including Kiyosi, stood over the

condemned men, their blades flashing in the sun. They swung their swords up at the same time.

Five blades fell, full force, on five necks. The blows propelled each head a short distance, and the kneeling bodies collapsed like sacks of rice. From each headless neck a bright pool of blood spread on the sand, which was as white as a snowdrift. There was a murmur of mingled excitement, approval and horror from the onlookers.

Moko's stomach heaved violently. As he had told Taniko, he had seen men killed before, but had never seen a public execution. It must be, he thought, the first time for many of the people below him as well. In his revulsion he almost forgot the danger of his own position, that he might, at any moment, be discovered and join the dead down there.

Several courtiers fainted, one almost falling into the pit but saved when his attendants grabbed his arms. The unconscious men were carried out of the crowd by their servants. Another courtier suddenly vomited all over his beautiful lavender cloak, to his great embarrassment and to the amusement of several of his fellows. How shameful to vomit in the sight of the Emperor, thought Moko, once again forgetting his own precarious position. Sogamori, from his position near the Emperor, smiled scornfully.

Slaves dragged the bodies out of the pit by the ankles, while foot soldiers drove a sharpened pole into the base of each skull and raised the heads up so that even people in the distant parts of the crowd could see. Moko held his breath, realizing that now he was in the greatest danger because people would be looking upward. He prayed to the ghost of the warrior facing him to turn the eyes of the living in any direction but his.

The ritual of execution was repeated twice more, each time with five victims. Domei was being saved till last, Moko realized. He would have to see his followers die, then his sons' heads hoisted on poles before he himself could find the release of death. What cruelty.

Before Domei's two elder sons knelt to be executed, they stood and looked long at their father. Were they accusing him of having led them to their deaths, or were they exchanging one last, affectionate look before going into the Great Void? Moko hoped it was the latter.

Domei's expression did not change as he saw his sons beheaded.

Now it was his own turn. He knelt and spoke. "The clan chieftain of the Muratomo dies proclaiming his unswerving loyalty and that of the Muratomo family to His Imperial Majesty. He begs his Imperial Majesty to remember that the Muratomo are ever the teeth and claws of the Emperor."

Kiyosi was to execute Domei. He raised his sword, its gold and silver mountings glittering, high over his head, then brought it down with a loud, "Ha!" While Domei's body was still shuddering in death, Kiyosi turned his back on it and bowed to the Emperor. The Emperor's face remained as soft and empty as bean curd in a bowl. I'll bet he's never seen a public execution before, either, thought Moko, and I'll bet he wishes he could look away, or even vomit. But he doesn't dare, because he's the Emperor. Odd, that the Emperor is less free than anyone else.

To his surprise, Moko noticed tears sparkling on Kiyosi's face. Even this enemy of the Muratomo is moved by these deaths, he thought. Then Kiyosi happened to glance upward. His eyes met Moko's.

Moko's heart stopped beating, and he almost let go of the tree limb. Be merciful, Buddha, he thought, and tried to prepare himself for death. He could not help shutting his eyes.

For a long moment nothing happened. Then Moko slowly opened his eyes again. Kiyosi was still looking at him, the dark brown pupils burning into him. In his terror, Moko saw Kiyosi's square, chiseled face with a luminous clarity, as if it were the face of a Buddha or a kami. This great lord must defend the sanctity of the Emperor. It is his duty to kill me.

Kiyosi smiled ever so slightly, and looked away.

It was a long time before Moko was able to breathe normally again. It began to look as if the great lord were going to spare his life. Of course, he might be waiting until the executions were over, so that the dignity of the occasion would not be spoiled by the skewering of one as lowly as he. But somehow Moko doubted that. There had been kindness in the smile. All Moko had to do was stay put until dark and hope that nobody else saw him. Which was quite a lot to hope for. He recalled the shike telling him the Zinja had been trained to hide in trees for days. Moko would have a tale to tell the shike now—if he ever saw him again.

Sogamori, rather than the Emperor, gave an imperceptible hand signal and two courtiers closed the curtains of the Emperor's palanquin. The multitude of men who carried the Emperor leaped up and raised the gilded palace on poles to their shoulders. The troop of Takashi guards formed their mounted ranks before and behind the palanquin. The forerunners raised their batons and began shouting.

Behind the Emperor the high nobility walked to their waiting carriages. Moko watched Kiyosi, the man who had spared his life, as the lean young man walked away with his short, heavy father, Sogamori. Sogamori climbed into a Chinese-style carriage, while Kiyosi mounted a chestnut horse and rode away.

For Moko, the remainder of the afternoon was the worst ordeal of his life. The major executions were over, and the Emperor and the great lords had left, but there were still nearly eighty rebels who had to kneel in the bloody pit and die. Trapped in the cherry tree, his arms and legs slowly growing numb, Moko had to watch all of it.

At last darkness fell. There was no moon that night. When he felt safe, Moko somehow managed to get his limbs working and he half climbed, half fell down from his perch in the tree. He was barely able to walk.

He found his way to a wine shop in a side street and revived his aching body with the help of a jar of warm sake. Amazing, he thought, that the young Takashi lord, who had not hesitated to chop off men's heads with his sword, had let a sacrilegious little carpenter live. Moko remembered the tears running down Kiyosi's cheeks after he beheaded Domei. There was a compassion in the young samurai such as Moko had seen in only two other people—the lady Taniko and the shike, Jebu.

Thinking of his lady, and still shaken from the horror and pain of what he had seen and endured that day, Moko forced himself to his feet, paid for his sake, and set out for the Imperial Palace.

14

It was early spring when Jebu and Hideyori stood in the presence of a trembling Shima no Bokuden.

"Does Domei reach from beyond the grave to destroy his friends? This house has always been known as a Takashi house. How could I shelter you here?" Lord Bukuden demanded.

"What do you mean, from beyond the grave?" Hideyori said quickly. "Is my father dead?"

"Yes, of course. And your brothers. Had you not heard?"

Jebu felt a pang of grief at the thought that the brave, strong Domei, in whose service he had spent two years, no longer lived. He looked at Hideyori, whose face was without emotion.

"How did they die?" Hideyori asked.

"One of your brothers was badly wounded, and your father helped him to die. Domei and the other two were captured, taken back to Heian Kyo and publicly executed."

"What of Yukio, my half brother?"

"I have heard nothing," said Lord Bokuden, waving away these family griefs as if he were trying to drive away a mosquito. "But you can see that your family's cause is hopeless. From now on the Shima must be thoroughly Takashi."

"I understand," said Hideyori. "I ask you in the name of whatever bond existed between you and my father to give me shelter for a few days. I think I will continue to travel north. I need time to make plans and to send out messages."

Standing beside him, Jebu turned and looked at Hideyori. It was a serene profile that bore the mark of authority. There

was an unbelievable calm and strength about this fifteen-
year-old boy, Jebu thought. Another youth might have prostrated himself before Lord Bokuden, blubbering for mercy.
Hideyori might be the last living male in his family, but he
was absolutely controlled. Jebu remembered *The Zinja Manual:*
"He who does not feel fear is dead." What was the price of
Hideyori's control?

After the monk and his charge had left the room, Lord
Bokuden took Taniko's letter out of his desk and reread it.
The letter was in Chinese.

> Honored Father,
>
> This is to warn you that Hideyori, the heir to the
> chieftainship of the Muratomo clan, is said to be headed in
> your direction. I have never questioned your dealings with
> these warring clans, but neither am I unobservant. I have
> reason to think, therefore, that Hideyori may come to you
> for help.
>
> At this moment the Takashi are in the ascendant, and you
> may be tempted to display your loyalty by sending Hideyori's
> head to Heian Kyo. I suggest that this young man may be
> worth more to you alive than dead.
>
> As the Takashi grow more powerful they grow more
> arrogant and make more enemies. If Hideyori is alive, he
> will be the natural person for those enemies to rally around.
> Whoever has protected Hideyori will then hold the key to
> the future.
>
> These suggestions are offered in all humility and in grati-
> tude to you for having placed me here, where I can observe
> great events.
>
> > Your loving daughter,
> > Taniko

Lord Bokuden grunted. What possessed this daughter of his
to think she could advise him in as perilous a matter as this?
Still, there was sense in what she said. But he had to assure
the Takashi of his loyalty.

Taking up his brush, Bokuden began a letter to Sogamori.

> Esteemed Minister of the Left,
>
> I have Muratomo no Hideyori. What shall I do with him?
> I shall hold him until I hear from you.

*   *   *

Tears formed rivulets in the white powder that coated Akimi's face. It is not pleasant to see a woman of the Court cry, thought Taniko.

"I loved Domei," Akimi said. "He was a warrior of force and fire, but he was a gentle, simple man as well. I loved him so much I went through the agony of going to see his head displayed at the execution ground. Now all I have left is Yukio, my sweet, beautiful boy. I fear his father may have condemned him to death."

"How?" asked Taniko.

"Domei's legacy to his family is a blood feud with the Takashi. The only way the Takashi can protect themselves is to kill all his sons. And Yukio is in their power."

Taniko put her hand on her friend's. "What can I do to help?" She understood how Akimi felt about Domei. She had only to compare the feeling with her own for Jebu. It could have been Jebu's head on a pole overlooking Rokujo-ga-hara.

Akimi said, "If you will permit me to speak of your husband."

"Of course." Be careful now, Taniko told herself. In this house anyone could be hiding behind the panels, listening. So far I have said nothing to endanger myself.

"Your husband has great influence with Sogamori. And I believe—excuse me for saying it, but fear for my son's life makes me bold—when blood might be shed, Prince Horigawa is in the forefront of those who call for shedding it."

"I do not think Prince Horigawa would deny that," said Taniko dryly. "He would speak of the need to strengthen the power of the Emperor and to protect the government from treasonous factions."

Akimi bowed her head. "Of course. Only—my son is not a danger to the Emperor and he does not think of treason. He is a child. His only thoughts are of watching the wild birds on Mount Higashi and playing the flute. His flute playing is— beautiful to hear—" She broke down in sobs.

Taniko felt tears fill her own eyes to overflowing. She pressed Akimi's hand in both her own. "I have no influence whatever with my husband, dear Akimi-san. But I will do what I can."

Akimi looked up. Weeping had destroyed her painted face.

"Believe me, Taniko-san, I will do anything—anything at all—to save the life of my son."

The scowling, florid face of Sogamori appeared in Taniko's mind. She recalled his look of frustrated lust when his son, Kiyosi, had ridiculed him for attempting to woo Akimi. Sogamori, she thought, might do anything—anything at all—to have Akimi.

"I believe you can win Sogamori over," Taniko said, "if you are willing to pay the price. I can say no more now. Don't give up hope. I'll send word to you when the moment seems right."

On the fifteenth day of the Fifth Month of the Year of the Horse, Horigawa held a winding water banquet. Such affairs were a tradition that went back centuries. Horigawa chose the evening of the full moon, so that the silver disk would be reflected in the stream that wound through his garden. For seven days before the banquet Taniko resided at Horigawa's house to help oversee preparations.

She sent Moko to Akimi with a special message. The chances that Horigawa would find out what she was doing were all too good, she realized. If he did find out, he would undoubtedly punish her severely. But Akimi had lost nearly everything. To lose her son would kill her. Something inside Taniko—perhaps it was what Jebu called the Self—would not let her abandon her friend.

The evening of the banquet, the landscaped gardens around Prince Horigawa's mansion were bright with lanterns. Carriages pulled by oxen bedecked with ribbons and flowers rolled up before the main gateway. Servants ushered each guest to a designated place along the twisting banks of the stream. To enhance the beauty of his artificial brook Horigawa had added a few bridges, ponds and small waterfalls, as well as a number of new plants along its edges.

The guest of honor was Sogamori. He arrived last of all and was seated approximately at midpoint along the stream's course, so that he need be neither the first nor the last to recite a poem. His son, Kiyosi, who had already arrived, was seated a few places downstream from his father. The other guests included courtiers, ministers and high-ranking Takashi.

Unknown to Horigawa, one other person was present. Lady

Akimi had left her carriage some distance from the Shima mansion and, cloaked and hooded, had come the rest of the way on foot. Taniko let her in by a side gate.

Taniko was painfully aware of the risks of her plan. She might have misjudged Sogamori. Meeting Akimi at this banquet could have the opposite effect on him from what she intended. He might even be provoked to take action against the boy Yukio and against Akimi as well. As for Horigawa, even if the plan were successful, only the kami knew what that cruel and bloodthirsty man might do. Taniko sent Akimi to a vacant chamber in the woman's pavilion, promising to come for her at an opportune time.

When the guests were seated, Horigawa gestured to Taniko, who filled a round-bottomed wine cup with hot sake and set it adrift at the head of the stream. As host, Horigawa began the recitation of poetry by picking up the cup, sipping from it and declaiming:

> Straw dogs turn to ash
> Under the Red Dragon's breath.

There was laughter and applause. No one doubted that the sacrificial straw dogs referred to the defeated Muratomo. From some courtiers, however, Taniko heard a murmur of distaste. For hundreds of years the best people of the capital had looked on fighting and bloodshed as activities fit only for savage beasts, certainly nothing to write poetry about.

The next guest along the stream bank took the cup out of the water, sipped the sake and said:

> That pale cloud in flight—
> White smoke or a dragon's tail?

Most of the guests laughed, Sogamori loudest of all. Taniko looked beyond him at the handsome Kiyosi, who was staring pensively into the stream.

Horigawa had set the tone for the banquet, and most of the guests followed with poems on the martial theme, many of them ancient Chinese ballads of war. A few who disapproved recited poetry on subjects more traditional for a winding water banquet: flowers, the seasons, the moon. Whenever this happened, Taniko noticed, Sogamori glowered at the offender. Clearly, he wanted to celebrate his triumph.

After one elderly doctor of literature had recited, in a stately, old-fashioned style of declamation, a poem about the moon's reflection on the water, Sogamori suddenly rose. As the noble next to the doctor of literature drank and began to recite, Sogamori quietly stepped away from the stream and drew a small, dark object shaped like a cherry from his sleeve. He went over to a lamp and set fire to the stem of the cherry, then tossed it within a few feet of the learned doctor.

There was a noise like a thunderclap and a blinding flash. The old scholar leaped to his feet and nearly fell into the stream. Taniko was shocked and frightened. A harsh, powerful stench filled the garden. A puff of smoke drifted past the dwarf pine trees. It was as if Sogamori had unleashed an ugly, vicious demon.

A horrified silence had fallen over the banquet. It was broken at last by Sogamori's laughter.

"There's a new subject for poetry," he said loudly. Taniko glanced at Kiyosi and saw that he had his head down, staring resolutely at the stream, his expression a mixture of embarrassment and disgust.

Horigawa, who should have been outraged at the disturbance, strolled over to Sogamori and said, "Most remarkable. Has the esteemed Minister of the Left taken up sorcery?"

Sogamori laughed and sat down. "Nothing magical. It's only a Chinese toy. I have a new man in my service, a barbarian from across the sea. He brought me a box of these little thunder balls. An amusing novelty, is it not?"

Taniko wondered about Sogamori's barbarian. Could he be from the same land Jebu's father had come from? Jebu had said nothing about these horrid fireballs.

Now it was Sogamori's turn to recite. He stood up, thrusting out his chest, and boomed out a Chinese poem about a battle that had been fought over a thousand years before:

> His chariot horses draped in tiger skins,
> Duke Wen charged the lords of Ch'en and Ts'ai.
> The Right Division of Ch'u collapsed,
> Its battle flag dragging in the dust.

* * *

This was greeted with appreciative murmurs. Taniko observed that the old scholar who had been Sogamori's victim had left the banquet. After a few more poems, it was Kiyosi's turn to recite. Would he try to match his father in belligerence? Taniko wondered. Kiyosi remained seated, a thoughtful, faraway look in his eyes. He spoke in Chinese, so softly Horigawa's guests had to strain to hear.

> Frontier war drums disrupt all men's travels.
> I am fortunate enough to have brothers, but all
>   are scattered;
> There's no longer a home where I might ask if they're
>   dead or alive.
> How terrible it is that the fighting cannot stop!

There was total silence after Kiyosi had finished. He set his wine cup adrift and gazed after it as if he were quite alone. All eyes turned to Sogamori. If he had been annoyed by poems that neglected warfare, what would he do when his own son recited a poem that deplored it? The man on Kiyosi's right took the cup out of the water and held it in a trembling hand, afraid to begin speaking.

"Who wrote that?" Sogamori asked in a low, hoarse voice.

"Tu Fu, honored Father," said Kiyosi. "One of the great poets of the T'ang dynasty."

Sogamori nodded. "What compassion. What depth of feeling. Truly, a poet who understands the sufferings of a war-torn land." With a lugubrious expression Sogamori reached for a wine cup and drank deeply.

Suddenly he grinned at Kiyosi. "My son's taste in poetry is flawless," he said proudly. "Just as his victory at the Imperial Palace shows that he has no peer in war."

Taniko could hear breaths being expelled throughout the group. An unpredictable man, Sogamori, she thought; a changeable man. There was no telling how he would react when she lured him to a secluded part of the garden to encounter Akimi.

The servants brought food, and the recitations resumed. Another cup of wine was launched down the stream, and another. The formality of the occasion began to dissolve.

People stood up and moved about. The flirtations constantly being conducted by courtiers took their toll of the guests, as this man or that woman slipped discreetly away from the stream to a rendezvous in the safe seclusion of the trees. Among the guests who stayed in their places, conversation gradually took the place of recitation.

Taniko quietly left Horigawa's side, motioning to a maid to take over waiting on the prince and those near him. She hurried to the room where she had secreted Akimi.

"Now is the time."

"Taniko-san, I'm terrified. What if something goes wrong?"

"I'm terrified, too. What else can we do?"

"You did not have to do this much. I'll always be grateful to you, Taniko-san."

Returning to the banquet, Taniko unfolded the fan she had had painted especially for the occasion and took up a dish of sweetened fruits. She carried the dish to Horigawa, Sogamori and Kiyosi, who were deep in discussion.

"Nits make lice," Horigawa declared flatly.

"Twice in recent years the Takashi have been responsible for public executions," said Kiyosi. "Many think this scandalous. We have lost the goodwill of many important men, many families, and the people in general, because they view these killings with horror."

Taniko offered Sogamori an orange slice skewered on a sliver of wood. The heavyset Takashi chieftain smiled broadly at her. Taniko could see he must have been a very handsome man tweny years ago.

Smacking his lips after the orange slice, Sogamori said, "What have those executions to do with this question?"

"The Takashi are already called butchers," Kiyosi said. "It is your advice that has gotten us that name, Prince Horigawa." The young man's dark eyes blazed at the prince. "Do you want us to be known as child murderers, too?"

"Nits make lice," Horigawa repeated. "Let Hideyori and Yukio live, and they will trouble the Takashi for years to come. Kill them now, and they will be forgotten tomorrow. To kill a grown man sometimes takes a war. To snuff out the life of a child is quite easy." He snapped his fingers.

Her heart pounding, Taniko chose that moment, when Kiyosi and Horigawa were glaring at each other, to reach out,

squeeze Sogamori's hand and place in it a slip of green-tinted
paper, folded, with twisted ends. On it Akimi had written:

> All must surrender
> To the Red Dragon's power
> And none disobey.
> In the forest he may work
> His will on her whom he meets.

The meaning should be plain enough, Taniko thought.

When he noticed the paper in his hand, Sogamori turned to
look at her, startled. Then his round face beamed knowingly.

Taniko hid behind her fan, letting him see the painting on
it. It was unmistakably a representation of the shrine of the
Beautiful Island Princess on Itsukushima, built and maintained
by the Takashi family. Sogamori and Kiyosi had been on
pilgrimage to that shrine when Domei raised his insurrection.
Taniko stood, bowed to the three men and withdrew into the
shadows. She hoped Horigawa was too intent on his argument
to notice her departure.

When she was among the trees on the edge of the garden a
hand caught her arm. It was Akimi. Taniko looked back over
her shoulder. Sogamori was reading the poem, holding it so
Horigawa and Kiyosi could not see it. He slipped it into his
sleeve and stood up. Squinting into the shadows, he tried to
see Taniko.

Taniko handed her fan to Akimi and withdrew behind a tall
stand of bamboo. Sogamori said something to Horigawa and
Kiyosi that made them both laugh. He stretched and strolled
toward the trees with an elaborate show of casualness.

Holding the fan before her face, Akimi stepped into
Sogamori's path. As he approached her, she drew him deeper
into the darkness.

"The painting on your fan shows exquisite taste, dear
lady," he said, reaching out for her.

"Thank you, my lord," said Akimi with a light laugh.

"You do not sound like—I must see you," said Sogamori,
taking Akimi's wrist and pulling the fan away from her face.
He gasped when he recognized her.

"Is this some trick?"

"You may call it so if you wish, my lord. It was my poem

that my friend Lady Taniko gave you. It was I who wished to meet you here."

Still holding Akimi's wrist, Sogamori looked down at her. "I was struck by your radiant beauty the first time I saw you at Court. I have never dared hope. You were always *his*. How can you come to me now, when it was I who destroyed him?"

"A woman can admire more than one man, my lord. The enmities of men do not mean so much to women. Because of him, I could never approach you. Now he is gone, and nothing stands between us, if you still deign to look upon me."

"You will be mine, then?" Sogamori was fairly panting.

Taniko felt tears burn her eyes as she thought of what her friend was sacrificing.

"My lord, I fear his angry ghost. But there is a way that we can set his spirit at rest. Then I can give myself to you fully."

"What is that?"

"That you promise to spare his children."

A few days later Horigawa came to the Shima mansion in a rage. Alone with Taniko, he seized her arm and twisted it violently until she pulled away from him.

"I have done nothing to deserve this treatment, Your Highness."

"Lord Sogamori has announced that he will spare the lives of the two Muratomo brats. An example of samurai benevolence, he calls it. The tenderness of a warrior. As if the samurai could know anything of ethics. It is like dressing a monkey in a courtier's robes. It is his lust for Lady Akimi that drives him to this foolishness. She beds with him now. This is your doing. Akimi came to visit you before my banquet. She met Sogamori at the banquet, even though she was not invited. I detect your hand in all this, my clever young lady of Kamakura." He advanced on her, his eyes narrowed to slits, his nostrils flaring, his face pale.

Taniko bowed her head. "As Your Highness says, I am just a child from the provinces. How could I possibly have any influence in these high matters?"

Horigawa turned from her, pacing the room. "That young

dog who came to kill me at Daidoji—he is to live. In the care of your father. Your father! After Domei was defeated he disappeared, and when he reappears it is in Kamakura, at your father's house."

"Do you think I sent him to my father, Your Highness? There is no way I could have done that. Doubtless, the young Muratomo was passing through Kamakura, and my father, being a loyal supporter of the Takashi, stopped him and held him."

"Oh, doubtless, doubtless. How do I know what passed between the two of you while I lay buried alive? When I think of the hours I spent under all that weight of dirt—well, you shall see what it is like to be buried alive." He stared at her with such hatred that Taniko, despite her contempt for him, was terrified.

"What do you mean?"

"You will not remain in Heian Kyo to thwart me again. As your husband I command you to move to my house at Daidoji. You will live there. I am not free to deal with you as I truly wish, because I need the support of your family. But I will keep you from tampering with my affairs. Prepare yourself. I expect you to be ready to move by tomorrow morning."

Oh, merciful Buddha, no, thought Taniko. He takes from me the only thing that makes life bearable. To leave the capital, to go into exile, no. If I can't be here at the center of things he might as well kill me. I'll die there at Daidoji, of grief and boredom.

She knew it was useless to plead with him. Any sign that she was suffering would please him and confirm him in his decision. Two women had virtually thrown their lives away to save Akimi's son, Yukio. She could only hope he would grow up to be worth it.

15

The Muratomo were finished, thought Jebu. Almost all the leaders of the clan were dead. Hideyori was as much Lord Bokuden's prisoner as his ward. Jebu himself could do no more for Domei's family. He worked his way southward toward the capital, still serving the Muratomo as the Order commanded. But the wings of the White Dragon had been clipped. Any lives lost now were being lost for nothing.

He was trudging over terraces of harvested rice. Behind him was another lost battle, if it deserved to be called a battle. The Takashi had ambushed a dozen hungry Muratomo samurai with whom Jebu had been riding. Jebu had warned them it might happen, but the Muratomo warriors had insisted that no true samurai would attack another samurai without proper warning and challenge. Whoever was leading the Takashi apparently didn't care about such niceties.

Outnumbered many times over, the Muratomo samurai had thrown away their lives. What good had their sacrifice done the dead Domei?

Jebu reminded himself to think as a Zinja. To a Zinja there was no good or evil, failure or success, life or death. The Zinja simply threw his energy into the task at hand and did not concern himself about the outcome. From that point of view, his Muratomo comrades, alive a few hours ago, now dead, had lost nothing. At the very least, they no longer suffered the pangs of hunger.

A rider emerged from the woods behind Jebu, galloping directly across the rice stubble. There was no point in trying to outrun him, and no place to hide. Jebu quickly slipped off his bow and arrows and laid them at his feet. He nocked one arrow and laid it across the bow. He drew his sword and waited.

The samurai approached to within ten feet of Jebu and stopped. He looked sleek, strong and prosperous, like a well-cared-for war-horse. Quite different from the ragged, half-starved Muratomo samurai Jebu had been riding with. The laces holding together the many small plates of his armor were dyed a deep magenta.

"I saw you riding with that pack of Muratomo dogs we jumped, and I saw you sneak away when the battle went against you. I will not tell you my name and lineage because you do not deserve the courtesy. You are merely to be exterminated, like vermin." He unslung his huge bow and positioned an arrow.

Jebu stood silently. The instant he saw the samurai's fingers twitch to release the bowstring he threw himself to the ground. The ordinary warrior always gives a warning—a movement of the hand or fingers, a tensing of the arm muscles—when he is about to move. He consciously commands his movements, unlike the Zinja, who acts as the Self directs.

As the thirteen-hand-span samurai arrow whistled overhead, Jebu had his own ready. He stood up and fired. The point of his willow-leaf arrow struck the samurai in the left eye and buried itself deep in his head. Jebu felt no pleasure as he watched the samurai slide out of his saddle. It was a bit too much like killing a duck sitting in the water.

Jebu seized the horse's reins. Holding the horse with one hand and speaking gently to it, he set his foot on the dead man's forehead and pulled the arrow from the crushed eye. He wiped the arrow and returned it to his quiver. He took the man's sword and scabbard and strapped them to the saddle. Then he asked forgiveness of the samurai he had killed and looked around, trying to decide which way to ride.

From horseback he could see farther. Behind him was the forest where they had been ambushed. All around him were rice fields. Before him were the hills and mountains, and beyond the mountains was Heian Kyo. It was the first time he had been this close to the capital since last winter when he had ridden out of it with the defeated Muratomo army.

Now it hardly mattered where he was. The Takashi controlled everywhere. Any place he went for food and a night's shelter would be the home of Takashi adherents or people who now claimed to be. He would have to say he was a Takashi man as well. A good thing about being a Zinja was that you could present yourself as serving one side or the other as you chose, or else you could pretend to be a simple monk minding his own business. Unless, of course, someone recognized you, as the now-dead Takashi samurai had.

But he had not eaten in over seven days. His Zinja training had inured him to going without food and even water for long stretches of time, but he could feel himself growing weaker. At this rate, soon he would no longer be able to draw his bow. He would have to stop somewhere. If we did not have to eat, he thought, all of us would be safe and free. It is when the bird lands on the ground to peck at seeds that the cat pounces.

Riding south toward the hills he caught sight of a manor house overlooking the rice paddies. Whoever owns that house is undoubtedly lord of this land, he thought. An important landowner would have to take one side or another. But this close to Heian Kyo and undamaged, it must be a Red Dragon house. The huts of peasants were clustered around the base of the hill on which the manor stood, and more huts climbed the hill behind it, where a high waterfall turned a mill wheel three times the height of a man.

He decided against asking the peasants for their hospitality. It would endanger them, and they had little enough to share. No, the thing to do was ride boldly in through the gate, present himself as a Takashi messenger on an important mission, and demand shelter, food and provisions. While he was at it, he might get some news of the Muratomo and find out where he could rejoin them.

He rode through the rice fields and up to the gate of the mansion. A group of guards stood by it.

"I am Yoshizo, a monk of the Order of Zinja," said Jebu, using the name of a brother he knew was working for the Takashi. "I am on my way to Heian Kyo with a message for His Excellency, the Minister of the Left from—" Jebu said the first name that came to him "—his kinsman, Lord Shima no Bokuden of Kamakura. I require a night's lodging and food."

The guards didn't move. "That's a samurai sword and a samurai saddle," one said, gesturing with the naginata. "I didn't think Zinja monks used such fancy equipment."

"Quiet," said another guard. "He can kill you so quickly you'd be dead a minute ago. We'll find out soon enough if he's from Lord Bokuden. Come on in, monk."

The first guard brightened up. "Yes! Come in, monk." He grinned, stepped aside and waved the long-handled naginata toward the open gateway.

The manor house was old, Jebu saw, perhaps a hundred years old, built at a time when there was no need for fortifications. Both the stone wall around it, twice the height of a man, and the gate were new. A gang of workmen was putting up a wooden guard tower at one corner of the wall.

Jebu dismounted. One of the guards said, "I'll take your horse down to the stables, monk."

"Very good," said Jebu. There would be no easy escape now. He was angry with himself for the vanity of his sword-collecting project and for not getting rid of the saddle, or disguising it. If the samurai he killed were a local personage, the sword, the saddle and the horse might be recognized. But it was now too late to do anything but keep walking onward.

The other guard took him into the courtyard and slammed and barred the gate. "Chief of guards!" he called. An armored man wearing a sword immediately stepped from a building to the right of the manor house, trailed by a group of men carrying naginatas. This household had its own little army, Jebu thought.

"Chief Goshin," the guard said, "this monk claims to be from Lord Shima no Bokuden on a mission to the Minister of the Left in Heian Kyo. But he has a samurai's horse and equipment. I thought to myself, we've got a way of testing whether he's really from Lord Bokuden."

"Of course," said Goshin. He was a squat man with a froglike face, huge eyes, flat nose, and wide mouth. "I'll go see her." He turned to his men. "Keep this monk at the ends of your naginatas. If he makes a move, skewer him at once. Don't hesitate, or you'll be dead. I've run up against these Zinja before." He spat out "Zinja" as if it were a foul word. Goshin turned and strode into the manor house.

Jebu stood in the center of a ring of leveled naginatas. He

looked at the guards calmly and kept his hands away from his swords and his bow. What kind of test did they have in mind, he wondered.

The sound of hammering distracted him. He looked over at the men building the guard tower. One of the carpenters, a short man who gestured and shouted orders to the others, looked familiar, but he was too far away for Jebu to see his face.

"All right," said Goshin. "There he is, my lady. Do you recognize him?"

Jebu turned away from the guard tower to the veranda of the manor house. Through the blinds he could just make out a shadowy figure.

Then he heard a light voice, like the chiming of temple bells. "I *have* seen this monk visit my father. Who could forget that hideous red hair?"

Jebu felt himself go cold and then hot. He wanted to laugh and call out to Taniko, run up the steps, push his way into the manor house and put his arms around her. He forced himself to look coldly in the direction of her voice as if he had never seen her before. He reminded himself that he was a monk named Yoshizo.

She went on, "Of course, he could know my father and still be working for the Muratomo. It is my father's custom to give his messengers a password to identify themselves to any members of the Shima family they might meet. Did Lord Bokuden give you such a word, monk?"

Jebu played along. "He did, my lady, but it is for your ears alone. I must take the liberty of whispering it to you."

"Come up, close to these blinds, then," came the icy voice.

"Careful, my lady," said the frog-faced Goshin. "He might just be trying to get close enough to you to seize you as a hostage."

"Goshin, I command you now, if he takes me hostage you are to kill both of us immediately." She paused significantly. "I'm quite sure Prince Horigawa would want it that way."

Jebu slowly and carefully laid his bow and arrows and his two swords on the raked earth of the courtyard.

"It would be rude of me to approach you armed, my

lady," he said. Then he looked coldly at the guards. "But let no one touch my weapons."

"A Zinja is armed even when empty-handed," a guard muttered.

Jebu strode forward, climbed the steps and stood beside the screen that hid Taniko. A faint scent of lilac came to him, and his head reeled. He feared the pounding of his heart must be visible to all. Goshin stood close to him, and Jebu gave him the same hard stare he had given the guards.

"This man is not authorized to hear the word," he said.

"Goshin?" said Taniko.

Grunting angrily, Goshin took a few steps away from Jebu. He drew his sword and stood poised to spring.

Leaning toward the screen until his lips were almost touching it, and looking into the bright eyes he glimpsed in the shadows beyond the screen, Jebu whispered, "The waterfowl is still snared in the lilac branch." He heard a faint sigh from within.

"Goshin," Taniko called, "this monk has given the correct password. He is a genuine messenger from my father. Since he is traveling to Minister Sogamori, he will see my husband. I have a message for my husband which I will give this monk."

Goshin glowered. "My lady, I still don't trust him. There are many ways he could have learned this password. And there is the business of the samurai equipment he was carrying."

Jebu turned to Goshin. "You are quite correct. Now that I have been identified as, I hope, a friend of this house, I can admit that I did steal the horse. Not far from here a party of Muratomo samurai was riding through the forest. I was with a Takashi band waiting in ambush. One of the enemy tried to escape on his horse. I jumped him from a tree, and took his horse away from him. He seemed so unhappy about losing his horse that I killed him to spare him further grief."

Taniko greeted this story with her tinkling laughter, and soon all the servants and guards nearby joined in. Only Goshin stood unsmiling, his bulging eyes filled with anger.

"Did you not already have a horse?" he demanded.

Jebu laughed. "Clearly you do not know Lord Shima no Bokuden, or you would not have asked that question. Lord

Bokuden is not the most generous of employers. He felt my legs were strong enough to take me to Heian Kyo."

Behind the screen Taniko laughed again.

Goshin broke in. "You do not behave as Prince Horigawa would want you to, my lady. You are too familiar with this monk.".

"Be silent, Goshin!" Taniko snapped. "My husband did not appoint you to teach me manners. I am mistress of this house, and in my husband's absence I rule here. You are dismissed. Monk, wait there. A maid will take you to my chamber when I am ready to receive you."

"May I collect my weapons, my lady?" Jebu asked.

Goshin said, "I will keep them for you, monk. You don't need weapons here, since you are such a great friend of this house. Ask for them when you are ready to leave."

Reluctant to entrust his bow and arrows and his swords to this man, Jebu saw that he had no choice. He bowed. "Thank you."

Shortly afterward, a maid led Jebu to the women's quarters and down a series of twisting corridors. As he had long ago been taught to do on entering a strange house, Jebu constructed and committed to memory a mental map of everything he could see.

At last he entered a large, dim room with a sleeping platform in the center. On the platform was a screen of state whose curtains were painted to depict snow-covered mountains. Overcome with excitement, Jebu strode straight for the screen, meaning to step around it and see Taniko.

"Stop," she called from behind the curtain in a warning tone. Of course, Jebu thought, they must be under surveillance. He had allowed himself to be carried away by emotion, just the thing a Zinja was not supposed to do.

In a low voice Taniko went on, "We can be watched, but if we speak softly enough we cannot be heard. Sit down and talk to me. I am so happy to see you, my heart is like a butterfly just burst from its cocoon."

"When we parted I told myself I must never expect to meet you again," said Jebu. "Yet I knew I would think of you for the rest of my life. Not a day has gone by that I have not remembered that night on Mount Higashi overlooking the lights of Heian Kyo."

"I have not forgotten, either. There has been nothing in my marriage to replace the memory of that night. I have known nothing but horror and sorrow and ugliness since we parted."

Jebu felt as if a hand were crushing his heart. "How sorry I am to hear that. It would be like death to know that you had forgotten me, but I would accept it if it meant you had found happiness. We should have run away together instead of letting you go to that man. Tell me about the prince."

"He is cold and ugly and cruel. Let us not speak of him. Why are you traveling under a false name? Are you really working for the Muratomo?"

"Yes. The cause of the White Dragon is collapsing, but the Order has commanded me to stay with it."

"It is unfortunate that you said you were going to Sogamori," Taniko said. "He is well known in this house. For you to claim a connection with him raises suspicion. Horigawa is with Sogamori now."

At that moment Jebu heard bare feet on the wooden floor behind him. He whirled.

"Shike!" It was Moko, scuttling toward them and bowing from across the room.

"You do not know him, Moko!" Taniko snapped from behind her screen. "He is dead if they find out who he really is."

Moko stopped where he was, his face pale. He threw himself down on his knees.

"Forgive me, mistress. Forgive me, shike. Moko is so stupid—"

Jebu smiled and patted him on the back.

"You can speak to him, but try to seem as if you are speaking to me," said Taniko. "Supposedly I am giving you instructions about the new guard tower."

Moko said, "I am so happy to see you, shike. I have missed you so much. But if you want to do the sensible thing you will run out of this room, through the garden over the wall and across the rice paddies and not stop until you reach the woods. These guards will not rest until they kill you."

"They have no reason to kill me."

"These are men who need no reason to kill."

"I will not leave here—not yet."

"I understand, shike." Moko nodded toward Taniko, behind her screen. "She is the reason I stay in this hellhole with Horigawa and his bandits."

"We can safely talk no longer," said Taniko. "Go now, Moko."

Moko bowed first to Taniko, then to Jebu. "My lady. Shike." He hurried away.

Taniko said, "You will have to leave me now. But I hope you can remember the way to my bedchamber. You will come here tonight." The words were more a demand than a request. Through a small opening at the top of the screen Jebu could see brown eyes looking into his.

"You must be silent as only a Zinja can be. I am watched constantly."

Smiling, Jebu stood and bowed. "As my lady commands." He turned and left the room, once again imprinting on his mind a picture of the corridors through which he passed.

Outside the women's quarters, Jebu found himself in the garden. He wished for brush and ink so that he might bring a poem to her tonight. The thought of the night to come filled him with a powerful yearning. Men whose constant companion was death needed women in a way most men couldn't understand, he thought. He wondered what Prince Horigawa had been doing to her. The thought that Horigawa might have hurt her filled him with rage. He hoped he could be tender enough with Taniko to wash away all the anguish she might have suffered.

The winter sky was empty and gray. The garden seemed bare and sad. How could a man such as Horigawa have a garden that would look anything but sad? Jebu stood awhile, letting pebbles drop through his fingers into the brook, then turned to leave.

The unseen sun was setting and the early winter evening was coming on, the empty gray sky turning to a cold black. Jebu walked through the main yard of the estate just as the gate was being shut for the night. He went into the building that housed the manor's guards.

The men lounging in the guard room eyed him closely. He saw his bow and arrows and his two swords—his own Zinja sword and the sword he had taken from the samurai who tried to kill him—hanging on the wall where all the other weapons had been gathered. He asked one of the men where he could get something to eat, and provisions for his departure in the morning.

"Just go to the kitchen and tell them you're a guest of the manor. There are so many people here, they're always cooking. If you have any trouble, just tell them you're a friend of Lady Taniko."

"Thank you." Jebu smiled at the man and left. In the kitchen a cook served him a meal of bean paste, rice, soup, cucumbers and slices of fish. The man seemed used to cooking for military men and transients, Jebu noted. With practiced swiftness the cook packed a box with enough provisions for a two-day journey.

"That's more than enough to get you to Heian Kyo, even if you travel slowly," he said.

Back in the barracks, Jebu settled down in a corner to meditate. He wanted very much to take his weapons from the wall, but knowing the guards probably had orders to stop him, he resisted the urge. He looked around for Goshin, but did not see him.

"Hey, monk!" It was the man who had directed him to the kitchen. "Want to share some of our warmth with us?" He pointed to a jar of sake being heated over a brazier.

"Monks don't drink sake, fool," one of the other men said.

"Thank you," said Jebu. "I'm not used to sake. I'm afraid it would go to my head."

The men talking around the brazier smiled and nodded to Jebu and went back to talking among themselves. Jebu sat cross-legged against the wall and closed his eyes. With Goshin gone, the atmosphere seemed much more friendly. One could even walk into this room and be unable to tell whether the samurai here fought for the Takashi or the Muratomo.

16

Jebu had deliberately chosen to sleep in a corner beside a crack in a screen. A stream of chill air came through the opening, but he ignored the discomfort, and as the long winter evening wore on he pushed the screen open by imperceptible degrees until there was a space about as wide as his hand. There were extra quilts scattered around the room for protection against the cold, and Jebu unobtrusively gathered several of these and carried them to his spot. The lamps burned out and one by one the men went to sleep.

When the room was dark Jebu bundled the quilts together on his futon so that it would look as if he were sleeping there. Then, glancing around the room to make sure he was not being watched, he pushed the screen open. On his hands and knees he slipped through and partially closed the screen again.

Looking around the darkened compound, he waited until he had spotted the spear-carrying guards walking their posts. Then, bent low, running silently on his bare feet and keeping to the shadows, he circled around the rear of the main house. Now he was in the garden. Neither moon nor stars shone tonight. He crept through the garden, making use of each small tree and shrub for cover.

At last he crouched by a corner of the women's house. He reviewed Taniko's directions as he searched the outer screens of the house for one that, as she had promised, was left partly ajar. When he found his opening, he thought of water and flowed up the steps and past the screen. Inside the women's house it was totally dark. He stood perfectly still for a moment, listening to rustlings and soft breathing coming from all directions. There was a strong scent of flower petals. After a

few moments his eyes adjusted to the darkness in the building
and he began to see where the walls and screens were. If he
made a mistake and entered the wrong room, the guards
would be on him instantly. He counted doorways and turn-
ings, re-creating his mental map of the building.

Small fingers seized his arm. He stopped moving instantly,
stifling the impulse to attack. He peered at his captor, putting
his face close to the pale face that looked up at him. It was
Taniko. He stood motionless for a long time, reveling in her
closeness, the light touch of her breath on his cheek. He
tangled his fingers in her unbound hair and, at last, pressed
his face against hers. He let her lead him the rest of the way
to her chamber.

Taniko's form was a slightly darker shadow against the
general darkness of the women's house. Most of the fires
were out, and there was a chill in the air. Together they
mounted the sleeping platform, and Jebu lay down, his head
resting on her single wooden pillow, while she drew curtains
around them. She lay down beside him. The long years they
had been apart, the danger of their coming together, roused
him and made him eager to touch her, but for the moment he
held himself back.

Taniko's arm went around him, and her cheek brushed his.
''I have longed for you every night since we parted,'' she
whispered. ''The hope that I might spend another night with
you has kept me alive. I have never forgotten Heian Kyo in
the moonlight.''

''Nor I,'' said Jebu. ''I weep when I think of what you
must be suffering.'' His fingertips stroked the nape of her
neck.

Taniko drew back from him a little. Even in the almost
total darkness he could see the glitter of intelligence in her
eyes. ''I will live. And I will learn. And some day, perhaps, I
will use the knowledge somehow. I am learning what power
is, and how men struggle for it.''

''Taniko. Run away with me tonight. We won't stop running till we reach Hokkaido. We'll live on a farm on a
mountainside unknown to everyone.''

''Do you really think you could give up being a Zinja and
become a farmer?'' she whispered. ''I know I could not give
up the world I am discovering, even though every day of my

marriage to Horigawa is torture. I will escape Horigawa somehow, but it will not be to hide in the north.''

Jebu felt his eyes grow hot and wet. Her life was so wretched that she was deceiving herself with wild dreams. But he knew she would remain firm about not running away with him. Tonight was all they would have. He put his hand under her robes, found her breast and held it gently, feeling the nipple tickle the palm of his hand. He made himself touch her as lightly as autumn leaves fall on a forest floor, even though he was raging inside to spring upon her as a tiger seizes a deer. He waited until she had warmed to him, till the insistence of her movements told him her eagerness matched his. Then he pressed himself upon her and she drew him in. Their bodies were fully united for the first time. In total silence they climbed a mountain of pleasure together, leaped together from the summit, and drifted down together like falling snow.

Jebu felt a pang of regret that it should be over so quickly. But he held her, his hands exploring her body, and he discovered that their union was not by any means over. This time he silently guided her into the position favored by the Zinja, she sitting on his crossed legs with her own legs locked behind his back. This time there was a whole mountain range of pleasure for her, while his own peak took exquisitely long to reach.

For most of the night they lay together, sometimes talking in whispers, sometimes joining their bodies. Jebu discovered energy and desire in himself surpassing all previous experience.

At last Taniko said, ''I heard a bird call. It will be dawn soon. You must go now while the night still protects us.''

''I would stop the sun from rising if I could.''

''That is not possible, Jebu. Least of all in the Sunrise Land.'' She laughed softly. ''You will live, and I will live, and we will do what we must, and other nights like this will be ours again.''

Tiptoeing on bare feet, she led Jebu through the dark corridors of the women's house to the open screen where he had entered. Again avoiding guards, Jebu crept back across the compound and pushed his way in through the space in the guard room screen. He lay down on top of the bundle of quilts he had used to represent himself. Pleasantly exhausted, he dozed.

He heard footsteps. The entrance screen to the guards' quarters slid back and the blaze of a torch filled the room. He sat up, then sprang to his feet as he saw Goshin and Horigawa enter.

"That one!" Goshin cried.

Horigawa's small, square face turned in Jebu's direction. The narrow eyes seemed to glow as he nodded.

"I know who this man is. He is a monk named Jebu, who fights for the Muratomo. He was hired by Domei himself. Who else could possess such outlandish looks?" He smiled and turned to Goshin. "Please kill him at once, Goshin-san." He stepped back to watch, with a look of relish on his face.

Goshin was accompanied by three samurai in full armor, but he roared, "Every man to arms! Get your weapons down off the walls and kill the spy!" The sleepy guardsmen scrambled for their swords, spears, and naginatas. Jebu saw his own bow and sword, untouched and unnoticed, still hanging on the wall.

If he must die, there would never be a better day than today, after the night with Taniko. To die now would simply spare him any more of the suffering of being parted from her.

A half circle of men came at him, spears leveled. He waited until they were at the right distance, then threw his body into a handstand, delivering a stunning kick to the jaw of one of the spear carriers, then somersaulted past the group. This put him among Goshin's three armored men, who were caught by surprise. Jebu drove his stiffened fingers into one man's throat and plucked the long samurai sword out of the suddenly strengthless hand.

Jebu whirled the sword in a huge, whistling arc, and the three men backed away. This left Goshin exposed. With a backhanded sweep of the sword, using all the strength in his right arm, Jebu beheaded the chief guard.

Now he was face-to-face with Horigawa. But beyond Horigawa he saw his weapons. The men in the room were recovering from the initial attack. By the time he killed Horigawa they would be upon him. If he went for his weapons he had a chance of getting out alive. He did not care that much for saving his own life, but something—the Self perhaps—told him he had a duty to go on living.

Horigawa cringed away from Jebu, not even drawing his sword to defend himself. Jebu darted past him to the weapons that hung unguarded on the wall. Into his belt he thrust the sheathed sword he had brought with him. He leaned the sword he had just taken from Horigawa's guardsman against the wall. Slinging his quiver over his back, he drew his bow and fired a volley of arrows into the crowd of guardsmen.

Make every arrow count. Demoralized by the death of one leader and the cowardice of the other, the guardsmen milled around uncertainly, and four of them died as Jebu's arrows struck home. One of them was the man who had offered him sake.

He took the Zinja sword down from the wall and buckled it around his waist. Slinging the bow over his shoulder, he drew the Zinja sword with his left hand and with his right hand picked up the samurai sword he had set down a moment before. Brandishing a blade in each hand, he advanced on the remaining guardsmen. Staring up at him, they started to back away, stumbling over the bodies on the floor.

"Protect me!" Horigawa screamed. "Protect me! He wants to kill me!" The guardsmen formed a ring around the prince.

Again Jebu saw that he could either attack Horigawa or escape. He praised the Zinja training that enabled him to keep anger and vindictiveness out of the fight. He bolted for the screen in the corner of the room where he had slept, smashed through the oiled paper and out into the predawn cold.

As he ran he slid the samurai sword into his belt beside the prize he had taken earlier, and sheathed his Zinja sword. Running still, he drew the grapple out of his inner pocket, unfolded it and threw it at the top of the wall. He pulled himself hand over hand up the silk cable, dropped down the other side and ran for the stable. There it was, a low building, black against the purple sky.

A guard stood at the entrance to the stable. "Get away," Jebu snarled. "I'll kill you if I have to." The man ran, shouting loudly for help. Looking after him, Jebu could see lanterns bobbing around the gate of the manor and he heard shouts of alarm and command.

He entered the stable, breathing in the strong, warm smell

of horses. It was too dark to find the horse he had ridden
here. He looked into the first stall and saw a big, dark shape.
There was a row of bridles hanging on the stable wall. He
took one down, went into the first stall and threw it on the
horse, buckling it in place quickly and pulling the horse
firmly out of the stable. The horse whickered fearfully and
tossed its head.

"I know you've never met me before," said Jebu, "but
you can save my life if you will." Hoping the horse would be
strong, fast and obedient, Jebu scrambled on its bare back and
dug his heels into its sides. The horse sprang forward and
broke immediately into a gallop, as much from fright as from
Jebu's command. Jebu slapped its neck encouragingly and
over the wind shouted, "Good! Good!" into its ear.

He looked over his shoulder. The lanterns were streaming
toward the stable. He would have a long start on them,
though. He would be all right if he could make it into the
wooded hills north of Heian Kyo. He might even find Zinja
monks who would shelter him.

It was foolhardy to ride this fast through unfamiliar country
in darkness, but he had no choice. He was glad he'd had to
fight his way out of Horigawa's manor; it had taken his mind
off the agony of leaving Taniko. But what was he leaving her
to face? He could only hope that, whatever happened between
her and Horigawa, she would live through it.

Sword drawn, Horigawa shoved aside the screen to Taniko's
bedchamber and strode in. Taniko had heard the commotion
at the guards' quarters and the men running across the compound. To quiet her pounding heart she insisted to herself that
Jebu must have escaped.

Horigawa lit a lamp. His black eyes glowed at her in its
reflected light.

She yawned and said, "You are discourteous to me, Your
Highness, bursting in and waking me at this hour. I am not
prepared to receive you properly."

"It appears you have had other guests this night," Horigawa
rasped.

"Why do you come here with sword drawn, my lord? Do
you expect to find enemies here in the women's quarters?"

"Yes. He might have fled to you. He killed Goshin and four other men."

He was still alive! He had escaped. Wonderful news! Goshin was the ablest of Horigawa's men. With him dead it was unlikely the others would be able to catch Jebu.

"The loss of Goshin, especially, is a great blow to me. It was he who rode to intercept me as I was returning here from Heian Kyo, and who persuaded me to speed my return to catch this deceitful monk."

Taniko could not resist taunting Horigawa. "It occurs to me that none of your men would be dead if you had not insisted on ordering them to attack a Zinja monk. The monk would have come and gone quietly without harming anyone."

Baring his teeth, Horigawa snarled, "You are to blame for those deaths. You knew who he was. You permitted him entry into this house under a false name."

"Yes, I tried to protect him. He is the man who brought me safely to you from Kamakura. He fought and killed to protect me. Your men would have executed him on the spot if I had revealed his identity."

"He fights for the Muratomo. It was your duty to order the death of any Muratomo supporter who entered this house." He glowered at her. "Just what is your interest in this monk, that you were at such pains to protect him? Is he your lover?"

"My conduct has always been correct, Your Highness."

"Has it? We shall see." Suddenly Horigawa lunged at her and threw her down on the bed platform. She felt helpless, and in a momentary panic she pushed and kicked against him. He was trying to part her robes.

"Don't fight me," he gasped. "If you've done nothing wrong, you have nothing to fear." He had exposed the lower part of her body now, and he was peering at her and probing at her with his nasty, skinny little fingers. How lucky that she had cleansed herself after being with Jebu. It was a practice her mother had taught her, explaining that it was a wise precaution for women who didn't want to have too many babies. Men, said her mother, knew nothing about such things.

"No sign," Horigawa muttered, releasing her and stepping back. "If I had caught you with this Jebu last night, I would surely have killed you. Perhaps I will kill you anyway." He seized her hand. "He was here in your chamber yesterday talking to you. You and that carpenter, that cross-eyed fool. What were you talking about? Are you spies for the Muratomo?"

"If anyone in this house has secret dealings with the Muratomo, it is not I or the carpenter, my lord," said Taniko pointedly. This cruel hypocrite would have killed Jebu as a Muratomo spy and was constantly howling in the councils of the Takashi for the deaths of all leaders of the Muratomo faction. But she knew that messages had passed between Horigawa and Muratomo no Hideyori, the young man who had come to kill him, who was still in exile at her father's house in Kamakura.

Horigawa turned white at her words. "How dare you?" he sputtered. "You could cost me my life if anyone believed—I think I *will* kill you!" His fear turned to rage, and he seized her little finger and bent it back, grinding his teeth. The finger broke, and she screamed. Without thinking she brought her fist around and drove it into his small, round belly. Gasping, he threw down her hand and backed away from her, holding his middle.

"You little snake!" he screamed. "I should cut you to pieces. I would have every right to. But I still need your father's goodwill. One day you will pay a high price for the indignities you have heaped upon me. And you will go on paying, for the rest of your life. That"—he pointed to the finger which she held tightly to ease the pain—"is only the beginning. Now I'm going to get that carpenter. He won't get off as easily as you have. He will suffer more than you can imagine, until he tells me all he knows about that Muratomo spy."

"He knows nothing. Spare him, please!"

"If his suffering causes you pain, then he shall surely suffer."

"If you plan on hurting me again," Taniko gasped, "you'd better bring your guards with you next time. You won't get near me by yourself."

"I have no wish to be near you," said Horigawa. "I will have my revenge in due time."

17

Early the following summer, Jebu was trudging up a mountain road on Kyushu, a road he had come to know very well as a boy. He reflected on the strangeness of perceived time. It had been three years since Taitaro sent him to Kamakura, but so much had happened to him, and he had done so much, that it seemed more like six. But also it seemed as if it were only this morning that Taitaro and he had stood before the steps of the Waterfowl Temple and said a final good-bye to each other.

The monastery buildings had never been visible from the landward side. One climbed toward what appeared to be an empty hilltop for hours before any of the outlying buildings became visible through the pines. The Zinja preferred seclusion. Still, it seemed to Jebu he should have seen the farm buildings and the gatehouse before now, even at this distance.

When he had climbed a little further, he was shocked to find that the wooden wall around the monastery was gone. The gatehouse was gone. Only the gateway itself, with its tall pillars and crossbeams, was still standing. A gateway in a nonexistent wall.

Now through the shrubbery he could see the foundation stones where the granary had stood. He walked to the gate. The bell that visitors used to announce themselves was still hanging from the gateway, along with the hammer for striking it. The Zinja had never bothered to guard the gate, but they were wary of trespassers. To enter without ringing the bell was considered a hostile act. Jebu struck the bell a resounding blow with the hammer and walked on in.

He passed the granary. It was not a ruin. There was simply

nothing left of it, no scrap of burnt or broken wood, just the foundation stones. Shrubs were growing where the floor had been. The path turned, and he was out of the pine forest that covered the hillside. Now he was shocked to see that all the buildings—the stable, the men's quarters, the women's quarters, the guest house, the library—all were gone. Only the temple itself, a simple, square building with a peaked, slightly curving roof of thatch, still stood.

As Jebu stood there, trying to guess what had happened, Taitaro emerged from the temple.

"Jebu."

"Sensei."

They ran to each other and embraced. Then they separated, still gripping the other's arms, and looked at each other. Taitaro's hair and beard were neatly trimmed, but a good deal grayer. His eyes were older and more tired, the lines in his face deeper.

"Well," he said, "you've seen a lot. I can tell that. Your face doesn't look as much like a blank sheet of paper as it did when you left. Experience has written on it."

"What happened here, Father? Where is everyone?"

"You've traveled a long road, Son. You must be tired and hungry. Come. I've built myself a little hut at the edge of the cliff. You can rest, and I'll give you something to eat."

Jebu looked around, perplexed, as he followed Taitaro. His father seemed smaller and thinner than he remembered. Taitaro's hut, made of cedar frame, paper walls, thatched roof, and dirt floor, was barely large enough for the two of them. His sword, bow, and quiver of arrows hung from pegs on a beam; he pointed to empty pegs where Jebu could hang his own weapons.

Taitaro had dug a square hole in the floor for a fire. Now he lit the fire and set a pot of water on a brazier over it.

"The Order has kept you hired out to the Muratomo. You will remember, I told you that your vision of a white dragon meant that your destiny would be bound up with that of the White Dragon clan."

Jebu shrugged. "I came back here to have done with the war. I hoped to find a refuge where I could refresh myself and perhaps make a new beginning."

"You must be sorely disappointed to find the place so

desolate. I rather like it this way. That's why I willingly stayed behind when the others left."

"But why did everyone leave?"

"About two years after we sent you away, we were attacked by surprise at night by a troop of samurai. The fact that we could be taken by surprise at all shows that we were getting soft and did not deserve the name Zinja. In any case, they killed our guards and rushed the monks' quarters. Of course, they made so much noise that we were awake and arming ourselves by the time they got there. They set fire to all the buildings. We lost most of our horses in the fire. A group of the samurai attacked the women's quarters, and the women fought bravely and ferociously."

"Is mother all right?"

"Yes, she's fine. After a short, fierce battle we drove off the samurai attacking the monks' quarters and killed many of them. Then we went to the aid of the women, who had fought their attackers to a standstill with sticks, needles, pots, boiling oil, and kitchen knives. We finished off nearly all of those samurai. I'm afraid we let our emotions get the better of us. They had killed some of the women and wounded many more. The remaining samurai retreated beyond the wall. Stupidly, they tried to besiege us, perhaps thinking that they could eventually starve us off the mountaintop. We gave them a few days to relax their guard, then went down the mountain through the tunnels and came up behind them. This time we gave a better account of ourselves, even though we had to fight uphill. We lost fewer and they lost more. When they started to run for it, we opened ranks and let them go."

"Were they Muratomo or Takashi?"

"Takashi. Now that the Muratomo clan is defeated and scattered, Sogamori intends to stamp out any other force in the land that does not submit to him utterly."

"But we work impartially with Takashi and Muratomo alike."

Taitaro shook his head. "That does not satisfy Sogamori. He distrusts us deeply because many of our brothers, such as you, have worked for the Muratomo. Also because our Order has connections with branches in other lands. He questions our loyalty to the Emperor. By which, of course, he means our loyalty to himself. He has eliminated nearly all the Zinja in the Takashi's employ. Thus his suspicion that we side with the Muratomo is fulfilled.''

"Did he himself order the attack on this temple?"

"No, we believe it was the governor of Fukuoka province, an appointee of Sogamori. The governor would have had no trouble finding samurai eager to go up against us. There are many who hate the Zinja. They fear our fighting skills and our stealth. They despise what they know of our child-rearing practices and the free relations between our men and our women. And they've heard rumors that we hoard vast treasures in our temples.''

"So, it's war between us and the Takashi.''

"Not at all. Our relations with Sogamori, even with the provincial governor, are officially cordial. This attack was a probe, to see how easy it would be to destroy one of our temples. We hope we convinced them that it would be too costly. But it was costly for us, as well. Many urns were emptied and refilled in the crypt the day after the battle. Many trees on this hillside were cut down for funeral pyres.''

"Is that why the monastery has been closed?''

"We could have stayed here, but other Zinja monasteries around the islands have suffered great losses as well, both from raids and in this War of the Dragons. The other abbots and I met at Yamatai and decided to combine several of our communities in temples nearer the more important cities.''

"Where is Mother?''

"After the decision to close this temple, the remaining monks and women cleaned up the debris, rebuilt the temple building, and left. Your mother went with them to the Teak Blossom Temple near Hakata.''

"Why didn't she stay here with you?''

"I wanted to be alone.''

"I don't understand. Why would you want Mother to leave you?''

"You cannot understand until you are as old as I am. Men and women go through stages in their lives. Each stage carries one on to the next, and all lead to the ultimate insight, to final realization of the Self. At one stage it is appropriate to lead the life of a young warrior, as you do. At another stage one marries and lives quietly and cheerfully with a spouse and carries out duties of leadership in the community, as your mother and I have. But then there comes a stage when one must sit alone on the brink of the infinite and contemplate one's impending leap into the dark. One can no more hold back or prevent these changes than a caterpillar can stop itself from becoming a butterfly. Indeed, not only do people pass through stages, but so do communities, nations, orders like the Zinja. As I sit here alone on this mountain it becomes more and more apparent to me that the Zinja are entering some final stage. It may be that the light of the Order is going out. I fear that this Sunrise Land is moving into a time of darkness. I believe that this temple will sooner or later be destroyed. The war will go on, and the marauders will come back.''

"I will stay here with you and defend it, Father."

"No. Spend the day with me, and tonight if you will. This evening I wish to show you certain things that will be of value to you. But you are too young, there is too much for you to do, for you to dedicate your life to caring for the ruins of a temple and of a Zinja abbot.''

That night Jebu and Taitaro went into the temple and seated themselves on the polished stone floor before the altar, facing each other just as they had after Jebu's initiation ordeal. Taitaro reached into a pocket hidden inside his robe and took out something small and round that sparkled in the candle-light. He leaned forward and held it up so that Jebu could look at it.

"Look deep into this jewel," said Taitaro. "Fix your gaze on it. Concentrate on it. Think only of it and nothing else."

Jebu saw that the surface of the transparent crystal was covered with an intricate maze of fine carved lines, made many times more complex because he could see through the jewel to the pattern on the other side. Taitaro held the sphere in his fingertips, turning it this way and that to display the tracery. In the depths tiny fires, hot red flames and hotter blue flames, twinkled and sparkled.

"As you look at the jewel, you will feel yourself getting drowsy," Taitaro. "You will feel yourself falling asleep . . . You will sleep . . . You will sleep."

Jebu was no longer in the temple. He seemed to be floating in midair through a dark forest. No dragon or bird bore him up; he was drifting as if swimming through the air. Ahead of him, in the blackness of the pines, there was light. It glowed, cool and white. He drifted toward the light.

He found himself in a clearing, about halfway between the top and the bottom of an enormous tree. Light came from the tree, and a strange, continuous murmuring. As Jebu drifted closer to the tree, he saw that the murmuring came from soft sounds made by thousands of living creatures. The creatures seemed to grow, like fruit, out of the tree's branches.

On the lower branches were the smaller animals, the worms, the insects, the fish, the lizards and snakes. In the middle branches, nearest Jebu, were birds, horses, monkeys, cats, dogs and the like. A magnificent striped tiger with glowing green eyes looked at him solemnly, the sort of beast he had seen once or twice in a painting. There were many animals that he did not recognize, many that amazed him. There was one huge creature with flapping ears, a nose as long as a rope that moved with a life of its own, and two white pointed teeth, each as long as a man, that protruded like spears from its mouth. There was a fish that was even larger, as big as a castle, with a mouth big enough for a man to stand upright inside it, yet somehow it seemed comfortably nestled in the branches of this tree. Floating upward, Jebu saw in the topmost branches men and women of all kinds, some a normal color, others as black as ebony or as white as snow, some richly dressed, others naked. And above these were beings who glowed as if they were arrayed in jewels, a glow so intense that it hurt Jebu's eyes to look at them and he could not clearly see their shapes. These must be the kami, he thought.

It came to him with great surprise, awe and joy that all life is one, that living things are not separate from one another but—just as all leaves are part of a tree—all animals, men and gods were one mighty living thing, the Self, manifested in many forms. He laughed aloud at the wonder and simplicity of it, and even as he did so the light from the tree began to dim and he began to move away from it, till he could no longer see the individual creatures in the tree, but only the tree itself, a glowing mountain of light. Then he drifted further away, back into the forest, and the light was only a tiny spark, far in the distance.

The spark became the spherical jewel Taitaro held up

before him. "You are awake now," Taitaro said. "Look at the jewel again."

The pattern of lines with its rising and falling movement somehow suggested the shape of the tree he had seen in his vision.

"This is called the Jewel of Life and Death," Taitaro said. "It is a shintai, the dwelling place of a kami. And now, Jebu, it is yours. Take it." His eyes glowing with a fire almost as bright as that in the Jewel, Taitaro held the crystal out to Jebu, who took it and held it in the palm of his hand.

"This is one of the jewels your father brought with him from far away," said Taitaro. "I do not know where he got it. He never had time to tell me. He gave it to me the night he was killed."

Jebu's eye would follow a particular line for a few of its twists and turns, then lose it again in a network of other lines.

Taitaro said, "The pattern carved on the Jewel is called the Tree of Life. It has a special influence on the inner life. When Jamuga, your father, brought it to me, he told me that while contemplating this Jewel he suddenly saw that he had to rebel and that he would have to flee from his homeland. As for me, after your father's death I looked at the pattern on this Jewel daily. When I took you and your mother in I was still a man with many illusions. I mourned your father, but I secretly rejoiced that his death had brought me a lovely woman for my wife and a fine son. I wanted to be first among all the Zinja abbots in the land. Over the years, as I kept looking steadily into this Jewel, day after day, my illusions faded. And when the time came, as it did after you left, I was able to decide that I no longer wanted to be a Zinja abbot but could happily spend my days living as a hermit and caring for this temple. In a few years, perhaps I can even cease congratulating myself for making such a wise choice." His deep-set brown eyes twinkled, and Jebu laughed.

Jebu said, "My father came from a land of barbarian cattle herders. Such people could not have carved this Jewel."

"Oh, certainly not. Undoubtedly your father or one of his comrades looted it from its original owners. But it changed him. It changed me, and it will change you, as well, if you let it. I do not know who made the Jewel, or how. I think it must be the work of great sorcerers, such as lived on the earth in the distant past. I know that if you will spend a little time each day focusing your awareness on this Jewel, concentrating on its design, trying to absorb it into your mind, each day you will become a little more aware of your true self. You will discover that, as we have always taught you, you are a man of insight, perfect just as you are.''

Tears flooded Jebu's eyes, blurring the fires of the Jewel. This was a gift that had come from both his natural father and his spiritual father. He held the Jewel in trembling hands and stared into its shifting, multicolored depths as if, with the sheer pressure of his gaze, he could penetrate to the answers to all the questions that had plagued him ever since he was a boy. He was half native of this Sunrise Land, but what was the other half? Who was his father? Who was the man who had killed his father? *Who am I?*

The vision of the Tree of Life Taitaro had shown him had already moved Jebu profoundly. Now he was shaken to the very core as he held the Jewel in his hands, turning it slowly and, in his mind's eye, superimposing on its design a memory of the Tree of Life. He would never let go of this Jewel, he resolved, unless to pass it to another as Taitaro had given it to him. Perhaps to a son of his own. And every day he would spend some time contemplating it.

A faraway look came into Taitaro's shadowed eyes. He turned away from the altar and looked through the temple entrance into the darkness outside. He hurried around the temple, blowing out candles until they were almost in darkness. One small candle remained in his hand.

''A group of mounted men just passed through the gateway. Hide yourself. I will meet them.''

18

Taitaro pressed down on a small block of stone in the floor, tipping it upward to expose an iron ring. Pulling on the ring, he raised a slab covering a chamber under the floor.

"Down there you'll be able to hear everything. There is an entrance to a tunnel leading from that chamber to what used to be the monks' quarters. Slip down the mountain and go to the Teak Blossom Temple at Hakata, where your mother and your old friends are."

"I don't want to hide. I will not abandon you."

Taitaro laughed. "Jebu, I have been a Zinja abbot for twenty-three years. Do you really think I'd have any trouble escaping from a party of samurai? No one can hurt me unless I permit it. Now, get down there."

It was so dark that Jebu could not see the floor of the chamber below. He jumped into the blackness and fell farther than he had expected to, his feet striking stone with an impact that stunned him. Taitaro closed the slab over him, and Jebu was in darkness. It was so like the night of his initiation that it brought back all the memories of that ordeal. He felt his way to a corner of the room, sat down and waited in total darkness.

Carrying his candle, Taitaro slowly crossed the temple to the entrance. He questioned himself, wondering why he had bothered to hide Jebu. The two of them could easily defeat or escape from a group of samurai.

It was because he was tired of bloodshed. He wanted to see if he could deal with these samurai quietly and send them away in peace. If Jebu were with him, there would inevitably be fighting.

The mounted warriors galloped up to the temple steps and stopped. Taitaro held up his candle to get a better look at the horsemen. They had Red Dragons embroidered on the breasts of their surcoats.

A deep voice addressed Taitaro. "Old monk, I remember you. You are the Abbot Taitaro." The voice spoke in Chinese.

With the aid of the candle Taitaro peered at the man who had spoken. Taitaro recognized him instantly, with a shiver of mingled anticipation and dread.

The huge man wore a fur-trimmed iron helmet topped by a single spike that came to a needle-sharp point. The collar of his red cloak was edged with silver-gray fur. His silk surcoat was a bright scarlet. His eyes were ice blue. His reddish-brown moustache hung in long strands on either side of his mouth. His cheekbones were broad and prominent, his face deeply lined and scarred, his skin tanned to brown leather by sun and wind and sand. He was wide through every part of his body—shoulders, chest, arms, legs.

"I know you, as well," said Taitaro, answering in Chinese. "But I do not know your name."

"I am Arghun Baghadur." The big man jumped from his horse, handing the rein to a samurai beside him, and climbed the steps of the temple with the rolling gait of one who has spent a lifetime in the saddle.

Taitaro said, "As you see, this temple is undefended. You and your men are welcome to enter and rest yourselves."

Following Taitaro into the temple, Arghun said, "We need not waste time, Abbot Taitaro. I seek the monk called Jebu. I have followed his trail all over Honshu and Kyushu. I know he came here." Arghun spoke Chinese heavily, gutturally.

Taitaro was delighted. This was a splendid stroke of good fortune for Jebu. With a little skillful prodding it might be possible to get this barbarian to tell the full story of Jebu's father, for Jebu's benefit.

Taitaro pointed to the Red Dragon on Arghun's surcoat. "Do you seek him on behalf of the Takashi, or for some other reason?"

"While in this Land of the Dwarfs it suits my convenience

to ally myself with the Takashi clan. But I pursue my own ends. I have come here, as you must know, to slay the monk Jebu. Where is he?''

Taitaro sighed and seated himself, gesturing that Arghun should do the same. He positioned himself at one side of the slab under which Jebu was hiding.

''I felt chilled and sent Jebu out into the forest to cut firewood for me.''

Arghun strode to the temple entrance. He wore felt riding boots and his tread was soft, despite his size.

He called out to his men. ''Search the woods around here for a tall, red-haired monk. Bring him to me unharmed.''

Taitaro said, ''Let the will of heaven be done. I can do no more to protect Jebu. But I do not understand. This young man was a baby when you came here last. He had done nothing to you then. He has done no harm to you now. Why do you want to kill him?''

''It is a sacred obligation I have undertaken, and I may not rest until I fulfill it. Surely, as a warrior monk you can understand that. Genghis Khan is dead now, but his command binds me: *Let Jamuga and all his seed be slain, let his blood vanish from the earth.*''

''Ah, yes,'' said Taitaro. ''Jamuga told me of his people. Herdsmen living in the cold, dry plains north of China.''

Arghun laughed. ''We Mongols are no longer tent-dwelling cattle herders, old man. We are conquerors, and we live in palaces.''

''It is a cruel thing to put a man to death for his father's offense.''

''At the will of Genghis Khan whole cities have been wiped out. Every man, woman and child has been killed, every building leveled. Now riders can pass over the spot and herdsmen graze their cattle without ever knowing there was a city there. It was a small matter for Genghis Khan to decree the destruction of one family. When the Great Khan is offended, expiation must be made throughout heaven and earth.''

Standing below in the darkness, Jebu felt himself trembling. It had taken him a few minutes to recall the spoken Chinese he had learned in the temple years ago. But he understood enough. This was the slayer of his father. Now this warrior had come across the sea again, hunting him. It was dreamlike, in a way. It was hard to believe they were actually talking about him.

There were still unanswered questions. Who, exactly, was Jamuga? Who was this Genghis Khan? What had Jamuga done to call down upon himself such relentless vindictiveness? But Jebu felt he had heard enough. It was time to act, while Arghun was still talking to Taitaro, before the Mongol became restless.

Mongol. Whatever a Mongol is, I'm partly one, too.

When he burst up through the temple floor, Arghun would be taken utterly by surprise. That, plus his Zinja training, should be enough to enable him to kill the man who had killed his father. In the darkness he reached up to move the stone slab.

He found he could not touch the ceiling. He paced the room from wall to wall, reaching above his head as high as he could. His fingertips touched empty air. He felt the walls for a handhold. Except for the low opening to the tunnel Taitaro had told him about, the walls were smooth. He was caught like a cricket in a jar. There was no way to climb out.

Jebu clenched his fists and growled to himself. Taitaro had known about this. The old devil had planned it this way, to protect him.

Promising himself he would have a word with Taitaro, Jebu crouched and crept through the low tunnel. In total darkness, he had to feel his way. The tunnel was lined with stones which formed a vaulted roof to prevent collapse. It must have taken many months to build it that well, even though it was only about fifty feet long. But the tunnels under the temple were bored through the solid rock of the mountain. How long had they taken? The Zinja were patient.

Now the tunnel began to slant upward. Jebu's fingers touched rough stone. He pushed gently. The stone moved easily. A crack of light appeared, and he cautiously raised the stone a little more.

He heard the crackling and crashing of Arghun's samurai stumbling around the brush-grown temple grounds searching for him. He raised the stone enough to be able to see his immediate vicinity. There was no one nearby. He pushed himself out of the tunnel, creeping flat along the ground, and dropped the stone back into place.

Through weeds and shrubbery, Jebu snaked toward the temple. He darted up the steps. Cautiously, he peered into the temple entrance. He could see two dark, seated figures, one small, the other a bulk like a mountain, facing each other near the altar, a candle on the floor between them. From this distance he could not see Arghun's face well. But the Mongol had his profile to Jebu and might detect a movement out of the corner of his eye if Jebu rushed him.

Thinking of shadows, Jebu edged around the entranceway and crept along the back wall of the temple to the rear corner. He drew the collar of his hood up over his nose and mouth to muffle the sound of his breathing. At last he was behind Arghun.

Your armor is your mind. A naked man can utterly destroy a man clad in steel. Rely on nothing but the Self.

Slowly, silently, he worked his way along the side wall of the temple. Taitaro would probably see him, but the abbot would give no sign. Jebu drew his Zinja sword. A further soundless progress toward the altar, and he was facing Arghun's broad back.

Rely on nothing under heaven. You will not do the fighting. The Self will do the fighting.

The ritual sentences of preparation for combat were swept aside by an overwhelming urge to kill the man who had killed Jamuga. Jebu poised the Zinja sword, aiming the point at Arghun's red-cloaked back. Then he sprang away from the wall, launching himself at Arghun.

Just before Jebu reached Arghun, the Mongol rolled to one side. Surprised, Jebu dived past him. Suddenly he was driving the point of his sword straight at Taitaro's heart.

"No! Father!" Jebu screamed. He heard Arghun laugh in the shadows.

Jebu's Zinja-trained reflexes came to his aid and he swung the sword wide. Taitaro also moved quickly, springing to his feet. But they could not help falling into each other.

"Idiot! He saw you reflected in my eyes," Taitaro snapped as the two of them went down together, disentangled themselves and quickly stood. Jebu was furious at himself. He had been taught about eye reflections and had forgotten.

Jebu saw that when Arghun evaded the sword thrust he had also seized the candle. It was on the altar now, and the Mongol was standing beside it. His sword, long and curved though not as long as a samurai sword, gleamed in his hand.

Arghun and Jebu stood looking at each other. Jebu could read nothing in the narrowed blue eyes. They were fierce and empty as the eyes of a falcon. The Mongol's hair was hidden under his helmet, but the red of his moustache was a surprise. It was the same color as his own hair. Why, he looks like me, Jebu realized.

Arghun grunted. "I knew if I kept the old man talking, you'd come sneaking around. You are Jamuga's son, no doubt of that. You are as big as he was. But I think you will be easier to kill than he was. You're just a child."

Jebu was stung by the contempt in Arghun's voice. "A very well-trained child, Arghun. Who intends to kill you this night."

Arghun shrugged. "There is training, and then there is experience."

Without warning, Arghun leaped at him, bringing his saber down in a stroke that would have cut Jebu in two had he not leaped backward. Arghun kept charging him, thrusting and slashing.

Jebu ducked around the hanging hollow log that served as a temple gong, keeping it between himself and Arghun, slowing down Arghun's rush. Jebu took a crouching attack position, his short sword held before him, waist-high. He was swept by a wave of exhilaration. This man had taken his father from him. Now he would pay with his life.

Jebu darted around the log, slashing at Arghun. He expected the big man to duck back, but Arghun stood firm, parrying Jebu's sword with a clang. They were almost chest to chest, and Jebu thought how unusual to be fighting someone as big as himself.

Arghun put his boot behind Jebu's bare heel and tripped him. Jebu saved himself by turning his fall into a somersault, rolling away from Arghun's thrust. Part of Jebu's anger turned against himself. He was fighting poorly tonight. He was making mistakes, letting himself be taken in by obvious tricks. He told himself that he must get the better of the Mongol. Otherwise he would be failing himself, his father and the Order. Not only his life but the *meaning* of his life depended upon it.

Jumping to his feet, Jebu wondered when the rest of Arghun's men would join in. Surely they could hear the ringing of sword on sword. Why didn't Arghun call them? Probably because he wanted to kill Jebu himself. What was Taitaro doing? Jebu dared not take his eyes from Arghun for an instant.

The Mongol was moving in on him again. Unlike the Zinja, who frequently fell back or feigned retreat in order to draw their opponents off-balance, Arghun stayed constantly on the attack, his blade slamming again and again into Jebu's. Jebu knew Arghun was trying to wear him down, overwhelm him with his strength. To break the momentum of Arghun's attack, Jebu crouched and swung his short sword at the Mongol warrior's legs.

Arghun leaped into the air, bringing his saber down on Jebu's blade with all his strength. Jebu lost his grip under the force of Arghun's blow. The Zinja sword went spinning across the room. Still crouched, reaching for the lost blade, Jebu saw Arghun poised over him, his sword upraised for the death blow.

Rolling himself into a ball, Jebu hit Arghun's legs. The Mongol started to topple, then caught himself with a dancer's grace and whirled to strike at Jebu again. Jebu felt the impact of the sword's point and edge biting into the flesh of his upper arm.

Then the candle went out.

Arghun's blade, seeking him again, rang on the temple's stone floor. Jebu realized instantly why Taitaro had been standing near the candle. He had given Jebu his chance, and had blown the candle out when he thought Arghun was going to kill him.

Now Arghun was roaring for his men. "Get in here and bring light! The monk I'm after is here!"

Jebu remembered where his Zinja sword had struck the far wall. He ran for it and snatched it up, then turned to look for Arghun.

"Jebu, you fool! Here!" Jebu felt Taitaro's powerful fingers on his arm. Taitaro propelled him around to the back of the altar. Jebu heard stone grind against stone. Then Taitaro was pulling him again, and he squeezed through the opening and heard the stone door slide shut behind him.

Taitaro lit a candle and beckoned Jebu. Soon they were in the tunnels in the mountain, far below the temple. Taitaro turned on him angrily.

"I told you precisely what to do, but you wouldn't listen. If you had, you'd be safely on your way to Hakata. Now you're wounded, and you've still got to walk to Hakata. Let me see that arm. You're bleeding heavily." He helped Jebu clean and bind the wound.

"You'll have a scar there. I hope you're proud of it."

"Sensei, you're angry because I put myself in danger. But what else could I do? The man who killed my father, sitting there talking about killing me— He has been hunting me, sensei. And you were in danger, too. I had to attack him."

"I don't want you to be killed by that man."

"I won't be. I will kill him some day."

"Jebu, he killed you tonight, on the plane of combat skill. You did not fight as a Zinja should fight. You were angry and vengeful, and therefore you were conscious and controlling at every moment. You did not let the Self fight. You hungered for revenge on Arghun as an ordinary man hungers for a beautiful woman. Think back on it."

Jebu remembered. He had entered the temple composing himself for battle in the usual way, but somehow when he had launched himself at Arghun he had forgotten all that. More than anything in the world he had wanted to kill the Mongol giant. Throughout the fight he had incessantly been telling himself what to do. And he had always been wrong. Remembering, he was crestfallen. Truly he had fallen far short of the Zinja ideal. Perhaps it was his Mongol blood.

"You are right. I am humiliated."

"Humiliation is our best teacher," said Taitaro. "It is as kind to us as an old grandmother. I wanted you to know this man. An empty space in your life was filled up tonight. But now you should forget the tale of your father and Arghun as you would forget yesterday's meal. It does not matter how you came to be born or where you came from or what men did injuries to your father. Until you can go against Arghun stripped bare in mind, he will always be able to get the better of you."

Shame was a leaden weight in Jebu's chest. "I am afraid, sensei, that I am a bad student. I hunger for beautiful women, like any ordinary man. I haven't learned not to care about winning and losing. With Arghun, the man who killed my father, the wish to win became my master."

"You are young, Jebu. The Zinja teachings aim at perfection, but you are not expected to be perfect. We hope you will learn to apply the teachings often enough at this stage of your life that you can live long enough to apply them still more."

The weight in Jebu's chest felt lighter. He smiled gratefully, looking into Taitaro's weary, kindly eyes.

"I will try to care less."

"Consult the shintai, the Jewel of Life and Death, every day. It will help you to see things more clearly."

Together, in silence, they made their way downward through the tunnel system. At last they were on the beach under the half moon and the stars. Another light caught Jebu's eye and he looked up in horror. The Waterfowl Temple was burning.

The temple had always reminded Jebu of a bird. Now the tongues of flame were like feathers and wings, and the temple was, not a waterfowl, but a great bird of fire poised for flight.

Rage followed shock. "I wish I could run back up the mountain and kill them all."

"They are stupid men, and burning the temple is a futile act," said Taitaro. "It doesn't matter. We set no great store by temples. They're just so much firewood in the end."

They embraced, and Jebu turned his back on Taitaro and on the blazing Waterfowl Temple and started walking down the beach toward Hakata.

19

From the pillow book of Shima Taniko:

One hears very little from the capital these days. Once in a while Akimi manages to slip me a letter or a present by way of a trusted servant. I can only guess how it makes her feel to be Sogamori's mistress. Poor Akimi-san. Her son Yukio is now a novice monk at the Buddhist temple on Mount Hiei.

Sogamori has had himself appointed chancellor. This is an ancient office, long left vacant, and is considered higher than the office of Regent. Fujiwara no Motofusa, who is now Regent, must be grinding his blackened teeth down to stumps. With the office of chancellor and with tens of thousands of Takashi samurai ready to spring to do his bidding, Sogamori is the real ruler of the Sunrise Land.

According to Akimi, Sogamori was recently heard to say, "Anyone who is not a Takashi is not a human being." That remark has been repeated all over the capital. People follow the Takashi fashion in everything from the way men wear their ceremonial hats to the style of the family crest on one's clothing. Anyone who wants to be in fashion must study and copy the way things are done in the Rokuhara.

A strange and frightening thing happened yesterday. A troop of Takashi samurai visited Daidoji. Their leader was a giant barbarian who spoke our language very poorly, with a thick accent. He questioned all the guards who fought with Jebu, then came to see me.

Arghun Baghadur, he said his name was. What sort of an outlandish name is that? He would tell me nothing of himself, save that he does the bidding of Sogamori and had old Squint-Eyes' permission to question me. He asked me many

166

questions about Jebu, to most of which I answered that I did not know. Having been told by Horigawa that I speak Chinese, he conversed with me in that language, which he spoke passably well.

I made one stupid mistake. After he had asked me many questions I declared that I had no interest in Zinja monks, especially those of barbarian descent. He pounced at once.

"Then you know of his descent. He must have told you about himself."

I had only intended to make an insulting reference to this Arghun Baghadur's own barbarian background. Led on by my wish to hurt, I forgot myself and made a serious error. It was as Jebu once told me: the warrior who acts out of anger or hatred is simply seeking his own defeat.

I answered that I had guessed Jebu's barbarian ancestry from his appearance. Suddenly I realized that Jebu had told me his father was killed by a giant barbarian with red hair and blue eyes, and that the barbarian wished also to kill Jebu. Instantly I felt sure this was the very man. If only there were some way I could warn Jebu.

The barbarian pressed me with questions for an hour more. I pray I told him nothing else that might help him. After he left, I fainted. Compassionate Buddha, help Jebu.

—First Month, eighth day
YEAR OF THE SHEEP

Arghun Baghadur's visit brought her last meeting with Jebu vividly back to her. Finally she forced herself to accept a fact she had only suspected in the months since she had seen Jebu. She was pregnant.

Compassionate Buddha, she whispered to herself, help me.

She waited another month to be sure, before telling Horigawa the news on one of his infrequent visits to Daidoji. She asked his permission to go to Kamakura for the lying-in. Any place was better, she thought, than this godforsaken country rathole. And once she got away from Horigawa, she might be able to find excuses to avoid returning to him.

"Out of the question," said Horigawa.

"But a woman of good family always returns to her home to give birth."

Horigawa smiled and tapped his fingertips together. "Not, I think, when the home is as far away as Kamakura. It would be entirely too dangerous to your health. What would your honored father think of me, if I let you journey so far? He who takes such good care of every passing traveler, such as the Muratomo boy."

Taniko's heart sank. "Then send me to my uncle's house in the capital."

"Oh, no. Never again will you go to the capital. You disgraced me there once. It will not happen again."

"I did not disgrace you."

"There are many there who know that you were the go-between for Akimi and Sogamori. Now Akimi acts the great lady as Sogamori's mistress. People know that you thwarted my efforts to have the Muratomo brats eliminated. Among those people I am a laughingstock because of you. Now, when you arrive in the capital with your belly swollen, there will be rumors that the child is not mine. I will not be laughed at because of you."

"Why should anyone think the child is not yours?"

"None of my wives has ever had a child. And the story of the armed monk who came here and killed my guards has made its way to the capital."

"That has no bearing on whether you are the father of my child."

"You will stay here. You will bear the child here at Daidoji." He smiled at her. "It is really best for you. Pregnant women should not travel. The custom of a woman going home for the lying-in was followed when all the best people lived right in the capital. Besides, there are excellent midwives here in the village. You will be very comfortable."

"You are holding me prisoner."

"Only for your own good." He stood up and left her.

Taniko felt more alone than she had at any time in her life. She read *The Tale of Genji*, a beautiful illustrated copy which Akimi had sent her. She liked it better than *The Tale of the Hollow Tree*. As her stomach started to bulge, she carried herself straighter and tried to hold it in.

"That is good," said the midwife from the village of rice farmers who worked the paddies around Daidoji and paid sixty percent of their harvest to Horigawa. "Girls who have

husbands and are proud of their babies always let their bellies
stick out. They have a bad time when they give birth. Girls
whose babies have no fathers are ashamed. They try to hide
their bellies, suck them in. And always, they have an easy
delivery, because all that holding in makes them strong through
here.'' She laughed and stroked her hands over her pelvis.
''Keep holding your belly in, my lady. But why are you
ashamed of this baby? You have a noble prince for a husband.''

Having no one else to confide in and liking the midwife's
smiling, moonlike face, Taniko said, ''I do not know whether
this baby has a noble prince for a father.''

Taniko considered the notion of going to the Shima house
in Heian Kyo without the prince's permission, but it seemed
impossible. From the way his dozens of samurai watched her,
she was sure they had orders to keep her on the estate. And
even if she were able to slip away, it was unsafe to travel on
foot or on horseback. How could she get a carriage and
driver? And how could a carriage escape the mounted samurai
who would inevitably come after her? No, she decided, she
would only distress herself by trying to run away.

The midwife came to examine her once a month. She told
Taniko the baby would probably be born in the Seventh
Month. Taniko noticed that when not talking to anyone the
midwife would constantly mutter under her breath, the same
words over and over again. At first Taniko thought the woman
was mad. It would not surprise her at all if Horigawa had
provided her with a demented midwife. But the woman was
pleasant and made so much sense most of the time that
Taniko dismissed that explanation.

''What is it you keep saying to yourself?'' she finally
asked.

''Homage to Amida Buddha.''

''Ah, a prayer.''

''It is more than a prayer. If you repeat it with sincerity,
you are saved for all time. When you die your spirit will be
reborn in the Pure Land far to the west, where it is possible
for even the weakest of us to attain enlightenment and achieve
Nirvana.''

''Is that why you say it over and over again?''

''Yes. Also because it is such a great comfort. When I

invoke the name of Amida Buddha over and over again, it feels as if I am carrying Buddha within me, just as you are carrying that baby inside you. Try it some time, my lady. When you are feeling sad or in pain, just say, 'Homage to Amida Buddha' over and over to yourself until you feel better.''

One particularly beautiful day in the Seventh Month, as she sat reading under a parasol, Taniko found herself thinking back to her ride with Jebu down the Tokaido Road to Heian Kyo. When she realized that those were very nearly the last happy days of her life, a great sadness swept over her. Feeling foolish, she said, ''Homage to Amida Buddha.'' She repeated it. After she had said it about twenty times the sharp edge of the sadness seemed blunted. It was as if she had drunk sake, but with none of its after effects.

The next time she tried the invocation was when she began to feel labor pains. She sent a servant to the village for the midwife, then went to the chamber that had been prepared as a lying-in room and lay on her futon, saying, ''Homage to Amida Buddha.''

The midwife came, and they recited the prayer together. Taniko was in labor all the rest of that day, all the night and most of the following day. Holding in her belly did not seem to have helped.

Taniko awoke to see Horigawa leaning over her. His sour breath made her feel sick, and she turned her head aside. He grasped her under the chin and forced her to look at him.

''Taniko, your baby has been born.''

''Yes.''

''It is alive. It is a daughter.''

''Good.''

''Taniko, it has red hair and gray eyes.''

Taniko felt her heart turn to ice. Feebly, she said, ''Many babies are born that way—''

''No, Taniko.'' Horigawa bared his teeth in what almost seemed a smile. ''It is his. The monk's.'' He turned abruptly.

Taniko, her whole pain-wracked body trembling, raised herself up on her elbows. ''What are you going to do?''

Horigawa snatched the infant from the midwife's arms, held the little, red naked body up as the baby squirmed and squalled. ''Look, Taniko. Behold the living proof of your faithlessness.'' The baby's eyes were shut and the hair looked light brown to Taniko. She reached for her daughter. Horigawa laughed at her helplessness and ran from the lying-in room. Swaying, staggering, knocking over the one feeble oil lamp that lit the room, Taniko forced herself to get to her feet and follow him.

''What are you going to do? What are you going to do?'' She ran after him through the rooms of the women's quarters.

On the veranda the midwife caught up with her. ''My lady! You'll hurt yourself. You must lie down.'' She held Taniko.

''Help me! He's going to kill my baby!'' Taniko fought free of the midwife. With a rapid stride Horigawa was crossing the front yard of the manor to the gate, the naked baby clutched to his chest. Samurai came out of the guardhouse to stare at him.

Heedless of the way her single robe flapped open, revealing her nakedness, Taniko ran after Horigawa and seized his arm. Horigawa whirled and knocked her to the ground with a backhanded slap. The midwife came and knelt by the gasping Taniko. She started to help Taniko rise, and Taniko gripped her hand.

''I'm too weak. I can't stop him. Help me.'' The midwife stared fearfully at Taniko, then scrambled to her feet and caught up with Horigawa. Blocking the prince's way, she fell to her knees.

''Please, my lord, give me the baby.'' She held out her arms.

Holding the baby with one arm, Horigawa drew his dagger and lunged at her.

''Homage to Amida—'' she screamed, but the invocation ended in a horrid choking sound. Horigawa stepped daintily around her, wiping his dagger on his sulfur-colored robe before sheathing it. Blood splashing her kimono like the petals of a giant scarlet peony, the midwife toppled forward and fell facedown in the dust. Taniko's scream was as much for the woman who had helped her as for the baby.

Again she dragged herself to her feet and ran after Horigawa. He stopped and called his samurai.

''Hold her here till I return.''

Tentatively at first, then more firmly as he saw that the prince was watching him, the guardsman nearest Taniko gripped her arm. With a nod, Horigawa turned and walked out the front gate as the two gate guards saluted with their naginatas. The guards stared after the little man holding the crying infant in his arms. A strange stillness fell over the manor.

Another samurai removed his obi and tied it around Taniko's waist. "You should go inside and lie down, my lady. A woman in your condition should not be up and about."

Suddenly, through her tears, Taniko was filled with rage. "What kind of samurai are you? You're nothing but worms! You tell me to lie down when my baby has been ripped from my arms? You let him take my baby. You let him kill a defenseless woman. You are the ones who should lie down. You're not men. No real men would stand by and let these things happen."

"The prince is our lord, my lady," said the man who had given her the sash. "We are sworn to obey him in all things."

"You call yourselves samurai. Where is the courage and the kindliness samurai are supposed to have? You are only samurai on the outside. You have the hearts of maids. I have the only samurai heart here." She glared at the men standing in a half circle around her. They looked at the ground. She turned to the man holding her. "Let go of me."

Still he held her. The samurai who spoke to her said, "Let go of her. Let her do as she wishes. This thing will bring bad karma on all who are part of it." Taniko felt the man's hand fall away. She raced for the gate. The guards with naginatas stepped aside.

What she saw made her scream in anguish. Horigawa was halfway up the stone steps that led up to the mill on the hilltop. Like a huge spider, he climbed rapidly.

Taniko ran to the mill and started to climb. Horigawa was far above her.

"Don't! I beg you, don't," she screamed at him. "I'll do anything you want. I'll be whatever you want me to be. Take the baby away from me. Sell her if you want. I'll be obedient to you. Don't hurt her!"

The sound of the waterfall and the creaking of the mill wheel drowned out her voice. She struggled on up the stone steps, feeling weaker each time she raised a foot. She felt blood running down the insides of her legs. Clawing at the steps, using her hands to drag herself upward, she climbed on.

She was screaming, but she did not know what she was screaming. She could not think. She could not hear herself above the roar of water tumbling over black rocks. She could no longer see Horigawa. She was almost at the top of the hill.

Horigawa was standing upstream. As she caught sight of him, he lifted her daughter up over his head with both arms and hurled the screaming baby into the middle of the stream.

The baby howled in terror as she struck the black water. That was the last sound Taniko ever heard from her child. She plunged into the water. Vainly she reached out as the little body swept past her and over the edge of the fall. She felt the current pulling her. She let herself fall forward into the cold water, wanting to be carried to her death with her daughter.

Just as she neared the edge she felt strong hands seize her and pull her out of the water, powerful arms carry her over to the bank of the stream. It was the samurai who had tried to help her. Without looking at Horigawa, who stood panting by the edge of the rushing stream, he carried Taniko slowly down the steep flight of stone steps.

At the bottom, Taniko raised her head weakly. She saw peasants standing around a morsel of dead flesh lying on the grass beside the mill pond. They stared at her, horror-struck. Then all of them knelt, and one covered the little body with a blanket. Taniko was silent. She closed her eyes. She could not comprehend what she had seen.

A man emerged from the gateway of the manor carrying the body of a woman in his arms. Some of the peasants went over to him and formed a small procession to follow the woman's body to the village at the base of the hills.

A puff of smoke rose from the women's quarters of the manor. Taniko suddenly remembered knocking over the oil lamp in her room. Soon the smoke became a thick, black cloud reaching to heaven. Crackling red flames leaped up after it.

Some of the servants tried to throw water on the fire, but it was useless. A strong breeze was blowing, and the flames quickly spread from the one building to all the others. Broken beams blackened in the fire, and torn paper walls turned to ashes and flew skyward like so many crows.

Within minutes the entire manor had burned to the ground.

The samurai standing with Taniko said, "It is a sign. The kami are angry at the prince for what he has done. They have destroyed his house."

Some peasants overheard him and made the gesture of warding off demons.

"Homage to Amida Buddha," Taniko said.

Immediately, those near her echoed it: "Homage to Amida Buddha."

A peasant woman touched Taniko on the arm. "Your home is gone, my lady. You are ill. If you will be so kind, come to my miserable cottage and we will care for you."

Taniko said, "Homage to Amida Buddha." The samurai and the peasant woman led her away.

20

His estate leveled, Prince Horigawa had no choice but to return Taniko to Heian Kyo. She was desperately ill, and he told her he hoped the carriage journey back to the capital would kill her. But she survived, and by the beginning of the new year her body had recovered. Her mind did not recover as quickly. He tried for a time to keep her in his palace, but her presence in his home unnerved him, and her bewildered manner and constant muttering of the invocation to Buddha disturbed the servants.

Finally, Horigawa took her in his state carriage to the house of Taniko's uncle Shima Ryuichi. He decided that shame would keep her from telling anyone what he had done to the baby, and that no one could blame him for casting off a wife who had become so obviously useless.

In the slow ride through the streets of the capital she

crouched on the straw mat across the carriage from him, staring at him and whispering to herself, while he directed his gaze out through the blinds, so as to avoid looking at her.

"Unfortunately, her baby was born dead," he told Ryuichi. "She is upset. Possibly she has succumbed to the influence of an evil spirit. I think it best she remain with her family for a while." He left abruptly, while Ryuichi looked in helpless horror at the disheveled, murmuring Taniko.

Sometimes Taniko found herself trying to imagine what her daughter would have been like. She had red hair and gray eyes. Would she have been strange-looking? Would everyone have thought her ugly? Would she have been unable to get a husband? It would not have mattered. Taniko would have loved her daughter. She would have called her Shikibu, after the author of *The Tale of Genji*, the book she had enjoyed while she was with child.

Gradually, Taniko once again became an accepted member of the house of Shima Ryuichi. She remained something of a recluse and spent her days reading, embroidering and incessantly reciting the invocation to Buddha. It appeared a foregone conclusion that she would not return to her husband.

Word of what had actually happened at Daidoji filtered back to Heian Kyo through the gossip of servants and samurai. Shima Ryuichi heard the story and accepted it because it was hard to believe a strong girl like Taniko could be reduced to this state by a stillbirth, a misfortune that happened to many women. He considered writing to Lord Bokuden about Horigawa's behavior but decided not to. Against so powerful a man as Prince Horigawa there was nothing to be done, and Bokuden might take it into his head to hold Ryuichi somehow to blame for whatever had gone wrong.

One day in the Fifth Month of the Year of the Ape Taniko was reading when a maidservant burst into her room. "You must prepare yourself, my lady. A great man has come to call upon you."

Puzzled, Taniko slowly laid down her book. "What great man has come?" A picture of Jebu rose in her mind.

"Lord Takashi no Kiyosi, Minister of the Interior and General of the Left, is waiting in the great hall."

Kiyosi. The image of a brown, handsome face with a small moustache replaced that of Jebu. Suddenly, she was frightened.

"I cannot possibly receive him. He cannot see me like this, and I don't have time to prepare myself."

"Be calm, my lady," said the maid. "No gentleman expects a lady to receive him at once, especially if she has had no advance warning that he is coming. You have time to prepare yourself. Your esteemed uncle told me to tell you that he would consider it a great favor if you would greet Lord Kiyosi courteously."

"Of course."

In less than an hour Taniko had changed all her robes and dresses, found her favorite hair ornament, a mother-of-pearl butterfly, and had chosen a screen painted with green shoots of young rice just emerging from pools of water, an appropriate selection for the season. In her chest of personal ornaments she found the fan with the painting of the Takashi family shrine, which Lady Akimi had long since returned to her.

She was seated comfortably, the screen was placed before her, and she sent her maid for Kiyosi.

Through the top of the screen Taniko was able to see that Kiyosi was wearing what was known at the capital as a hunting costume—a long green cloak with a yellow plum blossom print, full tan trousers and a pointed black cap. Coming from the provinces as she did, Taniko always found the term "hunting costume" laughable. Any man who actually attempted to hunt in such cumbersome clothing would soon find himself eating dust. She had heard that Kiyosi was a splendid sight in his samurai armor. She hoped she might see him that way, some day.

To control her nervousness, Taniko whispered the invocation.

"What was that you said?" Kiyosi asked. "Were you speaking to me?"

"Nothing, my lord." Then, feeling she was betraying both Amida and the midwife who taught her, she explained. "I was reciting a prayer to the Buddha."

"Ah, yes." The light in the room was dim and it was difficult to see Kiyosi through the screen, but he seemed to be smiling kindly. "I have heard of such prayers. This is the teaching of the Pure Land school, is it not? Invoke Amida and you will be reborn in the Western Paradise?"

"I have studied under no school, my lord," said Taniko. "I learned the prayer from a very kind woman who helped me in an hour when I needed help badly."

"I hope you will forgive my presumption in coming to visit you, Lady Taniko. If I may say so, having met you on several occasions I have most pleasant memories of you. I heard that you were back in the capital at your family's house. I notice that your screen depicts sprouting rice. Perhaps in this month of rice-sprouting a new friendship might begin to grow between us."

"I am most grateful for your thought, my lord. I am overwhelmed by your kindness." It must be pity that had brought him here, she thought. I am old. My baby was killed. I am unattractive. Many people must think me mad.

They talked, through the screen for a long time. Taniko found herself again becoming interested in the affairs of Heian Kyo and Kiyosi seemed happy enough to tell her about them. He was modest, almost embarrassed, about the rise to power of the Takashi. Under Taniko's tactful questioning he acknowledged that his father was now virtually unquestioned ruler of the Sacred Islands.

"How fortunate you are to have such a mighty father," said Taniko.

"How fortunate is my father to have such a family," Kiyosi answered. "I do not speak of myself, but of the many ancestors who have paved the way for his rise to greatness— of his father, my grandfather, who wiped out the pirates on the Inland Sea, of his uncles, his brothers, even his cousins, who help him by holding high offices in the land. In a mountain range one peak always stands taller than the others, but it is all the mountains together that help the tallest stand."

"Not least among the peaks is the samurai general who defeated the Muratomo at the battle of the Imperial Palace," said Taniko. "But sometimes a man cannot achieve greatness unless he thinks he stands alone."

Kiyosi slapped his thigh and laughed softly. "How true! I worry about the destiny of my family, and I do not think my accomplishments will ever match those of my father."

He stood up suddenly. "I must leave you now, Lady Taniko. You have been most kind to receive me. I will call on you again, if I may. I—I am married, of course, and I know many women. But the conversation of women does not usually interest me. I find you fascinating to talk to."

"You are always welcome here, Lord Kiyosi."

A few moments after he was gone, Ryuichi hurried into the room. "This is splendid! To be quite frank, my dear, I thought your usefulness to the family had ended when Prince Horigawa cast you off, but Kiyosi is a hundred times more important than the prince. I shall write your father at once. He will be proud of you."

"The Takashi general is not going to marry me, Uncle."

"But he will come back?"

"He said he would."

"That is as much as we could hope for. That is far, far better for you than mooning about the house reading old books and mumbling prayers. You are a young woman. Even if he only makes you his mistress, you can do something for the family."

"Any small contribution I could make would be an honor, of course," said Taniko tartly. "But I think you are selling the rice when it hasn't even been planted."

"That's done all the time," said Ryuichi with mild surprise. "Here in the capital, people barter future crops on land they own to get what they need today. Your father has neglected your education in trade."

"Well, no seeds have been sown in this field yet."

"Only a matter of time," said Ryuichi with an airy wave of his hand. They both laughed.

Taniko realized it was the first time she had laughed since Shikibu's death. It was the first time since than that she had felt fully alive. She whispered her thanks to Amida, the Lord of Boundless Light.

21

Like the Waterfowl Temple to the north, the Teak Blossom Temple of the Zinja stood at the crown of a hill overlooking the sea, which was here contained within Hakata Bay, a great, circular inlet with the small fishing town of Hakata at its head. Hakata could have been a major port, being an excellent harbor and close to Korea and China. But the wealthy families involved in foreign trade lived mostly at the capital, and it was more convenient for them to conduct their shipping from Hyogo on the Inland Sea.

Many of Jebu's friends from the Waterfowl Temple were now living at the Teak Blossom Temple. Weicho, the short, rotund monk who had so impressed Jebu with his wickedness during his initiation, was the abbot. No longer required to pretend to play at being a bad Zinja, Weicho was now free to be his true self, a genial, simple man with only one vice, an inordinate fondness for eating.

"What's become of Fudo, your partner in wickedness?" Jebu asked him.

A shadow crossed Weicho's face. "He's left the Order."

"Left the Order? I can't imagine anyone leaving the Order."

Weicho shrugged. "Many strange things happen these days. Others have broken with the Order as well. In Fudo's case his duties—the pretense, the cruelty, the occasional need to kill an innocent young novice—became too much for him. He's converted to Buddhism. The last I heard, he was in a monastery in the eastern provinces, sitting on his arse day and night, trying to find happiness by meditating. He's a cripple. He wasn't strong enough to be a Zinja. Forget him." Weicho waved the irritating memory away. Strange, Jebu thought, but

179

Weicho almost reverted to his old role of sharp-tongued cruelty when he talked about Fudo.

Most important of all, Nyosan, Jebu's mother, lived at the Teak Blossom Temple. Jebu had not seen her since his initiation, and whenever the busy routine of the temple permitted, mother and son spent hours in conversation.

Nyosan had charge of Jebu's collection of swords. There were now over sixty. Many of them were the lower-grade sort turned out quickly by the swordsmiths to serve poor samurai in combat. Others were magnificent creations signed by such legendary sword makers as Yasatsuna, Sanjo and Amakuni, heirlooms whose capture by Jebu was a tragedy for the families of the samurai who had carried them. It was four years since Jebu had first vowed to undertake the project.

It was evident to Jebu that Nyosan deeply missed Taitaro. It seemed to him a cruelty that Taitaro should deliberately cut himself off from his wife and choose to live alone, but Nyosan herself never questioned his decision. From hints in her conversation, Jebu gathered that her life was not without its compensations. Indeed, it seemed the older men and women among the Zinja enjoyed their own sort of unions with one another, which were bound by no rules except that of secrecy from the younger members of the Order. So Nyosan apparently did not lack for whatever comfort might be drawn from the joys of the body. She was not alone, though she might be lonely, and she never complained. Still, Jebu resented the way Taitaro had left her. Could he not find whatever insight he sought within his union with Nyosan, rather than off in the woods by himself?

During his stay at the Teak Blossom Temple, Jebu followed the usual routine of a Zinja monk at home base—up at dawn, meditation and exercises before breakfast, practice in the military arts until noon, manual labor in the afternoon, study of Zinja lore in the evening. Each day he spent some time staring into the flickering depths of the Jewel of Life and Death. He found that it really did seem to enhance his peace of mind. The obsession with his father and Arghun, the longing for Taniko, were still there, but he accepted them, as a veteran samurai learns to live with the pain of old wounds.

He entered into a liaison with one of the temple women. It was pleasant and gave him a feeling of greater completeness.

Together they studied and practiced sexual magic, following ancient books from India and China. It was a fascinating pursuit. But more than once when he and his partner had devoted themselves to the sexual yoga for hours and the moment of supreme bliss should have been a moment of profound insight into the Self, instead he seemed to make contact with Taniko. At such times her face would appear in his mind as clearly as if she had supplanted the partner who sat with him in ecstatic union. Sometimes she spoke to him: "The lilac branch will always be there for the waterfowl." Once Jebu asked his partner if she had spoken. "I don't remember," she answered. It remained a mystery.

One afternoon while Jebu was weeding the vegetable garden, a monk approached followed by a small, ragged figure carrying a travel box. The man had a heavy, untrimmed black beard that almost covered his entire face. Jebu did not recognize him.

"Shike!"

Now Jebu saw the gaps in the teeth and the crossed eyes, and he knew who it was. "Moko!"

"Shike, it has taken me this long to find my way to you. I have been over a year on the road, going from one Zinja temple to another, begging for my meals, hiding from samurai and bandits. Luckily I was able to escape with my dogu box. With my Instruments of the Way of Carpentry I was able to earn my living as I traveled. Every place I went, you had been there, but you were gone. Where you seemed to travel on wings, I followed on wooden feet."

Jebu threw his arms around the little man and led him to the edge of the garden, where they sat on a pair of boulders. "Tell me all the news you can. Is Taniko-san well?"

Moko's face fell and he was silent. Jebu seized his arm. "What is it?"

Moko hesitantly put his hand on Jebu's. "Shike, after you found us at Horigawa's estate, I had to flee as well. The prince discovered I was your friend. I hated to leave the Lady Taniko alone with him, but I felt that my ghost would afford her small protection, so I went on my way."

"Did he hurt her?"

"Whatever I know is only what I've been told by others." And Moko told the story of the red-haired baby born to

Taniko, its death, the fire and Taniko's return to Heian Kyo. Tears streamed from Jebu's eyes. When Moko's story was over, Jebu sat covering his face with his hands.

Suddenly he stood up, gave a great cry of anguish and rushed to the edge of the sea. There he threw himself on the stony ground and wept. A dark cloud covered his mind. At first he felt no more than a blackness and numbness within, as if a naginata blade had cloven his chest. Gradually, images rose within him: Taniko, the baby he had never seen, Horigawa.

If only she had listened to him. They could have run away together. Waves of sadness swept through him like the surf below in Hakata Bay. Two lives were in bondage to sorrow and a third snuffed out because Taniko refused to give up her status, to forget this marriage that had been made for her by fools and run away with him. Their daughter was dead. How Taniko must have suffered. Jebu wept for the drowned child and for Taniko's agony.

He would go and kill Horigawa. He had never hated anyone this way before, not even Arghun. His enmity toward Arghun was a matter of principle; it was only right to hate the man who had killed his father and who wanted to kill him. But even though he had fought with Arghun, he felt he hardly knew the man, and from what little he did know, he felt a degree of respect for the Mongol.

With Horigawa, it was different. Horigawa had used and abused Taniko's body. He had killed their baby. The thought of Horigawa made his stomach churn and his fingers clench, aching to be wrapped around the man's scrawny neck. He hated the cruelty, the waste, the stupidity of Horigawa's act. It was Horigawa, too, who had egged on the Takashi and thereby set the great samurai families at each other's throats. Because of Horigawa thousands of good men were dead and much of the land lay in ruins. If Horigawa were to die, how many lives might be changed for the better?

If only he had killed him when he had the chance at Daidoji. He had been a fool to let him live. Some of the hatred he felt for Horigawa was directed at himself as well. It was because of his error that Horigawa had lived to kill Jebu's daughter.

The spasm of hatred recalled him to himself. He reached inside his robe to the secret place sewn into it, and he took out the shintai. Sitting up, he held the Jewel in both hands before his face, staring into the shifting planes of color and light in its depths. For a moment he seemed to see the great glowing Tree of Life and some of the creatures that grew from it.

Peace spread slowly through his body. The grief was still there, a dull ache, but the hatred was gone.

Horigawa and I are one, he told himself. For me to kill him in hatred, thinking that I am ridding the world of evil, is as mad as cutting off my left hand with my right hand. Horigawa acts according to his nature and I act according to mine. If I kill him someday, it will be because it is necessary, not because I hate him and desire his death.

That, he thought with surprise, is the deepest level of insight I have achieved since Taitaro gave me the shintai.

He stood up and walked back to Moko, who was staring at him. "Shike, what is that precious stone?"

"It is a gift to me from my fathers. Both of them." He put his hand on Moko's shoulder. "I'm all right now."

"Shike, I want to stay with you. Let me be your servant, your bannerman, your foot soldier—anything."

"A Zinja monk does not normally have servants. But these are not normal times. Yes, from now on you will travel with me."

A few days later Abbot Weicho called Jebu into his chamber. "You will continue to serve the Muratomo. The Council of Abbots is convinced that there is a doom hanging over the house of Takashi. It is important to the Order that Zinja be fighting on the winning side. When the Muratomo do win, we may see the revival of the Order for which we have long hoped."

Jebu was sent to the island of Shikoku to help a band of samurai besiege the castle of an oryoshi who was oppressing the countryside in the service of the Red Dragon. Jebu proposed to assassinate the oryoshi and was contemptuously told that it was impossible. The castle was so impregnable that a mouse could not get into it, and the oryoshi was guarded in shifts by samurai who even stood over his bed and watched him while he slept.

"He does not even send his guards away when he takes a woman," the local Muratomo leader said.

"Assassination is a Zinja specialty," said Jebu. "Leave this to me."

Jebu infiltrated the castle by way of a sewer outlet into the moat around it. He hid in the castle privy for a day and a night, using Zinja meditative techniques to remain motionless and silent. When his intended victim came to relieve himself, Jebu ran his sword into his bowels and escaped by the same route he had entered. Leaderless, the castle fell to the Muratomo samurai, who looked on Jebu with superstitious horror. Moko helped him to wash his clothing and equipment, and would not let him out of the bath, which he constantly replenished with fresh, steaming water, for an entire day.

Jebu fought along with one band of samurai, then another, staying at one castle for a night, at another for a week, at a few for months. He besieged and was besieged, ambushed enemies in the forest and fought pitched battles in the streets of cities and villages. It was a way of life he had grown used to after Domei's insurrection, and one to which Moko quickly adapted.

But in spite of the Council of Abbots' hopes, the Muratomo leaders who held out against the Takashi were, one by one, captured or killed. The insurrection came to seem more like the scattered depredations of outlaw bands than an organized rebellion. The two surviving sons of Domei remained under guard in the hands of the Takashi. The elder, Hideyori, was still under the watchful eye of Taniko's father, Lord Shima Bokuden. His half brother, Yukio, remained in Sogamori's custody in the Rokuhara, the Takashi stronghold in the capital. Both publicly disavowed any warfare conducted in their family's behalf, declaring it to be the work of bandits. They repeatedly swore their loyalty to the Emperor and to Sogamori.

Jebu's collection of swords grew month by month. After a battle, with Moko's help, he would find the swords of any samurai he killed, and Moko would carry them to the nearest Zinja monastery. Eventually the swords would make their way to the Teak Blossom Temple. Months later a message would arrive from Nyosan by some circuitous route, telling Jebu that the swords had arrived, and giving him the current tally.

Jebu continued his daily practice of contemplating the Jewel of Life and Death. Carefully secluding himself so that his samurai companions would not see and covet the Jewel, he would lose himself in the maze traced on the transparent sphere's surface.

Moko felt that the Jewel must be magic, and he feared its power over his master. Jebu had told Moko the whole story of Jamuga, Taitaro, Arghun and the shintai. The Jewel was beautiful, Moko thought, but why did the shike spend so much time staring at it?

22

From the pillow book of Shima Taniko:

Sogamori has commanded that the young Muratomo no Yukio be moved from the Buddhist monastery on Mount Hiei to the Takashi palace, the Rokuhara. Sogamori claims he has heard of threats on the young man's life, but everyone agrees that the main threat to the Muratomo heir is Sogamori himself. Akimi, it is said, no longer has much influence on Sogamori, who has fallen foolishly in love with a sixteen-year-old white rhythm dancer from Kaga province named Hotoke.

I wonder what Father would do if Sogamori ordered him to execute Hideyori.

—*Seventh Month, eleventh day*
YEAR OF THE APE

Kiyosi's visits had become the high points of Taniko's life. He now came in the evening and brought his lute with him, and while he played, they sang together. First, though, they would spend an hour or two discussing the gossip of the day.

Kiyosi found that nothing concerning the intrigues at the Court was beyond Taniko's comprehension, and he had even fallen into the habit of asking her opinion on difficult affairs of state in which he was involved.

"Father is beside himself with glee," he said one evening. "He says he has finally matched the accomplishment of the greatest Fujiwara."

"How so?"

"He has arranged for my sister, Kenreimon, to marry the Imperial Prince Takakura. And he intends to have Takakura succeed to the throne when Emperor Rokujo retires."

The year before in the Year of the Sheep, Emperor Nijo, whose Empress, Sadako, Taniko had served as a lady-in-waiting, had died after a short illness. Sogamori, the Retired Emperor Go-Shirakawa, and the Regent, Fujiwara no Motofusa, had agreed that the new Son of Heaven should be Nijo's son, Rokujo, who was now only four years old. Next in succession were two sons of Go-Shirakawa, Mochihito and Takakura.

Taniko pointed this out. "Prince Mochihito is next in line for the throne after Emperor Rokujo."

"He will be persuaded to step aside." Kiyosi looked away uneasily. For his visits, Taniko sent the servants away and put aside the screen of state. They had long since been conversing face-to-face. The Shima family had no fear of scandal. Indeed, Ryuichi was frankly hoping for something scandalous to occur.

"Kiyosi-san, this is a mistake. Your father is now tampering with the Imperial succession. His appetite is boundless. He is like the frog in the peasant tale who puffs himself up until he bursts. As you know, I hear things from people who would never talk to you or to a member of your family. People are afraid of the Takashi, and some are growing to hate them. What will they think when they learn that Sogamori intends to put a Takashi on the Imperial throne?"

"Just to marry the Emperor, not to *be* Emperor—"

"That wouldn't fool the stupidest street sweeper, and it doesn't fool me. Obviously Takakura and your sister will have a child, quite possibly a son. That child will be Sogamori's grandson. And as soon as that happens Takakura will conveniently abdicate and the Emperor will be a Takashi. Sogamori's ambition is as plain as Mount Hiei. I tell you, he overreaches himself.''

''What Father intends is not unheard of,'' said Kiyosi. ''The Fujiwara married their daughters to the Imperial heirs many times. The Imperial house today is as much descended from the Fujiwara as it is from Emperor Jimmu. And besides, we Takashi have Imperial blood. We are all descended from Emperor Kammu.''

''It's not the same,'' said Taniko. ''The Fujiwara were as close to the throne as a river to its banks when they intermarried with the Imperial house. Emperor Kammu lived a long time ago, and since then the Takashi have been provincial land-owners, traders and samurai. People see you as rustic up-starts. And what's more, the Fujiwara themselves are among those you should be concerned about. They are envious of the power of the Takashi. Your worst enemy at Court is the Regent, Fujiwara no Motofusa.''

''Motofusa is no danger to us.''

''The Fujiwara still have enormous influence in the coun-try.''

''Influence. What difference does that make? You speak of people fearing and hating the Takashi. Why should we be concerned? The day of the Fujiwara, the day of the nobility, is over. They had authority, and we respected and obeyed them. They despised us, the samurai, because we did the fighting, we shed the blood. The nobles of Heian Kyo were above all that. When Go-Shirakawa's brother tried to over-throw him, and later, during Domei's insurrection, we dis-covered that it was our arrows and our swords that decided events. It is from the sword that authority springs. And now that the Muratomo have been crushed, every sword in the land does the bidding of the Takashi. My father holds the country in the palm of his hand.''

Taniko shook her head. ''You are talking like your father now. I think you know better. You cannot rule this land with swords alone. If the nobles, the priests, the landowners great and small, the peasants and the people in the streets all turn against the Takashi, they can bring you down. The swords that serve you today will turn against you, if your enemies seem to have right on their side.''

Kiyosi said nothing for a moment. Then he spoke in a wondering voice. "You offend me."

Taniko bowed her head. "I have overstepped myself with the august Minister of the Interior."

"No one says such things to me any more."

"I ask your pardon."

"You don't understand. I need someone to remind me that the world still looks on the Takashi as uncouth butchers. We deceive ourselves. Only you, Taniko-san, of all the people I know, speak to me of things as they really are." He did something he had never done before in all the times he had visited her. He moved across the floor until he was sitting beside her. He took her hand.

Taniko's hand felt as if she had put it close to a fire. A warmth spread through her arm to her entire body. It was a sensation she had felt many times on looking at Kiyosi, but never had it burned like this. She sighed with the pleasure of it.

"Have you nothing to say now?" he whispered.

"Words are not the only language." She put her hand on top of his.

"I only came close to you. If that silences you, you are easily silenced."

"It has been very long since I was silenced so, Kiyosi-san," she said, letting her head fall against his chest.

Delicately his hands found their way into her robes. With the sure touch of a very experienced man his fingers penetrated the many layers of dresses and skirts she wore and found the recesses of her hungry body. She melted with joy at the sensation, and reached up to stroke his cheek again and again with an almost frantic insistence.

They undressed each other, not stripping away all their garments, but peeling away the layers of silk just enough to reveal each to the other, like a partially unwrapped gift. With a pang of regret Taniko thought fleetingly of Jebu, only to say to herself, as the samurai often said, that the past was the past and the present was the present, and this shining lord was someone she desperately needed and could not deny herself.

His face shadowed in the lamplight, he looked at her intently, seriously, his nostrils flaring as he drew deep breaths. Always, before now, she had seen him fully dressed in the clothing of a courtier. Now, for the first time, she saw and felt the power in him—the solid, broad neck, the wide, square shoulders, the great, flat muscles across his chest. She stroked his arms delicately with her fingers. These were the thick forearms of a swordsman, strong as tree trunks.

This was the body of a man trained from childhood to kill. He was, and would always be, a samurai, a man whose way of life was death. To such a man, who faced death constantly, a moment like this must be very precious. Each time he was with a woman he must know that it might be the last time, and this knowledge must give the union a painful sweetness which no man but a samurai could ever know. With Kiyosi she shared that poignancy, that transience.

This beautiful man might be cut down tomorrow, like a flower in a field. Shuddering with pleasure, she gave herself to him.

For the first time, Taniko experienced what it was to spend night after night with a man she loved. Her days passed with a honey-warm delight she had never known before. It was as if she had gone hungry all her life and was only now discovering the taste of good food.

Examining her body in privacy, she found her hips and breasts growing rounder, fuller, though her waist and legs were still slender. She had the figure of a woman now, no longer the body of a girl. Her mirror told her that her cheeks were a healthy pink, which, of course, she had to hide with white powder when she dressed. Her eyes sparkled and her hair was thick and glossy. How far she had come from the wraithlike creature invoking Amida Buddha in the corner of her chamber! How far Kiyosi had taken her! She had never been more beautiful.

They began to travel together. Kiyosi took her for carriage rides through the city and on visits to nearby shrines. During the autumn they went several times to one of the Takashi country estates, where they spent the day riding and hunting with falcons. They sailed the length of the Inland Sea from the port of Hyogo, which the Takashi virtually owned, to Shimonoseki Strait, opening into the great western sea.

Since she was no longer connected with the Court, and since their relationship had no official status, she was unable to accompany him to any of the great state banquets and festivals he frequently attended. But she was always with him at the smaller, intimate dinners and parties he and his close friends gave for one another. Kiyosi was the center of a circle of young nobles and courtiers who wrote poetry, patronized sculptors and painters, talked and drank and played the flute and the koto and the lute until dawn and went on long, rollicking visits to one another's country houses.

Taniko found the young Takashi men to be brilliant, evanescent creatures. A few years ago these young men would have been going to war instead of reciting poetry or riding after their falcons. One day war might strike Heian Kyo again, and some of these young men might fall. In their poems, the samurai often compared themselves to cherry blossoms, beautiful but blown away by the first strong wind. Taniko thought the comparison apt.

She knew that Kiyosi had a principal wife and two secondary wives, as well as sons and daughters. In matters involving affairs of state, this was the family to which Kiyosi was responsible. She did not resent them, and she hoped they did not resent her. They had possessed Kiyosi long before she knew him, and they would have him back long after she lost him. Somehow or other she would lose him, of that she was sure. All joy, she had learned, lasts only for a moment. Cherry blossoms. She wrote a poem for Kiyosi.

> Many are the nights
> We sleep in each other's arms.
> In years to come
> We will think these nights all too few.

Kiyosi didn't like it. It was depressing, he told her, to dwell on the instability of life. Such matters should be left to monks. As for himself, he intended to live forever.

> We have slept together
> And your long black hair is tangled in the dawn.
> We will remain together
> Till your black hair turns white.

Sogamori, Kiyosi's awesome father, approved of her. They

had met several times at Takashi banquets, and the stout chancellor had smiled benignly and spoken pleasantly to her.

Aunt Chogao beamed and little Munetaki peepèd, awestruck, as the Takashi hero strode through the Shima galleries. Uncle Ryuichi was beside himself with delight and sent glowing reports to Lord Bokuden in Kamakura about the way Taniko had charmed herself into the highest circles of the Takashi. Bokuden wrote letters back praising Taniko and mentioning in passing that Muratomo no Hideyori was growing up to be a dutiful subject of the Emperor and was no danger to the social order.

He was already fully grown when I met him five years ago, Taniko thought, even if he was only fifteen.

She managed, while being honest with Kiyosi, to be of help to her family. She told Kiyosi in a straightforward way that she wanted to do things for the Shima, and he gladly supplied her with information and sometimes with more tangible gifts to pass on. Several times he told Taniko where Chinese trading ships were going to land their goods secretly to avoid the Emperor's tax officers. Though the Takashi held the highest government offices in the land, much of their wealth was based on tax avoidance.

It amused Kiyosi to help the fortunes of what seemed to him a smaller and poorer branch of his own family. He persuaded Sogamori to double the allowance sent annually for the maintenance of Muratomo no Hideyori in Lord Bokuden's household. Grants of tax-free rice land descended on the Shima family unexpectedly.

Kiyosi smiled when she thanked him for his benevolence to her family. He said, "There are certain small fish that attach themselves to a shark, and when he feeds, they enjoy the morsels that fall from his mouth."

Taniko laughed. "That is a disgusting comparison, Kiyosi-san."

"Not at all. The small fish are said to help the shark find his way. It is my hope that your family will similarly be helpful to us."

From the pillow book of Shima Taniko:

This has been a good year for me, but a bad year for the realm. Famine and pestilence are laying waste both the

capital and the countryside. Every day carts piled high with
the bodies of those dead of disease or starvation are taken
out through the Rasho Mon to be burned. People are robbed
on the streets in broad daylight. Crowds of beggars surround
the mansions of the wealthy. The Shima house has its
regular contingent, who appear at our door every morning
like a flock of sparrows. Uncle Ryuichi lets me feed them,
because he feels I have brought good luck to the family. But
I tell the beggars not to let it be known that I am giving
them anything, or the flock will double in size, and I will be
sent out into the street to join them.

The Takashi seem unable to do anything about these
steadily worsening conditions, or perhaps they do not care.
But they permit no criticism of themselves. They have over
three hundred young men between fourteen and sixteen who
cut their hair short, wear robes of Takashi red, and patrol
the streets. Let someone whisper a word against the Takashi,
and before he knows what is happening he is whisked off to
the dungeon in the Rokuhara and beaten almost to death.
More than once the bodies of men and women have been
found in the Kamo River. It is said officially that they were
killed by robbers. But often the last time these unfortunates
were seen alive was when they were dragged into the Takashi
stronghold. In past times, when the people complained, the
rulers tried to improve conditions. The Takashi have found a
cheaper way to stop complaints.

Although my young lord likes me to be frank with him,
we do not talk much about these things. He knows about
them. He often seems troubled when he talks to me, and he
is silent for long moments. When we do talk of matters of
state he pours out his fears for the future of the land, his
unhappiness over the suffering of the people. But his father
will have things as they are, and my young lord can do
nothing but try to advise him. I hear that Sogamori's rages
are becoming more frequent and lasting longer. Just the day
before yesterday he smashed to pieces a precious vase from
China because Motofusa, the Fujiwara Regent, made a speech
criticizing him in the Great Council of State.

I yield myself to my young lord because he is noble and
strong and beautiful. He possesses everything that my husband has not at all and that only Jebu has in greater abundance. I yield myself because life is short and I cannot sit in

lonely sorrow. I need the arms of a strong man around me. I know Amida Buddha sees, and has compassion on me. But—oh, Jebu! Where are you?

—*Tenth Month, sixteenth day*
YEAR OF THE APE

In the Eleventh Month Taniko discovered that, as the ladies of the Court sometimes put it, she was not alone. She was surprised that her immediate reaction was joy. She had not thought that she would ever care about having a child, after the loss of her daughter. For over two months after she was sure, she concealed her condition from Kiyosi. She was not sure whether he would be pleased or displeased when he learned.

One night he touched her bare belly with his fingertips. "I think you are attending too many banquets and drinking too much sake. You seem to be getting rounder in the middle."

Taniko smiled, then laughed outright. Kiyosi sat smiling at her.

At last she said, "Can't you guess why my belly is fuller?"

"Spoken like a true country wench. Yes, I suspected. I sensed something different about you. Ah, Taniko-san, I am glad. I had hoped that some day you would tell me this news."

"You're glad? Why? You already have many sons and daughters."

He smiled. "I have wanted to give you a special gift."

She held out her arms to him, and they drew together.

The voluminous clothing worn by the wellborn women of Heian Kyo concealed pregnancy until the very last moment. Taniko was able, as she wished, to accompany Kiyosi on short journeys, to go to banquets and other celebrations and to venture out in public by herself from time to time. The physician who attended the Takashi in war and peace, a man who had watched over Sogamori's health for thirty years, came to examine and prescribe for Taniko and promised that he would be there when she delivered. Taniko hoped that this childbirth would not be as long and as painful as the last.

Her hope was fulfilled. She felt the first labor pains at dawn on the fourteenth day of the Fifth Month in the Year of the Rooster. By midmorning the Takashi physician and a midwife under his direction were with her in the Shima lying-in room. Early in the afternoon Taniko gave one last, agonized push and the midwife drew the baby out of her body.

"He will be called Atsue," Taniko said when the physician held the baby up for her to see.

Kiyosi came to see her and the baby at sunset. Surprisingly, his father was with him. Through the blinds of the lying-in room Taniko could hear the clatter of Sogamori's mounted samurai attendants. Ryuichi was beside himself with delight and apprehension. Sogamori's presence filled the house as if Mount Hiei itself had come down to the city and was walking among them.

"There cannot be enough of us," he declared. "The boy Atsue is Takashi on both his mother's and his father's side. He will learn the arts of war, but he will also learn poetry, musicianship, calligraphy, and the dance. He will be able to appear before the Emperor without concern." He looked sternly at Taniko. "You will see to it. For now he will remain with you. No expense will be spared for his education."

Taniko looked at Kiyosi who stood beside his father. In Sogamori's presence the younger man seemed diminished, a youth without a mind of his own. Taniko saw that Kiyosi might well be the wiser of the two, as many people said, but it was the strength and will of Sogamori that made the Takashi all-powerful.

She felt a chill at Sogamori's ominous words, "for now." Kiyosi smiled reassuringly at her. Tomorrow, she thought, he would come, and they would talk as they always had.

23

Early in the spring of Jebu's twenty-third year, he and Moko were camped near the Rasho Mon gate of Heian Kyo with a group of samurai disguised as silk merchants. They had been commissioned by the surviving Muratomo leaders to attempt the rescue from the Rokuhara of Muratomo no Yukio, who, it was rumored, was in grave danger of being murdered by the suspicious Sogamori.

"The boy is a constant reproach to Sogamori," said Shenzo Saburo, the leader of Jebu's band. "He reminds Sogamori that the Takashi murdered his father and grandfather and his older brothers. The tyrant will not rest easy till he has killed off all the generations of Muratomo."

None of the samurai, it turned out, had ever been in Heian Kyo except for Jebu and Moko, and none of them had seen the Rokuhara. Holding a council, the samurai agreed that Jebu would go into the city first, a scout.

"Dress as a Buddhist warrior monk, a sohei, Jebu," said Shenzo Saburo. "Go into the city and inquire about Lord Yukio. Observe the Rokuhara and report back to me how strongly guarded it is and how we might get Lord Yukio out. And shave your head, Jebu. It's your red hair that makes you conspicuous. There are plenty of tall monks and peasants in the world."

As Moko shaved his head, Jebu drew his tally scroll out of an inside pocket in his robe. "I have collected ninety-nine swords. Only one to go."

"Shike, this sword collecting of yours is madness."

"Yes, it is foolish. But in an impulsive moment I made a vow. When I collect one more sword I can stop."

195

After several hours of wandering the broad avenues and smaller side streets of Heian Kyo with his naginata over his shoulder, Jebu was frustrated. He found it difficult to approach people on the streets and in the wine shops, and the people he did speak to were terrified of talking to a stranger. He had only to mention the name "Muratomo" and the conversation would abruptly be broken off. The red-robed young men who patrolled the streets for Sogamori had terrorized the whole city. Several times Jebu encountered groups of them, and like the other citizens of Heian Kyo he prudently crossed over to the other side of the street.

No one would tell Jebu anything useful about Lord Yukio's condition, his whereabouts in the Rokuhara, how well he was guarded, or the strength of the Takashi samurai. But the Takashi were so unpopular that his guarded questions aroused no hostility, only warnings that he was broaching matters better left alone. Jebu decided that he would go and look at the Takashi stronghold for himself and report back on its apparent defenses. That would give him something to show for his journey into the city.

Then it appeared that his one-man expedition might produce another result. At the darkest hour of the night, Jebu, wandering westward toward the Kamo River to get to the Rokuhara, heard the music of a flute. Someone was playing an air of the eastern provinces. There was something almost magical in the pure, sweet sound carrying on the still night air. Jebu smiled appreciatively.

He stepped onto the bridge called Gojo, over the Kamo River. This was the very bridge on which he had first crossed into Heian Kyo with Taniko. In the moonless dark he could faintly make out the three towers of the Rokuhara on the far side of the bridge.

Then he saw the flute player strolling toward him from the other end of the bridge. It was a man dressed in a green and yellow hunting costume, with his long sword hanging from his belt. He was small and slender and looked very young. His long black hair hung unbound below his shoulders. He had no samurai topknot, but he wore a samurai sword. He must be very young, indeed. Strange that such a boy should be out so late.

To fight and perhaps kill this flute-playing lad would be a

shameful way to collect his last sword. But an armed man in Heian Kyo must be on the Takashi side. Perhaps this was one of Sogamori's young bullies, off duty and out of his red robe. If so, it was time he was taught some humility.

Swinging his naginata down from his shoulder, Jebu fell into an at-the-ready stance, barring the young man's path across the bridge.

"You play very well."

"Thank you, sohei," said the boy politely, raising his eyebrows ever so slightly as his glance fell on the long pole arm in Jebu's hands. "Can I be of service to you?"

"I want your sword. Give it to me and I'll let you pass."

Calmly the young man sheathed his flute, drew a fan from his sash and snapped it open. It was white, with a red disk painted on it. What on earth did he intend to do with that? He was a good-looking boy, Jebu saw, though the eyes under his high forehead were larger than normal, which gave him a somewhat feminine prettiness. When he smiled, he displayed slightly protruding teeth.

"My sword is my most valuable possession, sohei. I find it rather an insult for you to suggest that I give it up without a fight."

"Do not force me to attack you, young man. Do you intend to defend yourself with that fan?"

"If you are a well-trained sohei, you must be acquainted with the art of the war fan. I'll use this until I see the need for a more puissant weapon. It is always better to use too little force than too much, don't you think?"

Jebu laughed. "So young and such a sage?"

"I have given some thought to military matters. Are you going to stand there talking, sohei, or are you going to come at me?" The youth crouched slightly, the absurd fan held out before him.

Very well, Jebu thought. He would try to subdue the young man without hurting him. Waving his naginata from side to side, he took a few menacing steps forward. Suddenly, he swung the naginata at the boy's feet, trying to knock him down with its long pole. At the last possible second the youth stepped quickly backward, and the naginata's sword blade sliced into the railing of the bridge. Jebu pulled the weapon free and stepped back, trying to draw his opponent into an attack. But what sort of attack could he make, armed with nothing but a fan? The flute player simply stood his ground, eyeing Jebu intently.

Once again Jebu lunged, whirling his naginata in a great arc that was intended, not to hurt, but to force the boy off-balance in evading it. This time, instead of stepping back, the young man made a prodigious leap into the air. Jebu's naginata whistled harmlessly through the space where he had been.

Jebu considered himself to be faster than any swordsman he had ever met, except for some Zinja teachers he had fenced with. But this lad's bursts of speed were absolutely blinding. From a position of perfect stillness the young man could move so quickly as to make the movement seem invisible. Jebu repeatedly attacked places where his opponent had been an instant before, only to realize that the young man was now six paces away.

Then the boy darted in past Jebu's guard, the fan thrust into Jebu's face, blinding him. Then, folding the fan, the youth stabbed its rigid ribs into the backs of Jebu's hands. The pain was excruciating, and it was all Jebu could do to keep his grip on his naginata. The boy beat him about the head and face with the folded fan, the blows coming as fast and furiously as the hammering of a woodpecker's beak on a tree trunk. Growling like an angry bear, Jebu managed to shove the boy away.

To be so discomfited by a lad fighting with a fan—this was humiliating. He must defeat him and take his sword.

No, Jebu thought then. Why must he defeat the young man? His opponent was excellent, he himself was excellent. They were brothers in the warrior's arts. It didn't matter which of them won.

Satisfied to fight now for the pleasure of using his skill, Jebu found himself doing much better. He was driving the young man back. He had him pinned against the railing of the bridge. He looked into his opponent's large eyes and saw there a slight amusement, and deeper than that, he saw the Self looking at him.

The young man leaped to the railing and stood there, balanced on the balls of his bare feet. He was laughing. Jebu slashed at his ankles and the young man jumped into the air, letting the blade pass under him. He landed and danced backward along the railing, parrying Jebu's thrusts with his open fan. His agility was awe-inspiring. Jebu remembered Moko's legend of the demon of the Rasho Mon, and suddenly wondered if he were fighting with a spirit.

Enough of this, he thought. He stopped fighting and lowered his naginata. He chuckled, then started to laugh aloud. He stood there on the bridge, roaring with laughter and delight.

"You are the best opponent I have ever fought! The best! Who are you?"

Smiling, not even out of breath, the young man dropped lightly to the planks of the bridge, folded his fan with elaborate care and tucked it back into his green sash.

"Who are you?" Jebu asked again.

"The samurai ask who their opponents are before a fight, but you ask afterward. I have known all along that you are Jebu, the Zinja shike."

"How do you know me?"

"For years I have been hearing tales of a huge brute of a monk, who goes up and down the countryside attacking samurai and collecting their swords. He is said to have red hair. Your head is shaved—I suppose you consider that a disguise. How many swords in your collection now, Jebu?"

"Ninety-nine. I vowed to collect a hundred. Yours would have been the last. But meeting you means far more to me than collecting another sword."

"I am glad of that. You fought beside my father and my brothers. I want to be your friend."

"Who *are* you?"

"I am Muratomo no Yukio."

Jebu fell to his knees and pressed his forehead against the wooden planking. "I have been seeking you."

"You have? Tonight I just escaped from the Rokuhara."

"And you stopped to fight with me? What if the Takashi were pursuing you? You should have simply given me the sword and hurried on."

Yukio laughed. "I could not miss the chance to learn the outcome of a contest with the great Jebu."

"How did you learn to use a fan like that? I heard you were being educated for the Buddhist priesthood."

"I was tutored in the martial arts by the tengu. Every night I used to slip out of the monastery to fence with them."

"The tengu?"

"Little creatures, half man and half bird, who live in the mountains. Very skilled with all weapons, including the war fan and the tea kettle."

"Do you expect me to believe that?"

Yukio laughed. "The monks of Mount Hiei did. Monks are generally very superstitious."

"Not Zinja monks," said Jebu. "Lord Yukio, I am part of a band of allies of your house who came here with the hope of rescuing you from Sogamori before he could harm you. We are camped outside the city near the Rasho Mon. I am delighted to see that you have rescued yourself, but we must get away from the city at once. Having fought you, I know that you are truly worthy to lead the house of Muratomo."

"The leader of the house of Muratomo is my elder brother Hideyori," said Yukio. "He is in exile at Kamakura, but he will come forward at the proper time."

"As you say, lord." Jebu bowed again. "No more sword collecting for me. This night I make a new vow. Because Lord Muratomo no Yukio had prevented me from fulfilling my vow of collecting one hundred swords and because he has shown me what the art of swordsmanship truly is, I vow to serve him faithfully and constantly as long as both he and I shall live. I swear it on the honor of the Order of Zinja. In token of this vow, I offer him my sword." Drawing his Zinja sword, he held it out to Yukio. The handsome young man extended his hand over the sword without touching it—the customary samurai gesture to indicate acceptance of an offer of service.

"I accept your sword and I am deeply honored. As a son of Muratomo no Domei, I expect many men to swear fealty to me as time passes. You are the first. I know that this is the sword that was presented to you by your Order at your initiation, and therefore it is a precious symbol of your holy calling. In the name of the house of Muratomo I accept your offer of service. I pledge you and your Order the same loyalty you offer me." He handed the sword back to Jebu, who sheathed it with tears in his eyes.

"And now," said Yukio, "let us go to join our friends at the Rasho Mon. Perhaps whoever shaved your head can perform the manhood ceremony for me. For some reason, even though I'm already fifteen, Lord Sogamori never would allow it."

24

Surprisingly, for a trio as unusual in appearance and easy to recognize as Jebu, Yukio and Moko, the three continually managed to elude the samurai sent out by the Takashi to hunt them down. Sometimes they were barely out one door when their pursuers entered through another. Sometimes they enjoyed long periods of peace under the protection of one or another friendly local lord. Sometimes the idleness of safety grew boring, and they were almost happy when word came that a group of samurai flying the Red Dragon pennon was riding their way.

Yukio's main objective was to survive and wait for the Takashi to make a mistake. They had risen so high, they must come down eventually. There was no possibility of the house of Muratomo's accepting the permanent supremacy of the house of Takashi. During his captivity Yukio had tried to remain on good terms with Sogamori, but still Sogamori had been on the verge of having him killed when he escaped.

Yukio finally explained to Jebu that he had secretly taught himself the martial arts and devised his own exercises for practice. Jebu was almost inclined to believe Yukio's tengu story. Somehow Yukio had made discoveries in the fighting skills that were not likely to occur to anyone who had learned in the usual way from a recognized teacher. Jebu and Yukio practiced together constantly, and Jebu was quite willing to admit that in this youth he had met his master. Together the two men progressed to unparalleled accomplishments with their weapons., When, on occasion, they were forced to fight, legends were born.

Yukio was also interested in the theoretical side of war, and when he learned that a landlord in the land of Oshu, at the far northern tip of Honshu island, had a copy of the Chinese classic, Sun Tzu's *Art of Warfare*, he could not rest until he had read it. The owner of the book being a Takashi adherent, Yukio could not simply present himself at the gate and ask permission to read the book. He had to gain entry to the household by stealth.

The landlord also had a beautiful daughter named Mirusu. Each night Yukio positioned himself outside her bedchamber and wooed her by playing the flute, so softly as not to wake the rest of her family. After he had charmed her for six nights with his flute playing, Mirusu invited him in. He spent the following nights making love to her, and when he had pleased her sufficiently, reading the thirteen books of Sun Tzu.

Yukio was also fascinated by ships. He had studied books on naval warfare and examined the records of the old battles with pirates that had won the Takashi renown in the last century. Yet he had never been on a ship. He questioned Jebu closely about his few voyages and asked Moko what he, as a carpenter, knew about shipbuilding.

"Ships are the key to Takashi power," Yukio declared one day. They were far to the north, enjoying the protection of the lord of Oshu, Fujiwara no Hidehira, who owed old debts of gratitude to the Muratomo and who bitterly hated the Takashi.

Yukio went on. "Half the Takashi wealth comes from overseas trade. My family can never defeat them as long as we are landlocked. We, too, must take to the sea. You may not know that the patron kami of the Muratomo, Hachiman, was once called Yawata and was a kami of the ocean. So our heritage is of the ocean, and in the ocean we will win the final victory over the Takashi."

"We should go to Kyushu," said Jebu. "It's time we left

here. We've imposed on Lord Hidehira long enough. My mother and my stepfather both live on Kyushu, and it has been years since I've seen them. My mother lives at the Zinja Teak Blossom Temple, and this is what will interest you—the temple is on Hakata Bay. There are fishing boats and a few bigger ships there, and you can study the sea and talk to seamen to your heart's content. Hakata is a small port, and the Takashi have no forces there. We can live there unseen for as long as we like."

"Might it be possible to cross the ocean from there?"

"Korea is very close."

"I was thinking of China," said Yukio pensively. "In China the arts of shipbuilding and navigation are advanced far beyond ours."

Disguised as yamabushi—wandering Buddhist monks—Jebu, Yukio and Moko worked their way down the west coast of Honshu, crossing to Kyushu at Shimonoseki Strait.

"This is a short run, but it's tricky," said the captain of the fishing boat that weaved a twisting course past hilly islands. "In midmorning at this time of year, the tide shifts and runs westward through the strait at eight knots, and we have to navigate across it."

"You see, that's the sort of thing I want to know," Yukio said to Jebu.

"You can't expect to pick up every bit of seafaring lore in all the land," said Jebu.

"We must learn as much as we can."

The three made their way down Kyushu toward Hakata. Jebu insisted on a side trip to the Waterfowl Temple, but though the temple had been rebuilt, it was deserted. His heart sank, wondering if anything had happened to Taitaro. Finally, they climbed the hill to the Teak Blossom Temple.

"Is there any news of my father?" Jebu asked roly-poly Abbot Weicho.

"The great Taitaro has left these Sacred Islands. He came to visit us here a year ago. His teachings on the Zinja way of life were incomparable. Unfortunately, though, he only stayed with us a few months. Then his Zinja insight told him that it was time for him to cross the great water. There are things to be learned in China, he said, that will be lost in another few years.''

''I have been thinking of making the voyage to China myself, Holiness,'' said Yukio.

Weicho nodded. ''If Lord Yukio goes, Jebu, you must go with him. The Order has decreed that your task now is to accompany him, to serve, protect and fight for him.''

Yukio joined with pleasure in the daily routine of the monks. Moko was set to work repairing the monastery's granary, which was old and about to fall down. He found occupation for his free time, he told Jebu with pride and pleasure, in the company of a woman of the village, who thought his tales of adventure more than adequate compensation for his odd appearance.

Jebu spent a day visiting with Nyosan. ''I can't understand why Taitaro does this to you,'' he said to his mother. ''This pursuit of insight without concern for others is a kind of spiritual greed.''

Nyosan patted Jebu's hand. ''I am pleased that you are indignant for me. But my life has given me three of the most splendid men I have ever known—my husband, Jamuga the barbarian, a giant of a man and a magnificent warrior, and my husband Taitaro, a giant of the spirit. And it has given me a son who combines the best of both. I am well content.''

''You may be content, Mother, but you have not gotten all you deserve.''

''If each of us got what we deserve we would have to be in both heaven and hell at the same time. The way things are makes more sense.''

One afternoon Abbot Weicho sent for Jebu and Yukio. They met in a cryptomeria-shaded grove at the base of the path leading to the peak overlooking the temple.

Weicho had a visitor with him, a round-faced, shaven-headed monk in a black robe. ''Normally,'' Weicho was saying to the visitor, ''our temples are placed at the very tops of mountains. But here the peak was too sharp, so we built the temple down here and put a small hut for meditation up there instead.''

The visitor smiled and nodded. Since the Buddhists wore saffron, the Shinto monks white and the Zinja gray, Jebu wondered what way this black-robed man followed. His eyes, as he looked at Jebu and Yukio, were somehow at once warm and stern. He seemed an inconsequential fellow, just another monk in a land where there were tens of thousands, until Jebu looked into his face. There was a rock-hard strength in the directness of his stare, the firmness of his lips and the set of his jaw. He looks at me as Taitaro did, thought Jebu.

"I am called Eisen. I bring a Buddhist teaching back from China. It is called Zen. In Chinese, *Ch'an.*"

Weicho chuckled. "You will not convert Jebu. He's the most stubborn Zinja in the land. And Lord Yukio is too interested in fighting to care about religion. But I thought you might tell them something about China, since they are considering going there. And in repayment they will escort you to the top of the mountain, since I'm too lazy to take you myself."

"A soft Zinja is no Zinja," Jebu quoted *The Zinja Manual*.

"You are also the most sententious Zinja in the land," said Weicho. "May I remind you that the *Manual* also says, 'On occasion the soft serves better than the hard. Where the sword cannot cut, the pillow may smother or the silken cord strangle.' You may escort Eisen-sensei to our meditation hut while amusing him with your borrowed wisdom."

As they began the climb, Jebu said, "What does the word Zen mean? I never heard it before."

Eisen laughed. "Some of us have spent years asking ourselves what Zen means. It comes from an Indian word, *dhyana*, which means meditation."

"So you teach meditation," said Jebu. "On what do you meditate?"

Eisen smiled. "Some of us meditate on a question, such as, 'What is Zen?' Others, like myself, meditate on nothing at all."

"To what end?" Jebu asked.

"We meditate to meditate; that's all."

"I don't understand."

"It's very simple. That's why it's hard to understand." They were halfway up the stone steps leading through the small pines that grew on the mountain. Though Eisen was a stocky man, he was breathing easily and seemed to have no difficulty with the climb.

They took up the conversation again, Jebu and Eisen doing most of the talking. Yukio, having spent his boyhood practicing the martial arts secretly at night and sleeping during the day when he was supposed to be studying philosophy, had little to say. Jebu doggedly argued that spiritual practices had to produce results of some sort, even if only rebirth in the Pure Land. Eisen sidestepped all his arguments with amusement, much as Yukio had evaded his sword thrusts on the Gojo Bridge. At last they reached the top of the mountain, where there was a small straw hut sheltered by pines that had dug precarious footholds among the boulders. Beyond the hut and the pines the shoreline stretched encircling arms out to the horizon to form Hakata Bay.

Eisen said, "Long ago men whose names we no longer know went into the forests and up to the tops of mountains and thought about why people are not happy. And they came to the same conclusion: we should seek happiness in nothing at all. The Brahmans of India learned from those original sages. The Buddha and Lao Tzu both restated their teachings. The same wisdom is at the heart of the lore of Zinja and Zen monks. I find there is much similarity between our two paths. Only, if you will forgive my saying so, we part company on the matter of warfare. We students of Zen believe that violence is an obstacle to enlightenment. The Zinja do not hesitate to kill or injure others."

"Like you, we seek enlightenment," Jebu said, "but we do it through the practice of the arts of warfare. We learn to be forgetful of the conscious mind. We learn to love our opponents and not to fear death. Even the samurai, if they learned the Zinja principles of fighting, could aspire to the same sort of enlightenment you teach, sensei."

"Perhaps I am wrong about the military arts," said Eisen. "If any samurai should come to me for teaching, I will not turn him away."

He sat down before the entrance to the hut, facing out to sea. Jebu and Yukio sat with him.

Yukio said, "Tell us about China, sensei. I hear the Emperor of China is fighting barbarians. I am thinking of taking fighting men over the water to serve the Chinese Emperor. There are many of us whose lives are forfeit if we stay here, many who have lost everything to the Takashi. Perhaps we will find better fortune in China.''

"Too bad you are not going, as I did, to learn from the Chinese. But if the Central Kingdom, as they call it, is not saved from the barbarians, there will be nothing left to learn.''

"Who are these barbarians?'' Yukio asked. Jebu knew these barbarians were his father's people, but he wondered what Eisen would say about them.

Eisen said, "There are many peoples who live in the grasslands north of the borders of China. They are called Cathayans, Kin, Manchus, Tartars—and Mongols. They spend their lives on horseback, herding cattle and other animals. They live in tents and have no fixed abode. From time to time they make war on the farming people to the south. Ages ago a Chinese Emperor built a Great Wall to keep them out, but as with all walls its promise of security was false. A hundred years ago people called Cathayans crossed the Wall and took the northern half of China for their own. Then a people called the Kin conquered the Cathayans. They seized all the riches, settled in the cities and learned Chinese ways. Now the Mongols have come. They have utterly destroyed the Kin. They threaten the native rulers of China, the Sung dynasty, who still hold the southern half of the country.''

Yukio said, "I have heard of these Mongols. I have heard that they have no human law and are more ferocious than tigers or bears.''

Eisen shrugged. "You know how men will exaggerate when describing their enemy. Actually, their laws are very strict, and among them many transgressions are punished by death. They are a fearless, energetic, intelligent people. They are capable of enduring incredible hardships. What they have achieved in recent years they owe to a leader called Genghis Khan. In their language his name means Mightiest Ruler. He wrote their code of laws, which is called the *Yassa*.''

He was the ruler who sent Arghun to kill my father and me, thought Jebu. He who commanded the obliteration of whole families, of whole cities.

"This Genghis Khan was a master of warfare," Eisen went on. "Other barbarian horsemen from the grasslands simply swarmed like locusts, overwhelming the civilized peoples with their numbers and ferocity. But Genghis Khan shaped the Mongols into a well-organized, well-drilled army. That is why their conquests extend beyond all others. Even though Genghis Khan died many years ago, long before I went to China, his successors have continued to use his methods of making war to extend the Mongol territories even further. Genghis Khan was a ruler more awesome and brilliant than any Emperor of China or Japan has been in the last thousand years."

Yukio looked shocked. "You would compare a barbarian warlord to our Emperor?"

Eisen raised a placating hand. "Not at all. Our Emperor is a manifest kami. He is the child of the sun goddess. But there are times when clouds obscure his light. At present, I think, the clouds are thick and numerous in this Sunrise Land."

Yukio nodded. "For many of us the clouds are too thick. That is why we are willing to seek service with the Emperor of the Land of Sunset."

"I wish you a safe journey, and may you return some day to a happier country." Eisen pulled himself into a more rigid sitting position, crossing his legs and hooking his feet over his thighs, then folding his hands in his lap.

He said, "I know the Zinja do not use any special position when they meditate. But I have found that once you have assumed this position, it is impossible to lose your balance and fall over, even if you drop off to sleep." And he rolled from side to side like a doll with a weighted bottom that cannot be tipped over. Jebu and Yukio laughed as they bade him good-bye.

"My mind is made up," Yukio said at the bottom of the hill. "I am going to China. Come with me only if you want to. I don't care that your Order says you must accompany me. I don't want you with me unless you want to come."

"Please let me come with you. I want to go to China for many reasons."

"Fine. I intend to send out a message secretly to our friends in all the provinces—Muratomo no Yukio is going to

China and calls for every samurai who supports the Muratomo cause to come with him. Normally it would not be proper for me to issue such a call without the permission of my brother Hideyori, our clan chieftain. But Hideyori is a prisoner in exile in Kamakura and cannot speak freely. His captors might even force him to denounce me for doing this. But I know that in his heart he will be cheering me on.''

Somehow, Jebu could not picture the grim, controlled Hideyori cheering for anything that did not benefit him directly.

Yukio went on, ''There is nothing left for us now in these islands. The Takashi rule everywhere. Those who have been loyal to the Muratomo have been stripped of their lands, many of them hunted as outlaws. All the wealth of the world is in China. We can help save the greatest civilization in the world from the barbarians. And the day will come when the Takashi will be weaker than they are now, and we may perhaps return when fortune favors us, and take back what is rightfully ours. Meanwhile, we will gather men and hire ships, and we will present ourselves to the Emperor of the Sung as a fighting force. You and I will lead.''

That night, when Moko was through working on the granary, Jebu told him of Yukio's decision. Moko smiled broadly.

''Long ago, shike, when we first met, I told you I would go to China with you if need be. Now, even though I have found the joys of love here in Hakata, I am ready to prove that I meant what I promised.''

25

The ox-drawn carriage rumbled down the rocky road from Mount Hiei. Before it walked ten unarmed samurai, while six more brought up the rear. In the front of the procession walked an aging bannerman, an honored veteran of the rebellions of past years, many times wounded. He carried a red Takashi banner. The dragon portrayed on the banner was at rest, indicating that this was not a war flag, but one to be displayed peacefully on family occasions.

In the carriage Atsue, aged nine, blew idle notes on his flute. He and Taniko were returning from his regular music lesson at the temple on Mount Hiei.

"I wish the koto was small enough to carry with us so I could practice on it now," he said.

"Some of the country folk play a little stringed instrument called the samisen," said Taniko. "I could get one of those for you."

"I don't want anything from country people," said the boy. "Country people are stupid and ugly and rude. I don't want to be anything like them."

"I'm from the country."

"No one would know it if you didn't tell them Mother. You're a fine lady."

Smiling, Taniko peered through the curtained window of the palm-leaf carriage. The procession had already entered the great covered gateway in the north wall of the city. The small group of Imperial police officers guarding the gate saluted the Takashi banner as the veteran carried it through. Now the carriage passed into the shadow of the gateway.

Suddenly, someone shouted at them to stop. The voice was angry, peremptory.

"Remove this carriage from the gate. Make way for the Imperial Regent, His Highness Fujiwara no Motofusa." The carriage came to a halt.

Taniko looked through the front curtains. The shouting man was wearing rich, orchid-colored chamberlain's robes. Four other men in black silk robes, wearing the long, slender swords of the Court in black and gold scabbards, had seized the head of the ox and halted its slow forward pace.

The bannerman, holding his staff as if there were a naginata blade at the end of it instead of a square of red cloth, cried, "This carriage carries Shima no Atsue, son of the esteemed Takashi no Kiyosi, commander-in-chief of the Imperial army, and grandson of the noble Takashi no Sogamori, Imperial chancellor and victor over the Emperor's rebellious enemies." The bannerman made it sound as if all those august personages were riding in the carriage with the child Atsue, Taniko thought.

More armed men in black silk surrounded the bannerman. The unarmed Takashi samurai moved closer to the carriage. Looking out the other window, Taniko saw that another carriage, this one three times the height of a man, ornamented with elaborate scrollwork and magnificent black and gold lacquer paneling, and drawn by two white oxen, was moving majestically toward the gate. Taniko's carriage was right in its path, and one or the other would have to give way.

She knew what was going to happen. It was inevitable. A carriage brawl. Heian Kyo had been notorious for these incidents for hundreds of years. Some of them even took place on the palace grounds.

"The family claims of the occupant of this carriage are ridiculous," said the chamberlain who had stopped them. "Prince Motofusa is the Regent and a Fujiwara."

The Fujiwara. So civilized and so old. And now so envious of the rising, vigorous Takashi who were shouldering them aside, who had cut off the heads of two Fujiwara princes during the rebellions and who even had adopted the old Fujiwara tactic of marrying into the Imperial family. The two most powerful men in Heian Kyo these days were Fujiwara no Motofusa, the Regent, with his high office, his wealth and his ancient family, and Takashi no Sogamori, the chancellor, with *his* high office and tens of thousands of samurai at his back. Perhaps Motofusa had chosen this moment for a test of strength.

"Come here," Taniko called to the bannerman in the strongest voice she could muster.

The old samurai limped over to Taniko's carriage. The Regent's chamberlain squinted at the curtains to see who else was in the carriage with Sogamori's grandson.

"Under no circumstances are you to back down," said Taniko firmly. "The Regent holds a higher office than this boy, but we are already in the gateway, and it would be unseemly and dishonorable for Lord Sogamori's grandson to back out of the gate. Tell the Chamberlain that we would yield place if we had arrived at the gate at the same time as His Highness, but under the circumstances we respectfully beg leave to continue through. Tell him that."

"They're going to fight us, my lady, no matter what we say."

"Then the disgrace will be upon them. Remember, the honor of the house of Takashi is involved."

The bannerman went back to the Fujiwara chamberlain and repeated the message.

"Nonsense!" the chamberlain retorted. He turned to the men holding the oxen. "Push this carriage out of the gateway."

The four men in black were now joined by others carrying naginatas. At the sight of the deadly blades a chill went through Taniko. The police who had been guarding the gate had long since disappeared. Taniko looked over at Motofusa's carriage, which was still slowly advancing. There were at least fifty men in Motofusa's entourage. They were not samurai, but armed courtiers, the remnants of the old army of aristocrats and conscripts that had policed the empire before the rise of the samurai. They didn't really know how to fight, but they knew how to hate, and the small band of Takashi men they faced was unarmed.

The courtiers pushed against the head of the ox, while the bannerman and the Takashi samurai tried to hold the animal where it was. A shoving match broke out. One of the courtiers fell. He rose up shouting curses, his black robe spattered with brown mud. Now the men with naginatas moved forward, holding the long poles with the blade ends sheathed and toward themselves, like fighting sticks. Taniko felt a little relief at this. At least they were not prepared to kill, though it might later come to that.

One courtier swung his pole and caught a samurai on the side of the head. Taniko winced at the thud of the pole against the man's skull. The samurai slowly sank to the ground.

"Kill them! Kill them!" Young Atsue had stuck his head out through the curtains and was cheering the Takashi samurai. Taniko pulled him back. The child had never seen bloodshed, but he was full of stories of glorious Takashi victories over pirates and the Muratomo, and he was wild with the excitement of his first battle.

But the courtiers' naginata poles rose and fell furiously, doing brutal work on the samurai. Several of the samurai were wrestling with the courtiers, trying to get the naginatas away from them. If they did, they would surely start to use the blades.

Then stark terror seized Taniko as, with a sudden rush, the courtiers attacked the carriage itself. A pale face, distorted with rage, shoved itself through the window curtains.

"You will make way for Prince Motofusa, Takashi garbage!"

Atsue struck at the man with the only weapon he had handy, his flute. The man jumped back as the flute thumped against the bridge of his nose.

The carriage began to rock and topple. Taniko screamed and took the boy in her arms as she felt the world giving way around her. She had never known such panic since Horigawa had snatched her newborn daughter from her arms and run off to kill her. Now another child of hers was in danger. She and the boy and all the rich furnishings of the carriage were falling, falling. With a crash that knocked the breath out of her, she landed on a side of the carriage that had now become its bottom. The wooden frame creaked and broke in several places. She looked at Atsue to see if his arms and legs were all right. The boy stared back at her, terrified. He was no longer enjoying the adventure.

The carriage shook under heavy blows. Taniko screamed as she saw a naginata blade bite through the wood. Scrambling to her feet and pulling Atsue with her, she made a dive for the door of the carriage.

She found herself in the center of the melee. The courtiers were hysterical with rage now, and one seized her and tore at her clothes.

"Here is the bitch who cuckolds Horigawa and whores for Kiyosi," he screamed. The courtier flung Taniko from him so that she fell into the mud. Others were flailing at the carriage with their naginatas. Feet trampled her. Wildly she tried to find Atsue.

The boy was struggling with a black-robed courtier, the same man he had struck with his flute. The man was tearing the flute out of Atsue's hands. Getting it away from the screaming child, he broke it over his knee.

"Look!" he shouted to the other courtiers, holding Atsue by the shoulder. "Dress the little rustic bastard in fine clothes and give him lessons on the flute and he thinks he lives above the clouds. Go back to the rice paddies, you vermin!" And he kicked the sobbing Atsue into a mud puddle.

Taniko sprang at the man. She saw a little ceremonial dagger dangling from his black sash by a gold chain. She pulled it loose and drew her arm back to stab the courtier.

Someone seized her from behind and pushed her to one side, firmly but gently. It was the bannerman.

"Don't dirty your hands, my lady." Still unarmed, he gave the courtier who had kicked Atsue a chop against the side of the neck that sent him rolling in the dirt, unconscious.

Taniko pulled Atsue into her arms, grabbing him up as she saw a naginata blade slice into the veteran's belly. The old man gave a grunt of pain and fell into the dirt, his blood pooling the ground.

The violet-robed chamberlain who had stopped them stepped forward with a grim smile. "Get out of the way, the rest of you bumpkins, or you'll share his fate."

The overturned carriage was a heap of kindling now. Even its wheels had been chopped to bits. The ox had run off. Contemptuously the courtiers pushed the wreckage to one side of the gateway as the carriage of Regent Motofusa continued its lordly advance.

Taniko knelt in the dirt beside the bannerman. She gagged when she saw his wound. Through his rose-colored tunic his stomach had been slashed across. There was blood everywhere.

"Don't distress yourself, my lady," the bannerman said. "Don't spoil your pretty cloak with an old man's blood."

The man had survived two great rebellions, a hero, only to die in the mud after a sordid little carraige brawl. "I'm sorry," said Taniko. "I'm so sorry." She pillowed his head on her lap.

"Don't feel bad about me, my lady," the old man said, trying to smile. "I've got the same sort of wound I'd give myself if I'd tried to kill myself in the samurai way."

Taniko raised her head at the rumble of wooden wheels. Far above her the Regent's state carriage lumbered past, a rolling palace. When it went by, she saw Motofusa himself looking out the near window at her. With his thin, small face and sparse moustache he looked very much like Horigawa. He wore the tall black hat of office. He looked at her with a faint, superior smile.

Defiantly, Taniko met his gaze. By your courtier's standards it is shameful for me to look you in the eyes, Motofusa, she tried to say with her gaze. But I want you to see the hatred in my eyes, and to show you that your courtier's world is passing away.

In response to her stare Motofusa's grin broadened, showing teeth dyed black after the fashion of the Court. He closed the curtains of his carriage.

Many of the Takashi samurai lay on the ground, badly beaten. A few appeared to be unconscious. Those on their feet looked angry, frustrated and ashamed, all at once.

Taniko turned to one of them. "Go to Lord Kiyosi. Tell him what has happened, and tell him we will wait for him here."

She looked down at the old samurai whose grizzled head lay in her lap. "Are you in great pain?"

He gave her a smile that was really a grimace. "Of course not, my lady. But I shall not live. You could—do me a great service."

"Anything."

"None of the men are armed. Except you."

"I? I'm not armed." Then she looked down at the hand that was still holding the dagger she had taken from the courtier. "I'll give this to one of the men and he can help you."

The deep-set eyes looked into Taniko's. "I would like you to do it, my lady, if you can bring yourself to. My lord Kiyosi is not here. You stand in his place. It is much to ask, I know."

Taniko hesitated. I must do it well. He must not suffer. I cannot say no. "Yes. You must tell me what to do."

His fingers feebly tapped a spot below his rib cage. "Strike here. As hard as you can. Drive upward toward the heart."

Taniko raised the gold-hilted ceremonial knife high, gripping it with both hands. Slowly she lowered it till the point touched the place he had indicated. Then she raised the knife again. Am I strong enough?

She said, "Say with me, homage to Amida Buddha."

"Homage to Amida Buddha," the old man whispered.

With all her might, not thinking, letting the Self do it, as Jebu would say, she brought the dagger down. She felt it meet flesh, but the force of her thrust and the sharpness of the blade pierced the flesh, and her fists struck against his chest.

She looked down. Please be dead. His eyes were open, and they did not blink. She had done it. She had given him what he asked for. She had stopped his heart. She said again, "Homage to Amida Buddha." Gently, with the index finger of her right hand, she pulled each of his eyelids down. Slowly she eased the gray head to the ground and stood up.

She looked around. A small group of Takashi samurai were standing around her in a circle. When she looked at them, they bowed deeply from the waist. She handed the dagger to one of them and looked around for Atsue.

He was standing beside one of the samurai, clinging to the man's leg. When she turned to him, he took a step back. She held out her arms, but he did not move. She started to go to him.

Terror filled his eyes. "You killed him. There's blood all over you."

She looked down. Her bright yellow cloak was speckled with blood. She hadn't realized the old samurai had bled so much. She felt that she must wash the fear of her from Atsue's eyes, or it would remain there forever. Determinedly, she strode over to him, took the whimpering boy in her arms and lifted him up.

Kiyosi himself came soon in one of the Takashi's finest Chinese-style carriages. It was surrounded by a hundred Takashi samurai in full armor. Kiyosi gave orders that the body of the bannerman was to be borne in state on a cart to the Rokuhara. He helped Taniko and Atsue into the carriage, climbed in himself, and sat Atsue on his lap. He patted Taniko's hand.

"You and the boy suffer because my father must have more and more power," Kiyosi said sadly. "Motofusa is our enemy because he wants Prince Mochihito, rather than my sister's husband, Prince Takakura, to succeed to the throne. Now we must avenge Motofusa's insult to our family. So it goes on and on."

He was not angry, Taniko saw, just sad and tired. "What is wrong Kiyosi-san?"

"I have come to realize that I will never know peace. All my life I've been fighting my father's battles, and still there are more battles to fight, and there will never be any end to it as long as I live."

"Give Motofusa a chance to apologize. When he realizes what his people have done, he will probably regret it." Actually, remembering the smug face at the window of the carriage of state, she could not imagine Motofusa apologizing for anything.

Kiyosi shook his head. "My father would accept no apology from Motofusa. And it's not just he. Yukio, the youngest son of Muratomo no Domei, has reappeared. He is raising an army in Kyushu. Our spies say he wants to sail across the sea to fight for the Emperor of China. My father is sure Yukio wants to raise another Muratomo rebellion. So I must go to Kyushu and crush Yukio at once."

Still shaken by the carriage brawl, still stunned by the realization that she had killed a man, Taniko felt a new fear clutch at her heart. "Must you go?"

"I am commander-in-chief of the army. I have advised my father to let Yukio go. All the malcontents in the Sacred Islands would flock to his banner, and we'd be rid of them once and for all. We wouldn't have to lose a man. But my father will not be satisfied unless blood is shed. No victory is

real to him unless men die for it." The anger in his face faded
and was replaced by a deep weariness.

"Oh, Taniko, I remember Yukio so well—that bright-eyed
boy who used to play in the gardens of the Rokuhara. Every
time I looked at him I felt a pang, knowing it was I who
beheaded his father. I wondered if he knew it, and I wondered what he thought of me. He wasn't much older than our
Atsue is now, the first time I saw him. And now my father
commands me to bring Yukio's head back to Heian Kyo."

Taniko held his hand while the carriage trundled along and
he, in turn, patted Atsue's head. "I'm so tired, Taniko. So
tired of it all. How terrible it is that the fighting cannot stop."

From the pillow book of Shima Taniko:

Last night my lord Kiyosi came to me and told me, with
no great satisfaction, that the carriage of the Regent Motofusa
was attacked by a troop of samurai as his procession was on
its way to the Special Festival at Iwashimizu. The samurai
killed eight of Motofusa's retainers, cut the oxen loose from
his carriage and drove them off.

Motofusa's carriage was too heavy for his remaining men
to pull. He could have waited for more oxen or a palaquin to
be brought, but he was afraid for his life, and so he walked
home through the streets like any commoner and missed the
ceremony. He has thus been publicly shamed.

Since Iwashimizu is one of Hachiman's shrines, and
Hachiman is the Muratomo patron, Sogamori thinks that in
some obscure way he is hurting the Muratomo. By offending
the god of war? This seems to me a dangerous way to get at
one's enemies.

Kiyosi brought a new flute for Atsue, a family heirloom
called Little Branch, which has been his own favorite flute
until now. At least, Kiyosi says, the Regent has paid many
times over for the death of our bannerman and the fright
he gave our little Atsue. Even the Regent, formerly the
most feared official in the land, who once controlled the
words and actions of the Emperor, can be chastised by
the Takashi.

Each night before I fall asleep, even when I lie in Kiyosi's
arms, the face of the man I killed appears in my mind. His
dead eyes seem to look at me and not to look at me. And in
the darkness and silence of my bedchamber I feel a horror in

the pit of my stomach. I have done a dreadful thing. Killed a man. There is blood on my hands and they will never be clean.

More than that, every night I see the look that was in the eyes of my little Atsue after he had seen me stab the bannerman to death. He knows now that his mother can kill. A nine-year-old boy should not have to live with such a memory. I see my own horror at what I have done reflected in his eyes. It is as Jebu told me. We are all part of one Self.

If that is so, the bannerman was I, and I was killing myself. Indeed, he asked me for death. The samurai often kill themselves or ask others to kill them, to avoid capture, mutilation and shame. What I did was not horrible. It was a mercy. Yet, the fact that I have killed another human being fills me with terror, because it is such a vast thing, such a final thing. Whether I have done it for right reasons or for wrong ones, it is taking for myself the powers of a kami. Such an act should be approached with fear, as one approaches a very holy place.

My Jebu—is he still mine after all these years?—has killed and killed again. By now he must have lost count of the numbers he has killed. I was there the first time Jebu killed a man. I remember how he stood looking down at the bodies of those he had killed for a long time after the fight was over. What was he thinking? I wish I could talk to him now.

I've asked Kiyosi how he feels about killing, but he doesn't want to talk about it. He says the part of his mind that thinks about killing is sealed off when he is with me.

How lonely I will be when Kiyosi is gone campaigning in Kyushu.

—*Third Month, twelfth day*
YEAR OF THE HORSE

26

One night in the Fourth Month of the Year of the Horse, Yukio, Jebu and Moko sat together in the monks' quarters of the Teak Blossom Temple and said farewell to the members of the Order who had been their hosts for so many months. In the morning their little fleet would embark for China.

Down in the town of Hakata over a thousand men were drinking, coupling, sleeping, writing or pacing about, waiting for dawn to come. At Yukio's summons they had come from all the Sacred Islands, the last, dogged supporters of the Muratomo cause in a realm in which everyone bowed to the Takashi. There were wild men, half Ainu, from northern Honshu; there were hard-bitten warriors from the eastern provinces; there were Shinto and Buddhist military monks from the temples around Heian Kyo; there were near cannibals from southern Kyushu. All of them saw Yukio's summons as a last chance to recoup the fortunes they had lost when the Takashi plundered the realm.

For the farewell to Jebu and Yukio, Abbot Weicho had ordered a hearty meal—the closest the Zinja ever had to a feast. There were raw fish, steamed vegetables, an abundance of rice, and a small jar of heated sake for each of the brothers and their guests. Though the women of the temple did not usually eat with the monks, Nyosan was also present.

They were halfway through the meal when one of the monks escorted a samurai to Yukio. He was one of the guards Yukio had posted some miles from the town.

"Perhaps this should be for your ears alone, Lord Yukio," the samurai said. He was out of breath and clearly tired.

"If it is bad news, tell it to all of us. The more we know, the better prepared we will be."

His calm manner seemed to reassure the samurai, who nodded and said, "It seems the Takashi have learned of your plans, and they mean to prevent you from going. An army of ten thousand men crossed over from Honshu two days ago. They are now less than a day's march from here. They'll be here tomorrow for certain."

"Then they'll arrive too late," said Jebu. "All they'll see will be our ships sailing out of the harbor."

"They may revenge themselves on the townspeople and the monks for helping us," said Yukio.

"Don't worry about that," said Weicho. "We'll protect our own. If need be, we'll teach them that the Order is still to be respected, even if we have lost a few members."

Yukio stood up. "There are still things to be done. I thought something like this might happen, and I have given some thought to preparing for it. I apologize for leaving this feast, Holiness, but there are arrangements I must make in town." With a smile and a bow, the slight figure turned and strode to the door, where he buckled on his dagger and sword and went out.

Before sunrise the next morning the quays of Hakata were alive with the thump of bales and boxes, the clank of weapons and the shouts of young male voices as Yukio's men assembled. In a few hours, according to word from scouts Yukio had sent out, the Takashi army would be upon them.

The warehouse workers sweated in the cool dawn air as they raced to load each ship with provisions for a voyage of ten days. The ten ships were oceangoing galleys designed to carry both passengers and freight. Each had sails stiffened with bamboo battens to catch any favorable wind that might help the oarsmen. At stem, stern and masthead the ships were bedecked with white Muratomo banners and pennants and streamers bearing the crests of other samurai families joining in the expedition.

As the sky above the hills around Hakata turned a paler blue, the samurai began to board the ships. Some of them bade good-bye to somber little family groups that had accompanied them this far on their journey. Others, reeling drunk, were half carried to the docks by the women with whom they'd spent their last night on shore.

Long before dawn Nyosan and Jebu made the long downhill walk from the Teak Blossom Temple. Now, dressed in the ankle-length gray robe and black cloak of a woman elder of the Order, Nyosan gazed up at Jebu with shining eyes. Jebu had to bend almost double to put his arms around her and kiss her.

"That such a great, huge man should have come out of a tiny creature like myself," she laughed.

"I will miss you, Mother."

She shook a finger at him. "We have said good-bye too many times in too many ways to feel sadness now. Perhaps you will find your way to the land of your father. I hope, if you do, that it sets your heart at rest."

Jebu looked out past Shiga Island, a sandspit at the tip of the northern arm of the bay, as if trying to see the fabled land that lay to the west. As he looked, a long, dark shape slid past the island. It was followed by another.

A silence fell over the quays. Then a murmur rose as ship after ship appeared in the entrance of the bay. The murmur grew as, oars sweeping rhythmically through the waves, the vessels sailed closer. The bright banners that bedecked the ships became visible. The banners were bloodred.

"We're trapped," said a man near Jebu.

"Might have known the Takashi wouldn't let us leave," said another.

The crowd parted and Yukio strode down to the edge of the water. For the occasion he wore his finest suit of armor, silver-chased with white laces. A silver dragon roared defiance from his helmet. The men watched him closely.

He smiled when he saw the Takashi ships. "They honor our departure with an escort." Some of the men laughed hesitantly.

Yukio stepped to the edge of the pier and raised his arms. Silence fell over the assembled samurai.

"Oh, Hachiman-Yawata, my great-grandfather was known as Hachiman Taro, your firstborn son. Now, in my family's hour of greatest need, I call upon you to give us your aid. Bless our journey across the great water. May we find the good fortune we seek in China. May we return one day, victorious, to this Land of the Gods.''

"May we escape from Hakata Bay to begin with," said Jebu in a low voice, eyeing the Takashi sails.

Hastily, bidding last farewells to those who had come to see them off, the samurai trooped up the gangplanks of their assigned ships. In every man's mind, Jebu thought, there must be the same question: am I really embarking for China, or am I going to die today? Jebu held Nyosan's hand for a moment, and their eyes locked; then he turned abruptly and went to Yukio's ship. On the quay Moko bade a tearful farewell to a woman holding an infant in her arms. At last he tore himself away. Carrying his precious box of carpenter's tools, his Instruments of the Way, he followed Jebu up the gangplank.

Yukio stood on the deck atop the after cabin of his galley. Beside him was his pilot, a gray-haired man in a black tunic who had made the voyage to China and back many times. Around him gathered his armored captains, each of whom would be responsible for one shipload of samurai. Of them all, Yukio was the smallest figure. Jebu joined the group.

"I'd prepared myself in case of an attack by sea," Yukio said. "I have consulted with the local fishermen on the winds and tides in Hakata Bay. I am certain that we can evade the Takashi and escape them."

A growl of dissent came from the other samurai. "Evade them?" said Shenzo Saburo, the samurai who had long ago been in charge of the expedition to rescue Yukio from the Rokuhara. "We don't want to evade them. We want to fight them. Why don't we attack immediately?"

Yukio laughed, a laugh of scorn that reddened Suburo's face. "Oh, well, if you want to fight and die, why go to the trouble of boarding these ships? There are ten thousand more Takashi warriors marching overland against us. If we wait here we can die fighting on our feet instead of floundering in the water."

The commanders shifted uneasily and fingered their sword hilts. Finally Saburo said, "Why not attack the Takashi ships at once and try to break through?"

Smiling, Yukio shook his head. "Our aim is to take this army overseas and win our fortunes in China. I am not going to allow the expedition to be destroyed before we are even out of sight of the Sacred Islands.''

The meeting broke up, and the commanders went to their respective ships. Yukio grinned at Jebu and clapped him on the arm. Still smiling, he turned to his pilot and gave the order to sail.

There was a moment of expectant silence. Then the cries went up from the pilots, and the mooring ropes were cast loose. On each ship a drummer raised his wooden sticks and brought them down thunderously on the monkey-leather head of his big taiko. The long white oars flashed through the green water at dockside.

Yukio stood on the afterdeck between the pilot and the two steersmen. Crouched near the rail was a signalman with a bundle of flags. Orders were relayed from Yukio to the pilot to the steersmen. Waving his multicolored flags, the signalman passed Yukio's orders to the other ships.

A brisk, salt-smelling breeze blew in from the sea, and a rising tide lapped against the quays. The advantage was with the ships sailing toward shore. The sails of the Muratomo ships were furled and only the arms of the rowers propelled the ships forward.

His bow slung across his back, Jebu leaned against the rail and stared across the wide expanse of water at the dark hulls and yellow sails of the Takashi. How far away they were! How large this bay was! It could hold thousands of ships. It would be a long time before the Muratomo came anywhere near the Takashi. In warfare on land, your enemy was sometimes upon you before you even saw him. At sea he might be visible for hours before the two of you drew close enough to fight.

The taiko on the ten ships rumbled, and Yukio watched the fish-shaped wind vane on the masthead. It pointed inexorably toward Hakata. Huge, puffy clouds sailed eastward across the sky like a fleet of heavy-laden trading vessels. Moko crouched at Jebu's feet, his back to the rail, and closed his eyes, his dogu box in his lap. The samurai drowsed at the rails. Only the men at the oars worked, rows of bare, brown shoulders rhythmically rising and falling. Gradually the Muratomo fleet drew into the center of the bay. The Takashi ships, their red banners fluttering, were much plainer now, but they had not left their position at the mouth of the bay. Jebu counted thirty of them.

Suddenly Yukio snapped out an order. At the sound of his voice heads turned all over the lead ship. The pilot spoke to the steersman, the signalman and the rowers' overseer. The right bank of oars held steady, while the left bank worked at doubled rhythm. A green flag flapped over the signalman's head. The steersmen braced their feet against the rail and pushed at the tiller. Within a few moments the Muratomo fleet had changed course and was steering for the little fishing village of Hakozaki, northernmost of the three towns around the bay.

One by one the Takashi ships changed direction and formed a pursuing column. Everything seems to be happening so slowly, Jebu thought. First we change course, then they react and some of them change course. And we're still hours apart. But every advantage gained at this distance could mean life or death for hundreds of men.

He might die today. He sat down on the deck with his back to the rail, took the shintai out of his robe and stared into its fiery core. Slowly he felt strength and calm flow into his veins. The power of the shintai worked as ever. Sitting nearby, Moko silently watched him.

Jebu stood up to look over the rail at the Takashi ships. A long way off, fifteen of them, a tight little group, came after the Muratomo fleet. Their sails were up, as were the Muratomo sails now, but they were drawing little wind and the oarsmen were still pushing the ships. The Takashi were far behind. The Muratomo oarsmen were fresh, while those rowing for the Takashi had been working for days.

Breakers thundered ahead on the rocks between Hakozaki and Shiga Island. Here and there black boulders jutted up like fangs in the white water. Yukio ordered another change of direction. The Muratomo were sailing parallel to the shore, past Hakozaki and back toward the town of Hakata. The sails of the Muratomo ships boomed, swelling with wind. Now the on-shore wind was pushing them. Yukio ordered the oarsmen to rest.

After a time, Yukio gave a whoop and pointed. One of the Takashi ships was slowly toppling over on its side, its sail folding, its mast crashing down, the red banner drooping into the water; soon the crew and fighting men were black dots in the green and white waves. Another of the pursuing ships had come to a dead halt, simply sitting in the waves as its companion ships left it behind, stuck on a sandbar.

"Our pilots know these waters," Yukio laughed. "Theirs don't."

Now he snapped another command to his signalman, who leaped to his feet and began waving a red flag and a yellow flag at the other ships. The two steersmen leaned into the tiller. The town of Hakata was still a long distance down the shore when Yukio's fleet changed course again and headed out toward the center of the bay.

Jebu watched once again the delayed reaction of the enemy craft as one by one they altered their course to continue the pursuit. Then cries from the other side of the ship drew him across the deck.

Through the green, terraced hills behind Hakata, streams of horsemen and foot soldiers were pouring into the town. Red pennons were fluttering on the town's ancient wall. Masses of men were gathering along the quays. The high sun of noon glittered on helmets, armor and naginata blades. Smaller contingents of Takashi appeared on the docks of Hakozaki on the north and Imazu, on the southern side of the harbor.

"Now they're going to take fishing boats and come out after us," Yukio said. "I expected this, too."

Even as they watched, Takashi samurai were crowding into every boat along the shore. Doubtless they would force the fishermen to row the boats out. Many of the fishing boats were overcrowded and low in the water.

The thousands of Takashi samurai left behind on shore waved their red banners and shot angry futile arrows into the water in the direction of the Muratomo ships. The waste disgusted Jebu. Samurai had no sense of the value of things.

Now there was no way the Muratomo could land again. They were cut off, committed to fight, to live or die on the water. Fifteen Takashi warships still blocked the harbor's mouth. Thirteen more pursued the Muratomo ships around the bay. And dozens of small craft from Hakata, Hakozaki and Imazu, their gunwales bristling with Takashi samurai like teeth in the mouth of a shark, formed a long sprawling line cutting across the Muratomo course.

The pilot spoke to Yukio and pointed upward. The wind vane on his ship had changed direction. Now the fish's head was pointing straight at the mouth of the harbor and beyond that to the open sea.

Yukio turned to the pilot. "Is the tide running out?" The gray-haired pilot grinned and nodded.

"Then Hachiman is with us," Yukio exulted. "It is time to say good-bye to our Takashi friends. We've shown them the beauties of Hakata Bay long enough. Now we leave for China. Up all sails. Rowers, row your hearts out. Head for the open sea!"

The signalman's flags blossomed on the afterdeck. In a moment the Muratomo fleet had made another course change. Now they were charging at top speed directly at the Takashi blockade.

The Takashi vessels, so distant for so long, now loomed larger. Faint cries came from the men on their decks. A few impetuous arrows arched toward the Muratomo ships and fell short, into the waves.

Yukio shouted to the captain in the nearest Muratomo ship, "Aim for the steersmen and rowers only! Don't bother with samurai! Pass the word!" He gripped Jebu's arm and pulled him to the rail.

"Come on. Our men think it's unworthy to shoot anyone lower in rank than a samurai. Let's set an example."

The column of Muratomo ships aimed for the head of the Takashi line. Takashi vessels were pulling out of formation and rushing to crowd in upon the Muratomo as Yukio's ship raced across the bow of the leading enemy galley. Yukio drew back on his samurai bow, as tall as himself, and a fourteen-hand arrow with a humming-bulb head screamed through the air to strike the throat of a steersman on the lead Takashi ship. Yukio had used the noise-making arrowhead to call the attention of his men to the target he had chosen.

Jebu's bow twanged and the steersman's companion collapsed over the tiller. A shame to kill unarmed seamen, but it would mean less bloodshed in the long run.

Yukio loosed two more arrows among the Takashi rowers. Out of control, the ship began to roll and flounder. Arrows fired by the Takashi samurai whistled over Jebu's head.

One armored man on the other ship was leaping over the

oarsmen, scrambling for the foredeck, holding his long bow high over his head. Standing in the bow of the ship, he braced himself, legs far apart, and aimed an arrow at Yukio. The man was bareheaded. In the instant that it took Jebu to jerk a blunt-headed armor-piercing arrow from his quiver, he saw a darkly handsome face with a small moustache. The arrow struck the Takashi samurai square in the chest. He dropped his bow, toppled slowly over the railing of the ship and fell into the sea. When the splash subsided, he was gone.

"I told you not to bother with samurai," Yukio shouted. Jebu started to explain that the warrior had been about to shoot Yukio, when a wail from beside them interrupted him. It was Moko, clinging to the railing, staring at the place where the Takashi samurai had gone down. He turned tearful eyes to Jebu.

"Accursed am I, that I should have seen this. Years ago that man saved my life. I will never forget his face. He was the only man in the world besides you, shike, to whom I could truly say I owed my life. And now you have killed him."

"He was aiming at Lord Yukio."

"I do not reproach you, shike. I only say that war is the evilest thing I know, and I hate it."

They were past the Takashi line now. The ocean, blue gray and limitless, lay ahead. Behind them, two more Muratomo ships were pushing through the blockade. More Takashi ships closed in. Flights of arrows whistled in both directions. Again the Takashi ships wallowed, disabled, and the Muratomo ships shot by them.

Móko told Yukio and Jebu of the day Domei was executed, and how Kiyosi had seen him hiding in the tree above the Emperor's head and had not denounced him.

"Of course," said Yukio. "I would have recognized him if I'd been looking in his direction. I saw him often, especially during the years I lived at the Rokuhara. How strange karma is. On the very day that Kiyosi spared your life, he beheaded my father."

"I saw him do it," said Moko. "But also, Lord Yukio, I saw him weep after he did it."

"That doesn't surprise me. He was always kind to me. He never said he was sorry that he killed my father; it would not have been proper for us to speak of that. But somehow I knew he did it because it was his duty, and I never held it against him. Just as it was his duty to aim an arrow at me just now. I hold others to blame for my father's death. Sogamori, Horigawa.''

''So that was Kiyosi,'' said Jebu. ''Years ago I shot at him, but it wasn't his karma to die that day. I have heard nothing but good of him. I am sorry that he died by my hand.'' Gripping the rail and bowing his head, Jebu mentally recited the Prayer to a Fallen Enemy with greater fervor than he had felt in years.

A Takashi vessel slammed up against the side of a Muratomo ship trying to break through the blockade. Takashi samurai leaped over the rails. Swords clashed. The decks of both ships were a jumble of fighting men. But two more Muratomo ships cut through to the open ocean.

Yukio gave orders to his signalman. In a few moments the Muratomo craft that had broken the blockade were sailing parallel to the line of Takashi warships, arrows devastating the enemy crews. More Muratomo ships came through. Clouds of arrows fell on the Takashi ships while their samurai, shouting challenges and insults, stood at the rails, futilely waving their swords.

Jebu looked past the crumbling blockade. The other Takashi ships and the commandeered fishing boats from Hakata had joined forces and were sailing toward the harbor entrance in hot pursuit of the Muratomo.

A bright flash caught Jebu's eye. Flames leaped up on a fishing vessel. The men on it were jumping overboard. Ribbons of fire sprang up all over the fishing boats. The flames spread to the Takashi warships.

''What's that? More of your planning ahead?''

Yukio nodded. ''It was easy to foresee that the Takashi would commandeer boats to come after us. So, aboard the boats today were, not the local fishermen, but Muratomo samurai dressed as fishermen. When the fishing boats were mixed in with the Takashi fleet, my men set fire to them and jumped overboard.''

A few of the Takashi ships seemed to have escaped, but the mouth of the harbor was now blocked by a great ball of fire, as if a piece of the sun had fallen into it. Takashi samurai splashed briefly in the water before their armor pulled them under. One of the fishing boats, manned by Muratomo men, darted here and there, pulling the unarmored Muratomo survivors out of the water. When they had all been pulled in, the boat followed after the Muratomo fleet. Yukio's ship fell behind to meet it.

Yukio ran amidships and helped pull wet, naked men from the fishing boat. "Marvelous!" he shouted. "Splendid! Let sake be brought for these men at once. They're cold from their swim."

Looking aft, all Jebu could see was rolling clouds of black smoke and a jumble of burning ships. Then his eyes narrowed. Two ships were coming after them. One, judging by its lines, was a Muratomo transport, while the other appeared to be a Takashi warship. He caught Yukio's arm.

"Look."

Yukio laughed wildly. "Look again." There were white banners waving from both ships. Jebu remembered the two ships that had come together and the masses of samurai locked in hand-to-hand combat. Evidently the Muratomo had won.

"We have eleven ships now instead of ten," said Yukio. "A gift from the Takashi." He suddenly seized Jebu violently by both arms and shook him with a strength surprising for such a small man.

"China, Jebu! China! A whole new world for us! Let the Takashi perish in the nine hells. The future is ours."

Yukio laughed again. "Out to sea," he called to the pilot. "Take us to China." The signal flags flapped, and the Muratomo vessels turned away from the mouth of the harbor and set their course westward. All sails were up, and all rattled as the strong wind from the east took them.

Yukio's feverish gaiety subsided. "If only we hadn't killed Kiyosi. That takes some of the joy out of this victory for me, Jebu-san. He was the wisest of all the Takashi, the best fighter, the noblest lord. In killing him we've dealt the Takashi a blow from which they may never recover. Still, I would rather he had lived, if karma allowed it."

Jebu shrugged. "It was his day to die. I'm sure he was as ready and willing as you and I are. And he was trying to kill you."

"You saved my life. Again. I am in your debt forever."
Yukio gripped Jebu's upper arm, hard. "But it's a great
sadness, not just for Kiyosi's sake. His death harms others for
whom I care. There was a woman, Kiyosi's woman. She was
very good to my mother and me. Remember I told you how
my mother became Sogamori's mistress to save my life?
Well, this lady acted as a go-between, for no other reason
than her affection for my mother. And she suffered for it. Her
husband was Prince Sasaki no Horigawa, who wanted Hideyori
and me dead. He punished his wife by—why are you staring
at me?"

Jebu's body went cold. Even now, he reminded himself,
the secret must be kept. He made himself assume a calm
expression.

"This lady. Was her name Shima Taniko?"

"Yes, that was she. Did you know her?"

"Long ago," Jebu said, waving his hand as if it were of no
consequence. "I'll tell you about it some time."

"She had a baby by Kiyosi, a son, while I was at the
Rokuhara. I suppose he'd be about nine by now. Another son
whose father has been torn from him. Moko is right. War is
an evil thing."

Yukio turned away and began to walk among the men on
his ship, praising them, even talking to the rowers and patting
their shoulders. Then he called for a small boat so he could
visit the other ships. A dinghy was lowered over the side, and
Yukio leaped into it with the astonishing, easy grace that Jebu
had first seen seven years ago on the Gojo Bridge.

Jebu walked along the deck to the forecastle and stood
staring into the empty blue sky. His eyes burned and his
cheeks were wet.

Why am I crying? he thought. If I hadn't killed Kiyosi my
friend would be dead now.

Instead, another son has lost his father. As Yukio did. As I
did.

Another woman has lost the man she loved, as my mother
did.

He had never wanted to know what Taniko was doing.
Only once had he asked, when Moko told him what happened
at Daidoji. That had been the worst moment of his life. He

had never asked about her, because it hurt too much. Hardly the attitude of a true Zinja.

What if he had known what Kiyosi was to her? Would he have hesitated to kill him? Or would jealous hatred have gone winging along with his arrow?

No, he had never wanted to invade her life. Even when Domei said he was sending men to kill Horigawa, his first thought had been that he must not go. How much less would he want to kill this Kiyosi. After all, he himself had given her nothing.

He didn't really know how much Kiyosi had meant to her. He might just have been a protector, someone to whom she could escape from Horigawa. Or he might have been a true lover, a man who made her cry out with delight in the darkness, as she had wanted to, but never could with Jebu.

Whatever she shared with him, Jebu had reached out from all this distance, after all this time, and destroyed it. Just by letting go of a string that propelled an arrow. Such a little thing. So easy to kill a man, end his whole life and whatever it meant, perhaps destroy many other lives at the same moment.

But even if he'd known what he was doing, he'd have done it anyway, to save Yukio.

Why was he crying? Because he'd done an evil thing? But a Zinja was beyond good and evil. A Zinja was always aware of his own perfection.

From a dark chamber in his memory a voice whispered, *The Zinja are devils.* He had not thought of the Saying of Supreme Power in years.

Was this what it meant? That in trying to do good the Zinja did evil, and then tried to tell themselves it didn't matter, that good and evil were the same thing? If war was an evil thing, as he had been shown today, and the Zinja were devoted to war, then truly they were devils.

He had hurt Taniko. Had hurt her child. And there was no way he could undo it. He couldn't even want to undo it, because the only other choice would have meant the death of his friend.

He wondered if she would ever hear a description of the man who killed Kiyosi. He wondered if she would realize that it was he.

The sun had crossed the sky and now hovered, white hot, ahead of the Muratomo fleet. It paved a road of dazzling white jewels in the sea before them. Somewhere at the end of that glittering pathway lay the land of his father, the empire of the Mongols. Perhaps he would actually see the land where his father was born and meet again his father's killer.

And perhaps, too, the great distances would help him forget for a time that small, white, lovely face that had haunted him ever since that journey down the Tokaido.

With trembling fingers he reached into his robe for the Jewel of Life and Death.

PART TWO

THE BOOK OF KUBLAI KHAN

Because men suffer, they fight and kill one another. The innocent, who begin by fighting to defend themselves against robbers and murderers, become robbers and murderers themselves. Someone must protect them, both from what happens to them and from what they become. It is our hope that we can take upon ourselves the duty of necessary fighting and killing. We think we can be trusted.

—*The Zinja Manual*

1

Summer came to Heian Kyo. The screens and lattices of houses were opened to the air as the days grew longer and the nights warmer. Rain and sun alternated to deepen the green of the huge old willows that grew along the avenues and canals. Moon and fireflies lit the night. Taniko found that she missed Kiyosi terribly. She wanted to share this beauty with him. Unable to talk to him, she wrote poems, two or three a day, and imagined herself reading them to him.

> The sun warms the wind,
> The wind strokes the willows,
> The willows reach down to caress the river.

She had little to record in her pillow book. She liked to write about the gossip of palace and Court, the problems of the country's rulers, the struggles of powerful men. About all this, she had heard in abundance from Kiyosi. Since he had sailed south to Kyushu her life had been one of isolation, monotony and boredom. It was no consolation to her that it was the same for almost all women of her station, except the few lucky enough to have duties at Court. She had no idea how other women managed to tolerate such lives.

Her one source of daily joy was the companionship of Atsue. The boy had quite forgotten his horror at seeing his mother stab a man to death, and the two spent hours together every day. Atsue was growing to look more and more like his grave, square-jawed father. Every fifth day she took him by carriage to the Buddhist temple on Mount Hiei for lessons on the flute and koto with a famous master. Daily she listened to his practice on these instruments. She finally convinced him the samisen was worth learning and gave him lessons herself. Kiyosi had taught him go, saying that every samurai should play the game well, and Taniko played it with Atsue night after night. She took him for walks through the garden, teaching him the names of summer herbs and flowers. Late in the evening, just before he went to bed, they would sit and watch the moon rise. Atsue would play on his flute just for pleasure, and his playing was often so beautiful it brought tears to her eyes.

A strange silence fell over the Shima household in the middle of the Fifth Month. Taniko's maids seemed nervous and chattered less than usual while helping her dress and undress. There was something furtive in the way her aunt and cousins greeted her in the women's quarters and hurried past on business of their own. Ryuichi's oldest son, Munetoki, now a fierce young samurai of nineteen, had gone off with Kiyosi's expedition to hunt down the last of the Muratomo. Uncle Ryuichi seemed to have disappeared completely. When she asked about him, Aunt Chogao said he had gone on a long journey by sea to Yasugi on the west coast. Yasugi, Taniko knew, was a stronghold for the pirates who preyed on the Korean coast and shipping. All her life she had been hearing rumors that her family was involved with pirates; this seemed to confirm it.

One afternoon a servant announced that the first secretary to Lord Takashi no Sogamori was in the main hall and had asked to visit her. She felt a little leap of pleasure. She had not had a letter from Kiyosi in nearly a month. She hurriedly prepared herself with her maid's help, set out the screen of state in her chamber and sent the maid for Sogamori's secretary.

She immediately noticed the willow-wood taboo tag tied to the secretary's black headdress and dangling down the side of his face. She wondered if the evil that beset him was a personal misfortune or something that had fallen upon the entire house of Takashi. It would not be polite to inquire. It was surprising that a man under taboo would even leave his house. He must consider the visit essential.

She had never seen the man before, but she recognized the type. His prim manner and old-fashioned, slightly tattered robe and trousers proclaimed him a Confucian scholar. Doubtless a man of good family whose declining fortunes had forced him to go into service with a rising clan like the Takashi.

They exchanged greetings, the secretary peering nervously at the screen as if trying to see through it. *He wants a look at the famous lady who delights Kiyosi,* she thought.

At last the secretary said, "Lord Sogamori has sent me to you to inform you of his wishes."

"I am honored," said Taniko. "But I had hoped you might have a message for me from Lord Kiyosi." Through the openings near the top of the screen she could see that the man's eyes had widened in surprise—and possibly fear—at the mention of Kiyosi's name.

"There was no message," he said hastily. "Lord Kiyosi sent no message." There was something in his voice that frightened Taniko.

"What is it then?" she said. "What are you doing here?"

"Lord Sogamori desires that his grandson be sent to him."

The secretary's words surprised Taniko and intensified the dread she felt. "For how long?"

Again the secretary seemed surprised. "Why, for the rest of his life, my lady. Lord Sogamori wants to give the boy the Takashi name and adopt him as his own son."

"His son? But he is Lord Kiyosi's son. He, if anybody, should adopt him."

"My lady," the secretary said, then stopped. He seemed at a loss for words. At last he blurted out, "A dead man cannot adopt a child."

It was as if he had plunged a sword into her body. She sat paralyzed, impaled on his words. At last, as the numbness of shock faded away, she began to feel pain and struggled to free herself.

"No, no, he is not dead. Someone would have told me. You can't come here and say that he is dead. I would have known about it if something had happened. You're wrong. You must be mistaken."

Even as she denied his words, it struck her with overwhelming force: Kiyosi had been killed in the fighting in Kyushu, and no one had told her.

The secretary blushed a deep scarlet. "Don't you know what happened, my lady?"

"I have heard nothing. Surely I would have heard if anything had happened to Lord Kiyosi."

Again the man seemed to grope for words. "Then I—I must tell you? How unfortunate. But seemingly it falls to me to do this duty where others have failed." He drew himself up and composed himself into a picture of Confucian rectitude. "My lady, it grieves me greatly to be the bearer of this news. Six days ago, we received word that there had been a great sea battle at Hakata Bay. The rebellious Muratomo forces were trying to escape. My lord Kiyosi was on the flagship of the Takashi fleet. During the fighting he was struck in the chest by an armor-piercing arrow. Those who were near say he died instantly. One arrow, no pain. His body fell into the sea and disappeared immediately. He is gone, my lady. He died faithfully carrying out his father's orders. You may take pride in that."

Taniko heard the man out. Then she stood up.

The next thing she knew, she was lying on the floor, her maid kneeling beside her, wiping her face with a damp cloth. She struggled to sit up. The screen was knocked over, and the Takashi family secretary was standing in a corner of the room with his face politely averted.

Then it came back to her. Kiyosi was dead.

She looked up at the maid, one of the women who had come with her to Heian Kyo years ago. The maid was crying.

"You knew," said Taniko. "You knew days ago and you didn't tell me."

"I could not, my lady," the maid sobbed. "I could not bear to be the one. Why should it have to be me?"

In spite of the shock of grief, Taniko's mind was still working. "Set up the screen." The first thing she must do was get rid of this man with his talk of taking Atsue. When the screen was raised, Taniko composed herself and sat behind it.

"Please tell Lord Sogamori that I am overwhelmed with gratitude at his offer to adopt the boy Atsue. However, with the greatest respect, the Takashi family has no obligation to do anything for either Atsue or me. Atsue is my son, and it is my desire that he stay with me."

The secretary stared. "My lady, the boy is Lord Kiyosi's son. Lord Sogamori has lost his own son, his eldest—the son he loved best in the world. He wants his grandson. You cannot deny him."

It was agony to sit upright, agony to hold her voice to a soft, polite tone, agony to speak at all. She clenched her hands in her lap, digging the fingernails of one into the back of the other. "I am very sorry, but Lord Sogamori has other children and grandchildren. I have only Atsue. I am sure he would not want to take my only child from me."

"Excuse me, Lady Taniko, but this is most unwise. You only bring more suffering upon yourself. Lord Sogamori is the most powerful man in the Sacred Islands."

"My son does not belong to Lord Sogamori. I do not belong to Lord Sogamori. I have nothing more to say."

His mouth drawn down, the secretary left her. Taniko sat without moving for as long as she could, while her grief welled up inside her until she felt it would tear her apart. She began to gasp like a deer with an arrow in its chest. Her gasps became sobs. At last she screamed. She threw herself full length on the floor, tearing at her robes and beating upon the polished floor with her fists.

Her maids rushed in and tried to hold her. She struck them away. Drawing her body into a knot, she shrieked and wept.

Atsue came in. Horrified at the sight of his mother, he turned to the maids, who stood whimpering and wringing their hands.

"What's happened to my mother?"

Still sobbing, Taniko pulled herself to a sitting position. Thank Amida Buddha I can be the first to tell him, she thought. At least he won't get the news from some servant. She reached out and pulled the boy to her, fighting for breath, trying to get her voice under control.

"Your father has—left us. He has gone to the Pure Land. He died in battle at sea off Kyushu. I have just heard it."

"Oh no, Mother, no, no, no." The boy's arms tightened

around her neck until she thought he would break it. But she
endured the small pain gladly. She had only Atsue to live for.

For hours they cried together in each other's arms.

In the evening the maids brought food to them. Taniko
could not eat. She watched Atsue pick at the small slivers of
fish with his chopsticks. In his green silk tunic and black
trousers he looked like a replica of Kiyosi.

Why didn't they chop me to bits with swords and be done
with it? Taniko thought. How long could she feel this pain
before she went mad?

"Homage to Amida Buddha." Taniko started to recite the
invocation. Atsue put down his chopsticks and joined her.

After the maid took away their dishes, Ryuichi pushed
back the screen to Taniko's chamber and peered in at them.
His face was pale. In the dim corridor he looked like a
goldfish trying to see up through the surface of a pond.
Taniko, murmuring the homage to Buddha, looked back at
him.

"You never went to Yasugi, Uncle."

"Forgive me, Taniko-san. I remembered how you were
when Horigawa brought you here. I couldn't bear to see you
like that again."

"So, instead of telling me yourself, you mercifully allowed
one of Sogamori's lackeys to give me the news by accident."

"Do not torment me, Taniko-san."

"Ah, are you the one who is being tormented? I see. Well,
don't stand there in the doorway like a frightened peasant. Sit
down with us."

Ryuichi snapped his fingers at a maid. "Sake." Still looking
apologetically at Taniko, he sat down.

Taniko said, "Atsue, go to your bedchamber. I have something to discuss with your uncle."

"Why can't I hear? I'm the head of our family now."

The words brought Taniko a renewed realization of her
loss. She burst into a storm of weeping, while Ryuichi sat
looking sadly at her. Atsue crept into her arms.

The maid brought hot sake. Taniko poured for Ryuichi and
herself. "All right," she said. "You will also have to decide
what you want, Atsue-chan." Atsue did not object to the
term of endearment for a child. "Stay and listen." The boy
sat down again, facing his mother and his uncle. She turned

to Ryuichi. "Sogamori has asked that I send the boy to him. He wants to take him from me and adopt him, make him a Takashi."

Ryuichi nodded. "This afternoon I received a summons to the Rokuhara. Of course, it was worded as an invitation. What did you say to Sogamori's secretary?"

"I refused. I want Atsue to stay with me."

Ryuichi quickly drained another cup of sake. "You refused?"

"Yes. But Atsue must be the one to decide in the end."

"Children do not decide their futures," Ryuichi cut in. "Of course he will want to stay with his mother. But he has no idea of what he would lose. What can you give him that would compare with the station in life he would have as Sogamori's son?"

"Kiyosi gave Sogamori other grandsons, and Kiyosi's younger brothers still live," said Taniko. "Why must Sogamori, who has so much, take this child from me?" Tears ran down her cheeks.

Ryuichi shrugged. "Aside from the late Kiyosi, Sogamori's male descendants are a rather undistinguished lot. This boy, on the other hand, is a paragon. Perhaps it is because you and Kiyosi enjoyed some powerful bond in a former life. You must be aware that Atsue's musicianship and his knowledge of the classics are remarkable. And his face—" Ryuichi sipped sake and contemplated the boy. Atsue, his eyes downcast, flushed a deep scarlet. That's one trait he gets from me, Taniko thought.

Ryuichi went on. "Anyone who knows anything about physiognomy can see Atsue has the face of one destined to hold a high place in the realm. In all respects, even at this young age, Atsue outshines Sogamori's other descendants. That cannot have escaped you, Taniko. Be sure that Sogamori himself is well aware of it."

Taniko turned to the boy. "Atsue-chan, what your uncle says is true. You can become an important member of the most powerful clan in the land. If you remain here, you'll merely be a fatherless boy, part of a rather undistinguished provincial family."

"I want to stay with you, Mother," Atsue said instantly. "I love you, and you love me. I am afraid of Lord Sogamori.

They say he is cruel and has a terrible temper. I don't want to live in the Rokuhara. I don't like the Rokuhara."

"This is not childish prattle," said Taniko. "The boy knows perfectly well what he is saying."

"We dare not defy Lord Sogamori," Ryuichi muttered.

"If Sogamori can take a child from us, he can take anything and everything from us."

That thought made Ryuichi frown. "But there is nothing I can do. What can I say to Lord Sogamori at the Rokuhara tomorrow?"

"You are a samurai, Uncle, as much as he is. You can present the case to him and let him make what he will of it. When you go to the Rokuhara, tell Sogamori that the boy does not want to go and his mother does not want to send him."

"Madness," said Ryuichi.

"Uncle-san," said Taniko, the tears coming again, "my champion is dead. You are the only defender I have left. If you won't protect me, I am lost."

Shaking his head, Ryuichi rose. "I will do what I can. Drink more sake. It will help you to sleep."

2

It was a sweltering morning when Ryuichi went to the Rokuhara. Alone, sweating and trembling in his carriage, he fanned himself incessantly. Six armed, mounted men escorted him, but their presence did nothing to make him feel more secure. He was going, perhaps, to his death. What else could he expect if he disobeyed the command of Lord Sogamori, who could annihilate him as a careless sandal crushes an ant?

The Rokuhara was at once magnificent and frightening. Its three donjon towers, bedecked with proud red Takashi banners,

dominated the surrounding district. Ryuichi saw them as soon
as his carriage crossed the Gojo Bridge. The stone outer walls
with their tile-roofed turrets were taller than those around the
Imperial Palace. The walls girdled a spacious park bounded
by four avenues. Three streams diverted from the Kamo River
fed the moat, itself wide as a river, and ran through the park
over beds of carefully chosen pebbles, beneath tiny ornamental bridges. Interior walls divided the grounds into parade
fields, gardens and graveled courts. The main buildings of the
Rokuhara were imposing structures in the Chinese style, with
red and green tiled roofs. Mixed in among these were a
Buddhist temple, a Shinto shrine and many stables.

The Takashi headquarters was across the Kamo River, east
of the original limits of Heian Kyo, outside the city's walls.
The land had been given to Sogamori's grandfather after a
victory over pirates on the Inland Sea. In those days the
Takashi estate was out in the countryside. Over the years,
with each new acquisition of power and wealth, the stronghold grew, as a coral reef rises out of the sea. At the same
time the capital spread eastward, and now the Rokuhara was
surrounded by innumerable lesser buildings, like a black rock
in a swiftly moving current.

It was palace, fortress, barracks and prison all in one.
Between the samurai quartered within its walls and those who
lived nearby with families and retainers of their own, the
Takashi could call up ten thousand warriors at a moment's
notice.

Even after crossing the moat and passing through the fortified
western gate, Ryuichi traveled a long time through a labyrinth
of inner walls before he finally came to the hall where Sogamori
awaited him. Ryuichi dismounted and dismissed his outriders,
who looked thoroughly cowed now that they were in the
Takashi stronghold. A group of Sogamori's red-robed youths
eyed Ryuichi's party with a threatening casualness.

Approached by two Takashi samurai, Ryuichi tried to appear calm and superior, a difficult feat for a sweating, trembling
fat man. Despite their deferential manner, the hard-faced
warriors frightened him. The Shima were supposedly samurai
themselves, but Ryuichi was more at home with ink, brush
and account books than with bow and sword. He allowed the
guards to lead him to Sogamori.

The chieftain of the Takashi clan, dressed in a billowing
white silk robe, sat on a raised platform, a naked sword in his
lap. His round skull was completely shaved; he had entered
the priesthood several years earlier after a nearly fatal illness.
Behind him, brightly lit by oil lamps, hung an enormous gold
banner bearing an angry Red Dragon, its eyes blazing, claws
extended, wings flapping, the scaly body, coil upon coil,
seeming about to leap out of golden silk and destroy all in
the room.

Ryuichi was grateful for the excuse to fall to his knees and
press his forehead to the cedar floor. He was shaking so
violently he felt he could no longer stand. Why did Sogamori
have a sword in his lap? Was it for him?

"You are welcome here, Shima no Ryuichi," said Sogamori
in his grating voice. Ryuichi looked up. The lines of Sogamori's
broad face were deep and shadowed. His eyes were red-
rimmed and bloodshot. The man must have been weeping for
days, Ryuichi thought. There were tears glistening on
Sogamori's brown cheeks even now.

Below the platform, to Sogamori's right and left, sat the
men of his family. The place just below and to the left, where
Kiyosi had always sat, was occupied by Sogamori's second
son, Notaro, his puffy, white-powdered features drooping
with a faint boredom. Beside Notaro sat the third son,
Tadanori, a famous dandy and poet, but not known to be
good at much else. Sogamori's other sons by his principal
wife and his other wives sat facing each other in two rows
leading up the platform. Dullards, weaklings, and fops, thought
Ryuichi. Other nobles, favorites of Sogamori, sat around the
room. With surprise, Ryuichi recognized Prince Sasaki no
Horigawa, smiling and gently fanning himself.

Sogamori took a sheet of paper from his sleeve. "We have
been reading my son's poems, Ryuichi-san. This is the last
one he wrote, aboard ship on his way to Kyushu.

> The shadow of the sail is my palace,
> These cedar planks my bed,
> My host, a seagull.

"Exquisite," Ryuichi whispered, dry-mouthed. Sogamori
sighed and wiped his face with his sleeve. In the silence

Ryuichi thought how Taniko would love to have one of Kiyosi's poems. But it was obvious Taniko had no friends here. Horigawa waved his fan before his face and smiled his secretive smile at Ryuichi.

Sogamori raised the sword, holding it by its gold and silver-mounted hilt. The blade glistened in the lamplight. It was sharply curved and double-edged for more than half its length.

"His sword," said Sogamori. "Kogarasu. He didn't want to risk losing it at sea, so he left it behind. If he had worn it, it would have gone down with him to the bottom of Hakata Bay. Kogarasu once belonged to our ancestor, Emperor Kammu, who received it from the priestess of the Grand Isle Shrine. I gave it to my son when we cut his hair and tied it in the topknot."

Ryuichi bowed his head. "The grief of your house is the grief of my house."

A silence fell. Sogamori studied Kogarasu, turning the sword this way and that to catch the light on its shadowy temper lines. Wrapping his white silk sleeve around his hand, he polished the blade lovingly. Gently, as if cradling a sleeping baby, he laid the sword in his lap.

"I am told that your own son, Munetoki, is well and is on his way home to you," said Sogamori softly. "I hear he performed bravely in the battle at Hakata Bay. The joy of your house is the joy of my house."

Was there irony in Sogamori's tone? "A thousand years would not be enough time for me to express my gratitude to the chancellor for noticing my son," said Ryuichi, bowing deeply.

"Can the Shima not control their women?" Sogamori whispered harshly. At the sudden change of tone Ryuichi's innards froze with terror.

"Your miserable servant begs forgiveness if we have offended," he mumbled, bowing his head.

"If you have offended?" Sogamori growled. "You should be ashamed to show your face before me, Ryuichi. You should have thrown yourself into the Kamo on the way here."

"She is overcome with grief," Ryuichi pleaded. "She does not know what she is saying."

Horigawa spoke. "I have warned my lord Sogamori that the woman is both willful and wicked."

Ryuichi was outraged. He wanted to cry out, to demand that Horigawa apologize. The Shima family was being insulted here. But he remained silent. He was too frightened to speak.

Sogamori held up the sword again. "This will belong to Atsue when he performs his manhood ceremony as a Takashi."

"We are overwhelmed by my lord's offer to adopt the boy Atsue," Ryuichi said. "Only, we plead for time. The boy's mother is so newly bereaved."

"Do you compare her suffering with mine?" Sogamori rasped. "What was she to my son but another courtesan? What right does she have to mourn? We will have the boy here today."

The realization that he would have to face Taniko drove Ryuichi to make one last effort. "But she is the boy's mother. She loves him."

"She is still married to me," Horigawa cut in. "By law I am the boy's father. I say he shall go to Lord Sogamori."

Ryuichi stared at Horigawa, astonished.

"Thus the woman is no obstacle, Ryuichi-san," said Sogamori.

"I have a further thought, Your Excellency," said Horigawa. "To insure that she is kept under proper control, I shall take her back into my household." He turned to Ryuichi and bared his blackened teeth. "You have borne the burden of caring for her long enough."

Ryuichi was overcome with horror. She'll kill herself, he thought. "No, no, that will not be necessary."

"Let her be taken to Horigawa's house at the same time Atsue comes here." Sogamori laughed mirthlessly. "Peace will be restored to Ryuichi's household."

Horigawa said, "My journey to China on Your Excellency's behalf will be an arduous one. It may be a year or more before I return. I will need the companionship and help of a wife. I have so immersed myself in my duties that I have not had time to seek one. On this voyage I shall have to make do with the one I have."

But Taniko hates you, Ryuichi thought. You killed her baby daughter, now you are helping to steal her son. Merciful Buddha, she has lost Kiyosi, and now she will lose Atsue. And then to fall into the hands of Horigawa again—she will surely go mad.

"Yukio has escaped to China after killing my son," Sogamori brooded. "Well, there is one Muratomo on whom I can avenge myself. Listen, Ryuichi."

Ryuichi shrank back. "Yes, my lord."

"Send your swiftest messenger to your brother Shima Bokuden in Kamakura. Tell him the Imperial chancellor finds the continued existence of Muratomo no Hideyori a danger to the serenity of the realm. He is commanded to execute Hideyori immediately. I want the head brought back to me by the same messenger."

If only Bokuden were here, Ryuichi thought. He would know what to do. In the midst of all his anguish, the prospect of Hideyori's death troubled Ryuichi least of all. Hideyori had never brought any good to the Shima house, and Yukio had destroyed their entire little world. Ryuichi had no tears to spare for the Muratomo.

"As you wish, my lord."

Horigawa said, "The other Muratomo will not escape your wrath in China, Your Excellency. Through me, your vengeance will follow him to the Central Kingdom."

"Prince Horigawa is a remarkable man, Ryuichi-san," said Sogamori. "He is small in body, but within that small head of his is encompassed the entire Chinese language, not only all its literary classics but all its terms of trade and warfare. The prince can equally well address the Sung Emperor or bandy words with the lowliest sailor on the docks. The messages he carries to China and the information he brings back will be precious to me. If he needs your niece, he must have her."

"I understand, my lord." Ryuichi quavered.

"I will send a carriage with you for the boy, Ryuichi-san. Do not let your family trouble me again."

Horigawa rose. "I will go along myself, with my own carriage, to bring my wife back to my house." He bowed to Sogamori. "Would His Excellency be pleased to send some of his samurai with us as an escort?"

"Tell the captain of the guard to assign twenty outriders to you."

Filled with despair, Ryuichi bowed, turned and shuffled out of Sogamori's presence.

3

Taniko and Atsue were playing go when they heard the carriages and mounted men come rumbling through the gate of the Shima mansion. Atsue's hand, about to place a white stone in a move that threatened a whole line of Taniko's black stones in a corner, hesitated in midair. He put the white stone down slowly, and they sat and looked at each other.

The returning party made much more noise than Uncle Ryuichi and his outriders had on leaving, as if there were more horses, perhaps more carriages, with him now. The nervousness Taniko had felt all morning turned to dread. Pushing the go table aside, she took Atsue in her arms.

After a time, the shoji screen to her chamber slid back, and Aunt Chogao's tear-streaked face appeared in the opening. One look, and Taniko's fear turned to a wild, despairing terror. Her aunt shook her head helplessly.

"Your uncle wants Atsue in the main hall."

Taniko kept her arms around the boy. "If he wants Atsue he will have to come and tear him from me."

Sobbing, Chogao left. Atsue was crying in Taniko's arms. She patted the small shoulder beneath the dark green robe.

"Mother, kill me like you killed that man, and then kill yourself. We'll meet Father in the Pure Land."

Taniko bit her lip. "You have a long life before you, Atsue-chan. I would rather lose you than harm you in any way. And even in the worst moments of my own life I've never wanted to kill myself. Let us commend ourselves to the mercy of Amida. Homage to Amida Buddha."

"Homage to Amida Buddha," Atsue repeated.

Ryuichi came into the room. Behind him there walked a

small, hatefully familiar figure wearing a tall black lacquer hat.

"Good day to you, Taniko-san," said Horigawa, baring his blackened teeth in a broad grin.

With a scream of rage Taniko reached for the nearest weapon, which happened to be a lighted oil lamp. She hurled it at Horigawa, who stepped aside, laughing at her. Ryuichi shouted an alarm as the small, orange flames raced up a paper wall. A servant rushed in with a pot of water and threw it on the fire, and Ryuichi beat out the remaining flames with a quilt.

"I see Lady Taniko is still given to setting houses on fire," said Horigawa.

"It was you who put this idea in Sogamori's mind," said Taniko, wanting to spring upon her husband and strangle him.

Horigawa spread his hands. "On the contrary, I suggested to Lord Sogamori that the offspring of a woman of unsound mind and low birth could hardly be worthy of his attention. But he insisted. I am merely here to see that his wishes are carried out. By law you are my wife, and this boy is my son. He will be adopted by Lord Sogamori, and you, from now on, will be part of my household."

His household. They were sending her back to Horigawa. Her mind reeled under the shock. For a moment she really did want to kill herself. Everything that had given her happiness in these past years was gone, as if swallowed by an earthquake.

She knelt and held Atsue. "We will not go."

"That man isn't my father," Atsue sobbed.

"Of course not," Taniko said through clenched teeth. "He is incapable of being anyone's father."

Ryuichi was pleading with Horigawa. "You don't want her as a wife, Your Highness. I'll see to it that she doesn't trouble Lord Sogamori."

A change came over Horigawa's face. His cheeks reddened under his courtier's white powder. His eyes narrowed and his thin lips drew back from the black teeth. In a voice choked with hatred he said, "She is my wife. Mine. I will dispose of her as I see fit. Do not interfere in this, Ryuichi." Horigawa turned away from Ryuichi and called through the shutters to men standing on the veranda.

"Taniko," said Ryuichi, "perhaps if you let the boy go without making a scene, we could persuade Prince Horigawa to allow you to stay with us."

"Don't deceive yourself, Uncle," Taniko said coldly. "The prince has old scores to settle with me. As for you, you failed me when I needed you most. Now I don't want to stay with you."

"Try to understand, Taniko. All the world bends before Lord Sogamori as grass before the wind. I can't withstand him."

"I thought a samurai could withstand anything."

Two men in red silk jackets and shin-length trousers, their long swords hanging from their belts, tramped into the room. They looked somewhat sheepish at entering the chamber of a lady unprotected by a screen. Standing against the wall, they kept their eyes averted from Taniko and looked questioningly at Horigawa.

"Really, Your Highness, this is unnecessary," Ryuichi said. "You insult me by bringing your samurai into my house."

"You have already shown yourself unable to make the members of your household obey the commands of Lord Sogamori," said Horigawa. He turned to the samurai. "Take the boy from her and put him in Lord Sogamori's carriage."

Taniko remained kneeling with her arms around Atsue. Ryuichi held out his hands to her.

"Please, Taniko. Do not disgrace us like this."

"It is you who disgrace yourself, Uncle."

"Take the boy," Horigawa snapped at the samurai.

The elder of the two men stepped forward and stood over Taniko. "Excuse me, my lady. Will you give us the boy?"

"I'm sorry," said Taniko, "but I cannot do that."

"We know you, my lady. It was you who helped one of our comrades into the beyond. You are held in great esteem by all samurai. But we must obey orders. Do not force us to shame you."

Taniko closed her eyes and bowed her head. "Forgive me." She tightened her grip on Atsue.

"It is you who must forgive us, my lady." The samurai bent over and took hold of her arms. Atsue screamed. Ryuichi stood moaning and wringing his hands.

Suddenly Taniko let go of Atsue and leaped at the younger of the two samurai, grabbing for his sword. She had it halfway out of its scabbard when the samurai's open hand smashed down on the side of her head. She fell, stunned, unable to move.

"She must have been a warrior in a former life," said the older samurai.

"Mother!" Atsue cried. Taniko opened her eyes and saw her son in the grip of the younger samurai. She held out her arms to him and he struggled to free himself.

"Get the boy out of here," Horigawa said. The man dragged Atsue from the room.

Shutting Atsue's screams out of her mind, Taniko turned to the older samurai. She had to speak very slowly to keep the sobs from breaking through.

"Before you leave, ask the servants to give you his flute, koto and samisen and take them with you to the Rokuhara. The flute, Little Branch, is a Takashi family heirloom given Atsue by his father. The boy's practice should not be interrupted. He is a very fine musician." She remembered years ago when Lady Akimi had said of Domei's son, Yukio, "His flute playing is beautiful to hear." Yukio, because of whom Kiyosi was now dead. Yukio, whose life she had helped save. Until this moment that had not occurred to her. Now the realization of it stunned her.

"Homage to Amida Buddha," she whispered. Only the Lord of Boundless Light could understand the tangled karma that made her somehow responsible for Kiyosi's death.

Taniko stood, turning to Horigawa. "Take me and do what you will."

Walking with the small steps of a lady, holding her back very straight, Taniko left the weeping family of Shima Ryuichi. She realized that she might never see any of them again, but she walked silently past them without saying good-bye. Her family had failed her once too often.

Horigawa commanded one of the Takashi samurai to get into the carriage with himself and Taniko. As they trundled through the streets of Heian Kyo, Taniko said, "Will you always have a guard present when you are with me, Your Highness?"

Horigawa smiled at her, a smile full of hatred. "You

cannot possibly imagine the fate I have in mind for you. It will be most interesting to see how a delicate, well-bred lady, used to life in the capital, withstands the rigors of a journey to China.''

Taniko stared at Horigawa, openmouthed. China? But if Yukio had fled to China, as she had heard, Jebu might have gone there, too. It was almost impossible to believe this was not some strange dream.

''Yes, my dear, China,'' Horigawa said. ''But that is only to be the beginning of your journey. Before you come to the end you will find yourself in hell.''

She was treated rather like a guest at Horigawa's house. The women's building had been unused for some time. It was dirty, and the roof leaked. But Horigawa's servants, evidently on orders from the prince, worked hard and quickly and had it put right the day Taniko arrived.

She was completely cut off from the rest of the world. The servants avoided conversation with her. She longed for just a word about Atsue. Sometimes, when she woke from a night's sleep, it would be a moment or two before she remembered that Kiyosi was dead and that Atsue had been taken from her. Then she would cry for hours before she could gather the strength to dress and take her morning meal. At night she would cry until she fell asleep.

There was absolutely nothing to do. She tried to write poetry, but she had no heart for it. She tried to write in her pillow book, which had followed her here from the Shima mansion along with her wardrobe and other personal possessions, but she had nothing to write about. Sometimes she thought about the tortures to which Horigawa might subject her, the kinds of death he might inflict on her, and she felt terror. But the realization of what she had lost and how hopeless her future was, numbed her to fear. Whenever the sadness and the fear seemed unbearable, sbe found comfort in invoking the Buddha.

More than once it occurred to her that by slitting her throat she could put an end to her suffering, once and for all. But empty as her life seemed, dreadful as Horigawa's plans for her might be, she was sustained by a feeling that somehow she would overcome all, that she still had a destiny to fulfill.

Then, too, it would give Horigawa too much satisfaction to look down on her corpse and think he had driven her to kill herself. Nor could she bear to leave this world while Jebu was still part of it. As long as he was alive, she had not lost everything.

Finally, there was the thought of China, that fabulous country across the sea, from which came all beauty, all wisdom and all law. She could not die without seeing China.

One day a maid came to her. "His Highness says that you are to pack your very best robes and gowns, because you may be presented to some of the great lords of China."

Strange, Taniko thought. Why would he present her to great lords, when he loathed her? With the help of Horigawa's maids she began to make lists of the things she wanted to take with her. Fear rose in her mind, and she tried to quell it with, "Homage to Amida Buddha."

There had not been an official mission from the Sunrise Land to the Land of Sunset in over two hundred years, and Horigawa's visit was not an embassy from the Son of Heaven to the Emperor of China either. But when he set out the prince visited retired Emperor Go-Shirakawa and Chancellor Sogamori and even paid a ceremonial visit to the young Emperor Takakura, Sogamori's son-in-law. These conversations took most of a day. In the late afternoon Horigawa, along with Taniko, his samurai and his servants, protected by a hundred Takashi outriders, set out through the Rasho Mon.

They followed the Sanyodo Road through pleasant plains divided into flooded rice paddies. They spent the night at the estate of a Takashi lord and continued south in the morning. The road led south to the coast and then west along the Inland Sea.

Through the screened window of her carriage, which she shared with three maids, Taniko could see islands sparkling on the sea like emeralds scattered on blue silk. Fishing boats and other small craft plied their way among the islands and along the shore.

At last they came to Hyogo. The Takashi banner was everywhere, fluttering on the tops of warehouses and the tall masts of ships in the harbor. The harbor itself had been specially dredged by Sogamori to admit fully loaded oceango-

ing vessels. The party rode along the stone wharves past
staring dock workers.

Three Takashi war galleys were docked in the harbor, their
sails down, their oars at rest. It was from here, thought
Taniko, that Kiyosi had embarked on his last voyage. Perhaps
it was in one of these very ships that he had sailed to his
death. Now, for part of her journey, she would be following
the same route he had, seeing the same sights he had seen.

She remembered her own voyage on the Inland Sea with
Kiyosi. That time, too, they had left from this same port. She
recalled the islands they had stopped at, the flowers they had
picked, the shrines and temples they had visited. Tears filled
her eyes, blurring the sights of the harbor.

The maids were both excited and terrified at the thought of
leaving their country, but had kept their conversation subdued
throughout the journey because of Taniko's presence in the
carriage. Now they burst into excited chatter. They had seen
the ship on which they would be sailing.

It was a Chinese seagoing junk, standing alone and majestic,
tied to the end of a long stone wharf. Taniko's first impression, as she pressed her head against the carriage screen
beside the maids, was of a floating castle. The ship had five
masts. Taniko had to twist her neck to see to the top of the
tallest one, where a gleaming, golden fish trailing red pennants swam through the sky, veering this way and that with
the wind. Eight-sided charms, looking like round, glaring
eyes, were painted on either side of the prow. In the center of
each was the yin-yang symbol. The sides and stern of the ship
were decorated, mostly in red, black and gold, with scenes of
warfare, with birds, fishes, flowers and dragons. As the
carriage approached closer to the huge junk, she read a verse
of good omen in Chinese on the stern: ''Water that sleeps in
the moonlight.'' This enormous, gaudy ship was like no
vessel built in the Sacred Islands. When she stepped aboard,
she would already be in China.

She was carried up the gangplank in a small sedan chair,
preceded and followed by maids. Around her rose the mur-
murings of the Chinese crew as the sedan chair bearers hurried along the deck. She was hastily whisked to a cabin in the
stern. The presence of women on the ship must greatly in-
crease the danger of disorder, she realized.

The cabin which she would share with one of her maids was small but reasonably elegant. There was a window and, one above the other, two wooden shelves were covered with mats and quilts for sleeping. Her traveling boxes would take up the remaining space.

From the pillow book of Shima Taniko:

We have been at sea five days now. Since we left Shimonoseki Strait behind, we have been in sight of land most of the time. We stopped at Tsushima Island, then at Pusan on the coast of Korea. I saw both places only through my cabin window.

Once a day we women are permitted to walk the deck for our health. The rest of the time we are confined to cabins which get tinier and smellier each day. When I see Horigawa he smiles at me in his ugly way. I wish I could push him overboard, but he is always surrounded by guards.

Since we entered the China Sea I have been sick. The ship rises and falls constantly and sometimes rolls from side to side. It is not so bad when I am on deck and can look out at the horizon, but when I am in my cabin and the sea is rough I cannot keep food in my stomach and ardently wish I could depart this life.

There must be over two hundred passengers on board. I can't imagine that there is enough room for them belowdecks. Some of the more important passengers, including Horigawa and myself, have cabins in the stern. Besides Horigawa's party there are priests, monks and merchants aboard. There are Chinese and Korean travelers as well as our own people. The crew, one of the maids told me, consists of about a hundred men.

The Chinese are much taller than we are, and lighter of skin, except for the sailors, who have been tanned a dark brown by the sun.

Sick and unhappy and frightened as I am, the adventure of crossing this vast ocean and the prospect of seeing the Central Kingdom fill me with excitement.

Sixth Month, Fifteenth Day
—YEAR OF THE HORSE

4

Two flags emblazoned with white dragons flew from the battlements of Kweilin. The larger was the ancient flag of the city, the smaller, the Muratomo family crest. When Yukio and his men arrived at Kweilin, dispatched there by the Sung Emperor's chief councillor, both they and the people of the city had been amazed by the coincidence of symbols. All considered it to be an auspicious omen.

Jebu, Yukio and Moko stood at the parapet on the south side of the city's wall, watching the coming of the Mongols. Like a storm moving in from the sea, the Mongol advance was heralded by a blurring of the horizon. The line between the distant blue hills and the blue sky vanished into a ribbon of gray. Gradually the gray blanketed the nearer hills. Dust clouds reared into the sky like giants.

There had been plenty of advance warning. Refugees had been streaming up from the south for days, by land and on the rivers near the city. For the past day and a half, on orders of the city's governor, the landowners, artisans and peasants living in the surrounding countryside had moved within the walls. They brought with them every scrap of food, including live animals—oxen, goats, pigs, sheep, chickens and horses. Nothing was left behind for the Mongols. It had amazed Yukio and Jebu that Kweilin could feed its huge population in normal times. Though not one of the larger cities in southern China, it was still many times more populous than Heian Kyo.

Now there would be no more refugees. The Mongols themselves had arrived.

Out of the billowing dust clouds came roars and rumblings,

258

the booming of drums, the blare of horns and shouts of command. The Mongols' standards rose above the dust—poles decorated with horns, spearheads, the wings of large birds or the fluttering tails of animals. The first riders appeared, dark figures advancing at a jog trot in silence.

"Do they frighten you?" Yukio asked Jebu with a smile. "There must be tens of thousands of them. The wings of their army spread from west to east."

"I am not frightened," said Jebu, "but I am amazed."

"I'm frightened," said Moko. "Even one warrior frightens me. Here there are as many warriors as there are raindrops in a *tai-phun.*"

"We will try to blow this *tai-phun* back where it came from," said Yukio. He was his usual cheerful self, but Jebu suspected he spoke with more confidence than he felt.

On and on the Mongols came. The thunder of their horses' hooves filled land and sky. Their advance guard was now a short ride from the two lakes, Rong hu and Shan hu, that formed the southern side of the moat around Kweilin's walls. They were heading straight for the Green Belt Bridge, the one bridge that Yukio had left standing. The wooden bridge divided the two lakes and led to the fortified south gate of the city. All the other bridges had been destroyed and the other gates, except for the river gate, walled up.

As he watched the Mongols, Jebu remembered a day years ago when he had stood with Yukio's father, Domei, on the wall of the Imperial Palace in Heian Kyo, watching the glittering advance of the Takashi. Would this day end as disastrously as that one had? He hoped not, and reminded himself that a Zinja does not hope.

Jebu felt a special excitement that he could not share with his comrades. These were his father's people. Until now the only Mongol he had seen was Arghun Baghadur. He strained his eyes to capture every detail of the dress, appearance and manner of the warriors swarming over the hills south of Kweilin. His first impression was one of fur and leather, slitted eyes and brown faces that preserved, as they rode, an implacable silence.

Jebu said, "I would advise that, for the spirits of our men and the spirits of the people of this city, we ride out and attack the Mongols before they get into position."

Yukio nodded. "Let's give them a taste of what they can expect from us."

Yukio called his samurai together at the base of the city wall. Four times the height of a man, the wall was built of yellow rock quarried from the limestone hills around Kweilin. The gates consisted of an inner and outer set of doors made of huge logs reinforced with iron bands. Square stone towers guarded either side of the gateway.

Besides the thousand men he had brought with him, Yukio had been placed in charge of two thousand Chinese troops. Twice that many civilians could be armed from the city's arsenal and pressed into service if need be. Yukio called only the samurai for this first sally, directing the other troops to man the walls. All mounted, all in full armor, the samurai crowded into the paved staging area behind the south gate.

Observers on the walls reported that the Mongols had reached the two lakes and were lining up facing the south wall. Yukio ordered the gates opened. With Yukio and Jebu leading the way, followed by a bannerman bearing the White Dragon, the samurai rode five abreast, at a trot, on to the bridge. Their taiko drummers beat out a rising, angry rhythm.

As he looked at the line of warriors facing him, Jebu could not see the Mongols—his people—clearly. They were mostly heavy framed, bigger than the samurai. Their faces were dark, burnt by sun and wind. They all wore moustaches with drooping wings, and their hair, where it protruded from under their helmets, was braided. Most of them had black hair, but here and there Jebu saw a red beard and moustache. Their eyes were narrow, the eyes of men who had spent their lives squinting into the sun.

Yukio drew his long, gleaming sword and spurred his horse to a gallop. Jebu did the same, and the wooden bridge quivered as the samurai behind them picked up the pace. The samurai shouted their battle cry, "Muratomo!" at the motionless Mongols. Jebu looked over his shoulder and saw a thicket of steel blades behind him. But about half of Yukio's men were still inside the city gate.

Jebu heard three notes of a horn, a Mongol signal. Now, he thought, they would attack. But those facing him wheeled in unison and rode away from the edge of the lakes, leaving a broad open space on the far end of the bridge to invite Yukio's warriors.

Over the clamor of the samurai charge, Yukio called, "Try to set fire to their seige engines."

Jebu was remembering that other battle, long ago, when he had watched the retreating Kiyosi lead the Takashi out of the grounds of the Imperial Palace, pursued by the Muratomo.

"Yukio," he called. "It's a trap."

"I can't stop them now."

Jebu whipped his horse to a burst of speed that carried him to the end of the bridge well ahead of Yukio. He pulled the big brown Chinese stallion to a sliding stop and swung him athwart the path of the charging samurai. He stood in his stirrups so Yukio's men could see him, and held up his arms in a halting gesture. A Mongol arrow shot past his neck.

Crying out to his men to stop their charge, Yukio pulled his horse up short. The riders immediately following him responded to his command, and the word was relayed in shouts back along the bridge. But the milling mass of leading horses and men crashed into Jebu's stallion, and Jebu fell to the wooden planking.

There came two long blasts on the Mongol horn. Almost at once arrows were raining down. The Mongols, still riding away from the moat, had turned in their saddles and were shooting back at the samurai. Jebu's horse screamed and reared as a dozen steel-tipped arrows thudded into its side.

Jebu grabbed Yukio's arm and pulled him out of his saddle. Using the dying horses as cover, they watched the slaughter of their men. Three Mongol arrows had embedded themselves in Jebu's armor. He broke off their shafts. The Mongols had stopped and turned to face the city. Again and again they fired volleys at the men on the bridge from their short, powerful, double-curved bows.

The man carrying the White Dragon banner had fallen. Even though it made him a special target, Yukio picked up the banner and ran with it back over the bridge to the gate. Seeing the banner, the samurai began to fall back. Jebu and Yukio stumbled over dying horses and men. The two lakes were stained crimson and filled with bodies. The arrows fell upon them in clouds. Now all the surviving samurai were rushing pell-mell for the south gate.

One mounted man galloped past Yukio and Jebu in the opposite direction, his eyes wild, his face a furious red. Yukio tried to stop him, but the warrior didn't even notice his leader as he charged by.

The Mongol horn sounded a single note, and the arrows stopped.

Standing up in his stirrups, the lone samurai shouted into the sudden silence, "Ho! I am Sakamoto Michihiko of Owara, descended in the tenth generation from Abe Yoritoki, the renowned warrior."

Yukio had paused to watch Michihiko. Pushing him fiercely, Jebu got him moving again.

The next Mongol signal was a braying fanfare. In spite of his Zinja training Jebu felt a shudder of fear at what happened next. Like an avalanche the Mongol cavalry rode at full gallop toward the Green Belt Bridge. Silent before, now they screamed like madmen, their faces distorted into masks of fury. Waving their sabers, they bore down on the lone samurai.

With as much deliberation as if he were at archery practice, Michihiko drew his bow, which was taller than a man, and fired a fourteen-hand arrow at the first Mongol in the wedge. The nomad fell from his horse, pierced through the eye. Michihiko fired one arrow after another at the charging warriors. He was a good shot, and soon fallen men and riderless horses were slowing the Mongol rush.

But now the Mongols were on Michihiko. Throwing down his bow, he had drawn his long sword. The blade rang against the curved swords of the Mongols. Jebu saw a Mongol sword break in two. At least our swordsmiths are better than theirs, he thought.

The Mongols encircling Michihiko drew back. One of them spun a looped rope over his head and with a flick of his wrist snaked it at the samurai. Another rope dropped over his head. He was trussed, his arms pinned. He was trying to cut himself free when the Mongols yanked him from his horse and he fell heavily to the bridge. Their shrill laughter rang out over the two lakes. They closed in, and a dozen lance points stabbed Michihiko's writhing body.

Yukio kept his eyes fixed on the scene. "An indecent death for a brave warrior. Barbarian butchers."

Most of the samurai were safely within the city wall. Inside the gate Moko was waiting with a lighted oil lamp. Jebu took it from him and went back to the bridge.

A Mongol raised Michihiko's head on the end of a spear. They shouted triumphantly, high-pitched war cries, as if killing this one man had been a great victory.

"They probably think he was our mightiest fighter," said Yukio. "They don't know he was just one samurai who thought today would be a good day to die."

Like the Zinja, the samurai had learned to see death as no evil, Jebu thought. But unlike the Zinja, some of them actually saw it as good. They rushed to embrace it.

Now the Mongols were galloping across the bridge, racing to stop the gates from being closed. "Stand back," Jebu said to Yukio.

Into the oil lamp's flame he plunged the end of a string that had been rubbed with the explosive black powder of the Chinese. A hissing spark ran down the string and branched out in several directions along the bridge. Jebu and Yukio darted behind the great wood and iron doors.

The instant the gates boomed shut there came a tremendous thunderclap. Too late, Yukio put his hands over his ears. Jebu, his own ears ringing, beckoned, and the two of them ran up the stone stairs leading to the parapet.

"Look what we've done," Jebu said.

A gray cloud of stinking smoke hung over Rong hu and Shan hu. The Green Belt Bridge, except for a few smoldering, blackened stumps of pilings, was entirely gone. The water was full of Mongols and their horses, many of them dead or badly wounded, a few struggling to swim to shore.

"That repays them," said Jebu.

"No it doesn't," said Yukio. "They can lose all those men and not miss them. For us, to lose two hundred men is to lose one out of every five. And we've lost that many, I'm sure, in our very first battle." He laughed bitterly. "I ought to cut my belly open to make up for it."

Jebu said, "It was my suggestion to launch an immediate attack."

Yukio's large eyes were liquid with sadness. "I gave the order. And if you had not stopped our charge when you did, the Mongols would have annihilated us. You also suggested using the thunder-and-lightning powder to destroy the bridge."

"Moko learned about the powder from the Chinese engineers." Jebu found that he had no regrets about the disastrous attack, but he wanted to help his friend. He put his hand on Yukio's armored sleeve.

"We Zinja say that to act is within the power of every person. To guarantee the success of an act is not under anyone's control. So, if you are victorious, do not be elated. If you are defeated do not be downcast. A warrior who cares too much about winning or losing is worthless. I have thought several times today of your father and the last day of his uprising in Heian Kyo, when you were still a child. He was defeated and forced to retreat from the city, but he was not discouraged. He said that the falcon stoops and sometimes comes up with empty claws, but flies on to hunt again. He was a joyous samurai."

Yukio smiled, showing the slightly protruding teeth that gave his face a boyish look. "I will try to be a joyous samurai."

5

Across the two lakes the Mongols set up their camp and their fortifications. In their numbers, energy and discipline they reminded Jebu of the fierce red ants that built their nests in the forest around the Waterfowl Temple and viciously attacked any trespassing creature, from insect to man. Once, as a child, he had unknowingly stepped on a red ant hill. Instantly, his legs had been covered with a swarm of tiny, biting insects. He had run screaming to an elder monk who laughed and rescued him by throwing him into a horse trough.

Yukio summoned his men and called the roll. Their losses were as he had predicted, over two hundred. Yukio announced that he was keeping a written record of every battle. The slain would be listed carefully, and all meritorious deeds would be recorded. Feats of sublime valor like that of Sakamoto Michihiko would be memorialized in full. Yukio promised that whatever befell them, even if they all died defending Kweilin, he would get the record of their deeds through the Emperor's Court at Linan, and from there it would be sent to the Sacred Islands. Thus, their families would remember their heroism forever. Had he promised his men riches and long life, he could not have done more to win their loyalty. To die was nothing to a samurai, but to die unnoticed would be a calamity.

Their cheers for Yukio echoed against the high limestone walls. If they had any doubts about his leadership, those doubts were resolved for the time being. The Chinese spectators, unable to understand the language of Ge-pen, as they called the Sunrise Land, wondered how the strange warriors could be so happy after such terrible losses.

Kweilin lay along the west bank of the Kwei Kiang River, a wide, deep, swift-running stream bordered by blue hills riddled with caves and sinkholes and eroded into fantastic shapes. The river was not only a natural moat but also provided the city with an easy supply route and escape route. Any relief troops that might be needed could sail up the Kwei Kiang from Canton.

The besiegers pitched their camp on the west and south sides of the city. Every hill, all the way to the horizon, was covered by round gray felt tents arranged in regular rows. At night the campfires twinkled, as innumerable as the stars.

After several days of watching, Yukio estimated that there were seventy thousand fighting men in the army camped around Kweilin. Thirty thousand were Mongols, organized into three *tumans*, divisions of ten thousand. The rest were auxiliary troops drawn from the various peoples the Mongols had conquered, mostly Kin Tartars, northern Chinese, Turks and Nan Chaoans. Accompanying these warriors was a host of camp followers, women, servants and slaves.

The Mongols were far from being the ragtag horde of savages Jebu and Yukio had imagined. They were better organized and more carefully equipped than many armies of civilized nations. They wore leather helmets, sometimes topped with spikes or other ornaments, and trimmed with felt and fur. Their armor was of fire-dried, black-lacquered rawhide, which, Jebu knew, was as strong as steel. Each rider carried two bows and two quivers of arrows in saddle cases, a curved saber in a scabbard slung across his back, a lance, an iron mace, and a round leather shield. Each warrior had at least six remounts—compact steppe ponies about the size of samurai horses, much smaller than those of the Chinese. The Mongol ponies had powerful necks, thick legs and dense coats. Their manes and tails hung almost to the ground. They foraged for themselves in huge herds in the hills near Kweilin.

Life in the city of felt domes seemed quiet and orderly, amazingly so, considering that these were supposedly barbarians whose only interests in life were conquest, killing, looting and rape. Jebu remembered what the Zen monk Eisen had said about the strict laws of the Mongols.

The head of Sakamato Michihiko remained on a pole at the spot where he had fallen, a trophy to be pecked at by birds, gradually changing from the head of a comrade to an anonymous skull. And close to the two lakes was an even more wretched sight. A huge corral had been built. Thousands of tattered, woebegone Chinese were penned within it, mostly men but with many women and even some children among them. They sat or lay on the ground without shelter from the hot sun and the frequent summer rains; the more energetic paced like caged animals. They were fed once a day. Every day parties of these prisoners, each herded by a single mounted warrior, would trudge out to the hills and return pulling cartloads of brush which they laid in a huge pile beside their stockade.

Jebu, Yukio and Moko spent hours every day watching the Mongols. In his few moments of leisure Jebu contemplated the play of light in the flashing depths of the Jewel of Life and Death. Even though he and his comrades had gone, seemingly, from certain death in their homeland to certain death in a foreign country, he felt calm and cheerful.

Across the moat from the city walls the besiegers built a wooden counterwall, with towers higher than those of the city. Behind it they deployed mobile towers, large and small catapults, giant crossbows, rams and the long-barreled iron firethrowers the Chinese called *hua pao*.

Moko studied the many different kinds of siege machines, explained their uses to Yukio and suggested how they might be countered. "They will send miners to dig under the moat and try to blast our walls with the black powder," he said. "They have contingents of engineers among their auxiliary troops. We must have men constantly posted along the base of the walls listening for sounds of digging."

Kweilin had *hua pao* of its own, which Yukio ordered positioned on the city's towers, to be manned night and day by shifts of Chinese. Pots of oil were set up along the walls, to be ignited and dropped on the wooden Mongol machines. Within the city people gathered barrels of water on every street, buckets of water in every house. Fire was the worst enemy of a city under siege.

They were as ready as they could be, but there were certain aspects of their situation that mystified Yukio and Jebu.

Jebu said, "We know nothing of siege warfare, we know nothing of these fire-throwing tubes. We are ignorant of Mongol tactics. A wise man would have placed us under a Chinese general, so that we could learn and be used according to our skills. Instead we have been put in command of this city. The Chinese officers here resent us. Is Chia Ssu-tao a fool, that he would risk a city in this fashion?"

Yukio shrugged. "Perhaps he was overly impressed by us. People are often respectful of the strange, and contemptuous of the familiar."

"Or perhaps he wants this city to fall," Jebu said.

"But he is of the war party at the Sung Emperor's Court. It was he who provoked the Mongols by breaking a treaty with them."

Jebu nodded. "What if the Mongols desired that provocation?"

Yukio's large eyes opened wider. "Are you suggesting that Chia Ssu-tao is a traitor? And that we are being sacrificed to his designs?"

"All we can do now is play the game out," said Jebu. "We are learning more quickly than those who sent us here may have expected us to."

At the time of their meeting with Chia Ssu-tao, it had seemed like the beginning of days of good fortune. For ten days, longer than it took to cross the China Sea, they had sweltered aboard their galleys in the almost tropical heat of the southern Chinese capital, Linan. Chinese troops guarded them. Yukio gave a port official a flowery letter to the Chinese Son of Heaven, offering the services of one thousand samurai, to be used as His Imperial Majesty saw fit. The letter had been written at the Teak Blossom Temple with the help of the Zen monk Eisen. After a time Yukio began to despair of receiving an answer. They would have to choose between rotting aboard these ships, setting sail for some other land where they might be more welcome, or breaking out, to become outlaws in the Chinese countryside.

Then a reply came. A huge red and gold palanquin borne by a dozen men and accompanied by a squad of clanking Chinese soldiers was set on the stone quay beside Yukio's ship. A Chinese officer invited Yukio and three of his officers to ride in the palanquin to the palace of His Celestial Majesty's chief councillor, the venerable Chia Ssu-tao. Yukio gaped at the palanquin.

"Back home, only the Emperor would be allowed to ride in a conveyance like that."

"Things are different here," Jebu said. "Get your best kimono on and let us visit this venerable councillor."

Yukio, Jebu and two other samurai leaders rode in the palanquin. Linan seemed to them a city of giants. Its many-storied buildings towered over innumerable canals and elaborate stone bridges. Each city block seemed to hold as many people as all of Heian Kyo. The Zinja were taught to memorize landmarks, but before they had gone very far, Jebu realized he was completely lost. It was all too strange.

Chia Ssu-tao's residence did not cover as much ground as the Rokuhara or the Imperial Palace back in Heian Kyo. Land was obviously precious in Linan. But the buildings were bigger and heavier than those of the Sunrise Land. Chia Ssu-tao's palace was surrounded by vermilion columns resting on the heads of painted stone dragons. He was guarded by huge soldiers in silver armor. The halls of his palace were covered with heavy carpet, so that not a footfall could be heard.

Chia Ssu-tao received them seated on a throne painted with gold leaf. He was a man in his early forties, tall and lean with a large nose, a pointed chin and a small mouth. He wore a round hat topped by a ball of red coral, the mark of his high office. His welcoming smile was cold.

"Your command of Chinese is good," he began, "but you write in the style of over three hundred years ago."

Yukio blushed. "Forgive my blundering efforts, Your Excellency. There has been so little contact between your land and mine that we have not kept up with the progress in your manner of writing."

Chia Ssu-tao nodded. "The last official embassy from your Emperor visited our Son of Heaven near the end of the T'ang dynasty. I presume you have heard of the T'ang dynasty?"

"Of course, Your Excellency," said Yukio. "Our system of government is modeled on that of the T'ang. Our capital, Heian Kyo, is a copy of the T'ang capital of Changan."

"Your people have a gift for aping their betters," said Chia Ssu-tao with a patronizing smile. "However, it is time you visited us again to acquire a few new skills. The Central Kingdom is always pleased to aid the struggles of barbarian nations toward higher civilization."

Yukio was good at masking his feelings, but Jebu knew from the tightness around his mouth that he was furious. "It is to help protect your great civilization against the barbarian invaders that we have come here, Your Excellency."

Chia Ssu-tao nodded. "You show the virtue of filial piety, since our civilization is the father of yours. I shall ask the Ministry of War what role can be found for you. We will provide you and your men with quarters. By the way, do you hold cricket fights in your country?"

"Our children keep crickets in cages as pets, Your Excellency."

"Indeed your people are backward if they consider such a sublime sport a pastime for children. Here we pit crickets against each other. They strive together like tiny dragons. We place bets on the outcome. You must attend my next evening of cricket fights."

In the days that followed, Chia Ssu-tao introduced Jebu, Yukio and other high-ranking samurai to the aristocracy of Linan. They even had a brief audience with Sung Emperor Li-tsung, a stout, motionless figure seated on a jade throne. They attended several cricket fights, an obsession with Chia

Ssu-tao that preoccupied him more than his duties as the Son of Heaven's chief councillor. On all these occasions Jebu felt that they were being paraded as curiosities, not taken seriously as fighting men.

So it was a surprise when, after a short stay in Linan, Yukio was given an Imperial appointment as military commander of Kweilin, the chief city of Kwangsi province on the western border of the Sung empire. The Mongols had invaded the independent kingdom of Nan Chao and taken its capital, Tali. Kweilin was their next likely target. If Kweilin fell, the nomads could move on to Changsha, the strongest city in the central region. The fall of Changsha would open the way to Linan. The Chinese rulers had given Yukio a crucial post.

After the Mongols had been camped outside the city's walls for three days, they sent an unarmed officer across Lake Rong hu in a sampan.

Yukio said, "Let's behead him in front of the gateway, where his countrymen can see it. That will encourage our people and teach the enemy that we are resolute."

Jebu, who had a strong distaste for unnecessary bloodshed despite his years of combat, was surprised at Yukio. "The governor of the city might want to decide how to deal with this envoy," he suggested mildly. "Let's not antagonize our Chinese friends further."

Governor Liu Mai-tse, an aged scholar, received Yukio, Jebu and the Mongol emissary in his marble hall of state. After bowing to the governor, who was seated on an ivory chair, Yukio addressed him in Chinese.

"I wanted to behead this Mongol at once, Your Excellency, without even hearing what he had to say. This weak-spirited monk who accompanies me persuaded me to bring the enemy to you instead. If it is your wish, though, I will gladly execute him now."

For the first time Yukio spoke in a language the envoy understood. He showed no fear, but glowered angrily. Despite his age—his hair and moustache were gray—he had the powerful build and quick movements of a young warrior.

Governor Liu smiled. "I am not familiar with the humor of Ge-pen, but I believe you are joking about this monk. I observed him from the wall the day you fought the Mongols, and he is anything but weak-spirited. His advice to you is wise. The Mongols consider the person of an ambassador to be sacred. To slay this man would be an unforgivable offense."

Yukio shook his head. "I'm sorry, Your Excellency. I was under the impression we had already offended the Mongols."

Liu raised a slender hand in admonition. "You will admit the possibility that they might eventually take this city?"

"With reluctance."

"Of course. If we had slain their ambassador they would assuredly put all the people of Kweilin to the sword. That is their custom. You do not have the right to condemn every person in this city to certain death. If we do not embark on a course that drives them to do their worst, there is hope. The Tao is infinite and infinitely surprising."

Now the grizzled enemy officer turned to Jebu. "Are you a Mongol?" he demanded angrily in Chinese. "How can you serve the degenerate Chinese and fight against your own people?"

"I am not a Mongol, though my father was," said Jebu. "I was born of mixed parentage in the Sunrise Land and was raised there."

The Mongol looked surprised and curious. He squinted at Jebu closely and seemed about to ask another question when Liu interrupted.

"If you are through quizzing this monk, tell us who you are and what you have to say to us."

The Mongol drew himself up and addressed the governor. "I am Torluk, a *tuman-bashi*—a leader of ten thousand. I come from the commander of the army outside your gates. He does not wish to waste men or destroy a valuable city. Therefore he gives you an opportunity to surrender now. Open your gates to us and all will be spared—even the warriors from the Land of the Dwarfs."

Land of the Dwarfs. Jebu had heard that expression once before, when he had listened in secret to Arghun's conversation with Taitaro. Was it true that his people might be ridiculed for their stature? Perhaps it was so, for had he not always been the butt of jokes because of his height?

"I see." Governor Liu stood and beckoned to Yukio and

Jebu, drawing them to a corner behind a gilded pillar and leaving his pikemen to watch the envoy.

In a low voice he said, "This commander who offers mercy is only second-in-command of the army outside. The *tarkhan* who leads all the Mongols in this region is in Szechwan conferring with their Emperor Mangu. The temporary commander has made many errors by Mongol standards. In the battle at the Green Belt Bridge his orders were delayed, and too many warriors died. Discipline in the camp is poor. The movements of his army are behind schedule. Now he fears that the *tarkhan* will punish him for his mistakes. He wants to take the city without a fight and present it to the *tarkhan* as a great conquest."

"How do you know so much about what the Mongols are thinking, Your Excellency?" Jebu asked.

"I have agents who are able to get in and out of their camp with ease. I know also that even though you suffered great losses at the Green Belt Bridge, the Mongol commander fears you. You are strange to him, and you seem fiercer than the Chinese he has encountered. And he doesn't know how few of you there really are."

"Your Excellency wishes us to fight on?" Yukio asked.

"I do."

Yukio nodded. "We will teach them that the men of the Sunrise Land are not dwarfs but dragons."

Jebu was pleased that Yukio did not promise victory. Perhaps he had begun to absorb some of the Zinja teachings.

Governor Liu returned to his throne. "We reject the terms offered us. We will fight on against the barbarian invaders who would steal our lands, our cities and our lives." He motioned his guards to escort the ambassador back to the south gate.

The grizzled *tuman-bashi* started to turn away, then swung around and said, "You will regret your stubbornness. You should surrender now, while you have the chance. There will be no mercy for Kweilin when our *tarkhan*, Arghun Baghadur, resumes command."

6

From the pillow book of Shima Taniko:

The barbarians who have invaded southern China are said to smell so bad that the very stench of their approach forces their foes to retreat. They are described as hideous creatures, hunchbacked and twisted of limb. I have even been told that they bite off the breasts of women. Somehow, I suspect that those terrifying reports are spread to excuse the absence of Chinese victories. Jebu is sprung from the barbarians, and surely he is not twisted of limb. And he bites women only with the best of intentions.

The Chinese also have many strange notions about us. They believe that we eat human flesh and worship gods with the heads of animals. It makes one wonder if the things they say about the Mongols are any more true.

From one of the Chinese servingmaids I have heard the tale of a band of warriors from across the China Sea, short-statured and ferocious, who came to fight in the Sung Emperor's service. That could only be Muratomo no Yukio's men, and Jebu must be with them. They are now at a city called Kweilin, farther from here than the Sacred Islands. I thought if I came here I would be closer to Jebu. We are in the same country, but this one country is as big as twenty countries. I am told they were in Linan a few months ago. Lord of Boundless Light, will I ever meet him again?

—*Eighth Month, twenty-sixth day*
YEAR OF THE HORSE

At its southern end, the brick-paved Imperial Way—which was to Linan what Redbird Avenue was to Heian Kyo—

curved past the Imperial Palace and the base of Phoenix Hill. Aristocrats and rich merchants built their palaces on Phoenix Hill, and it was here Horigawa took up residence. The gateway of his mansion led into a formal courtyard surrounded by three imposing pavilions with blue and gold pillars. The window of Taniko's room on the second story of the women's pavilion looked toward a lagoon covered with lily pads. The weeping willows and peach trees around it were green. At home this would have been the beginning of autumn, but here in Linan there was no autumn.

Horigawa's negotiations with officials in the Chinese Court dragged on for months. He had arrived in Linan with the names of a few people who might be useful—mostly merchants who traded with the Takashi—and he used these like the rungs of a ladder to reach higher personages. But frequently there were waits of many days between his appointments with various great men. Hardest of all to arrange was an audience with the most important official in Linan, the Emperor's chief councillor and the real ruler of southern China, Chia Ssu-tao.

Taniko remained in isolation, in effect a prisoner. As happened wherever she went, she quickly made friends with the servants, both her own people and the newly hired Chinese. Horigawa had instructed the household staff to keep a close watch on her and warned them that she was not to be trusted. But, consciously employing charm, candor and kindness, she eventually won them all over. Through the servants she was able to make contact with the outer world. An elderly Chinese secretary was especially helpful.

From him she learned some of the history of the Sung Emperors. Their dynasty had been founded, almost three centuries earlier by a general who seized the throne. A hundred years ago they had lost northern China, first to the barbarian Cathayans, then to the Kin tartars. And now the Mongols, having in turn overrun the Kin, had decided to unite the two halves of China under their rule. They had pierced the Sung territories from three directions with three armies: their Emperor, the Great Khan Mangu, in the far west; Mangu's younger brother, Kublai Khan, in the west nearer the capital; and a famed and feared general, Arghun Baghadur, in the south. She thought she had heard of Arghun Baghadur before, but she could not remember where or when.

At first it seemed to Taniko that all Chinese were tall, grave and silent. Then she met several who were short, passionate and talkative. She thought the Chinese greedy, then heard tales of poor scholars and met beggar monks at the mansion kitchen. Gradually she realized that her quickly formed beliefs about the Chinese were as foolish as the Chinese notion that her people ate human flesh, and she settled down to studying the Chinese one by one.

One of their customs was utterly strange to her. She did not meet any upper-class women, but the servants assured her it was quite true that the feet of wealthy and wellborn Chinese women were tightly bound when they were small girls, to keep them from growing. The deformed results, which looked something like the hooves of horses, were known as lily feet, and the Chinese women were proud of them. Taniko could not imagine why, nor why the Chinese men would find such feet attractive, as they evidently did. Only a man like Horigawa, she thought, would want a crippled woman.

Toward the end of the Year of the Horse, the prince's Chinese secretary told her that Horigawa had finally made contact with Chia Ssu-tao. Because of the chief councillor's passion for sponsoring cricket fights, Horigawa had scoured the ten major marketplaces of Linan and all the lesser ones till he found a truly formidable fighting cricket, for which he paid one hundred bolts of silk. He sent the cricket to the great minister in an ivory cage, with the compliments of one who served the Emperor of Ge-pen in the same capacity that Chia served the Sung Emperor. It was an exaggeration, but there was no way Chia Ssu-tao could discover that. Chia sent for Horigawa. What they had discussed, precisely, the secretary had no idea.

Horigawa was invited to Chia Ssu-tao's celebration ushering in the Year of the Sheep. The chief councillor entertained his guests on Linan's great Western Lake, chartering a fleet of flower-bedecked pleasure boats, crewed by women and heavily laden with casks of spiced rice wine. Horigawa was among the most favored guests, those who accompanied Chia Ssu-tao himself on the dragon barge that led the fleet. Not long after this, Horigawa sent a sealed dispatch on a trading junk to Takashi no Sogamori.

Taniko passed the days writing in her pillow book, embroidering, and playing mah-jongg with a Chinese maid who taught her the game. The elderly secretary taught her the art of painting in the Chinese manner. She compared languages with him, both of them fascinated by the way Taniko's language was written in Chinese characters, but with the characters standing for completely different words. The old man explained that China was known as the Central Kingdom because all the other nations of the earth must come to China to learn.

One day in early spring of the Year of the Sheep, Horigawa came to her. His small, squarish face was alight with pleasure and triumph.

"I have come to advise my honored wife to prepare herself for a long and arduous journey by land. We leave in three days' time."

"Where are we going?" Taniko asked coldly.

"West." Horigawa waved expansively in that direction.

"There is war in the west."

"Yes. Are you afraid?" He watched her keenly. Perhaps he hoped that the long months of suspense and confinement would have broken her down.

"I am not," Taniko said firmly. "Wherever we are going, if you are not frightened, I can be quite certain I will not be frightened."

"You have more to fear than I do."

Once again Taniko carefully packed away her silks, jewels, combs and the other belongings she had brought with her from Heian Kyo. She had not yet worn any of her finery.

The day before they were to leave she sought out the old secretary to say good-bye. He prostrated himself before her and looked up with tears in his eyes.

Taniko smiled. "I hardly deserve such an outpouring of feeling. Perhaps if you knew me better you would weep less at this parting."

He shook his head. "Escape, honored lady. Run away. Do not go with the prince."

"How can I escape? Where could I go?"

"You are being taken to your destruction. To think that I should advise a wife to defy her husband—it is a great wrong I do. But the evil he contemplates is greater."

He would say nothing more. She passed that day and night

in dread. Of course, she had always known Horigawa had some cruelty in store for her, though the uneventful voyage and the quiet months in Linan had lulled her into a feeling of safety. There was danger in the west.

How could she run away from Horigawa in an utterly strange land? Could she find her way to Jebu? How would she eat? Where would she sleep? She would either be returned to Horigawa or fall into the hands of criminals. She could only escape if she had help. She decided to ask the secretary, since he had warned her, to help her get away.

After a sleepless night she dressed quickly. As she finished, Horigawa swept into the room.

"We depart at once."

"I—I am not ready."

"That is unfortunate. I'm sorry, but we leave in any case." The little man beckoned, and two large Chinese serving women came into the room.

"I am not going with you."

"I suspected as much. Rumor of our destination has somehow reached you. One can appreciate at such times the usefulness of the Chinese custom of binding women's feet."

"I am sure the idea of torturing and deforming women appeals to you."

Horigawa nodded to the two large women. With blank faces they stepped forward and reached for Taniko. She remembered her samurai training. She stepped toward the maid on her left, tripped her and sent her sprawling on her back. The other big woman threw her arms around Taniko from behind. Taniko drove her elbow into the woman's stomach.

Horigawa tried to block the doorway, but Taniko thrust the heel of her hand into his chin. He fell back against the wall of the corridor.

She ran out of the room and into the arms of a steel-helmeted guard with a three-pointed sword swinging from his broad belt. He picked her up off her feet in a bear hug and held her there impassively while she kicked against his massive body.

"Take her to the carriage and lock her in," said Horigawa, panting as he picked himself up off the floor with the help of one of the maids. He bared his black-dyed teeth at Taniko. "I might say I will make things worse for you, to repay you for this. But your fate cannot be made any worse."

7

They set out that morning escorted by a clanking company of soldiers carrying long spears and shields painted with fire-breathing dragons' heads. The prince rode in solitary splendor in a vermilion and gold official state carriage of the Sung Emperor's Court, drawn by a pure white ox. His entourage followed in less ornate vehicles, their belongings packed on the roofs of the carriages. Five big carts, each pulled by three oxen, carried bales of silk, boxes of silver bars and other valuables.

Taniko rode with three Chinese maids, the two she had knocked down and another, grim-looking woman taller and broader than either of the others. All were strangers to her. When she tried to speak to them, they silently looked away.

The caravan rode north on the Imperial Way, passing canals and bridges and vast marketplaces. Around the market squares stood tall buildings, some as high as five stories, a necessity in this overcrowded city. They passed through a fortified gateway and crossed a wide moat, and Taniko looked back at walls so thick, chariots could be driven along their tops.

As they traveled slowly westward, they passed flooded rice paddies, whose green shoots were just beginning to break through the water's surface, alternating with woodlands full of leafy trees. At night they stayed at inns, places that intrigued Taniko. People paid in silk, silver coins or the paper money issued by the Emperor, and were given food and sleeping quarters for the night. How much easier it would make traveling in her own country if such establishments existed there.

She decided that whatever was to happen to her, she must meet it looking her best. Each morning she selected a set of her finest robes and dressed in them, layer on layer, folded back one on the other at throat, sleeves and skirt to show their variegated edges. She combed and arranged her hair and adorned it with jeweled combs and pins. She powdered her face and painted her lips, carefully making her mouth, her worst feature in her opinion, look smaller than it actually was. Horigawa had taken none of the maids from their homeland on this journey, but she was able to teach the Chinese women to help her dress in the style of a great lady of Heian Kyo.

They began to pass long lines of refugees, bundles on their heads, trudging east along either side of the road. Horigawa was heading directly for the war zone. Taniko refused to give in to fear, knowing that was just what Horigawa wanted. She remembered Jebu's telling her that once she made direct contact with the Self, she would no longer feel fear. "There will be no necessity for it," was the way he put it. She tried to reach the Self by invoking Amida Buddha. Perhaps Amida was the Self.

They encountered a Chinese army, its yellow and black silk tents dotting the spring-green hills, its general a tall figure in gilded armor mounted on a splendid black charger. Horigawa showed the general a scroll which he took from a carved ivory case.

They went on, but now the Chinese guards who had accompanied them from Linan were no longer with them. They had no protection whatever. This was madness, Taniko thought. Yet she knew Horigawa would never risk his person unnecessarily.

Drowsing as their carriage bumped westward, Taniko was awakened by the screams of the Chinese women. "Mongols!"

She looked up. Pale with fear, the maids were staring out the carriage window. Taniko pushed in among them.

They were on a road running through green young wheat fields. Nearby were the burnt ruins of a cluster of houses. In the distance she could see the walls and pagoda towers of a city above which hung a cloud of gray smoke. And across the empty fields, riders were galloping toward them. Horigawa stepped down from his carriage and stood waiting for them.

They skidded to a stop with shrill cries. Their faces were very broad and a dark brown. For the first time Taniko was seeing Jebu's people. They looked nothing like him. Then she noticed that two of them had moustaches the exact shade of red of Jebu's hair. That was a shock to her, making real something she had only half believed, as if a kami should suddenly appear to her in the living flesh.

Horigawa addressed the riders in Chinese and showed them something. He was too far away for Taniko to hear what he was saying. She hoped they would ride him down and impale him with their lances. She would be content to die, if she could first see that.

Several of the warriors dismounted and began to walk down the line of carriages, looking in the windows. Would they really smell as bad as the Chinese claimed?

A round face with a long black moustache, surrounded by a felt headpiece, thrust itself in at the window. The Mongol's eyes widened, and he exclaimed in his harsh tongue. Pulling the rear door of the carriage open, he seized the maid nearest him by the arm and yanked her out of the carriage. It was the biggest of the women. The Mongol was tall, but she was a bit taller.

The bowlegged warrior pulled the stout, pleading woman away from the road and into the knee-high green wheat. He threw her down on her back as his comrades, laughing and calling to each other, rode over and climbed down from their ponies. Taniko could hear Horigawa call out a protest, but the Mongols ignored him. Chattering gleefully, they tore the screaming woman's robes from her body. Two of them pulled her legs apart. The one who had taken her from the carriage threw himself upon her.

Her stomach churning, Taniko watched while the Mongols proceeded to take turns raping the woman. Her cries and groans brought tears to Taniko's eyes. The other two maids crouched on the carriage floor and covered their ears with their hands. Horigawa, his back turned, was talking to the leader of the Mongols, some distance away.

The last of them was through with the woman. He stood, drawing up his leather trousers, while she lay on her back

sobbing. With a snarl the Mongol reached down and pulled
her to her feet by her hair. He drew the saber slung over his
back, stretched her neck by pulling downward on her hair,
and in one swift motion struck off her head.

Taniko bit down on her fist to stifle her scream. If they
heard her, they might come back. "Homage to Amida Buddha," she whispered. Sickened and grief-stricken, she fell
back into a corner of the carriage, turned her face to the wall,
and cried in anguish.

Horigawa's voice came to her from the carriage window.
"I regret the loss of a useful servant, but perhaps this specta-
cle has given you an inkling of what is in store for you."

Taniko's pain turned to rage. "If I should die today, I will
die happy, knowing I no longer have to walk in the same
world with you."

Horigawa laughed, inclined his head mockingly and turned
away.

With the scouts riding in a loose circle around them, the
caravan began to move again. Taniko looked back. The raped
woman's body lay partly hidden in the tall grass, her severed
head a pale blur beside it. The undulations of the plain were
gentle, and Taniko was able to see the body for a long time.
Even after she could no longer see it, she continued to
tremble.

Why couldn't he let the poor woman live? Wasn't it enough
to have raped her? She was no more than a used receptacle, to
be destroyed as one might smash an empty wine cup. And to
Horigawa, Taniko was no more than an unruly slave who
must be made to suffer. She thought of the baby Horigawa
had murdered, Shikibu, a girl. But her son, Atsue, was so
valued that Sogamori had torn him from her side. Her protest,
the protest of a woman, was worthless. She had been power-
less to stop Sogamori and Horigawa. Always, to be a woman
was to be something less than a man.

And now I, too, shall be destroyed. All I can do is meet
death with courage.

"Homage to Amida Buddha."

Now they entered the Mongol camp. It smelled of wood-
smoke, horses, and roasting meat. The soldiers sat before
their round tents and looked up calmly and somewhat curi-

ously as Horigawa's procession passed. Beyond the rows of
felt tents the besieged Chinese city smoldered in the dusk.

"What city is that?" Taniko asked a maid.

"Wuchow."

The camp was quiet. She had seen these barbarians rape
and murder a woman, but among themselves they seemed
orderly enough. She had often heard the Mongols compared
to wild beasts, but the men she saw working, cleaning their
equipment, currying horses, and repairing tall wooden siege
machines, had a busy, purposeful air. They were human,
even civilized in their own way. That could only make them
more dangerous.

Taniko had been carrying with her a box containing a
mirror and paints and powders. She set about restoring her
makeup.

The carriages came to a stop in the center of the camp.
Before a large white pavilion on the crest of a small hill,
Horigawa got out of his carriage. A group of Mongol officers
wearing red and blue satin coats, gold medallions and silver-
hilted sabers, approached him. Horigawa held up the same
object he had shown the scouts. Now Taniko saw that it was a
rectangular gold tablet. The Mongol officers inclined their
heads courteously.

An aged Chinese official emerged from the large tent. He
and Horigawa conferred, then the official gave orders. A
group of servants, closely watched by a warrior, began to
unload the valuables from Horigawa's carts.

The old Chinese man came over to Taniko's carriage. "I
am Yao Chow, the khan's servant," he said. "You will
please come out now." The two maids hesitated.

"Go on," said Taniko. "We're safe in this camp, I think.
Unless you annoy them." That thought impelled the big
women to scramble from the carriage.

Taniko had carried a carved ivory fan all the way from
Heian Kyo. Now she stood poised in the doorway of the
carriage, drew the fan from her sleeve and opened it with an
imperious snap. Her outer robe was of orange silk with
dazzling gold embroidery. She wore her favorite hair ornament, a mother-of-pearl butterfly. Her lips were scarlet, her
face white as a snow-covered field.

For a moment all motion stopped in the center of the

Mongol camp. Out of the corner of her eye Taniko saw, with satisfaction, several barbarian mouths open in wonder. Perhaps it is only that I look strange to them, she thought, but I know I look beautiful. The maids helped her down the carriage's steep ladder.

Swift as a spider, Horigawa was beside her. "A grand entrance, Taniko-san," he whispered in their own language. "You could have been a great lady in our land, had you not been so foolish as to betray me. Now, however, you are among those who can teach you to respect and fear a man."

Taniko tossed her head. "It seems they respect me well enough."

"That is because they do not know what you are," he spat. "I intend to tell them. I will tell them you are no highborn lady, but simply a courtesan sent by my lord Sogamori as a gift to the Mongol warriors. They will use you and throw you away like rubbish, Taniko. Your fate will the the same as that Chinese maid's, only it will take much, much longer. At first, perhaps, you will be the plaything of the generals. But even now you are no longer as young and attractive as you once were. They will tire of you and you will be cast off to the lesser officers. Eventually, you will be kicked like a football back and forth among the dirty, greasy men in the ranks. At last you will be worn out and old before your time, diseased, toothless. You will end your days among strangers who cannot speak our language, who neither know you or care about you, far from home, forgotten. Can there be a more miserable end for a gently reared woman of the Sacred Islands than to live out her life in exile as a slave of filthy barbarians?" Grinning, he reached out a long-fingered hand and stroked her cheek softly. She turned away.

I will not give in to despair, she thought. Not in front of him. Later, perhaps, I will weep for all that I have lost and I will fear for my future. Later I will decide whether now, at last, I ought to kill myself. But now I will show him that he cannot hurt me.

She turned back to him with a faint smile. "You forget, Your Highness, that while I lived with you as your wife, my lover was a man of the same blood as these filthy barbarians. Perhaps I shall be quite happy here."

Horigawa laughed. "Ah, yes, I had almost forgotten your

warrior monk. He and the rebel Yukio are at large in this country. Indeed, it was their escape that put an end to the noble Kiyosi and placed you back in my power again. Kiyosi, with whom you publicly dishonored me before all of Heian Kyo. Dinner for fishes now. Poor Kiyosi.'' He stopped and eyed her with a gleeful hatred.

She would show no feeling. "If Lord Sogamori heard you speak that way of his son, you yourself would be dinner for dogs.''

"But through me, Lord Sogamori will be avenged for the death of his son. I come to the Mongols as a secret envoy from His Excellency, Chia Ssu-tao. As a neutral, I have been asked to tell the Mongols that His Excellency recognizes the futility of resistance. He intends to make it easy for them to defeat the Sung, in return for which he asks high office in the empire of the Great Khan. I have already persuaded Chia Ssu-tao that Yukio, the monk and their men are traitors and outlaws in their own land and a potential danger to him. A Mongol army now besieges Kweilin, the city in the southwest which Yukio and his samurai are defending. Now, to rid himself of these undesirables, and to prove his good faith to the Mongols, Chia Ssu-tao intends to let them take Kweilin. The city cannot hold out without reinforcements. None will be sent. Kweilin will be overrun, and the surviving samurai, in accordance with Mongol practice, will be put to death. So your beloved Zinja, my dear, will die. Think of that while the Mongols are using you for their pleasure.''

Taniko raised her head, her long fingernails poised to rake his face. But she held herself back.

"Please strike at me.'' Horigawa smiled. "It would give me such pleasure to knock you into the dirt before these barbarians who imagine you to be such a great lady.''

The wrinkled Chinese who served the Mongols called out, "Your Highness. Our lord the Kahn is prepared to see you now.''

Horigawa nodded. "Good-bye, Taniko. I shall never look upon you again, but I shall always revel in the thought of your utter degradation.''

As Horigawa accompanied the Chinese official into the

presence of the Mongol overlord, another Chinese ushered Taniko to a smaller tent, where, with the rest of Horigawa's retinue, she awaited her fate.

8.

The day after *tuman-bashi* Torluk's mission to Kweilin, the drums in the Mongol camp began to beat in the late afternoon. The Chinese prisoners were herded out of their pen and set to pulling the siege machines to the edges of the moat. Dismounted, the Mongol troops marched in rows to the attack. The three white horsetails of their battle standard moved forward. Yukio ordered all available men in the city to the walls. His drummers struck up a rhythm to inspire the defenders.

Shortly before sunset the Mongols' portable bridges crashed down across the west side of the moat. The *hua pao* at the base of the Mongols' wooden wall boomed in unison. Iron balls smashed into the ramparts of Kweilin. Catapults flung explosive balls and huge stones into the streets of the city.

Kweilin's *hua pao* replied, blowing holes in the Mongols' wooden wall. The samurai dropped pots of burning oil on the enemy bridges and set them afire before more than a handful of men could cross the moat.

The Mongols forced their Chinese prisoners to lead the attack as human shields. The prisoners were slaughtered by volleys of arrows from the walls fired by men who pretended not to know whom they were killing.

All that night the Mongols kept coming. Using horses, siege machines, cartloads of earth and human bodies to bridge the moat, they fought to get at Kweilin's walls. They seemed determined to press the attack unceasingly until they took the city. Such a lust for victory, Jebu's Zinja training had taught him, often led to failure.

But he was awed by their sheer energy. Growing up on Kyushu, he had been through many of the great storms the Chinese called *tai-phun*. The Mongols attacked like a *tai-phun*, threatening to destroy all in its path. Even as he fought them off with arrows, with naginata and with sword, Jebu recognized in himself a contrary pride that these demons in human form were his people.

At last, at dawn, the assault waves stopped. The few troops remaining on the strip of ground just below the walls scrambled back across the moat, chased by samurai and Chinese arrows. The *hua pao* stopped spitting fire. The Mongol catapults kept hurling stones and fire bombs over, but less frequently. The many fires throughout the city were under control.

There was no sunrise. Thick gray clouds rolled in from the south and, to Yukio's satisfaction, it began to rain heavily. Rain would protect the city from fire and greatly hamper the besiegers.

Jebu and Yukio sat by the parapet and wiped the blood from their swords to keep them from becoming pitted. "We lose so many each time we fight the Mongols that soon there will be none of us left," Yukio said wearily. "What a poor leader I am, having brought these men this far, for them all to die in a strange land."

Governor Liu came down from his ivory chair of state and gripped Yukio and Jebu by the arms. "You should be sleeping, not wasting your time talking to this old man."

Jebu smiled into the governor's red-rimmed eyes. "I doubt that His Excellency has slept this night."

Yukio reported that two hundred Chinese troops and over a hundred samurai were dead or badly wounded. But the two white dragons were still flying over Kweilin.

The governor said, "My scouts say the Mongol *tarkhan*, Arghun Baghadur, is on his way with reinforcements of two more *tumans*, twenty thousand men, which his master, the Great Khan Mangu, has assigned to him. With a general like Arghun leading them and outnumbering us so greatly, the Mongols will surely take Kweilin. We are entering the season of heavy rains, and that may slow them down, but the end is still inevitable.''

''We have been promised that if we need reinforcements they could be sent here by way of the Kwei Kiang from Canton,'' Yukio said.

''It is time to send for them,'' said Liu. He beckoned to his son, an officer of high rank among the Chinese troops. The younger Liu's armor was nicked and battered. He stepped away from the wall of the governor's audience room and knelt at his feet.

''You will go to Canton, my son. You will sail tonight from the river gate.''

Five of the nomads, men too badly wounded to fight to the death, had been taken prisoner, and Jebu managed to convince the samurai that these men would be more useful to them alive than dead. Each day he spent some time visiting the prisoners in the stone building near the governor's palace, doctoring their wounds and conversing with them.

At first they talked in Chinese, which most Mongols knew because northern China had been part of their territory for almost a generation. It was hard for Jebu to understand their dialect, almost a different language from the southern Chinese he was used to. Among themselves the nomad warriors spoke Mongolian, and Jebu learned some of the words and used them when he talked to them. In time their conversation was more and more in Mongolian.

The Mongols distrusted Jebu. Aside from the suspicion of prisoners of war toward any captor, they recognized, as Torluk had, his Mongol features. They assumed he was a traitor, captured in an earlier battle, who had agreed to serve the Chinese in order to save his life. They guessed he had been sent to persuade them to do the same, and they offered to kill him if he would only come close enough.

To the distress of the Chinese guards, Jebu selected the biggest Mongol and fought him barehanded in the courtyard of the prison building. His opponent was the only one of the prisoners who had not been seriously wounded; he had been found unconscious on Kweilin's wall, where a rock, apparently catapulted from his own side, had struck him. It was traditional, bone-cracking, Mongol-style wrestling against Zinja unarmed combat techniques. Jebu threw the big Mongol five times.

Once he had earned their respect and convinced them he wanted no military information, the Mongols grew friendlier. They came to realize that Jebu really did not know Mongolian and therefore could not be a turncoat from their own side.

For his part, Jebu soon felt a certain affection for his near countrymen. These five, four of them wounded and sitting in a prison cell, bored and apprehensive, seemed far from being the brutal warriors of legend. Jebu found them simple, illiterate, young, quick to laugh, courageous and kind to one another.

He also discovered that they were fond of drink. He ordered a few jars of rice wine sent into their cell. Within an hour it was gone and they were calling for more. Their appetite for wine was bottomless, and Jebu had to limit their ration to prevent them from being drunk all the time. In their cups they tended to be merry, not belligerent. The language lessons went better with the help of a little wine.

He was starting to understand the Mongol way of life. These young Mongols had grown up enjoying the ease and wealth of the empire Genghis Khan had created, but their parents and grandparents had told them of the older times when not a season went by without at least one death in every family. The world of ice and desert and steppe never relaxes, never gives a second chance. The laws and customs of the Mongols were modeled after the laws of nature, or as the Mongols themselves called it, Eternal Heaven.

Days of inactivity passed behind the wooden wall of the besiegers and the stone walls of Kweilin. Jebu acquired a smattering of Mongolian. Yukio and Governor Liu directed repairs on the city and its fortifications. Everyone watched the river for signs of transport junks bringing a relief expedition.

Twelve days after the unsuccessful assault on Kweilin, word came from Governor Liu's scouts that Arghun Baghadur had returned from his visit to Mangu Khan in Szechwan province.

"Do we launch another attack on them to demonstrate how much we are to be feared?" Yukio asked Jebu as they stood on the wall watching the two additional *tumans* Arghun had brought with him set up camp.

"Suppose I toss you off the wall into their midst. That should frighten them."

Moko, who was on the walls with them, watching the arrival of the Mongol reinforcements, said, "I have been trying to design a catapult that would toss me out of this city and safely across the Kwei Kiang to the opposite bank."

After setting up their *yurts*, as they called their round felt tents, the new arrivals remounted their horses. They formed up in squares of a hundred mounted men, a whole *tuman* containing a hundred such squares, ten across and ten deep. The five *tumans* that made up the army besieging Kweilin formed in a semicircle wider than the city itself on the southern shore of the two lakes. Fifty thousand cavalrymen faced the city. Beyond them, drawn up in parade formation, were new siege machines and masses of auxiliary troops from the nations the Mongols had conquered.

Jebu felt a chill go through his body. Even for a Zinja—a Zinja hardened by fifteen years of almost continuous combat— the Mongol army was a terrifying sight. He had never seen an army this large. He doubted whether all the samurai in the Sunrise Land, gathered together, would present a specatcle like this. No wonder men were so terrified of the Mongols that some of them surrendered at the first news of their approach.

Yukio, beside him, let out a deep breath. "How foolish I was to think my little band could stand against something like this." He shook his head sadly.

A bannerman rode out before the massed Mongol troops, carrying the three-horsetail battle standard of the army. Now Jebu noticed that each *tuman* had a standard of its own planted in the ground before the massed squares of cavalry. The banner carrier drove the pointed base of his standard pole into the ground in the center of the field, just by the joining of the two lakes. How many battles, Jebu wondered, had these six standards seen? Over how many nations had they triumphed?

Five more horsemen rode into the open center of the field, one from each *tuman*. They formed a semicircle behind the battle standard.

"The *tuman-bashis*," Yukio said.

The army before the city and the spectators on the walls

seemed to hold their breath. A horn blared. Down from the hills beyond Kweilin rode a single horseman on a steppe pony.

He could have his pick of any horse in the conquered territories, Jebu thought. He could ride a huge black stallion or a white charger. He could have a horse worth a kingdom. But he chooses, when he shows himself to his army and to his enemy, the same sort of pony he has ridden all his life, the sort his ancestors have ridden for thousands of years before him.

The only sound was the clatter of one horse's hooves. The rider's red cloak streamed out behind him, showing his red lacquered armor.

It's strange, thought Jebu. I'm seeing the man who murdered my father, and yet he makes me think of my father. My father must have been a man very like him, and so he restores my father to me.

Arghun Baghadur rode out before the battle standard of his army. The five generals facing him got down from their horses, ceremoniously unbuckled their belts and draped them over their shoulders, took off their helmets and put them on the ground.

Arghun spoke to them and acknowledged their submission with an inclination of his head. The *tuman-bashis* stood up and remounted. Arghun turned to face his troops. Again there was a moment as if the world held its breath. Then a roar went up from fifty thousand throats.

Arghun stood in his stirrups and addressed his *tumans*. His voice boomed across the parade ground, but he was too far away for those on the walls of the city to hear him.

"We'll find out later what he is saying," a voice said beside Jebu. "My scouts will tell us."

Yukio bowed to the governor. "Your Excellency need not expose yourself to danger in order to see what is happening among the barbarians."

Liu smiled. A party of Chinese guardsmen and silk-robed city officials stood behind him. Jebu saw that he had been carried to the top of the wall in a sedan chair.

"When those who govern refuse to go out and see for themselves, the country is lost," said Liu.

Across the two lakes Arghun raised his arm in a signal. A

hill in the distant camp seemed to move. It lumbered down toward Arghun, followed by another gigantic gray shape, then another. For a moment Jebu could not understand what he was seeing. Finally he recognized that four enormous animals, the largest creatures he had ever seen, were moving toward Arghun. They were covered with brightly colored cloths under which armor gleamed. High on the back of each animal was a rider who occupied a little castle. The beasts were fantastic under their armor—a high, domed head; a nose as long as a tree limb, with a serpentine life of its own; two white spears, each the length of a man and the thickness of a leg, jutting out from either side of the mouth.

Jebu had seen such a beast before. After a moment he remembered where. It had been one of the strange animals he had seen in his vision of the Tree of Life, when Taitaro first gave him the shintai. He reached into his robe and rubbed the Jewel with his fingertips.

"Is it some kind of dragon?" Yukio whispered.

"It is a creature that is as terrible for the fear it inspires as for the damage it can do," said Liu. "They are much used in warfare by the nations to the south of us. I had heard that the Mongols acquired some war elephants when they invaded Nan Chao and Annam some years ago."

The elephants formed a line before Arghun, and the Mongols cheered the beasts with a roar. The elephants answered with a sound as of trumpets blown by giants.

Jebu felt an impulse from deep within, perhaps from the Self. "We have been tame spectators of Arghun's parade long enough." Drawing a willow-leaf arrow from his quiver, Jebu nocked it and took aim at the center of Arghun's back.

"That little bow will never carry that far," said Liu.

"That little bow may surprise you, Your Excellency," said Yukio.

Jebu fired. A gust of wind sweeping down the river valley deflected the arrow. It arced over the counterwall and landed at the feet of Arghun's horse.

Immediately the Mongol dismounted and picked up the arrow. He examined it for a moment, then turned and looked up at the wall. A great distance separated them, but Jebu could see clearly the upturned face, the deep-set eyes, the rocklike cheekbones, the thick red moustache. He could not see Arghun's eyes, but he knew the *tarkhan* must be looking right at him.

He realized now that he had wanted Arghun to know that he was here. That was why he had shot at him. He had no wish to kill Arghun from this distance. Some day Arghun must die by his hand and must know that it was he, Jebu, son of Jamuga, who had done it.

Across the gulf that separated the walls of the Chinese city from the Mongol camp, the two men stared at each other.

Yukio took his longbow from the wall where it had been leaning and sent an arrow winging at Arghun. Other samurai followed his example. A hail of arrows fell around the Mongol leader.

With their bodies, the *tuman-bashis* shielded Arghun from the flights of arrows. They led him under the wooden wall of their encampment. A line of Mongol heavy cavalry, mounted archers with powerful crossbows, trotted out into the parade ground and returned the fire from the city. A *hua pao* mounted on a wooden Mongol tower boomed; then another. An iron ball crashed into the parapet, sending splinters of rock flying in all directions, and a man fell with a head wound.

Jebu positioned himself in front of the governor. "This is too dangerous a place for you, Your Excellency."

Liu waved away Jebu's words with a slender hand. "I am the least important person on these walls." But he allowed Jebu to hurry him to his sedan chair.

The duel of arrows had turned into a general battle of archery and artillery. Across the lake the Mongol formations were moving aside as the auxiliary troops and siege machines, shielded by civilian prisoners, began to advance. The battle for Kweilin had begun in earnest. It would not end, Jebu thought, until the city had fallen.

9

"Until yesterday, I had not seen Arghun again since that night," Jebu said. "He did not continue to pursue me but left the Sacred Islands."

"When was that?" asked Governor Liu.

"In the last Year of the Ape, Your Excellency."

"Eleven years ago," said Liu. "That was when the Great Khan Kuyuk died. Whenever a Great Khan dies, the Mongols stop whatever they are doing, wherever they are, and return to their homeland to elect a new Great Khan. Kuyuk was the grandson of Genghis Khan. He was the third of the Great Khans. Mangu is the fourth."

A Chinese officer entered the governor's audience chamber. "The Mongol commander has sent another emissary, Your Excellency. He asks for a meeting with the governor and the military commander of the city."

Liu turned to Jebu. "You have met this man before. Your observations might be valuable. Please come with us."

"I would be honored," said Jebu.

Yukio said, "He has been determined to kill you since you were an infant. If we cross the moat to parley with him, he might very well have you assassinated on the spot."

"We will not cross the moat," said Liu. "We will meet with him on the temple island in Lake Shan hu. He will not have his men with him, and he will be covered by our archers on the walls."

"If I come as an envoy he will not harm me," said Jebu. "That is the Mongol law."

On an island in the center of Lake Shan hu stood a small, exquisite Buddhist temple built centuries before. Neither the

293

Mongols nor the Chinese cared to damage it, and the octago-
nal stupa with its copper ornament had miraculously escaped
accidental harm despite the many rocks and fire missiles that
had flown over it. Still, the Buddha taught the Middle Way,
neither self-indulgence nor self-destruction, and the monks of
the temple were not foolhardy. In accordance with the Middle
Way they had long since abandoned the temple. Liu and
Arghun now agreed on it as a site for their meeting.

A gold and red boat with a dragon figurehead, brought
around through the moat from the river gate, carried Liu,
Yukio and Jebu to the island. Two flag bearers, a Chinese
carrying the White Dragon of Kweilin and a samurai with the
White Dragon of Muratomo, made up the rest of the party.
They disembarked and stood before the gateway of the low
wall around the little temple.

Arghun and an officer carrying the standard of the three
white horsetails were borne from the opposite shore in a
sampan. Arghun's only adornment was the square gold
medallion of rank, which he wore on a chain around his neck.

His face had changed little since Jebu had last seen him,
eleven years ago. The long wings of his red moustache hung
below his beardless chin. His eyes, narrow and icy blue,
stared implacably at Jebu. Jebu stared back and heard Yukio
draw a breath and move defensively closer to him.

He tried to control his emotions as he had been taught. He
admitted to himself that he was afraid. He could not visualize
himself defeating Arghun in battle. At the same time, he
could not forget the old saying, "A man may not live under
the same heaven with the slayer of his father." Sooner or
later, he must kill Arghun.

But that was not a Zinja saying. As a Zinja, he was not the
son of Jamuga, he was not the person Arghun wanted to kill,
he was not the person who had a blood debt to kill Arghun.
He was simply a manifestation of the Self, and the Self was
everywhere, in Arghun as well as in Jebu.

Still, he could not resist addressing Arghun in a Mongol
speech he had learned and memorized, "Greetings, murderer
of my father."

Arghun stopped walking toward them and stared at Jebu
with his cold blue eyes. In Mongol he said, "So you have

learned the language of your father. Yet you fight against your father's people.''

''I fight my father's murderer.''

''There is no place for you in the world. You will not find your home on earth until you lie in it.''

Liu spoke. ''Have you come to exchange threats with this monk or to meet with the rulers of Kweilin?''

Arghun bowed politely to the governor. ''This monk is the reason I called this parley,'' he said in Chinese. ''I have a duty to fulfill. The spirit of Genghis Khan will not rest until this monk is dead.''

''It appears that your Great Khan demands death for all of us,'' said Yukio. ''That you harbor a particular hunger to take vengeance on our comrade is nothing to us.''

Arghun's hard mouth curved in a faint smile. ''You are wrong. It is important to you. It may save your lives. Were the decision mine, I would kill all of you when the city falls.''

''You insult us,'' said Yukio. ''You speak as if the outcome were already decided.''

Arghun nodded. ''I merely say what is so. I do not think that it will be difficult to take this city. I have conquered fourteen cities since the Great Khan graciously made me one of his *tarkhans*. Some were larger and better defended than this one. I do not think a handful of men from the Land of the Dwarfs will trouble us for long.''

''You know better than that, Arghun,'' said Jebu. ''You have been to our land. You have seen samurai fight. You have fought alongside them.''

''Do you, half Mongol and half dwarf, think of it as your land?'' Arghun spoke the very thought that sometimes darkened Jebu's life when he was alone—his feeling of being a stranger everywhere. There were moments when even the Zinja doctrine, even the contemplation of the Jewel of Life and Death, was not enough to drive away the sadness. He reminds me of this now, Jebu thought, because he wants to weaken me by discouraging me, to make me easier to kill. I must remember that I am the Self, and that is all I need to know.

Arghun turned to Yukio and Liu. ''The men of the Land of

the Dwarfs are fierce fighters, but they are ignorant of siege warfare."

"We will give them the benefit of our knowledge," said Liu.

"Even so, I will take your city. When I do, unless you agree to one condition, I will level it to the ground and execute every soul living in it."

"What condition?" said Liu.

Arghun pointed at Jebu. "Let me take the monk back with me when I return to my camp. He will die an honorable death. He is related to our ruling family. According to the law, the *Yassa*, the blood of such a person may not be spilled. He will be strangled with a bow string. It is a death reserved for those of high birth."

"Let me defend myself with my sword, and you may attempt to kill me with a bow string," said Jebu.

"You jest, but you have it in your power to save the lives of these men here, of your samurai comrades and of all the people of the city."

"We will not consider it," said Liu quietly.

It is my death we are discussing, Jebu thought. I find this hard to believe.

"Suppose we surrender the entire city here and now," Liu said.

"Surrender the city and the monk, and you will contine as governor. The dwarfs we will take prisoner, but they will be treated well. The Great Khan Mangu's younger brother, Kublai Khan, has expressed a desire to see them."

"But Jebu will die?"

"The monk must die."

"And if we permit him to escape and then surrender?" Liu persisted.

"The city will be destroyed and its people put to the sword."

Liu said, "Because you have a yearning to kill this monk, you are willing to sacrifice the lives of thousands of your men, who will surely die trying to take this city. And you will throw away the city and the lives of all in it."

Arghun raised his gauntleted hands in an appeal to heaven. "They have understood nothing." He shook his head at Liu. "It is the command of Genghis Khan that all those of the blood of Jamuga be slain. Any Mongol would die happily to carry out his command.''

Jebu had a sudden overwhelming conviction of what he must do. He saw it so clearly, he knew it must be what Taitaro called a Zinja insight.

He stepped forward. ''Give us your oath that you will spare the city, whether it is surrendered to you or whether you take it by force, and I will go with you now.''

He hoped that none of them would hear the slight tremor he himself detected in his voice. It was absurd that Liu and Yukio should think his life worth the lives of all the people of Kweilin and the warriors who defended them. They might believe it dishonorable to yield a comrade to death at an enemy's hands. But if so many lives could be saved in that way, it made no sense to protect one life.

''No,'' said Yukio. ''I forbid it.''

''I also,'' said Liu. ''You would die for nothing. He would simply find another excuse to destroy the city.''

''I believe that he will abide by his word.''

Liu said, ''Let me speak with you.'' Taking Jebu by the arm, he led him down to the rocky shore of the island. Yukio and Arghun waited in silence.

Jebu said, ''I am a Zinja monk, Your Excellency. I do not cling to anything, even life.''

''Here in our land your Order is called *Ch'in-cha*,'' said Liu. ''I know something of its teachings. If you did not offer to die to save so many thousands of lives, you would not be a true *Ch'in-cha*. But for you actually to sacrifice yourself would be foolish. And it would show you lack the *Ch'in-cha* wisdom.''

Jebu studied the old man's calm face curiously. Liu's black eyes seemed to give off a radiance.

''I am prepared to listen,'' Jebu said.

''If you accept Arghun's view of things, he has already imprisoned your mind, and he can kill you whenever he chooses. The future is closed to you. But as a member of the Order, you should know that no single view of anything is true, that the number of gates we face is always infinite. If you choose to go on living, many things might happen. You might be killed anyway, in battle. The Emperor might send reinforcements and drive the Mongols off. Arghun might be

killed in battle and his accursed quest for your death would
perhaps die with him. A plague might strike and wipe out all
of us, besiegers and defenders. Or the Mongols might suddenly decide to lift the siege and go away.''

"That will never happen. The Mongols never give up.''

"You are quite an authority on Mongols, young monk. But
I forget you are part Mongol yourself. Withdraw your offer to
give yourself up to Arghun. I believe that life has more to
teach you, and that this is not your time to die.''

"I see nothing ahead of me.'' Jebu had tasted the sweetness of life and now life seemed altogether bitter. He had
known Taniko and lost her. He had known victory in battle
and then had been driven from his homeland in defeat.

Liu said, ''The Ch'in-cha finds his happiness in nothing.''

"You know that?''

Liu smiled. "And the Ch'in-cha believes in nothing. Yet,
you believe it is right for you to sacrifice yourself. But you
have been taught that there is no right and wrong. The
Ch'in-cha do not believe in good or evil.'' He paused, and
his black eyes held Jebu's. "The Ch'in-cha are devils.''

Jebu did not think, after all he had seen and done, that he
could ever be greatly surprised again. But this moment left
him voiceless. He could only stand and stare at Liu in wonder. He did not know if he dared say anything at all.

"Not all of us wear gray robes and live in monasteries,''
said Liu. "Have I convinced you not to throw away your life
because of Arghun?''

Jebu bowed. "For now, Excellency, you have. I do not
know why you have spoken to me as you have. I do not know
if there is any reason why I should listen to you. I have no
way of knowing if you are truly one of us or simply a person
who has learned some of our secrets. But your words convince me, and I must follow my convictions.''

"That is all I hoped for.''

They went back to where Yukio and Arghun were standing, Liu walking first, Jebu a respectful distance behind.

"The young monk has decided that you have no right to
demand his life,'' Liu said to Arghun. Yukio shot a relieved
grin at Jebu.

Arghun's expression did not change. "He condemns your
city to death.''

''If you do conquer the city and kill all who live here,'' Liu said, ''the guilt will be upon you. Nothing requires that you put so many people to death but your own thirst for blood.''

Arghun turned to his standard-bearer and beckoned. The warrior went back to their sampan and took a large mahogany box from the bow. He carried it back to Arghun and laid it at his feet.

''I have brought this gift for you, Governor Liu Mai-tse,'' said Arghun. ''You have been expecting reinforcements to help you withstand the siege. Understand now that you are doomed.'' Arghun bent down, undid the catch on the box and stepped back.

Yukio looked questioningly at Liu. Jebu held his breath, a terrible suspicion of what the box contained sweeping over him. Governor Liu signaled to Jebu to open the box.

Within it lay the pale, bloodless head of Governor Liu's son, on a bed of straw.

10

''I will not let them crush me,'' Taniko told herself over and over again. Not Horigawa and not the Mongols. They might rape and kill her, as they had that poor woman on the road. They might, as Horigawa predicted, enslave her and grind her down until she ended her life as a ravaged old woman. But there was that within her, that which was not Shima Taniko, the vulnerable woman, which no one could destroy. That could be what Jebu meant by the Self.

After she had waited a long time in a felt tent with the other members of Horigawa's party, two Chinese men beckoned her and escorted her a short distance to another tent. She heard the voices of men singing around the campfires. She couldn't understand the words, but the songs were plaintive and moving. The Chinese men left her alone.

The tent was dark and reeked of smoke and sweat. It had a cylindrical latticework wall and a flattened conical ceiling whose spokes, radiating from two central poles, reminded her of a parasol. There were layers of thick, soft rugs on the floor, woven in intricate patterns, and she sat on silk cushions. So this was the sort of place in which Jebu's people lived. Thinking of Jebu reminded her of Horigawa's prediction that Jebu would be killed by the Mongols. Horigawa had tried to kill him before and failed. She prayed to the Buddha to help Jebu live.

Unable to keep track of the time, she brooded, circling again and again through boredom, fear and hopelessness. She would probably never see the Sacred Islands again. Or Jebu. She threw herself down on the cushions and wept.

She had had chances to kill Horigawa. Why had she never done it? She decided that if she ever met him again she would cut his throat without a word of warning and take the consequences. What a fool she had been to imagine that some good might come of this journey to China.

She sat up. The pillow on which her head had rested was soaked with tears. Her face was ruined. She found a pitcher of water and a basin and washed her hands and face. Her makeup box had been taken from her along with all her other clothes. There was no mirror. She desperately wanted a bath. The air in the tent was warm and close, and she could feel herself sweating. These Mongols probably never bathed. Just as the rumors foretold, they did stink abominably. The entire camp smelled of the greasy, unwashed bodies of meat eaters.

One small oil lamp struggled vainly with the shadows around her in the circular room. Through a round opening in the center of the tent roof she could see a patch of black sky with a single star in it. It was a warm, windless night.

As the oil lamp flickered lower, she lay in the near darkness and called upon the Lord of Boundless Light. "Homage to Amida Buddha." After awhile she sank into the long, heavy sleep of the despairing.

* * *

In the morning one of the Chinese men brought her food, coarse cakes and wine, and put more coals on the fire. She tried to ask him questions, but he would not answer her.

The tent was provided with a porcelain pot for her to relieve herself. She had fresh water now, and she took off all her clothes and washed herself thoroughly. The cool water refreshed her.

After dressing, she went to the doorway of the tent and opened the low wooden door. Bright sunlight and dust assailed her. All around her she had heard the bustle of men and horses. She had not realized until now how quiet the Mongol tents were.

A guard in a silk coat snapped at her in his language and waved her back into the tent. She went back and sat down, and considered how she might escape.

She had as much chance of eluding the Mongol horsemen as a baby rabbit trying to escape a falcon. And even if she did, how could she survive in an unknown, war-ravaged countryside? She was even more likely to meet injury or death if she ran away from here than if she stayed.

She had lost everyone and everything she loved. It scarcely mattered what the Mongols did with her. Again she sat down and buried her face in her hands and cried.

After a time, though, the tears stopped flowing. She was doing precisely what Horigawa would want her to, letting herself be ground between the millstones of monotony and despair until she had no power to resist her fate. She reminded herself that she was samurai. She remembered that she had resolved not to let them crush her. She stood and clenched her fists.

A Mongol woman's round face appeared in the doorway.

"May Eternal Heaven send you good fortune," she greeted Taniko in Chinese. "I am Bourkina, servant of our lord Kublai Khan."

Bourkina might be anywhere from thirty to seventy years of age. She wore a yellow Chinese silk robe and a heavy necklace of gold and jade that hung down to her waist. Her stride was long, her gestures commanding, almost mannish. She reminded Taniko of peasant women she had seen, women who worked constantly and lacked the delicate manners of well born ladies. She might enjoy silk and jade now, but she had surely been born in poverty. Her hair and eyes were dark, and Taniko could see in her no resemblance to Jebu.

Bourkina was solicitous. Was Taniko comfortable? Did she need anything? All Taniko's belongings would be delivered to her later in the day, as soon as they could be located. Bourkina asked what sort of food Taniko preferred and said she would do her best to see that she enjoyed her meals. In all this concern Taniko sensed little warmth. It was as if Bourkina had been placed in charge of a valuable horse and were seeing to its needs. With the advantage, in this case, that the horse could talk. But this horse wanted to do more than talk.

"May I have writing materials?"

Bourkina looked astonished. "What for?"

"I like to write down what I see and think."

Bourkina looked at her as if she had suddenly sprouted wings. "How did you learn to write?"

"In my country all people of good family are taught to read and write. Women, of course, write a language different from that of men, but it serves our purposes quite well."

"Among our people women do not read or write at all, and only a few men do. Our Great Khan Mangu and our lord Kublai Khan and their two brothers are all considered scholars. But they are most unusual men.

"You speak Chinese. That is a mark of learning in my country."

Bourkina smiled proudly. "It is a necessity for us Mongols. How else could we give orders to our slaves?"

"What has become of Prince Horigawa and his party?"

"Your master delivered his message from the Sung Emperor's Court to Kublai Khan and left."

"He is my husband, not my master." Since Horigawa had told the Mongols she was a mere courtesan, she must try to show that she was a person of consequence.

"Your husband left you with us as a gift?" Bourkina's face showed mingled shock and disbelief.

"A husband and wife can be enemies."

Bourkina shrugged. "It does not matter what you were before you came to us. My task now is to determine your present value."

Taniko felt her face grow hot. "I know what my value is." I will not be treated like a sack of rice, she thought.

The Mongol woman thrust her round face into Taniko's "Listen. Those who can't live with us, die. You must realize, if you want to live, that Eternal Heaven has given my people the whole earth to rule as we see fit. Forget what you were before. You will find your proper place among us."

Taniko sighed and nodded. This woman's talk might sound like wild boasting, but it was simply the truth as the Mongols saw it. Unless Taniko chose to die at once, she would have to learn the ways of this new world.

"I simply meant that I do not want—I want to be something more than a woman for your men to use."

Bourkin smiled. "Our lord Kublai Khan requires us to be most careful in determining the value of each person and thing."

"How will you determine my value?"

Bourkina sat down on the cushions and gestured to Taniko to sit beside her. She snapped her fingers and a Chinese boy hurried in with a lacquer tray bearing blue and white porcelain cups and a pot of Chinese *ch'ai*—the same beverage the Takashi had been importing into the Sacred Islands.

"Tell me about yourself," Bourkina said.

Sipping the steaming green liquid, Taniko began the story of her life, not in any orderly way, but taking each fact as it came to mind. She realized that, pleasant as Bourkina seemed, it was her task to pass judgment on the strange woman from across the sea. Therefore, like a calligrapher, concerned as much with the beautiful appearance of each word as with its meaning, Taniko tried to shape each part of her story to present herself to Bourkina in the best possible light. She stressed her breeding and learning, her association with the great men of her own land, her marriage to a prince.

"He said nothing about your being his wife."

"What did he say of me?"

"In China there are many women who sell their bodies for gold or silver—or for a bowl of rice. The prince said that in your land you were such a woman. He said you were the concubine of a nobleman in your country. The nobleman was killed, and you threatened to make a scandal because he left you no part of his wealth. As a favor to the family, the prince took you away with him on his journey to China."

Taniko shut her eyes. She felt herself about to cry, remembering Kiyosi and Atsue. But this Mongol woman would only despise her for her tears. She masked her feelings.

"I was, as I told you, a woman of noble family married to Prince Horigawa. He and I were estranged and I did, indeed, become the consort of a man who was not simply a noble, but the heir of the most powerful family on our islands and commander of all our warriors. I had a son by him. When he was killed in battle, I wanted none of his wealth. I only asked to keep our son, but he was torn from me by his father's family. I was taken out of the country so I could not protest."

"How many children have you had?"

"Two. I had a daughter, and Prince Horigawa killed her because she was not his."

Bourkina said, "Among my people the penalty for adultery is death. For both the man and the woman."

Taniko was astonished. "Death? If that were the law in my land, all the best families would be wiped out." Instantly she wished she had not said so. If the Mongols considered it a great crime to couple with someone other than your spouse, perhaps Bourkina would think Horigawa's low estimate of her to be accurate.

"The prince despised me long before I lay with any other man," she said. "He married me only because my family is wealthy."

Bourkina patted her hand. "I have seen the prince. He is not much of a man. And he is a fool to have given away a woman as clever and pretty as you. You have every reason to have strayed from his pasture." She stood up. "Now let me help you undress."

"Undress? Must I?"

"We have talked for a while now, and I know something of your life and your mind. But you are not being considered for a post as a general or an ambassador. I want to see whether your body is beautiful and without blemish."

Taniko sighed and stood. "Then it is true that I am nothing more than a vessel to be used by men."

There was a note of irritation in Bourkina's voice. "You know too much of the world to talk that way. A woman's fortune is founded on her beauty, just as a man's rests on his strength. It is obvious enough, though, that your worth does not end with your body. If you were merely to be given to the troops for their pleasure, do you think I would have spent this much time with you?''

It took Taniko some time to undress. She removed robe, jacket, skirts and dresses. She had bound her hair up for convenience while traveling. Now she let it fall to her waist, and the Mongol woman's thin eyebrows went up. Finally Taniko undid the last robe and handed it to Bourkina, who let it fall to the cushions as she appraised Taniko.

Taniko had never been embarrassed by nudity, especially in front of other women. When a man and a woman came together, they did not desire complete nakedness. The most attractive way was to open your clothes just enough to permit glimpses of your body and to give your lover access to yourself. But complete nudity for practical reasons, such as when bathing or changing clothes, was commonplace, and in her own household Taniko often saw women and even men naked.

No one, however, had ever examined her as closely as Bourkina did. Without a word the Mongol woman walked all around her, squinting at her from the crown of her head to her toes.

''You do not bind your feet like the Chinese. That is good. We find that custom ugly.''

Now Bourkina began to touch her. Taniko shrank from the Mongol woman's rough hands, and Bourkina ordered her sharply to stand still. Taniko felt like a melon being probed by a household cook. Bourkina peeled back her lips and poked at her teeth. She smelled her breath. She kneaded Taniko's breasts, pinched her nipples and felt her buttocks. She ran her fingertips over Taniko's belly.

''Not bad. Only a few stretch marks. You had two children, you say? How old are you?''

Taniko quickly decided that she could have lost five years in the China Sea. ''Twenty-three.''

''You are between twenty-five and thirty. But your small size and light weight have kept your body young. To a man, you might pass for even younger than twenty-three. Now lie on your back and open your legs.''

Taniko knew better by now than to protest. She lay back on the cushions, turning her head away and gritting her teeth as the Mongol woman peered and probed inside her.

"Good. Childbearing has not made you slack. You appear to be free of disease. Put some clothing on." Bourkina beamed, the round, brown face stretched by a broad grin. "May I presume that you are as expert in the arts of the bed as a married woman who has also had two lovers should be?"

"I suppose so," said Taniko.

"Are you prepared to use those arts with enthusiasm, in order to live well among us?"

"What is to become of me? You must tell me that."

Bourkina held up her hand. "I don't yet know for sure. I have to make my report. Then it will be decided. Meanwhile, your clothing and possessions will be brought to you. You will bathe. You will array yourself in your finest robes, as for your wedding night. Make yourself as beautiful as you know how to. You have until sunset." Bourkina moved to the doorway of the *yurt*, her yellow silk robe swirling about her.

"You come from a land so different from my own that I find it hard to see it in my mind. Yet there are qualities in you I like. You are strong. You are quick-witted, and you have lived long enough to acquire some wisdom. I will give you a little advice. Do not try, because you are among Mongols, to appear beautiful in the Mongol manner. Make yourself beautiful according to the custom of your land, no matter how strange you think it might seem to us. You are a woman of experience. You understand men and you have attracted great ones to you. Do not be frightened. Try to be calm and cheerful. Behave as you would in your own home among friends and family."

"Why do you assume that I am calm and cheerful in my own home?" asked Taniko. Bourkina laughed.

"I understand your advice," Taniko said. "You are kind. Thank you." Remembering that Bourkina was one of Jebu's people, Taniko felt a sudden surge of affection for the big woman.

Bourkina smiled at her again. "I am always happy to help a woman who deserves it. Prepare yourself now, little lady."

"I will. Please remember to send paper, ink and brush."

11

Taniko asked the Chinese maid holding the large mirror to circle her slowly. She held a small mirror in her own hand, and when the maid was behind her, she swept her long black hair to one side and studied the nape of her neck. Pure white, slender, defenseless. As it should look.

Red, she felt, was her most seductive color, so she had chosen a costume built up of layers of red. Outermost, though, was a richly embroidered overrobe of light green. It made her look young and innocent. The innocence would cover passion, a dark red robe. The sleeves of an unlined dress of deep red damask peeped from beneath the two outer robes. Beneath these she wore three underrobes of different shades of plum red, all visible at her throat, sleeves and skirt.

When she was fully dressed, only her fingertips and her face were visible in the midst of the flowing silks. The two Chinese women who were helping her to dress tried to keep blank, impassive expressions, but Taniko caught them darting curious looks at her. Would she be laughed at tonight? She could imagine how the courtiers at Heian Kyo would make fun of a Mongol woman trying, in her native clothing, to make a good impression.

But she knew that she had not beautified herself this much since Kiyosi died. Horigawa might hope for her degradation, but she would thwart his hopes. She would not let them crush her. She called on the Lord of Boundless Light.

She had one of the maids tuck a cloth into her neckline to protect her outer robe. She seated herself on cushions and drew her box of makeup to her, asking one of the maids to hold up the mirror. She applied a layer of white paint to her face. From this moment her face must remain frozen. She could neither smile nor weep. She dipped a brush into a jar of red pigment and painted her lips, a bow shape for the upper lip, a narrower red line for the lower; her natural mouth was too wide for perfect beauty. With rouge she filled in a circle of pink on either cheek. Now her face was no longer that of an individual. It was the face of ideal Woman. It might as easily be the face of the sun goddess or the Empress or a peasant girl as that of Taniko.

She glanced up at the two Chinese women. They were not laughing; they were awed, looking at her as if they were seeing a statue in a strange shrine.

Now she opened her jewelry box. Horigawa was a fool to have left me all this, she thought. With these weapons I will conquer. For a pendant she selected a jade necklace with an image of the seated Buddha. And of course she would wear the mother-of-pearl butterfly in her hair.

Now she was finished. She looked up at the circular smoke opening in the ceiling of the felt tent. The sky was indigo. The sun must be setting. Bourkina had told her to be ready by sunset.

She seated herself on the cushions and waited. She remembered the writing materials and pointed to the writing box, adorned with a landscape of trees and mountains, set on top of her clothes chest.

"If you get ink on your robe—" one of the maids protested.

"I never do."

She did not want to write for her pillow book. That could come later, when she knew what was going to happen to her. She would attempt a poem. She began rubbing the ink stick on the stone. One of the maids offered to do it for her, but she waved her away. By the time the ink was made she had her poem. She dipped the brush and wrote:

> Fire warms all who come near.
> Only the light of the Buddha
> Can warm the fire.

She sat back, wondering what the poem meant. The two maids sat humbly against the wall of the tent to Taniko's right

so she would not have to look at them unless she wanted to.
They, at least, see me as a great lady, she thought.

But how would she be treated tonight? Was all this some
trick, she wondered. The interview with Bourkina, the opportunity to make all these elaborate preparations, was it all
preparation for a band of Mongol officers·to make sport of
her at a drunken feast? No, Bourkina appeared, though a hard
woman, to be honest enough. Probably some officer of the
khan, some commander of a thousand or ten thousand men,
would enjoy her tonight. Or perhaps he would find her dwarfish
and freakish and would contemptuously send her away or
throw her to the brutes in the ranks.

Now she could really feel how Jebu must have felt, living
among people to whom she looked strange.

She must not lie to herself. Even if this Mongol general
should find her pleasing, what would she have gained? A man
she did not care for would enter her body and use her. Like
those first years with Horigawa. Disgusting. And she must
feign delight. And this, just so she could eat and sleep and be
allowed to live. She still did not want to kill herself, but how
much shame was she willing to endure just to stay alive?

And sooner or later this great one of the Mongols would
tire of her, just as Horigawa said, and would cast her off.
What affection could there be between people of nations so
different?

Sooner or later she would begin the slow descent through
the ranks of the Mongols. It could only end one way. Horigawa
would have his revenge.

She sat, looking at her fingertips peeping from beneath her
sleeves. The maids were silent, she was silent. The bleak
thoughts kept pursuing one another through her mind. She
brooded back over the course of her life. She had never·been
permitted to decide on a course of action for herself and by
herself. She had always been subject to the whims of one man
or another.

She wanted to weep, but held back her tears. She dared not
spoil her makeup, or the great Mongol would not want her.
She must take her mind off these thoughts.

She knew only one way to distract herself. In her mind she
said, ``Homage to Amida Buddha,'' over and over again. She
did not want to recite the invocation to the Lord of Boundless

Light aloud. She did not want to be the object of the maids'
idle curiosity. And besides. she might end up hoarse before
Bourkina came for her.

After a time she found it easiest to let the mental recitation
fall in with the rhythm of her breathing. and she repeated the
invocation each time she breathed out. just as if she were
saying it aloud. Whenever she found her mind wandering to
her wretchedness. she gently drew it back to the invocation.

She began to see Amida Buddha seated in his paradise. His
face was round and golden. like the sun. His expression.
bearing the faintest of smiles. was one of infinite peace.
Gradually she was able to see all of him, sitting in the clouds,
his hands touching together in his lap. surrounded by circling
flocks of angels and seated bodhisattvas.

A vast peace filled her. She forgot all her sorrows. She
forgot the passage of time.

The face of the Buddha was replaced by the deeply tanned
face of Bourkina. peering into hers.

"I'm sorry you have had to wait so long. There is always
so much happening here."

Taniko smiled. "It is quite all right."

Bourkina peered at her. "What has happened to you? Have
you been using the Arabian drug?"

Still smiling. Taniko shook her head. "Drug? No. I simply
have tried to take your advice. I'm not frightened any more."

Bourkina nodded. "I sensed you had possibilites. Good.
Well. then. let us go."

In spite of what Taniko said. she did feel a faint twinge of
fear as she rose smoothly to her feet. What would happen to
her now?

Bourkina looked at her appraisingly. "We have only a
short way to go. I hope you won't be too warm with all those
robes you have on. You look very lovely. though strange.
I've never seen a woman dressed as you are. But that's all to
the good."

The two Chinese maids sat like statues as Bourkina and
Taniko walked out into the warm night. At first Taniko was
unable to see. She hesitated. and the big Mongol woman
reached down and took her hand.

When Taniko's eyes adjusted to the darkness. she could
see the round tents on all sides. The fear was gone again. She

had discovered that she carried the paradise of Amida Buddha within her and could enter it, without having to die, any time she wanted to. No longer could anyone harm her. She could always escape.

They were walking toward the large white pavilion in the center of the camp where Horigawa had gone the day before. Though it was only a tent, it was as large as the house of a noble in the Sunrise Land. It covered the top of a low hill. Before it stood two standards, one the horns and tails of some great beast, the other a silk banner inscribed with the Chinese word *Yuan*, "a beginning."

There was a front entrance facing south, the most auspicious direction, protected by six warriors armed with lances. Bourkina went around to the side of the felt-covered tent, where there was another, smaller entrance guarded by only one huge man with a broad, curving sword in his belt. He bowed to Bourkina.

"Now you must know," Bourkina said, suddenly turning to Taniko. "I did not want to give you time to be frightened. You must not be afraid now. You are about to enter the presence of one of the greatest among us. If you please him, your future happiness is assured. Prepare now to meet the grandson of Genghis Khan, the brother of the Great Khan Mangu, the overlord of China, the commander of this army and the favored of Eternal Heaven, Kublai Khan."

Then Bourkina took Taniko by the hand and led her through the entrance of the tent. Within, all was cloth of gold, and it seemed as if hundreds of hanging lamps were blazing. Taniko was momentarily blinded as she entered the dome-shaped chamber filled with dazzling light.

12

The clouds that rolled across the night sky reflected red light. Missiles poured over Kweilin's walls, while bands of Mongols and their Kin Tartar and Turk auxiliaries pressed forward with siege towers and ladders. Four war elephants smashed a stone-filled battering ram against the south gate, arrows glancing off their armor like raindrops off a sedge hat.

Jebu expected the city's defenses to crumble at any moment, but he stood on the walls, smiling. There was beauty in war, the fire, the color, the flow and ebb of human waves, the enormous power of the elephants and siege artillery.

"No wonder this people has conquered half the world," Jebu called to Yukio over the roar of battle.

"You admire them?"

"I simply find it remarkable what human beings can do."

He did not admire the Mongols for their conquests, but he was impressed by their ability to throw all their energies into action, by their discipline and by the carefree way they faced hardship and death. These qualities reminded him of the Zinja. Now that he saw Arghun among his people, no longer a mysterious assassin from an unknown world, he was able to understand him better.

Kweilin had held out much longer than it had any right to. The Mongols had arrived before the city in the Fourth Month of the Year of the Sheep. It was now the Seventh Month, and the city remained unconquered. Rarely, since Genghis Khan first led them out of the steppes, had the Mongols found a city so troublesome.

Rain had helped Kweilin's defenders. The timing of the siege was bad for the attackers. The monsoons began just

312

about the time Arghun arrived to direct the siege. The rain slowed down the Mongol assaults, dampened their explosive powder, put out the fires they started, and provided the people of the city with plenty of fresh water.

Disease helped too. The Mongol camp quickly turned into a steaming swamp. Inured for generations to a chill northern climate, they were an easy prey to the fevers of this almost tropical country. By order of the governor, the human waste of the large population of Kweilin, which in peacetime would have fertilized the rice fields around the city, went into the moat and the Kwei Kiang River. Some of it, as Liu intended, poisoned the Mongol drinking water. Thousands of the nomads were felled by dysentery.

But the rain and the sickness had only slowed the Mongols down. It was the samurai who held them off. For the first time since they had emerged from the steppes, the Mongols were encountering warriors as tough, as energetic, as ferocious as themselves. Without help the samurai could not hold out much longer, but they had already wrecked the Mongol schedule for the conquest of the Sung empire.

Daily during those months Jebu looked into the heart of the Jewel of Life and Death. Taitaro, who had given him the Jewel, was somewhere in this land. They would never meet, though, because the city would fall at any moment, and soon after that he would be dead.

He found he could face the prospect with serenity.

But now a strange thing was happening. The noise that had been deafening Jebu for months was slowly dying down. A silence was spreading almost visibly like a blanket of snow. The boulders came hurtling over the walls less often. A single fire pot tore through the air like a shooting star. No more followed it. The *hua pao* were silent.

At the base of the wall where thousands of prisoners had died filling in the moat with stones and brushwood and human flesh, a detachment of Kin Tartar foot soldiers was rushing forward with a long ladder. A volley of samurai arrows fell among them. The ladder dropped to the ground. In response to a shouted command from across the moat, the surviving Tartars turned and ran back to the Mongol camp.

The sun had started to rise above the Kwei Kiang. In the pale light the elephants' handlers were unchaining the batter-

ing ram. It fell with a crush. Now the elephants turned and
lumbered over the stone causeway the Mongols' prisoners had
built across the junction of the two lakes. Flights of arrows
followed them, leaving the armored elephants unharmed but
killing several of the men with them.

In the full light of morning the samurai and the Chinese
watched, dumfounded, as the Mongols broke down their camp
and made preparations to withdraw.

"They expect us to throw open the gates as soon as they
disappear over the horizon," said Yukio. "Then they'll come
roaring back and catch us off guard."

"But they would have had the city today or tomorrow
anyway," Jebu said. "And they could hardly take us by
surprise if we sent scouts after them."

Governor Liu picked his way over the broken stone covering the top of the wall. "So, what I heard is true. They do
seem to be leaving."

Jebu watched the Mongols mount some of their larger *yurts*
on carts, while they stripped the felt covering away from the
wooden poles of the smaller ones and packed them away on
wagons. The Kin engineers were untying the ropes and knocking out the pegs that held the siege machines together. Others
were digging out the bases of the *hua pao*.

Yukio remained convinced that the whole withdrawal was a
deception. Liu suggested that there might be a Chinese relief
army on the way, or perhaps this army had been called away
to meet a Chinese counterattack in one of the other war
zones. Jebu thought that only some requirement of their own
law could draw the Mongols away from an almost certain
victory.

"It can only be something that affects them in the most
profound way," he said.

The besiegers had stationed a protective screen of heavy
cavalry across Lake Rong hu, not far from the pen where the
thousands of prisoners who had survived the siege sat on the
bare ground. The prisoners, Jebu thought, were probably
rejoicing that they were still alive and might return home
soon.

A high voice shouted a command to the riders on guard.
They formed a long line and began to trot in a circle around
the pen. Another shrill order and they were firing arrows into

the prisoners. Jebu shut his eyes momentarily and clenched his fists as the screams and pleas for mercy stabbed his ears. The Chinese soldiers on the wall shouted curses at the enemy and prayers for the dying. They tried to shoot at the Mongols, but their arrows would not carry that far. For Jebu, the pain of seeing the killing of so many innocents was like a barbed arrow in his own chest.

Again and again the Mongols circled the slave corral, shooting at any movement.

"They will have their massacre, one way or the other," Yukio said.

Jebu saw that Liu had turned his back on the slaughter and stood with tears trickling down his pale cheeks.

"I do not know which is worse," he whispered, "to see the severed head of my own son, or to see my helpless people slaughtered."

Now the Mongols had dismounted and were walking in a line through the pen. They had their sabers out and were inspecting the bodies, beheading or stabbing to death any who were still alive. Auxiliary troops moved behind them, retrieving arrows from the corpses.

Yukio also turned away. "There is no need for this. No need at all," he said hoarsely. "It is true that the Mongols are less than human."

And if they are, Jebu wondered, what am I? These are also my people. But I was not reared in their ways. I would sooner die than do what they are doing. To kill poor peasants is bad enough, but how can they kill women and children by the hundreds?

Genghis Khan, Arghun's master, had commanded the death of all Jamuga's seed, and Arghun had tried to kill Jebu when Jebu was a baby. That would not seem a task repugnant to a man who could shoot an arrow into a screaming child clinging to its mother's skirts.

Yukio, his face crimson with rage, said, "We have our prisoners, too. Let us show that we can be as merciless as these Mongols." In the months of the siege, the defenders had captured over a hundred Mongols and nearly three hundred auxiliaries.

"No," said Jebu. "I will not shame myself by killing those who cannot fight back."

"The Mongols almost always kill their prisoners," said Liu. "Perhaps, if we were to let our captured Mongols live, even return them to their people, it would show them there is another way. Our Master Confucious said, 'Do not do to others what you would not want others to do to you.' If we do not kill Mongols today, perhaps they will spare Chinese lives tomorrow."

"We always execute captured fighting men in our land," said Yukio. "To let men live so that they may attack you again is foolish."

"The few hundred Mongols and their auxiliaries that we captured are no great danger to us," said Jebu. "I will personally conduct them to Arghun."

"I'm sorry, Jebu-san," Yukio said, "but you must be completely mad."

"I will go as an envoy. The life of an ambassador is sacred to them."

Liu said, "You put too much temptation before Arghun."

"He has spent years of his life and made long and dangerous journeys to try to kill me. His very fidelity to his law is my protection."

Yukio stared at Jebu, large-eyed. "I can forbid you to take those men back to Arghun. I can order you to execute them."

Jebu nodded. "Yes, Lord Yukio, you can."

Yukio turned away. "Go ahead. Do whatever foolish thing you like."

When Jebu entered the Mongol camp, he was able to address an officer in the barbarian language, presenting himself as an envoy from Kweilin and requesting a meeting with Arghun Baghadur. His language practice with the prisoners had served him well.

The *tarkhan* sat astride a barrel-chested gray steppe pony, one gauntleted fist resting on his hip. His eyes were the color of a cloudy winter day.

"An envoy, are you? You are viler than a diseased dog to mock the laws of my people."

"I meant no mockery, *tarkhan*," said Jebu, looking back at him calmly. Arghun's reaction did not surprise him. He must hate me as much as I have been hating him, Jebu thought.

"So, you've learned a few more words in the language of your father," said Arghun with an ironic smile. "Perhaps you'd like to become one of us. Unfortunately, if you submitted yourself to our law, you'd die at once." His face darkened. "If you are an ambassador as you claim, approach me properly. Off your horse. Down on your face."

Jebu hesitated. But Arghun was within his rights to demand obeisance from an ambassador. And did not *The Zinja Manual* say, "Whatsoever role you play, manifest your inner perfection by acting it perfectly." Jebu climbed down from his horse. The muddy ground had been churned into a brown soup by thousands of hooves. He knelt and pressed his hands and forehead into the mud. He waited there.

At last Arghun said irritably, "Get up, that's not what I want from you."

Jebu stood up, wiping the mud from his forehead with the back of his hand. "Will nothing less than my death satisfy you, *tarkhan*?"

"Nothing less will satisfy the spirit of Genghis Khan. I cannot take your life today, but I will have it one day. Why did you come here?"

"First, to propose, since you seem to be leaving us, a treaty of eternal peace between the Mongols and the city of Kweilin."

"That is an absurdity. We make peace only with those who surrender. What else?"

"Also, to return to you the men we captured. We do not consider it necessary to murder helpless prisoners."

Arghun shrugged. "Then you are fools." Arghun turned to an officer beside him. "Have those men taken away." The officer shouted orders, and guards led away the men brought by Jebu. The returned prisoners walked with pale faces and downcast eyes.

"It may interest you to know that they will be strangled with bowstrings before we leave here," said Arghun, smiling.

Jebu's heart sank. "They don't deserve punishment. They are brave men. They were all wounded or unconscious when we captured them."

"It is not a punishment. We must send a detachment of warriors to the next world to serve the Great Khan. It is an honor to be chosen. These men will be part of the Great

Khan's spirit guard. We have our ways of mourning, monk, which you could not possibly understand.''

Amazed, Jebu saw at once what was happening. ''Your Great Khan is dead?''

''He is.'' Arghun's rough-hewn face was bleak. ''For now, our war with Sung China is ended, by our own choosing. It is our unalterable law that when a Great Khan dies, all of us shall return to the homeland to bury him and to choose his successor. Tell the people of Kweilin to thank Eternal Heaven for granting them this respite. But let them remember that it is only a respite.''

He fixed his strangely empty eyes on Jebu. ''For you also, son of Jamuga, this is only a respite. Three times now I have tried to carry out the command of Ghenghis Khan that you die. Each time you have been saved, but never by your own power. A man who must rely on others or on chance events to protect him is a poor creature. Destiny will bring you and me together again, and the next time I will surely kill you.''

13

Jebu and Yukio stood on the broken western parapet of Kweilin and watched the Mongols depart, as they had come, in a dust cloud that obscured the sunset.

''You see?'' said Yukio. ''You may have saved those prisoners from my anger, but they were fated to die. It was their karma.''

Jebu shook his head. ''Not karma. Arghun's ruthlessness.''

Yukio shrugged. ''Karma put him there to end the lives of those men.''

''What do you foresee as our karma?'' Jebu asked, recognizing that the argument was like a ko situation in go, where players endlessly repeated the same move, taking and losing the same stones again and again.

Yukio laughed. "We have little choice. We'll simply stay here at Kweilin until we get new orders from the Sung Emperor."

"If the Mongols have called off their war with China, perhaps Chia Ssu-tao will decide that he doesn't need us."

Yukio shook his head. "The chief councillor may not be a very wise man, but he must know that the Mongols will be back once they have a new Great Khan."

But judging by the news brought back by Governor Liu's intelligence network, it might be some time before the Mongols returned. Factions were forming behind two of the late Great Khan's younger brothers, Kublai Khan and Arik Buka. Supporters of Arik Buka declared him a true Mongol, untainted by the Chinese influences that surrounded Kublai Khan. Arghun Baghadur had thrown his weight behind Arik Buka. The opposing party claimed Kublai Khan was far better fitted to rule the vast empire than Arik Buka, whose name in Mongol meant Little Man because he was the youngest of his family. Kublai's backers frequently quoted the words of Genghis Khan, who said, when his grandson was but eleven years old, "Heed well the words of the boy Kublai. They are full of wisdom."

If the Mongols chose peacably between Kublai Khan and Arik Buka, China would feel the weight of a new onslaught in a year or so. But if the divisions were deep enough to lead to war among the Mongols, the Central Kingdom might be safe for generations.

Throughout the city which all summer long had heard nothing but the crash of stone and the roaring of fire and the screams of the dying, the most noticeable sound now was the rapping of hammers. Moko joined in the rebuilding, learning Chinese methods of carpentry, suggesting more economical ways of doing things from his own practice and spending hours down by the docks watching the building of new river-going junks.

Less then six hundred samurai had lived through the siege. Day by day, as it became clear that the Mongols were really gone, Yukio eased them down from a war footing. Even though they heard nothing from Linan, much less received any payment for their services, the warriors were well fed and comfortable. Governor Liu gave Yukio whatever he asked. Weapons were repaired or replaced. The precious swords of the fallen were distributed among the living. With the governor's help Yukio obtained three horses for each of his men.

After the samurai had rested for about a month, Yukio reintroduced discipline and training. Each day bands of mounted warriors rode through the beautiful blue hills around Kweilin, practicing Mongol-style cavalry tactics. About a hundred of the Chinese soldiers garrisoned at Kweilin who had come to admire the samurai and their way of fighting asked permission to join them. Since idle troops could become a problem, Governor Liu persuaded the soldiers' commander to release them to Yukio. Yukio put Jebu to work bringing the new recruits up to samurai standards of fighting skill.

"You're the best-trained among us, Jebu-san, and you're always practicing."

"That's because I don't spend as much time in the Quarter of Ten Thousand Delights as you do."

"I said you were well trained, Jebu-san. That doesn't mean you're as much of a man as I am. Though more than once my arrival in the quarter has been greeted with mournful looks because I haven't brought the red-haired giant with me."

Jebu mulled over his education as a Zinja and his current practices and put together a basic course of exercises that combined physical and mental discipline. He chose the most competent samurai to help him conduct the training. The recruits took up the work eagerly, and after they had studied some days under Jebu, more Chinese soldiers were asking to join the group. After a month some of the samurai themselves were coming to Jebu to ask whether they could take the training as well, "to brush up their skills."

"Clearly you are a great master," Yukio said. "Everyone is clamoring to study under you."

"Clearly I must be doing something wrong," said Jebu. "If I were teaching as I should, I would be driving them away."

Two months after the Mongols left, Jebu and Yukio heard that a Chinese army of five thousand was marching toward Kweilin. Their general sent word ahead that he had been dispatched there by the Emperor, to restore order in the regions invaded by the barbarians. Governor Liu had gone forth to greet them.

Jebu was in the great hall of the compound where the samurai were quartered, presenting the Chinese recruits who had survived his training program with swords, when a samurai entered and called Jebu.

"Forgive my interrupting you, shike, but Lord Yukio requests that within this stick of time, you have your men ready in full parade armor to honor the Chinese general."

Acknowledging the disruption as a problem set for him by the Self, Jebu finished the sword presentation ceremony quickly and set the recruits to polishing and donning their armor. He had hardly finished giving this order when Yukio sent for him.

Yukio was in a small room on the second floor of the samurai hall, which he used as a headquarters. A White Dragon banner hung on the wall behind him. Yukio sat cross-legged on a flat cushion, his face flushed with anger. A tall, grave-looking mandarin knelt before him.

"What would you say of a chief minister who repaid all the fighting we did for him by ordering us arrested and brought to him in chains?"

Jebu's chest contracted. "I'd say he was a fool. But a fool such as many rulers have been."

"If such behavior is customary for rulers, then fighting men are the fools, to give their lives for them. We are betrayed, Jebu."

The mandarin had come with a message from Liu. The general said he had orders from the Emperor to disarm and arrest the samurai and bring them back to Linan in chains. Chia Ssu-tao had accused Yukio of coming to China to overthrow the Son of Heaven and make himself Emperor of China. He accused the samurai of ending the siege of Kweilin by making a secret pact with the Mongols.

"Such charges are incredible," said Jebu. "Why do they really want to destroy us?"

The mandarin shrugged. "Someone has convinced the Emperor's chief councillor that you are a danger."

"We may have been fools to fight for the Sung Emperor,

but we would be greater fools to surrender," said Jebu.
"We'll have to fight our way out. Do we try to escape
overland, or should we take some junks and sail down the
river to Canton?"

"No," said Yukio. "This gentleman tells me that Governor Liu intends to help. If the governor's plan works, we'll
leave Kweilin without losing a single man."

Jebu stood beside Yukio as six men pushed open the iron
and wood outer doors of the double gateway. Solemn faces
peered in at him. The people of Kweilin had cleared away the
causeway built by the Mongols and had constructed a new
wooden bridge at the juncture of the two lakes, calling it once
again the Green Belt Bridge. There was a line of people along
each rail of the bridge, leaving a broad aisle through which
the samurai could ride. At the far end Jebu could see Governor Liu in his vermilion robes of state.

Beyond Liu, on the far shore of the lakes, were thousands
and thousands of people crowding the land where the Mongols
had been camped two months ago. Past the people, Jebu
could see the long, gleaming spears of soldiers. The Chinese
army.

"Are we sure this isn't a trap?" said Yukio beside him.

"Nothing is certain," said Jebu. "But I trust Liu. And I
trust our horses, our swords and our bows."

The sun, low in the southwest, sparkled on the silver
dragon on Yukio's helmet. He and Jebu mounted their horses.
Behind them, the samurai followed suit. Yukio raised his
arm.

"Forward."

Holding their mounts to a walk, Jebu on Yukio's left, they
stepped out on the bridge. Jebu wore his black-laced armor
with his sword at his side and his bow in a saddle case, the
long pole of a naginata held in his right hand and resting on
his shoulder, the reins in his left.

The bridge shook as the horses of the samurai stepped on
it. As they crossed, the people on either side were speaking
softly to them.

"Good-bye. Thank you."

"The gods be kind to you."

At the far end of the bridge, Liu held up his arms to them.

"If my son were alive, he would be marching with you today."

Yukio held out a hand in appeal. "Why have the rulers of China turned against us?"

"Perhaps someone has poisoned Chia Ssu-tao's mind against you," said Liu. "But perhaps it is simply that the Court is afraid of you. At first it was thought you were ignorant barbarians. Now it is known that you are formidable fighters. Victorious generals have always been a menace to the throne. This Sung dynasty was founded by a successful general who overthrew his Emperor. Many times before and since, generals who fought too well have been imprisoned and executed."

"I am ashamed to accept the protection of unarmed civilians," Yukio said. "And you, Honorable Governor, are risking your career and your life for us."

Liu pointed over the heads of the crowd. "There are five thousand soldiers there, sent to arrest you. You could fight them, of course, and you would kill many of them. But what a waste of lives on both sides."

"We are grateful to you," said Yukio.

Liu beckoned to Jebu. "A word with you." Jebu dismounted from his horse and followed Liu a little way along the shore of Lake Rong hu.

"Head north and west, toward Szechwan and Tibet," Liu said softly. "The Order has temples in that direction. You will be contacted."

"Thank you," said Jebu. He looked into Liu's eyes and saw a warmth like a distant fire on a cold night. That sense of remoteness, he realized, was the remoteness of the Self, communicating with him from deep within Liu.

They returned to Yukio. "You will have to live off the land," said Liu. "Which means you will take what you need from the peasants. In your baggage train you will find a cart carrying as much gold as I could spare from the city's treasury. Pay the peasants as much as you can. They suffer abominably when any army passes through." He reached into his sleeve and took out a scroll. "Here is a map of some of the lands through which you will pass." He reached up and took each man's hand. "I doubt that I will ever see you again, but you are sons to me. You saved the thousands of lives that were in my keeping."

''The fortunate death of the Great Khan of the Mongols saved them,'' said Jebu.

Liu shook his head. ''Only because you held out so long did the death of the Great Khan make any difference. You fought like—'' he smiled up at Jebu ''—like devils.''

Liu turned and gestured to the people around him. A hundred red-robed officials of the city grouped themselves in front of the samurai leaders. Liu nodded, and the procession of samurai and their unarmed protectors started off.

The Chinese troops were massed west of the city. Between them and the samurai stood almost the entire population of Kweilin. Led by Yukio and Jebu, like a river flowing between steep banks, the mounted samurai moved slowly along a road that led northwest, the direction Liu had suggested.

In the distance, people were parting to let through a single chariot drawn by two horses. They pressed close around it, and then closed ranks behind it. In the chariot stood a stout man wearing a flowing scarlet cloak. His cuirass was shaped to cover and protect a huge pot belly, and it was plated with gold and decorated with a peacock design worked out in precious stones.

''The general who's come to take us back to Linan in chains,'' said Yukio.

The general drew his chariot up before Liu. The procession of samurai and their protectors stopped.

The general smiled. ''A most impressive demonstration of public feeling. I imagine you, esteemed Governor Liu, arranged it?''

Liu shook his head. ''I am but one of the thousands who wish to be here. For over three months these men defended us with their lives. Now we protect them with out bodies.''

''Such heroism,'' said the general. He smiled at Yukio. ''Are you their commander?''

Yukio bowed. ''I am.''

''As one military man to another, I'm sure this is all a mistake. Come with us now, and the governor and some of the distinguished citizens of Kweilin can travel with you and testify to your worthy deeds. Doubtless the charges against you will be dropped.''

Yukio smiled back. ''We agree to come, as long as we are not disarmed and do not have to wear chains.''

The general looked sorrowful. "I wish I could allow that, but I am forbidden to do so. Your arms will be kept safe and will be returned to you as soon as this unpleasantness is settled. And the chains will only be token chains—children's toys, nothing more."

Yukio bowed. "I'm sorry, but we must decline your offer."

The general turned to Liu, his face darkening. "If you continue to protect these men, you will certainly lose your post and probably your head as well."

Liu shrugged. "I am disgusted with my government. I am resolved to give up this post. And I may very well end my own life as a protest against this vile treatment of faithful warriors."

"Good for you," said Yukio.

"You must not," Jebu said at almost the same moment. They looked at each other.

"I can command my troops to cut their way through your people," the general blustered. "Will you let them be destroyed just to protect these ridiculous dwarfs?"

Yukio reddened, and Jebu put a restraining hand on his arm.

Liu said, "I do not know where you and your army were when we desperately needed reinforcements here. Doubtless you have never seen a Mongol. If you cut your way through my people to attack these brave men, a Chinese general will have done what the Mongols could not do. You will have massacred the Chinese people of Kweilin. You will dishonor your ancestors and shame your descendants."

Yukio said, "We dwarfs, as you call us, will fight to the death, and we will take five of your troops with us for each one of us you kill."

"And I will make it my business to see that you yourself do not survive, esteemed general," Jebu added.

The general looked at Jebu, Yukio and Liu for a long, silent moment. His pudgy face was set in a stern military mask, but Jebu could see indecision in his eyes.

He got down from his chariot and approached Liu, saying in a low voice, "It could be reported to the Emperor that the dwarfs got word of our coming and fled before we arrived."

"The saviors of Kweilin are not be called dwarfs."

"Of course. I do not want to fight these warriors. I do not

want to kill your people. But I cannot simply let the foreigners go. Chia Ssu-tao would have my head."

"What tale you tell back in Linan doesn't concern me," said Liu.

"But you must swear to support my story, otherwise I might as well cut my throat here and now." The general thought a moment. "Yes, and you must agree to come to Linan with me, otherwise I will not be able to trust you."

"No," Jebu said before Liu could agree. "It is too great a sacrifice. This actor in general's clothing will take you to Linan to blame you for letting us escape. Chia Ssu-tao will have you executed. Remember, you stopped me from giving up my life for your people."

Liu shook his head. "If you escape, this general is in as much danger from Chia Ssu-tao as I am. Whether it is my lot to live or die, I am content."

"If you are not afraid of death, no one has power over you," said Yukio.

"If you understand that, you understand everything," Jebu said to Yukio, and Liu nodded.

Again Yukio gave the order to march, and the samurai and the people of Kweilin moved off together, leaving Governor Liu standing beside the general from Linan. Jebu turned in his saddle and made a gesture that was part a wave, part a reaching back. He felt he was leaving a father behind, never to see him again, and sorrow filled him.

14

Laughing, Taniko kicked her pony into a gallop and quickly left Seremeter behind. Ahead there was a creek still swollen with melted snow. Spring came late to this northern country.

Taniko raced her horse through the water, splashing her riding skirt. Behind her, Seremeter dashed through the creek, wincing at the spray.

"How dare a mere consort try to outrun the wife of the khan?" Seremeter had ivory-white skin and fathomless brown eyes. She had bound her long black hair up under a jeweled cap.

"The wife of the khan encourages familiarity by her own undignified behavior," said Taniko sweetly.

From the hills through which the creek ran, they could look back at Kublai Khan's city of Shangtu, newly built on a fertile plain beside a slate-gray river. Shangtu had been erected on territory that had always belonged to the nomadic tribes, about two days' ride north of the Great Wall of China. The city's raw wooden palaces were little more than warehouses built to contain the loot gathered from below the Great Wall. Around the permanent buildings clustered the round tents of Kublai Khan's army. Kublai's command was called the Left Wing and included one third of all the Mongols under arms.

Taniko and Seremeter heard the hoofbeats of other horses and turned to see Hotai, a Mongol woman of the Chestnut Horse tribe. She was followed by a servant carrying a wicker cage in which the dark, hunched shaped of a hooded falcon brooded.

"It's a shame to waste our good Mongol horses on foreign women," Hotai sniffed. "You treat them like toys. You know nothing about real riding. I cannot imagine what charm the khan finds in women like you."

Taniko stared at Hotai. She was not joking, as Taniko and Seremeter had been. Kublai Khan's Mongol wives and consorts deeply resented his interest in women of other lands.

"Perhaps the khan likes us because you Mongol women, being such marvelous riders, are all bowlegged," Seremeter said.

Hotai's broad cheeks flushed a dull red. "You have a sharp tongue, but my dagger is also sharp. Take care." She and her servant rode away.

"Your answer to her was splendid," Taniko said. "I wouldn't know how to talk like that to anyone."

"In my country that would be considered a passing pleasantry,'' said Seremeter. ''When the people of Persia really insult each other, the earth shakes.''

''In my land men are polite even when they are about to kill each other. Especially then.''

It was amazing, Taniko thought, the freedoms people of other countries allowed themselves. One of the delights of living among the Mongols was the liberty she enjoyed. She did not have to stay cooped up in her house, hiding behind a screen whenever a man appeared. The Mongol women came and went as they pleased in Shangtu; indeed, throughout the Mongol empire women went about without fear. So rigorously did the Mongols enforce their laws that it was said a virgin with a sack of gold could ride from Korea to Russia without being molested. Warriors might rape and loot in newly invaded territories, but where the Mongol peace was established, it was absolute.

Taniko made full use of her freedom. There was so much to be seen. The Persian princess, Seremeter, ten years younger than she and eager for good company, followed Taniko eagerly as she explored the city Kublai Khan was building as headquarters and resort on the edge of the steppes.

Seremeter had been sent to Kublai by his brother Hulagu, campaigning far away to the southwest in the lands of peoples called Persians, Turks and Arabians. She traced her lineage back to Cyrus the Great, founder of her country, but her family was Zoroastrian, she explained, not Moslem. These were two religions, Taniko gathered, but in the West religions did not blend with one another as Buddhism and Shinto did in the Sacred Islands. The Moslems ruled Persia, and families like Seremeter's, who belonged to a rival religion, had been stripped of their position. Seremeter's family welcomed the Mongols as deliverers and gladly married their daughters to the family of the Great Khans. Seremeter had lived with the Mongols three years now and spoke passable Chinese.

''Look.'' Seremeter pointed to a procession of mounted warriors winding slowly toward the palace, through the rows of tents. Crowds gathered along the way to cheer them.

''That must be Bayan of the Hundred Eyes,'' Taniko said. ''I heard that he arrived this morning from Shensi. He and Uriangkatai, the son of the great general Subotai Baghadur, are the best generals in Kublai's service. But Bayan is much younger than Uriangkatai, and—''

''How do you know so much?'' Seremeter interrupted her.

''I ask a lot of questions, princess.''

They turned their horses and started riding back toward Shangtu. ''Perhaps that's why Kublai sends for you so often,'' Seremeter said. ''Most of his women don't understand what he does. He can talk to you about it.''

''Oh yes,'' said Taniko. ''That must be it. I can't imagine why else he would want to spend time with a withered hag like me.''

Seremeter waved Taniko's mock modesty away. ''In my country we have a story about a sultan who used to behead his wives after spending one night with them. One wife kept herself alive by telling him stories that were so good, he couldn't bear to kill her. You are somewhat like that. Kublai doesn't behead his women, but he does forget them. Of course, it is important to be beautiful, too, and you are. But Kublai has his pick of all the beautiful women in the world. Yet you are among the women he sees most often.''

They were closer to the city now, and Taniko noticed a woman coming toward them, riding out on the road they had taken. ''He hasn't sent for anyone in days and days,'' Taniko said.

Seremeter nodded. ''The *kuriltai*.''

''Most of the officers and nobles seem to think a *kuriltai* is a fine time for sport with women,'' said Taniko.

''Some men, at times like this, are overwhelmed with excitement and must lie with a woman before they can sleep,'' said Seremeter. ''If they can sleep at all. Other men put all their powers into thinking and acting. They have no interest in women at such times. Kublai is that kind of man. Once the succession is settled, he'll wear us all out with his demands.''

Bourkina, lightly dressed in bright blue coat and trousers, galloped up to them. ''Ladies, there is to be a great gathering today, starting at the Hour of the Rooster. Everyone will be there, including the wives and consorts of Kublai Khan. You will want to return to our quarters and begin dressing now, if you are to be ready on time.''

''What has he decided, Bourkina?''

The round-faced woman shrugged. "I don't know. He whispers his secrets to you ladies under the quilts, if he tells them to anyone at all."

"He will have himself proclaimed Great Khan tonight," said Seremeter. "I'm sure of it."

"I'm not," said Taniko. "If he makes himself Great Khan, he may wreck the empire of the Mongols. If he doesn't, whoever becomes Great Khan may destroy him. If I were he, I could never decide what to do."

"His enemies are many and powerful," said Seremeter. "What will happen to us if there is a war and he is defeated?"

"You know what will happen," said Taniko, thinking that if such were the case, Horigawa would have his vengeance on her after all.

"It's better not to talk about it, ladies," said Bourkina briskly. "Let's ride back to the city."

Taniko and Seremeter sat on silk cushions in a gallery overlooking the great hall Kublai Khan had built for the *kuriltai*. The hall smelled of newly cut wood and fresh paint. There were hundreds of Kublai's women in the gallery, including the great lady herself, the principal wife, Jamui Khatun, a serene woman who looked a good deal like Bourkina.

Hotai and several other young Mongol women sat near Taniko and Seremeter. Hotai sighed loudly. "These are strange times indeed, when we must share our places with a cannibal and fire worshiper."

Taniko, who as a good Buddhist had never eaten meat, could not understand how the story had started that her people were cannibals. She wondered what Seremeter's reply to Hotai would be. To disparage Hotai's Mongol background would hardly be politic, especially at a *kuriltai*.

"You know as much about the customs of our lands as a lump of camel dung knows about the sea," said Seremeter, tossing her head.

Poetry, thought Taniko, sheer poetry. I wish I could teach Seremeter to write tanka. But first she'd have to learn our language.

She turned her attention to the main floor of the hall. In a space as vast as a public square, men from three quarters of the world were gathered—Kin, Cathayans, Tibetans, Manchus,

Koreans. Annamese. Kampuchans. Burmese. Nan Chaoans.
Turks. Persians. Arabs. Alans. Kipchaks. Armenians. Bulgars.
Russians. and men of many other nations whose names Taniko
had not yet learned. Lording it over all were those of the
many northern nomad tribes who now called themselves
Mongols—dark Kiraits. broad-shouldered Merkits. talkative
Uighurs. tall Kankalis. silent. secretive Reindeer People. The
most splendid. in furs. silks and jewels looted from half the
kingdoms of the earth. were those whose grandfathers had
been Yakka Mongols. the tribe of Genghis Khan himself.

On a raised dais under a cloth of gold canopy was the
place. still empty at this hour. where Kublai Khan and his
chief advisers would sit. They were meeting elsewhere. Taniko
knew. deciding what this gathering of leaders of the Mongol
empire should proclaim as its collective decision.

Besides those who had a vote in the *kuriltai*. there were
many who came simply to be present and to observe. There
were lamas in red; black-robed monks from the lands of the
Franks. the white-skinned people to the west; men with turbans and long white beards from the Moslem countries where
Seremeter's people lived. There was even a sohei from the
lands of the Franks—a warrior-monk with yellow hair who
wore a white cross-shaped crest on one shoulder of his black
cloak. He reminded her a little bit of Jebu.

The *kuriltai* was the knot that held together the Mongol
empire. At the *kuriltai* all members of the house of Genghis
Khan. all Mongol nobles and generals. all the princes of the
kingdoms that had submitted to the Mongols came together in
council to vote on great decisions. At a *kuriltai*. Genghis
Khan had proclaimed one government for the warring tribes
of Mongolia with himself as its head. At *kuriltais* his successors. Ogodai. Kuyuk and Mangu had each in turn been
elected Great Khan. At a *kuriltai* the Great Khan Mangu had
reopened the war against China that had ended in his untimely
death.

Now Kublai Khan. Mangu's younger brother. had called a
kuriltai to choose the next Great Khan. Whoever was elected
would lay claim to all the lands from Korea in the east to
Russia in the west. from Siberia in the north to Burma and
Annam in the south. He would rule. not only the largest

empire in the world, but the largest empire mankind had ever known.

There was a blast of horns and a rumble of drums. Hangings parted, and Kublai Khan, surrounded by *noyans, orkhons* and *tarkhans,* entered the hall. The assembled chieftains, most of whom had been seated on the carpeted floor eating, drinking and talking, rose to their feet.

When Kublai opened his mouth to speak, a total silence fell. "Ten months have passed since my brother, the Great Khan that was, died of his illness at Hochwan." His voice, deep and powerful, carried to the farthest parts of the hall. "Thirty days ago the summons went out to this *kuriltai.* Four days we have been meeting here. There has been time for all to come to this *kuriltai.* The Ancestor said, 'All they who do not come to a *kuriltai* shall be as arrows shot into reeds. They shall disappear.' So let it be with all those who have not come to this *kuriltai.*"

Though Taniko had by now spent many hours with Kublai Khan, the sight and sound of him appearing before this group of powerful men was breathtaking. He wore robes heavy with gold embroidery, and his shoulders were draped with collars of gold and jade and precious stones; on his head was the jeweled headdress of a Chinese Emperor, making him look even taller than he was. But he would have dominated this gathering physically even without such a display of magnificence. He was a huge man, towering over the Mongol commanders who stood at his side. He was heavy as well, with the build of a wrestler. His broad face was swarthy, his eyes so black they seemed to draw light from the room—light radiated again by his glittering robes.

"I demand the right to speak."

All heads turned to look for the source of this new voice. Taniko saw a man pushing his way forward, striding from the center of the hall toward Kublai's dais.

"I am of the Yakka Mongols, oh khan, and I have served the Golden Family all my life." The descendants of Genghis Khan were known as the Golden Family.

An *orkhon* beside Kublai called, "Be silent now, Torluk, if you want to be able to speak tomorrow."

"This is no true *kuriltai* if we cannot make our voices

heard,'' the gray-haired Mongol answered back. Taniko heard
a murmur of agreement from other Mongols in the crowd.

Kublai Khan raised a large hand. ''The *tuman-bashi* Torluk
is quite right. All men may speak freely at the *kuriltai*.
Torluk's years of service are three times my own, and his
words deserve our respect.''

Torluk walked up to the dais with the rolling gait of a
Mongol horseman and turned so that all in the room could
hear and see him.

''I urge the khan to call an end to this *kuriltai* at once. This
meeting has no right to choose the next Great Khan.''

Now there was a shocked murmur. Taniko could see those
who did not understand Chinese asking others near them what
the *tuman-bashi* Torluk had said. The *orkhon* beside Kublai
who had spoken before cried, ''Treason!''

Taniko felt a chill of fear. Torluk clearly spoke with the
voice of those who were in league against Kublai. Everyone
in the hall was watching the khan now, waiting to see how he
would meet this challenge.

15

Taniko had come to know Kublai well, but she had never
before seen him presiding as a khan among his chieftains.
Always when they met he had been alone, or at most with a
few other people, in his chambers.

She had been utterly terrified the first time she had met
him. He seemed, at first sight, a monstrous man. Since she
expected that he would want to lie with her, she thanked the
Buddha that she had known Jebu as a lover; at least she knew
it was possible to couple with a man so tall and heavy and not
be hurt.

"Sit here beside me," he had said in a rumbling voice, patting a cushion with a large hand. "Will you have wine?"

"Thank you, my lord," she murmured. Wine might make this easier. He picked up a beautiful silver drinking vessel from a low table before him and poured dark yellow wine into an alabaster cup. She took the cup and then held it out to him with her right hand, the left hand underneath to steady it; this was the proper way for a lady to offer wine to a man of rank.

"You must let me serve you, my lord. It is the custom in my country." He took the cup from her, smiling, and drank. She poured a second cup for herself.

His eyes were very narrow and very black—splinters of ebony. The bones of his face were heavy, like the bones of a horse. It was a strong face, but the alertness of the eyes, the mobility of the mouth, suggested an acute intelligence.

"Your country, the Land of the Dwarfs. You may have heard that I—what is your name?"

"Taniko, my lord. I am the daughter of Lord Shima Bokuden of Kamakura."

"You may have heard that I am a very inquisitive man, Taniko. I know nothing about the Land of the Dwarfs, and I would like to know everything."

There could only be one reason why he would ask questions about the Sunrise Land. If she told him anything, she might betray her people. But she dismissed the fear. To get through this night she would have to laugh at everything and be serious about nothing, not even about herself, not even about the Sacred Islands.

"Perhaps, my lord, I can begin by correcting some of the fantastic tales you may have heard. First of all, we are not dwarfs. You and the Chinese are giants. And we do not worship gods with the heads of animals. Nor does our Emperor live in a palace made of solid gold. Nor are we cannibals."

"Not cannibals?" Kublai's eyebrows went up. "What a pity. I had a fine, fat Chinese sage especially roasted for you. Now I will have to feed him to my hunting dogs. My people are also the subject of many false reports. The stories say we also eat human flesh. They do not say we worship gods with the heads of animals, they say we ourselves have animal heads. We are supposedly not even human, but devils spawned to scourge mankind for its sins. But tell me what is true about your country. What sort of palace does your Emperor really live in?''

The questions went on long into the night. Uneasy about Kublai's purpose, she stressed that hers was a poor land compared to China. The Emperor's palace in Heian Kyo would look small and bare beside the house of any rich man in Linan. Always Kublai pressed her for details of law, of custom, of daily life, details that most people would consider too obvious or trivial to notice. Three times during the evening he struck a small gong with a hammer, and the wine was replenished by a Mongol guard armed with a huge scimitar. Kublai showed her a silver table at the entrance to the tent laden with fruit and meat and pitchers of milk.

''Eat what you want,'' he said. ''No one goes hungry in the khan's tent.'' She helped herself daintily, never forgetting that this giant had the power of life and death over her. His manner might be gentle and pleasant, but his questions assaulted her mind with the relentlessness of a Mongol army storming a city.

But, she reminded herself, knowledge is the one thing I can still possess, even after another has taken it from me. And I am discovering that I know things about my own land that I never thought were important or did not even realize I knew. Her country reshaped itself in her mind under his questioning. She saw its people and events through the eyes of a master of strategy.

After she explained the complexities of the feud between the Takashi and the Muratomo, he commented, ''How like my own people yours are. Both peoples live on the edge of China, both learn from China, both are poor compared to China. Both peoples breed fierce fighters, so fierce that we weaken our nations by fighting among ourselves. With us, the feuding was stopped by the Ancestor, my grandfther Genghis Khan. Perhaps this *orkhon* Sogamori will do the same for your people.''

He stood up, towering over her. Hastily she rose to her feet. He patted her shoulder with a large, brown hand.

''I have had much wine, and I have worked long and hard today. I will sleep now. One of my guards will escort you back to your *yurt*.''

Taniko was startled. No rape of the body to follow the rape of the mind? Perhaps he thought her unattractive.

He seemed to notice her surprise. ''That's another tale they tell about us, that we take women brutally, without ceremony. It's not true. Please believe that I find you most attractive. You are an exquisite little creature.''

''Thank you, my lord,'' she said, bowing with apparent shyness and seething inwardly at ''little creature.''

''If you were to lie with me tonight, you would do so as my prisoner. I know that you are not a courtesan, despite what Prince Horigawa told me when he presented you to me. Bourkina told me your version of the story. It amuses me greatly that giving you to us was the most horrible fate your husband could imagine for you. Tonight, talking to you, I became convinced that you are a lady of rank, as you say. I find you a beautiful and singularly interesting woman. I intend to give you time to become accustomed to me. Go now.''

She had seen him about once a month after that. Since there were over four hundred women in his household, and new women were constantly being sent to him, for him to send for her that often was a mark of high favor. He continued to question her about her homeland, but gradually the range of their topics broadened. She had begun to counter with questions of her own. Kublai's answers revealed to her the landscape of a world staggeringly larger than she had ever imagined existed. And much of that world, she learned, was ruled by the family of Genghis Khan.

The Ancestor, Kublai told her, had had four sons by his principal wife. These were his heirs. Each son had been given a separate domain within the empire. Genghis Khan had indicated that he wanted Ogodai, the third son, to reign after him as Great Khan. After the death of Genghis Khan, Ogodai had been elected Great Khan at a *kuriltai*. The *orkhons*, *tarkhans*, *noyans* and *baghadurs* swore that the Great Khan would always be a member of the house of Ogodai. Ogodai commanded the Banners to ride westward, where they completed the conquest of Russia begun by Genghis Khan and overran lands beyond called Poland and Hungary. The campaign ended when Ogodai died.

Kublai's own father was Genghis Khan's youngest son,

Tuli. He was a brilliant, daring and merciless warrior who had inherited something of his father's strategic genius. He was known as the Master of War. The portion of the empire given him to govern was the Mongol homeland, and with it the title Keeper of the Hearth. Tuli died nine years before Ogodai.

For five years after Ogodai's death, his widow ruled as Regent. She was a proud and foolish woman, and she made many enemies. She was rude and overbearing to members of the Golden Family and veteran commanders. She demanded excessive gifts from vassals and allies, showed favoritism to the Nestorian Christian religion, and threatened to impose it on the whole empire.

Finally a *kuriltai* elected Ogodai's son, Kuyuk, Great Khan. He was sickly and a heavy drinker. He died after reigning a little over two years.

Kuyuk's widow was rumored to be a witch. Together with Ogodai's widow she ruled the empire for two years. Then they put forward Ogodai's grandson as their candidate for Great Khan.

The two widows of the house of Ogodai never suspected that yet another great lady would bring about their downfall—the widow of Tuli, Kublai's mother, Princess Sarkuktani. She was as wise and discreet as the women of Ogodai's house were headstrong and arrogant. Like Genghis Khan himself, Tuli had four able sons. Princess Sarkuktani saw to it that the four young men were trained in the Chinese classics of statesmanship and philosophy as well as in the Mongol arts of warfare. She quietly made alliances with the leading men of the empire.

When the *kuriltai* to elect Kuyuk's successor was finally convened, the Mongol leaders ignored their promise that the house of Ogodai would always rule them. Instead they elected Mangu, the oldest son of Tuli.

A year after his election Mangu discovered a plot against his life led by the widows of Ogodai and Kuyuk. The Mongol law forbade shedding the blood of any person of high rank. So the bodily orifices of the two women were sewn shut to prevent the escape of evil spirits, and they were tied up in leather bags and thrown into a river. Mangu commanded the execution of hundreds of other members of the house of Ogodai and their supporters.

Mangu then set out to extend the Mongol empire further. He sent his second brother, Hulagu, westward to invade the Moslem lands of the Middle East.

Kublai invaded China on Mangu's order, and then Mangu decided to go to war himself. Under Kublai Khan, the Great Khan Mangu, and Arghun Baghadur, three armies invaded southern China.

A chill went through Taniko when she heard the name Arghun Baghadur on Kublai's lips. At once she remembered the giant red-haired warrior who had come to Daidoji looking for Jebu. Could this be the same one, or were there other Mongols of that name?

Mangu left his youngest brother, Arik Buka, behind at Karakorum, the Black Walls, the Mongol capital built by Genghis Khan. Just as Tuli, the youngest son of Genghis Khan, had been Keeper of the Hearth, so now Arik Buka, Tuli's youngest son, was given that title. He was ruler of the homeland and commander of the army of the Center.

The Sung empire was a more populous land than any the Mongols had ever invaded, and its cities were bigger and better fortified. Kublai frankly admitted to Taniko that the invaders had bogged down. Arghun was besieging Kweilin in Kwangsi province, Mangu's army was before Hochwan in Szechwan, and Kublai was here in Hupeh, trying to take Wuchow. The war had been going on for two years.

"By the way, a number of your countrymen are making the war more difficult for us," said Kublai with a smile. "Arghun reports that a contingent of warriors from the Land of the Dwarfs is in command of the defense of Kweilin. They fight like devils, almost as well as Mongols. They have considerably delayed Arghun's capture of the city."

Taniko carefully kept her face expressionless, though her heart was pounding like a taiko drum. What strange karma brought Jebu and his enemy together at a remote city in China?

"I did not know there were any warriors from my country in China," she said.

Kublai's broad face creased in a smile. "Didn't you? Prince Horigawa knew about them. They are members and supporters of that warrior family you told me about, the one on the losing side."

"The Muratomo?"

"Yes. They won't delay Arghun much longer. Through Prince Horigawa we have made an arrangement with a Chinese statesman that will lead to their being overrun shortly." He was watching her closely, searching for a reaction.

Taniko smiled. "My lord, my country may seem small to you, but it is full of people I don't know, whose karma is of no interest to me. My family is related to the Takashi, and I have always been close to them, rather than to the Muratomo."

Later, in her *yurt*, she wept for herself and Jebu, who must be with the samurai at Kweilin if he were alive at all. She remembered Horigawa's saying the samurai would be sacrificed by the Sung Emperor's chief councillor as part of a secret peace offer. They would be destroyed at Kweilin, and the Chinese, whom they had come to help, would not lift a finger to save them.

Her heart was a pit of ashes. It would be with Jebu as it had been with Kiyosi. One day, almost casually, someone would tell her that he was dead.

A few days after that conversation with Kublai came stunning news of another death. On the eleventh day of the Seventh Month of the Year of the Sheep, the Great Khan Mangu, Kublai's elder brother, had died of dysentery at Hochwan. Bourkina told her to prepare for a long journey.

"It will take us at least a month to get to Shangtu."

"Who besides us is going there?"

"All of the khan's household that is not there already. His advisers and ministers. And the entire Left Wing of our army."

"What will we do there?"

"We will wait and watch what the other great ones of the empire do—the khan's brothers, the survivors of the house of Ogodai, the members of the other families descended from Genghis Khan, the *noyans*, the *orkhons*, the *tarkhans*."

"What about the siege of Wuchow?"

"That's over. It's of no importance now."

"What about Kweilin? Has Kweilin fallen?"

Bourkina smiled. "Ah, that's where the men from your country are, isn't it? It will take awhile for a messenger from the *tarkhan* Arghun to reach us, but at last report Kweilin still held out. There is no more war with China, lady. We have a more important question to settle now, one that will decide the future of Mongolia and China and the whole world. To say nothing of your future and my future. Who is to be the next Great Khan?''

16

Now Taniko sat in the gallery of the great hall at Shangtu with the wives and consorts of Kublai Khan, watching as he met an open challenge from those opposing his election.

Kublai seated himself on an ivory chair that had once belonged to the Kin Emperor who reigned in Yenking. His manner was casual, rather than ceremonious, as if he were making himself comfortable in his *yurt* with a few close friends.

In the same easy manner he said, ''You mystify me, Torluk. It has been ten months since my elder brother was taken from us by the will of Eternal Heaven. With great tasks to perform, we stand like tethered horses. How long would you have us wait?''

Torluk, a commander of ten thousand troops, had a voice that carried through the hall. ''This is the first time a *kuriltai* has not been held in our homeland, by the waters of the Kerulan,'' he said. ''All members of the Golden Family have been present. Why does this *kuriltai* meet in a pleasure city in a conquered land? And why are there so few of the blood kin of Genghis Khan here? Where is Birkai, khan of the Golden Horde of Russia? Where is Kaidu, Ogodai's grandson? Where is your brother Hulagu? Where is Arghun Baghadur, the great general of the southwest China campaign? Why are you counseled only by your own officers of the Left Wing, Bayan and Uriangkatai, and by foreigners—Chinese, Turks, Tibetan lamas? Can these men of small account rightfully elect a Great Khan? Will the Mongol nation accept their choice? Above all, where is your brother Arik Buka? It is our Mongol custom that the youngest son inherits. Arik Buka is the youngest son of Tuli, ruler of the homeland, Keeper of the Hearth. Let him call a proper *kuriltai* in the homeland, oh khan, and you will be keeping faith with the Ancestor.''

One of Kublai's generals shouted, ''The voice is yours, Torluk, but the words are those of the khan's enemies.''

''Peace,'' said Kublai. ''Many will attack what we do here for the reasons Torluk gives. It is good that we have this chance to answer.''

Kublai stood up. Most of the Mongols were big men, but he was one of the biggest among them. Taniko had heard that his grandfather, Genghis Khan, was also very tall.

''As to the place of the *kuriltai*. We are north of the Great Wall here. This country has always been part of the home-land. We were fighting in the south when the news of my brother's death came. From here we can return to that fight-ing more quickly than if we go all the way to Karakorum. Let any who would have a voice in ruling the empire come here, where we are building the empire.''

His deep voice, calm at first, grew fiercer as he spoke. When he paused, the assembled leaders cheered until he raised his hand for silence.

''As for those who are not here. The khans of Russia have not attended a *kuriltai* since my grandfather's day. They will have to support whomever we choose. My brother Hulagu is just as far away, fighting in the lands of the Arabs. The Mameluks of Egypt press upon him, and he cannot disen-gage without the loss of everything we have gained in thirty years of fighting there. Hulagu has sent me permission to cast his vote as I see fit. As for Kaidu, Arghun and my brother Arik Buka, perhaps you can tell me where they are, Torluk. Why have the elderly dung eaters who advise my young brother persuaded him to remain in his *yurt* by the Gobi when he could be my guest, enjoying the delights of Shangtu?''

There was laughter, which died away when Torluk replied, ''Let me remind the khan that those who dwell in *yurts* have always triumphed over those who live in palaces. And this is no true *kuriltai* while your brother remains in Karakorum.''

A young *tarkhan* beside Kublai, whom Taniko recognized as Bayan, stepped forward and drew his saber. Taniko held her breath. In the Sacred Islands when a warrior bared his sword he could not honorably sheathe it again until he had drawn blood. But Kublai rumbled softly to Bayan, who put his sword away and sat down.

''I am at home in both *yurts* and palaces, Torluk,'' said Kublai with a smile. ''But I advise you now to have a care.'' The smile fell away and the broad, dark face was as stern as the visage of a carved god. ''You come close to saying that you will not accept the judgment of this *kuriltai*. That would be treason.''

Torluk remained on his feet but stood silent, while Kublai stared him down. At last he turned away from the khan and pushed his way through the crowd. Kublai began speaking quietly to the councillors around him. Gradually the huge room filled with the roar of many different conversations.

What a strange way to conduct the business of an empire, Taniko thought. She had never been to a public gathering in which men talked all at once to one another and ignored their leaders, while their leaders ignored them and also talked among themselves. She tried to imagine what it would be like if the Son of Heaven were elected at a meeting conducted by the great men of the realm. It was unthinkable, sacrilegious. But the Emperor of the Sacred Islands, of course, was a god.

Now the *tarkhan* Bayan was calling for silence. He made a long speech in Mongolian. Taniko had lived with Mongols long enough to understand the drift of it. He called upon the *kuriltai* to choose Kublai as Great Khan. He gave many reasons. The reasons were all obvious. They added up to one reason: that there was no one else in the world who could govern, maintain and expand the huge Mongol empire. She wondered why Arik Buka and those around him couldn't see that.

The chieftains responded to Bayan's speech with a roar of assent. Now Kublai was protesting that he was not worthy. He held out his hands in a gesture rejecting the honor offered him. Bourkina had told Taniko exactly how this part would go, so that even though she understood little Mongolian, she could follow what was happening. Shouts went up from the crowd. They were demanding that he accept the Great Khanate. How rude and strange, subjects shouting orders at the man they had chosen to be their ruler. No more rude and strange, though, than the very idea that people could choose their ruler.

The roar became insistent, even frightening in its intensity. Some of them were chanting his name, "Kublai, Kublai," over and over. Still he shook his head and tried to make his refusal heard above their clamor, ludicrous behavior for a man wearing crown jewels and sitting on an Emperor's chair of state. But it was expected of him, as Bourkina had explained.

At last Kublai stood up. He held out his hands again, but this time the gesture was one of yielding. He bows to accept the supreme power, Taniko thought, still bemused by it all.

The shout of the leaders of the Mongol empire was deafening.

Bayan and an older general—she supposed it was Uriang-katai—held up a long strip of dark gray felt. This, Bourkina had told her, had been traditional for Mongol khans from the days when their tribe was created by the spirits of snow and ice. The two generals draped the felt over the seat and arms of the throne. Slowly Kublai Khan sat down.

So simple, thought Taniko. A man plants his buttocks on a piece of felt and becomes lord of the world.

The cheering redoubled in volume, then died away. One by one the men removed whatever head covering they wore—fur hats, steel helmets, Chinese-style caps of office, turbans, burnouses. As a silence fell over the room they unbuckled their belts. Swords and daggers thudded to the carpeting. The standing men draped their belts over their shoulders. Thus they made the traditional submission to the new Great Khan.

One by one the chieftains moved forward to greet Kublai and to make individual pledges of loyalty to him. Servants bearing large porcelain wine jars and silver platters laden with smoking roasts of beef and mutton began to move through the crowd. Taniko saw the *tuman-bashi* Torluk pushing his way out of the hall. His felt hat was on his head and his sword buckled at his side, but nobody seemed to notice him.

In the gallery Bourkina called out, "Ladies, it's time we

were leaving. It won't be long before the level of feasting and rejoicing here passes what is safe. Each of us will surely have her opportunity to congratulate the Great Khan in her way and in her own time." There were cries of protest.

Hotai said, "That may be well enough for foreign women, but I've grown up attending Mongol feasts. I will be quite safe and comfortable, and I will stay."

"Indeed, she's safe enough," Seremeter said quietly to Taniko. "What man would look twice at that cow?"

One of Kublai's Chinese consorts smirked. "Cows are what the Mongols like best."

Taniko stared at the Chinese woman. "You could lose your head if any Mongol heard that."

The woman laughed. "Not at all. To call a woman a great cow is considered a high compliment among the Mongols. Didn't you know that?"

Except for Hotai and several of the older and more prestigious Mongol wives, such as the principal wife, the lady Jamui, Kublai's women permitted themselves to be shepherded by Bourkina down the gallery stairs and out of the place. Across a wide courtyard with a fountain in its center was the woman's palace. Though it was the Fifth Month, the beginning of summer, the wind was from the steppes of the north, and it was cold. Taniko could see why Kublai had chosen Shangtu for his summer residence.

The women crossed the courtyard in a group. Like a flock of geese, Taniko thought. A monk approached them, one of the many who had come from the farthest corners of the world to observe the *kuriltai* and see what these new world conquerors portended for the various religions. This one was only slightly taller than Taniko, with white hair and a white beard. He wore a gray robe.

"Stand aside," Bourkina called loudly. "No man is permitted to approach the Great Khan's wives."

The elderly monk chuckled and stood his ground. "Surely, my lady, one my age and wearing the robe of a monk is harmless enough."

"Many a monk's robe has concealed a pestiferous weapon," said Bourkina in a slightly more pleasant tone.

"The range of my weapon is not so great these days, lady," said the monk with a smile. "I assure you, you're well beyond it." Taniko wondered about him. From his size and general appearance he looked neither Chinese nor Mongol, but as if he might have come from her own country. Immediately after that thought came the shocking recognition that on his robe was the same willow tree symbol she had seen on Jebu's. The old man was a Zinja from the Sacred Islands. She was sure of it.

She had no idea until that moment how much she had been missing her country and her people. She wanted to cry.

"What do you want, old monk?" Bourkina snapped. "If it weren't for your white hair, I'd have had the guards take your head by now."

The old man bowed as only the men of the Sacred Islands knew how to bow, with respect and yet with dignity.

"I realize that I may not speak directly to one of the Great Khan's consorts," said the monk. "But I see among you a lady whom I recognize as a countrywoman of mine." He looked directly at Taniko and his eyes twinkled. "I have news for her."

"Indeed," said Bourkina. "I should have recognized from your imposing stature that you are from the Land of the Dwarfs." Several women snickered, and Taniko glared at them. She wanted to rush across the courtyard to the old monk and throw herself at his feet, but she dared not even speak to him directly.

The monk said, "Last year a small band of our dwarfish warriors succeeded in holding off a huge army under Arghun Baghadur equipped with siege engines, elephants and all, at the city of Kweilin. When the Great Khan Mangu died, the siege was lifted, as you know. Since Arghun is no friend to your newly elected Great Khan, I'm sure Arghun's lack of success will please all the ladies. But what may especially please the lady from my land in this. Were she to read a list of the dead, she would recognize none of the names."

Bourkina eyed Taniko narrowly. "Once one has become a subject of the Great Khan, she leaves old attachments behind. Is it not so, Lady Taniko?"

"Oh, certainly," said Taniko, her heart beating furiously. "But I would like to know the name of this monk who has been kind enough to pass on this interesting news."

"I am Taitaro of the Order of Zinja," the old monk replied. "I was once abbot of the Waterfowl Temple."

The Waterfowl Temple. Jebu's temple. He had said once that the abbot was his stepfather. This was the man who had raised Jebu. Dangerous or not, she had to talk more with him. But the old monk was gone.

Her head reeled. She thought she was going to faint and put her hand on Seremeter's arm to steady herself. Jebu was alive. He was alive, and she had just talked to his father. It was as if Jebu had just reached out and touched her himself. In this land where she felt so far from home, forsaken by the gods, Jebu and his father had been able to find her. The surge of joy and longing within her made her gasp for breath. Bourkina was still looking at her. She had to hide her feelings. She managed to smile at Bourkina and they started walking again toward the palace of the women.

Bourkina said, "I told you once that we are making a new world. The world you came from will only cause trouble for you."

Seremeter said, "She has a lover among those warriors from her country, is it not so, Taniko?"

"Certainly not," Taniko said, angry at Seremeter for harping on a subject she wanted dropped. Didn't any of these people know the value of silence?

"She'd best put him out of her mind if she does," said Bourkina. "She belongs to the Great Khan now."

"Along with how many hundred other women?" said Seremeter. "At last count, four hundred and fifty-seven. When the Great Khan spreads his attentions so widely, a woman can't be blamed for at least thinking of a former lover."

"I wonder who will receive his attentions on this night of nights," said Taniko to change the subject.

Bourkina chuckled shortly. "I wouldn't want it to be me. These Golden Family men, when they win a victory, they're like bulls in springtime. His father and grandfather were that way."

"Do you speak from personal knowledge, Bourkina?" said Seremeter sweetly. Before Bourkina could answer she went on, "Bulls in springtime. I think I'd like to experience that."

Bourkina shook her head. "He'd tear you apart."

"Taniko. I really do believe Bourkina has bedded all three, Genghis Khan. Tuli. and Kublai Khan. Tell me, wouldn't you like to see our lord like a bull in springtime?"

Taniko was embarrassed to admit that Kublai had yet to take her to bed. "I'm thoroughly pleased with him as he usually is." Bourkina looked at her shrewdly. She probably knows, Taniko thought.

They had arrived at the women's palace. Guards admitted them and they went up to their chambers. Music, shouts and laughter from the hall of the *kuriltai* reached them even here. Taniko undressed with the help of a maidservant and lay down to rest. The events of the night had been so exciting that she found it hard to drop off to sleep. Her last thought before drifting into dreams was, Jebu is alive.

Bourkina awakened her suddenly.

"Is it morning? How long have I slept?"

"No, you've been here just few hours. You must get up, my child. He has sent for you."

"For me? Why me?"

"It is not your place to question. You are to attend the Great Khan in his chambers. Don't keep him waiting."

17

She entered Kublai Khan's chambers with as much fear as she had felt at their first meeting. The pale green silk hangings suspended from the ceiling and covering the walls gave the room a domelike shape. The floor was covered with thick Chinese carpeting. He's managed to make it look like a *yurt*, she thought.

Hidden musicians played wind and string instruments. A

pleasant tang of incense floated on the air. In the center of the room stood a silver swan on a marble pedestal.

A circular dais guarded by porcelain lions took up half the room. Heavy brocade curtains gathered above would drop down at the pull of a cord, to form a *yurt* within the *yurt*, screening Kublai's bed from the rest of the room.

There were no windows, therefore there was no way to tell whether it was night or day outside. A man living in a room like this could make his own time.

Kublai sprawled on the cushions on the dais. He was wearing a simple dark green robe, belted at the waist. The embroidered garments and jewels that had adorned him earlier in the evening were gone. Taniko bowed to him.

"Well, my little lady, what did you think of tonight?" he said in his deep voice, rising to his feet with a smile. She would have thought the question casual except for the way his black eyes glittered. She found herself at a loss for words, and the terror at being in his presence persisted. Uncertainly, she bowed again.

"Do speak," he said. "Try to think of me as just an ordinary man." He walked toward her slowly. She wondered again, why me? Of all those four hundred and more women, why me?

She tried to smile back at him. "It's no use, my lord. Your Majesty. The ways in which you are not ordinary shine out too brightly. There is nothing I can say that can possibly match the event I witnessed tonight. I feel so foolish. I can't imagine why you should have sent for me, when there are many women more beautiful and more clever than I who might have shared this moment with you."

Kublai shrugged. "There may be a few as beautiful. None so clever."

"If cleverness is what you want, there are a thousand sages here in Shangtu able to talk much more cleverly than I can."

"Yes, and some of them may even be honest men. But there are only a few as clever as you, and none at all are beautiful. Tonight I want the company of a woman. Women are very important in my family, you know. In many ways, it was the women of the house who shaped us."

"I don't understand, Your Majesty."

"We were raised by our mothers. My grandfather, Temujin,

whom we call Genghis Khan, was eleven years old when his father was poisoned. His mother ruled over the tribe until Temujin was of age. And my grandmother had to care alone for all four of the sons of Genghis Khan, while my grandfather was gone campaigning.

"When my father, Tuli, died, we were still young, my brothers and I. I was sixteen. We were in great danger, because the house of Ogodai feared us as possible rivals. My mother, Princess Sarkuktani, guided us through those dangerous years. She engaged Yao Chow to teach me to write and to read the Chinese classics. She taught my brothers and me to show deference to the ladies and princes of the house of Ogodai and to bide our time."

Taniko said, "It's all so different from my land. Here women can be powerful. The grandson of a destitute orphan can be ruler of the largest empire that has ever been."

"A destitute orphan, yes." There was a faraway note in his voice. She sensed that having made his claim to the supreme place in his world, he wanted to talk about who he was and where he had come from.

"My grandfather was the lowest of the low," he went on. "He had nothing, nothing at all. His tribe was scattered. When the Taidjuts caught him, they didn't even think him worth killing. They put a wooden yoke on his neck and made a slave of him. He was strong and resolute, but he was as far down as it is possible for a man to be. He did not even own his body. Could he have foreseen then that he would one day make his name feared among all nations, that men would call him Genghis Khan, the Mightiest Ruler? With all the powers of his mind, he could not have predicted that.

"What he intended at the beginning will always be a mystery. I do not think he knew what he could accomplish. After he escaped from the Taidjuts, he just set out to fight back. He was like a man climbing a mountain who does not think of what he has left behind or where he is going, but simply takes the next step, climbs over the next rock. Suddenly, to his surprise, there are no more rocks to climb. He has reached the summit, and he looks around and down and he sees all at once what he has become, and he is full of joy in himself and his achievement."

Taniko wondered if that was how it was for Kublai this night when he was proclaimed Great Khan.

Kublai walked over to the sculptured swan in the center of the room and beckoned her. He held a goblet under the swan's beak and struck a bell with a small hammer. After a moment a pale stream of wine spurted from the beak and splashed into the cup. Taniko laughed as he handed the cup to her and tapped the bell for another goblet for himself.

"It's almost like magic, Your Majesty."

"No need to have servants running in and out, disturbing us. In his palace at Karakorum my brother Mangu had a tree of silver with four serpents twining up its trunk. From the mouth of each serpent came a different kind of wine, and at the top was a silver angel that blew a trumpet whenever the Great Khan drank."

Kublai reached out a hand to stroke the silver swan. "Drinking has destroyed many members of my family. Every one of the four sons of Genghis Khan died an early death. My grandfather died at seventy-two, but none of his sons reached the age of fifty. The eldest, Juchi, died before Genghis Khan did, a gout-crippled wreck, in Russia. My father, the youngest of the four, was the next to die, at forty. He was addicted to wine. Chagatai and Ogodai died a year apart. Ogodai was only fifty-six. I never saw either of those uncles sober. Once one of Uncle Ogodai's ministers showed him an iron jug that was corroded because wine had been standing in it. Ogodai promised to drink only half as often as he had been. Then he had a goblet made for himself that was twice as big. My cousin Kuyuk, the third Great Khan, was a drunk. He was already a dying man when the *kuriltai* elected him. He reigned less than two years."

Taniko sat on a cushion, looking down at the golden wine in the silver goblet. "But a man getting drunk is nothing to worry about. Men need to get drunk once in a while to relax."

"That was so among my people before the victories of Genghis Khan. That still seems to be so for my brothers and me. We have escaped the family curse. But in the old days Mongols drank *kumiss*, fermented mare's milk, which is not as strong as wine. They drank when they could spare the time, which was not very often. After the wars of Genghis

Khan, wine went through our people like a plague. We had nothing else to do. We had servants or slaves to do our work for us. We were forbidden by the *Yassa* to fight among ourselves. We could not spend all our time with women. What is left, if you can't read or write, if you are more ignorant of civilization than the poorest Chinese dung carrier? Water flows downhill, and men prefer to do what is easy. The easiest thing to do is drink. It makes life seem interesting. Now we drink from sleep to sleep. We poison ourselves by the hundreds and thousands, we lords of the earth.''

Again Taniko looked down at the wine. Astonishing, that it should be the death of so many of these hardy Mongols, that they should be, in their way, such vulnerable creatures. Like wild flowers that withered instantly when plucked and brought indoors.

''There are other reasons why many of us drink too much,'' Kublai went on. ''We've seen too much. Often, when we take a city, we kill all its people. Tens of thousands, hundred of thousands, sometimes.''

Taniko looked at him in horror. ''I've heard that. I always thought it was just one more of the lies your enemies spread about you.''

He looked at her somberly. ''No. It's true. I myself haven't done it, and I don't intend to do it. It's stupid and wasteful. We did it more often in my grandfather's day. We saw no use in cities then. When my grandfather sacked Yenking, the capital of northern China, it burned for more than a month. I was born a year after the destruction of Yenking, and one day I will build my own capital there.

''We felt no regret for the thousands of lives we ended, but neither did we enjoy the killing. It was simply work that we did, as one would butcher sheep, because it seemed necessary. Usually victims would be divided up among the warriors. Give each man five people to kill, and an army of twenty thousand can exterminate the population of a city in moments.''

A city just the size of Heian Kyo, Taniko thought.

''We killed conquered people because we didn't know what else to do with them.'' Kublai said. ''Then, too, the policy of annihilating whole cities struck such terror into our enemies that they often gave up in despair. Of course, we had to destroy the cities of those who slew our ambassadors. In Khwaresmia, where they murdered our emissaries, my father directed the storming of Merv from a golden throne set up on the plain before the city. When Merv fell, he ordered all the people brought out before him. They were divided into three herds, men, women and children. People submit to death more easily when families are broken up. They were told to lie down, and my father's troops beheaded every one, to make sure that none might survive by feigning death. The heads of men, women and children were stacked in separate pyramids. Even the dogs and cats were killed. Then the city was burned to the ground and stones pulled down. A few thousand people survived by hiding in the cellars. Later my father sent some of his horde back to hunt them down. In the end there was no life left in that place. So it went with many other cities of Khwaresmia and Persia.

"My father did not escape unscathed, however. He used to have nightmares about Merv and other places where he had ordered massacres. Many of the men who took part in the killings suffered from it later."

Taniko drained her goblet. Her hands were trembling. Did he actually expect her to feel sorry for his father and those like him? The picture of her baby being swept over the waterfall at Daidoji forced its way into her mind.

"Why the children?"

Kublai took the goblet from her cold hand. She made an effort to get up and pour wine for herself, but he waved her down. As he handed her the full goblet, she looked up at him and thought he seemed like an enormous tree.

He said, "If we let the children live they would only have starved to death."

She laughed shakily. "So you killed them out of your overflowing compassion."

Kublai looked irritated. "I have already told you that I never ordered such massacres. Besides, in every country it is the law that when one person commits a misdeed, the whole family is punished, including the children. Is that not so, even in your land?"

"Yes." She recalled the many questions he had asked her about her country on other occasions, and fear took hold of her. "Why do you go on and on? How many lands must your people conquer before you say you have enough?"

"Our ambitions change. My grandfather did not set out to conquer the world. He wanted to take horses and cattle and women from his enemies and force them to submit to him, to protect himself. But each time he won a war, he made new enemies, who feared his increasing strength. So he had no choice but to go on and fight again. By the end of his life, though, we had won so many wars that we began to feel we had a special destiny. The Ancestor often said, 'There is only one sun in the sky and one Power in Eternal Heaven. Only one Great Khan should be upon the earth.' He and those who succeeded him sent messages to rulers all over the world demanding that they come to Karakorum with tribute and offer their submission to the Great Khan.

"Grandfather in his day dreamed of reshaping the world so that all of it would be one enormous pasture. Even so, he didn't talk, as Arik Buka and his councillors do, of preserving the old ways. He never cared whether a way of doing things was old or new. He cared only for what would make the Mongols great and powerful.

"In the end my Ancestor realized that destroying all the cities and killing all their people, reducing farms and manors to wastelands, these things would not keep the Mongols powerful. He saw that there is a power that comes from the cities, from knowledge and wealth, that could be greater than the war-making strength and skills of the Mongols.

"Now the cities are a part of our empire, with the knowledge they hold. When my grandfather's generation took cities, they were like men who have starved a long time and are suddenly given meat rich with grease. They could not disgest it. It made them ill.

"I and my generation are Mongol enough to be able to conquer cities, but civilized enough to know what to do with our conquests. To be a nomad is not to be uncivilized, after all. I have read the history of China and its endless wars with my people, and I know what we Mongols are. For as long as men can remember, we have lived on the edge of the civilized world, hounded and harried by its armies, learning from it, sometimes stealing from it, an unrecognized part of it. We did not spring full grown from the steppes. It was civilized men who first learned to ride horses and camels, to herd cattle and sheep. They developed law, and it is law that binds our nomad world together like the leather thongs that hold together the frame of a *yurt*. They invented warfare. Civilized men moved slowly northward from the fertile plains of China, building their houses, raising their crops and their animals. They came to a land not so fertile, the land where I was born, poor for crops but good for herds. They cut themselves loose from the land and began to follow their herds with the seasons. They taught the hunters and forest people who already lived in the north, and they intermarried with them. That is how my people came to be.

"When the Emperors of China were strong, they warred on my people. When the Emperors were weak, my people took lands and tribute from them. The herdsman and the farmer are not different kinds of men, they are right hand and left hand. Through their constant warfare, each developed new weapons and new strategies.

"Now, for a time, perhaps for all time, we Mongols are bringing that warfare to an end. We have united the cities, the farmlands and the steppes in peace, prosperity, and order. There is no reason why all men cannot dwell under one government, even as the Ancestor said. Combining the foundation my Ancestor laid in the *Yassa* with the Imperial wisdom of China, we can create a perfect government, a government based on Mongol strength to guarantee that it will endure forever. We will use the old Confucian system of examinations to find the most talented administrators. It is the best system of government in the world—appointment of the most fit. Of course, we must never let the Chinese get the upper hand. We will take their ideas, use their skills, but never let them rise to positions of power. I will bring in able men from all the countries of the earth—Turks, Arabs, Franks, and Mongols, of course—to rule over the Chinese and humble them. If we allowed the Chinese power, they would corrupt us, weaken us, make us forget who we are, until there were no Mongols left, only decadent Chinese whose ancestors had once been Mongols. I am often accused of wanting to deliver the Mongol empire into the hands of the Chinese, but I am not so stupid as that. I will devour China, China will not devour me.

"After all of China is ours, we will turn west again. With the wealth and wisdom of China, we will go on to the conquest of the Franks. It will not be difficult. We would have swept through Europe twenty years ago, had my uncle Ogodai not died at the wrong moment. You asked me how far we mean to go. Once we have China and Europe, how much of the world will be left?

"We will be herdsmen of nations. There are many kinds of riches besides animals, besides precious stones and metals. There is the wealth of beauty, the wealth of wisdom, the wealth of comfort. We will possess and enjoy all of it, all the goods this world has to offer."

"The kind of wealth you speak of is only accumulated in time of peace," Taniko said.

Kublai eyed her with amusement. "Those islands of yours have never been invaded. There must be a great deal piled up there."

"You would be surprised at our poverty. Having seen China, I realize that our people have no idea what wealth is." Don't overdo it, she warned herself.

"You fear me. That is why you keep telling me how poor your country is." She realized that he had been sitting beside her for quite awhile now.

"Your Majesty is the most powerful man in the world. How could I not fear you?"

His dark eyes impaled her. "You know me better now than you did when we met. Why still fear me?"

She saw what was happening to him. His eyes were heavy-lidded, his breathing quicker. A slight flush crept into his cheeks. Like a bull in springtime, she remembered. Amazingly and almost instantly, she felt a warmth between her thighs in response to his stare. She had not known a man in the two years since Kiyosi's death.

He is such a big man. I could close my eyes and pretend I'm with Jebu. If he lies on me, though, he'll crush me.

"Your elephant trainers know their elephants, Your Majesty, but still—and wisely—they fear them."

"Stop calling me Your Majesty. It reminds me of things I would like to forget for a while."

"What shall I call you?"

His body lay across the bed like a boulder. He smiled up at

her. She put her hand on his silk robe and let it rest there, feeling the beating heart of the most powerful man in the world.

"You must think of your own name for me," he said. "One that we will share with no one else."

He is so big, so strong. "I shall call you Elephant."

Kublai laughed and pulled her down so that she lay on his chest. His hands plucked at her clothes. Gown by gown he stripped her. She was surprised when he didn't stop until she was completely undressed.

"You are exquisite," he said. "But you are blushing. Does it bother you to be naked? I prefer it this way." His thick fingers gently explored her body.

"It's strange to couple with a man in complete naked-ness," she said. "I don't like it or dislike it." Then she gasped. "I like what you are doing now. Very much."

She had forgotten her fears of how he might crush her if he lay on top of her. He never did. When she was ready for him he clasped her waist in his huge hands and lifted her into the air with an easy heave of his muscular arms. Lying on his back, he slowly lowered her over his loins.

She was awakened by the sound of voices arguing.

"I don't care what you think is proper. If you don't wake him right now, your head will go the way your stones have already gone."

A softer voice protested.

She opened her eyes and thought for a moment that she was in a Mongol tent. Then she remembered he had drawn down the curtains around the dais before they fell asleep amid the tumbled cushions and quilts. There was a pleasant ache in her groin, where muscles long unused had been overworked last night. Kublai lay beside her, an enormous dark bulk. Even though he was motionless, she could tell from his shallow breathing that he was awake.

The curtains parted and a fierce young Mongol face framed by braided black hair thrust itself in. Taniko shrank back and pulled a quilt around her. Kublai sat up quickly.

The man spoke an urgent sentence in Mongolian, in which Taniko caught the word Karakorum. She recognized him now. It was the *tarkhan* Bayan. The general didn't look at

Taniko but stared intently at Kublai, who asked him a question in the same tongue.

Kublai sighed at Bayan's reply. He stood up on the dais, naked, towering, and the household eunuch who had tried to stop Bayan from waking him brought him a robe. He looked down at Taniko.

"What I feared and expected has happened. Even while this *kuriltai* was electing me Great Khan, Arik Buka's people were claiming the title for him at Karakorum. Now there are two Great Khans, and it will be war. It will be years before we can proceed with the conquest of the Sung."

And even more years before you can threaten my homeland, Taniko thought with faint satisfaction.

Lying with a quilt pulled around her to cover her nakedness, she said. "I grieve for your people, Your Majesty. A civil war is a horrible thing."

"It's a wasteful thing," said Kublai. "To avoid it, I'd almost be willing to yield the empire to Arik Buka and his people. But they wouldn't know what to do with it."

The Great Khan and his *tarkhan* strode out of the bedchamber, deep in excited conversation. It's a game to them, Taniko thought. They relish it.

18

Jebu stood with his back to a willow tree as four Chinese pikemen closed in on him warily. The cries and clash of battle were loud nearby, but the mist was too heavy for him to see anything. They had been fighting almost blind for hours. He was exhausted and panting heavily.

The burble of a river sounded at his right, through the mist. He feinted with his sword, driving the four Chinese back. He raised both arms over his head, crouched and sprang. He almost didn't make it. The rough bark of the willow tree scratched the palm of his left hand. For a moment his left arm was pulling all his weight. Then he managed to hook the right arm, which held the sword, over the tree limb. A willow can't fail me, he thought.

He hauled himself up, climbing like a monkey. The four pikes thrust through the space he had occupied. He swung into the lower branches of the tree and ran out along a limb toward the river. When the branch would no longer hold his weight he dropped off and landed feetfirst in the water. The current carried him away from the shouting pikemen.

Even near the shore the river was deep. Encumbered by his armor, Jebu swam with difficulty. This was one of the many channels that irrigated the Red Basin. Jebu heard voices speaking his own language and swam to the riverbank. Clambering over the big boulders that held the river in its manmade bed, he called out to two nearby samurai.

"We've won, shike," said one of them. "They're running away."

"He can't tell," said another. "For all we can see in this fog, we may be running away."

"Where's Lord Yukio?" Jebu asked.

"Somewhere," said the second samurai. "I don't even know where I am."

Jebu walked along the riverbank calling for Yukio. At last he found him sitting on a boulder, his dragon-crowned helmet in his hands. Jebu looked around. There was a thick white wall of mist in every direction. Near Yukio's feet three bodies lay.

"Did we drive them off?" Jebu asked. He sheathed his sword and sat next to Yukio.

"Do you think I'd be sitting here with my helmet off if we hadn't? In a little while I'll get up and order a roll call, and find out how many we lost this time. I'm sick of this. I still say we should go south to Nan Chao."

"We'll find what we're looking for if we keep going north," said Jebu.

"For eight months we have wandered in this land of mists and rivers and rice paddies, looking for what? Only you seem to know. I'm tired of you playing the mysterious shike with supernatural knowledge who keeps insisting we should head north but won't tell us why."

Jebu sighed and shook his head. "I've told you everything I know. Governor Liu advised me strongly that our best prospects lay in this direction. That's all. He didn't tell me any more. I have no mysterious knowledge. If you consider my advice faulty, give the order. We'll march south and offer our services to the King of Nan Chao against Annam. Or is it to the King of Annam against Nan Chao?"

"I have the burden of deciding the future for all of us, and you mock me."

"You make a burden of it."

"We're nothing but bandits. The Chinese have put a price on our heads. Every so often they send an army after us and we kill a few of them and they kill a few of us. Our silk and silver have run out and we have to steal food and fodder from the peasants. Everybody hates us."

Jebu snorted. "And you can't stand to be among people who don't worship you as the people of Kweilin did."

Yukio stood up. "Are you laughing at me?"

Jebu remained seated. "Yes."

Yukio's fingers tapped the hilt of his sword. "I am Muratomo no Yukio, son of Muratomo no Domei, chieftain of the Muratomo, the most illustrious warriors in the Sacred Islands."

"That means nothing here."

"You are goading me. I'm a better swordsman than you are."

"Possibly." He's right, Jebu thought, I'm goading him. These last six months have been as trackless as this white mist we're in. It bothers me as much as it does him. It puts me at the mercy of my feelings. I have no direction, no purpose. I'm lost. There's nothing to hold to.

Moko suddenly appeared, looking comical in a broad, flat Chinese helmet. "I beg of you, masters, don't quarrel. The only thing the men have left is their faith in your leadership. And as for me, if either one of you hurt the other, I would kill myself."

"You're more liable to be killed by one of us," said Jebu gruffly, glad to see him, "if you wear that Chinese helmet."

"Anyone who can get close enough to kill me can get close

enough to recognize me," said Moko. "And I have no right to wear a samurai helmet." On their long march Moko had become a sort of quartermaster for samurai. He led the baggage train, kept track of stocks of food and trading goods, and saw to the welfare of the women and servants. He negotiated with the peasants whose rice and vegetables they took, giving them promissory notes and persuading them that the samurai might actually return one day to pay for what they took. Honest or not, it made it easier for the peasants to give and the samurai to take.

"These troops you've just defeated were sent out by the governor of Hockwan," Moko said. "He doesn't know whether he's subject to the Sung Emperor or to the Mongols. Like most of Szechwan, he hasn't had a message from either overlord in six months. But he knows that both sides consider us an enemy, so he thought he'd perform a service to his masters, whomever they turn out to be, by eliminating us from the countryside."

"How do you know all this, Moko?" Yukio asked.

"Our warriors took some prisoners and they brought them to me for safekeeping. They were quite willing to talk to me."

"Good, now kill them."

Jebu's stomach contracted. "Why not let them go?"

"We are samurai. We do not suffer from confusion about whether we are fighting men or monks. Moko, round up the first six samurai you meet and tell them they are ordered to behead all prisoners." He turned to Jebu, his rounded eyes blazing. "Don't argue with me." Jebu held his tongue and turned away, his shoulders sagging.

Shaking his head slightly, Moko bowed. "One more thing," he said. "There is an old monk who came along after the battle looking for both of you. He is short, white-haired and wears a gray robe, like a Zinja."

Jebu felt his heart beat faster.

"Finally," said Yukio.

"Shall I bring him to you?" said Moko.

"At once," said Jebu.

The old man emerged out of the mist looking little changed from the night, years ago, when Jebu had left him on the beach below the burning Waterfowl Temple. His beard had grown almost to his waist, hiding the white rope around his neck. Age was thinning his white hair.

He and Jebu looked at each other a long time in silence. Droplets of water dripped from a tree branch to a puddle on the ground.

"Why did you not come to me before, sensei?" Jebu whispered.

"I had other things to attend to."

Jebu turned to Yukio, whose eyes were big with awe. "Lord Muratomo no Yukio, I present my father, Taitaro, former abbot of the Waterfowl Temple."

Yukio bowed deeply. "Sensei."

Taitaro bowed in turn. "Lord Yukio, your fame has spread throughout the Sacred Islands and a good part of China. Future generations of Muratomo, when they go into battle, will proudly claim you among their ancestors."

"You are too generous, sensei," Yukio said, bowing again to express his reverence for Taitaro's attainment. "I have been hearing of the great Abbot Taitaro ever since I met your son."

Jebu and Taitaro embraced. Jebu felt happy and at peace for the first time in many months. Affection surged up within him like a spring bursting out of the ground and spread to Taitaro, to Yukio, to Moko. Moko, who had never met Taitaro before, stood to one side, his bowl-shaped helmet in his hands, tears running down his cheeks.

"Did Governor Liu tell you how to find us, sensei?" Yukio asked.

"The word was passed from him to me through the Order," said Taitaro. "I must tell you, though—that good, wise and strong man is gone. Both he and the general who was sent to arrest you were executed by Chia Ssu-tao for letting you escape."

Grief was a great weight in Jebu's chest. "I warned him not to go back to the capital with that general. I mourn him."

"He was one of us, Jebu," said Taitaro. "He is no more to be mourned than the ashes of our dead which we scatter on the wind. He would not want it."

"Chia Ssu-tao would have let Kweilin be overwhelmed by the Mongols," said Yukio. "He tried to punish us for defending it. Now he has slain one of the finest officials in the land.

He is a poison at the heart of the Sung empire. How can it survive with such as him ruling it?''

"I am more concerned about how you are to survive," said Taitaro. "I have come to invite you to accompany me to a temple of the *Ch'in-cha*, where this little river forks away from the Min. It is a day's ride from here. There I hope to be granted a vision that will help to guide you."

"Just you, Jebu and I?" asked Yukio. "This countryside is hostile."

"It only seems so to you. Now that you have driven off the troops of Hochwan, you need fear no further attacks."

"Perhaps only Jebu should go," said Yukio. "He is your son and a member of your Order."

"But—" Jebu started to say. A motion of Taitaro's hand silenced him.

"You are the leader of these samurai," said Taitaro. "It is not fitting that a monk who serves you should have any special knowledge that is not fully known to you as well."

It was almost as if Taitaro knew what had been happening between the two of them, Jebu thought.

19

The temple of the *Ch'in-cha* was near the top of a steep, forested hill. They were exhausted when they got there. The journey began before sunrise, continued through a plesant summer day, and ended with their horses climbing a steep mountain path long after dark with the aid of the seventh full moon of the Year of the Ape.

That night, for a change, there was none of Szechwan's usual mist. Tall pine trees concealed the temple until they were almost upon it. It was dug into the side of the hill, the only external structure a carved stone entrance with a tiled roof.

Taking a tinder box and an oil-soaked pine knot torch from his saddlebag, Taitaro made a light for them. Inside the temple entrance was a surprisingly large room, carved out of solid rock. It was five-sided, and in each side there was a triangular opening to chambers beyond. Taitaro led the way to the farther opening on the left side of the entrance. They entered a tunnel.

"This temple was here when the ancestors of the first Emperors of China were village overlords," Taitaro said.

"Is it deserted?" Yukio asked.

"At the moment, yes."

"What happened, did the Mongols sack it?"

"No," Taitaro said. "The Mongols respect the holy places of all religions. In this land the *Ch'in-cha* have long since given up living in communities of their own. The temple is used only when there is a need for it."

Jebu had to crouch to walk through the tunnel, though the rounded roof was high enough for Yukio and Taitaro. The cool air around him had the pleasantly dank smell of a cave.

The chamber at the end of the tunnel was spacious. The scraping of their footsteps echoed from the dome-shaped ceiling. Looking down, Jebu saw that there was a mosaic design in the floor. Taitaro placed himself in the center of the design. The intertwining lines were worked out in the six colors of the rainbow, against a background of concentric rings of black and white. So rich were the colors that the entire design seemed to vibrate under Jebu's torch.

He noticed something on the wall of the room opposite to where he was standing. It was an eye painted on the rock wall of the chamber, the paint fading with age. In the center of the eye was a red and white version of the yin-yang symbol. A bunch of wilting flowers was set in a small jade vase on a pedestal before the painted eye. Someone had been here a day or two ago.

Jebu looked back at the mosaic on the floor. Now he recognized it. It was the Tree of Life, the intricately knotted maze he had seen in a vision with Taitaro, a version of which was carved on the precious stone he carried concealed in his Zinja robe. This version of the tree seemed to radiate from the center of the circular room, as if one were looking down upon it from above its many-colored branches.

Taitaro seated himself on the floor in the center of the mosaic, dropping down easily and gracefully despite his age. "Do you know how to meditate, Lord Yukio?"

"I spent a good many years in a monastery, sensei. Though I never could see the point of sitting on one's buttocks and thinking about nothing."

"I understand," said Taitaro. "But there is a point tonight. Please seat yourself and try to meditate. Jebu, give me the Jewel of Life and Death."

Jebu set his torch in a holder beside the entrance and reached inside his robe for the Jewel. He walked slowly to Taitaro, holding it out before him.

"What is that?" whispered Yukio.

"A shintai," said Jebu.

"Have you been carrying it with you as long as I've known you? Why haven't we had better fortune?"

Taitaro took the stone from Jebu. "It is the belief of our Order that fortune is neither good nor bad, Lord Yukio, and that in any case neither prayers nor spells nor deeds can affect it." He held the Jewel up between his thumbs and forefingers and gazed into it.

After a moment he said, "Put out the torch." Jebu stamped out the torch in the tunnel outside the room.

The chamber was not totally dark. Jebu noticed a shaft of soft, white light falling from the ceiling, striking the mosaic floor near Taitaro. It was moonlight, entering through a small circular opening in the center of the dome. The moments when the moon was in precisely the right position to send its light through the opening must be rare, Jebu thought.

The three sat in silence until Jebu lost track of time. From long habit, he kept his eyes fixed on the Jewel in Taitaro's lap, feeling that he could see its intricate pattern even though it was across the room. He seemed to be floating in a sea which had no surface, no bottom and no shore in any direction.

Gradually the shaft of light changed position as the moon moved across the sky. It struck Taitaro's knee, then his forearm. At last the light fell upon the Jewel, which seemed to blaze up instantly like a newly kindled fire. A cool, green radiance filled the room. The eye painted on the wall was fixed on the back of Taitaro's head. Taitaro's eyes were fixed unblinkingly on the Jewel.

Jebu expected the Tree of Life to spring up before him in all its glory. But he saw only the burning seed in Taitaro's palm. At last, as the light moved on with the passage of the moon from east to west, the Jewel ceased to glow.

Taitaro spoke, and his voice was calm and pleasant, but Jebu felt that he was hearing the voice, not of his father, but of the Self.

"You will go into the north, where the Wise One contends with the Keeper of the Hearth. You will join the Wise One, who has gathered men from many lands to serve him. You will fight for the Wise One, then you will return to the Sacred Islands. One of you will be betrayed by his own blood. The other will seem to die but live. The jewels created by Izanami and Izanagi shall be protected by the Hurricane of the Kami. Each of you will be worthy of his father."

Taitaro's voice died away. The three sat in silent meditation again for a long time.

"Take the Jewel again, Jebu," Taitaro said. Jebu stood and took the Jewel from Taitaro's hand. Taitaro rose fluidly to his feet and stretched himself casually, as if he had only been napping.

"Come," he said, "let's camp outside for the night."

Their horses tethered to a pine tree, they sat on the ground a short distance above the entrance to the temple. Fog was beginning to fill the valley below their hill, so that they seemed to be on an island rising out of a pearly sea.

"What happened to you in there?" asked Jebu.

"It was as if I were dreaming," said Taitaro. "The words I spoke were not mine. They came to me."

"Who are the Wise One and the Keeper of the Hearth?" Jebu asked.

"Two members of the Mongol ruling family are preparing to claim the title of Great Khan—Kublai Khan and his brother, Arik Buka. Kublai Khan's grandfather, Genghis Khan, called him *Sechen*, which means the Wise One. Arik Buka is ruler of the Mongol homeland. His title is Keeper of the Hearth. The first part of the prophecy means that you will serve Kublai Khan. He gives high place to foreigners and has adopted many foreign ways. You will be welcome among his Banners. One wing of his army is moving westward, south of the Great Wall. You can meet them at Lanchow, directly north of here.''

''How kind of the gods—or whoever it is who prophesies with your tongue, sensei—to arrange things for me,'' said Yukio bitterly. ''I need only get to Lanchow and there join the army of this Kublai Khan. How simple.''

''What is it, Yukio?'' asked Jebu softly.

Yukio shook his head. ''Only twice in my life have I felt in control of my own destiny. Once was when I escaped from the Rokuhara. The other, when I decided to lead this expedition to China. Whatever mistakes my father made, they were his mistakes. He was no one's plaything. I did not know what a glorious feeling that could be until the night I went over Sogamori's wall.''

''And now?'' said Taitaro.

''Since we left Kweilin, sensei, I've been following your son blindly. And now I am following you. Jebu decided that we must wander through Szechwan. Now you tell me I must go and fight for this Kublai Khan.''

''Not must, Yukio. The path has been suggested to you, nothing more. You will find Kublai Khan a wiser and more generous lord than the Emperor of China.''

''To serve Kublai Khan now is simply the best choice open to me, as you see it?''

''I thought so before,'' said Taitaro. ''But I could not be entirely sure of it until tonight, when I had the opportunity to read the Jewel of Life and Death in this temple. Now I know. If you choose this path, Lord Yukio, it will ultimately lead you back to the Sacred Islands and to glory.''

Yukio's large brown eyes seemed to glow in the moonlight. ''That is the road I want to travel, sensei. I left the Sunrise Land only with the thought that I might return one day to avenge my family and overthrow our enemies. I may die on that path, but as long as I know I am on the path, I don't mind. These past months I felt I had lost my way.''

''My vision tonight tells me you are on that path.''

Yukio shook his head. ''And yet my father told me that a military commander who pays attention to the flights of birds or the cracks in a tortoiseshell is sure to lose. He used to tap his forehead and say, 'The only auguries worth listening to are in here.' ''

Taitaro nodded. ''But you came to China not only to escape the Takashi and make your fortune, but to learn more about the art of warfare. In today's world the Mongols are the masters of war. Of Kublai Khan, the Mongols say he has the military genius of his grandfather, Genghis Khan. How could you learn more than in the service of Kublai Khan?''

Yukio smiled wryly. ''How foolish you make my notion seem, of getting involved in the wars between Nan Chao and Annam.''

Taitaro patted Yukio's arm. ''You are no man's plaything, Muratomo no Yukio. You're only twenty-five years old. You'll be a great general.''

''Forgive me, sensei, for not being more grateful to you for your efforts in my behalf.'' Yukio went over to the horse he had tethered nearby and said, ''I think I want to be alone for a while.'' He took his ivory flute out of his saddle case.

They watched him climb to the top of the boulder where he could see the moon sink toward the western horizon. It was the yellow moon of midsummer, not the great lantern moon of autumn. But it was beautiful enough in its way. To Jebu, the sight of Yukio seated on his boulder was reminiscent of a stone on top of a stone. Yukio raised the flute to his lips.

The tune he played was a simple country air, such as one might hear greeting the fishing boats as they sailed into Hakata Bay late in the afternoon. Yukio had not played his flute in a long time. Jebu felt his eyes grow moist. The melody made him think of home. And that reminded him of Nyosan.

''Sensei. Father. There is something I have to ask you.''

Taitaro said, ''I hear the note of an impending quarrel in your voice. Couldn't you at least wait until he's finished playing?''

They were silent as Yukio's melody soared over the pines, then dipped its wings like a crane and glided to a landing. Jebu waited a moment more out of respect for the music and Taitaro's appreciation of it. Then he plunged in.

''Sensei. Many years ago you sent Mother away while you remained at the Waterfowl Temple to pursue your studies in solitude. Later you saw her at the Teak Blossom Temple, then left her again to travel to China. You have abandoned your wife, my mother. I know you to be a good man, if there is any such thing. I don't see how you could leave her alone and lonely."

Taitaro was silent for so long that Jebu began to think he was not going to answer. Finally he said, "I have had word from the Sacred Islands. From the Order. Your mother is dead, Jebu."

"What?" He must have mistaken Taitaro's words.

"Whatever I should or should not have done for your mother, it is too late. She is gone, my son. The best woman I ever knew."

"Did she know you thought that?" Jebu asked bitterly. He felt the tears starting to come. There had been a moment when he couldn't believe what Taitaro was saying, a moment when it seemed the old man must be posing one of his philosophical problems. But he heard the sadness in Taitaro's voice and knew it was real. He felt as if the bottom had dropped out of his heart.

"Yes, she knew it," said Taitaro. "There wasn't much we didn't talk about."

"Except during these last years," said Jebu. "What did you have against her, that you could leave her like that?" His voice broke as he said the last few words. He put his hand to his face and sobbed.

"She and I were very close after our parting. We believed— I believe—that each of us is a manifestation of the Self. We felt that we could never be separated. I saw her in everything around me, and she, I believe, saw me in the same way."

"Monk's talk. She would have called that monk's talk. She knew the difference between a flesh-and-blood man and a manifestation of the Self."

Taitaro sighed. "She lives in you, Jebu, as she does in me."

"Yes, but that's not her, don't you see? What did she die of?"

"It is going to hurt you a great deal to hear this." Taitaro moved closer to him and spoke in a lower voice. Even though Jebu knew Nyosan was dead and nothing could hurt her any more, he felt frightened. Taitaro rested his forehead on his hand.

"Jebu, when Yukio and his army sailed from Hakata Bay it was a terrible defeat for Sogamori. His son, Kiyosi, was killed."

"I know. Kiyosi was in the bow of the lead ship, aiming an arrow at Yukio. I didn't know who it was until after I had shot him in the chest and he had fallen overboard. Moko told me."

"I had no idea it was you who had killed him."

"I suppose no one except Yukio and Moko and I know."

"Had Sogamori known it was a Zinja who killed his son, he would have felt even more justified in what he did."

Jebu's body went cold. "What did he do?"

"All that summer of the Year of the Horse he was secretly sending infiltrators disguised as monks, merchants, and land-less peasants, into Kyushu. Then in the Ninth Month he sent a huge armed force across Shimonoseki Strait. Before word could reach the Teak Blossom Temple, his agents had cut off all communications and all escape routes. Ten thousand sam-urai surrounded the monastery buildings. Those who tried to escape were pushed back into the flames. Of course, the monks fought back, and over two thousand Takashi died, I am told. Weicho, the abbot, went down fighting. A master of the naginata, that one. The women and children took refuge in the temple building itself. They all died in the flames. It's said their screams could be heard all over Kyushu. When the fire was cold there was no one left. Every person in the temple perished."

Jebu was unable to speak for a long time after Taitaro finished. He sat there gasping, his thoughts incoherent. He felt as if someone had thrown him to the ground and beaten him with a club.

At last, he said, "My mother was burned to death?" It was both impossible to put the half-formed picture out of his mind and impossible to see it clearly. The packed bodies. The screams of women and children. The towering golden flames.

Taitaro gripped his arm. "Listen, Jebu. This world kills people in all manner of horrible ways. You are not the only person who has lost a parent by violence. You must bear this. You are a Zinja."

Jebu tried to see into Taitaro's eyes, but the moon was behind the old man's head, and his face was in shadow. "Two parents, sensei. Two." He started to sob brokenly. He had not cried like this since Moko told him of the death of his and Taniko's baby.

"I hate this world," he said suddenly.

"There is only this world."

"Then better to be out of it. The samurai are right to pursue death."

"Neither your father nor your mother sought death. If you turn to death because they died, you'll be betraying them."

He remembered Nyosan at the Waterfowl Temple so many years ago saying, "Live, Jebu." He burst into sobs again.

"Some day I'll go back there. I'll leave a flower in the ashes of the temple. And then I'll go and kill Sogamori."

"You've already killed his son. Perhaps you can feel, a little, how Sogamori must have felt about that."

Jebu stood up, towering over Taitaro. "Oh, you're so wise, sensei. Why can't your wisdom show you how to weep for my mother?"

"I have wept for her, Jebu."

Jebu wanted to kneel beside the old man and put his arms around him. But he was still angry.

"Can your wisdom tell me why you were on the other side of the world when my mother was killed? And why she had to pine for you for so many years before that?"

Taitaro spoke in a sad, yielding voice. "When you scold me for giving a higher place to monkish wisdom than to human feelings, I can almost hear your mother's voice. You are so very much like her. One day, Jebu, you will come to understand the separateness of beings. We Zinja teach the oneness of all beings. Because we understand that oneness, perhaps we are able to grasp separateness better than most."

"You did love her. I know you did."

"I do love her."

"Then how could you leave her?"

"I feel I have a mission. I have had an insight, if you will. There are certain things I am called to do. The world is entering a new age. The years of solitary meditation were my preparation. My being here in China is part of my task. I know you can understand this, my son, because you have followed the same path yourself."

Jebu slowly sat down again beside Taitaro. "What do you mean?"

"My son, when last we met at the Waterfowl Temple, I didn't know everything you had been doing, nor did you have time to tell me. I always wondered if there was a woman who meant as much to you as your mother meant to me. On my brief .visit to the Teak Blossom Temple before I left for China, I learned about you and the Lady Shima Taniko."

"What did you learn?" Jebu's face felt hot.

"That the very first task I sent you on, so many years ago, is a task you have never completed. That your life and the life of Lady Taniko have been linked together ever since. And yet, my son, both you and she decided long ago to go your separate ways. I suspect she means more to you than any other women in the world does, and that you mean more to her than any other man. Yet each of you feels a destiny drawing you that makes it impossible for you to be together."

"That may be true," said Jebu.

"But she is closer to you than you realize, my son."

"More of your Zinja wisdom about seeing everybody everywhere, sensei?"

"Not at all, Jebu-chan. I mean that the Lady Taniko is here in China. She is in the household of Kublai Khan."

20

The hot south wind that blew over the steppes of Mongolia all through the night wailed mournfully. The long grasses barely stirred. Eternal Heaven, worshiped by the Mongols, was utterly black, adorned with innumerable stars. Men who

had wandered these wastes all their lives, as the Mongols and
their ancestors had for generations beyond memory, read the
stars easily.

The portents were good. "When the Northern Fish comes
near the Great Dog," said Kublai's astrologers, "the khan
will be mighty and his enemies overwhelmed." Tonight those
two wandering stars were the closest they would be this year.

The wind's keening was barely audible above the drumming
of tens of thousands of horses' hooves. Birds sleeping in the
grass, alarmed by the approaching thunder, took flight. Their
cries were the only voices raised over the rumbling of the
oncoming horde.

The faces of the riders were bound with cloths against the
wind and dust. Officers shuttled back and forth before the
long lines of horsemen, checking the order of the formations
and passing whispered commands.

Behind the riders, ox-drawn wagon trains groaned along in
the darkness, the solid wooden wheels creaking, each wagon
bearing its mushroom-shaped *yurt*. In the center of the rolling
city of *yurts* lumbered black, enormous shapes. The war
elephants padded over the grass, crushing it under foot, moving more silently, despite all their bulk, than the horses or the
oxen.

The host of Kublai Khan was marching northward toward the
Gobi. It was the Tenth Month of the Year of the Rat, four
years since the war between Kublai and his brother Arik Buka
had begun.

Countless times over thousands of years, armies had clashed
on these grassy plains. Hsiung-nu, Yueh-cheh, Turks, Tartars, Mongols, as well as races and tribes whose names were
forever lost, had battled here with one another and with the
chariots and legions of China. The steppe grasses had been
watered with warriors' blood and fed with their flesh. The
earth was enriched with their bones.

The first pink of sunrise shone in the east. Scouts rode back
to the advancing front ranks to report campfires beyond the
hills to the north. Colored lanterns, shielded so they could
only be seen from one direction, signaled the Banners to halt.

Arik Buka was caught. His back was to the desert.

The *yurts* stopped rolling, holy men stepped forth. Shamans sacrificed sheep, Buddhist lamas spun their prayer wheels,

Nestorian Christian priests chanted half-forgotten Latin over portable altars, and *muezzins* called their faithful to prayer. Men of every faith and of no faith at all, men of every nation from the rising to the setting of the sun, prepared their minds and bodies for battle.

In the left wing, so far across the steppes from the center of the arm that they could not see it, rode the samurai under the command of Muratomo no Yukio, beneath the standard of the *orkhon* Uriangkatai. As the first sliver of crimson broke the flat line of the horizon, the samurai dismounted and bowed deeply from the waist toward the sun, toward the Sacred Islands, toward the Emperor. Glancing at Yukio, Jebu saw that his friend's eyes were glistening with tears.

Some groups of samurai performed Shinto rites of purification while others listened to the chanting of Tibetan lamas, whose words meant nothing to them but whose ceremonies gave comfort.

For those who wished, Taitaro held the Zinja equivalent of a service. It was more a philosophical discourse than a religious ritual. Taitaro repeated the sayings that had given the Zinja courage since the founding of the Order. "Your armor is your mind . . . Act, and do not concern yourself with results . . . Death is neither good nor evil."

Yukio and Jebu went to confer with the general, Uriangkatai. The *orkhon* was a big man, as tall as Jebu and broader. He had gathered his *tuman-bashis* under his standard, an iron spear with a collar made of long white horsehairs.

"Our wing will attack first," said Uriangkatai. "We face their right wing, commanded by Arghun Baghadur."

Jebu and Yukio looked at each other.

"What is it?"

"We fought Arghun at Kweilin four years ago," Jebu answered, "when we were serving the Sung Emperor."

Uriangkatai grunted. "Now you fight for a better master and he for a worse. The Great Khan has chosen to try the *tulughma*, the standard sweep. It's a tactic Arik Buka knows as well as we do, but he may be drawn to attack us anyway, because he was the desert behind him and nowhere to go but forward. Also, we've taken him by surprise, and he may not be aware of how strong we are. Our right wing under Bayan will lie back while the center under the Great Khan will strike at Arik Buka's center. The Great Khan will retreat, seemingly driven back by Arik Buka's resistance." Suddenly Jebu was reminded that Uriangkatai, ten years older than he, was the son of Subotai Baghadur, a companion of Genghis Khan's youth who became his greatest general, a master of strategy second only to the Conqueror himself.

A *tuman-bashi* asked, "What if Arik Buka's right attacks the Great Khan?"

"It's our job to keep their right wing occupied. When we attack Arghun, we can expect him to retreat. Remember, they're heavy cavalry. Their bows will have much longer range than ours. We'll take a lot of punishment before we can give any back. Get them moving away from us, then turn and run yourselves. Get them to chase us. That's all we have to do. Meanwhile, if Arik Buka's center and left wing advance against the Great Khan, Bayan with all the heavy *tumans* will sweep around Arik Buka's flank, envelope it and crush it. Then Kublai Khan will hit them with all the strength of his center, war elephants and all."

Jebu remembered a battle long ago at the Imperial Palace in Heian Kyo when Kiyosi's Red Dragon helmet led the feigned retreat.

"The Great Khan has promised that all the treasures piled up in Karakorum will be divided among his horde," Uriangkatai said. "That's more than fifty years' accumulated loot. If we win this, each man will be a khan in his own right."

"Generals always make everything sound easy," Yukio said as they rode back to their own ranks on their Mongol ponies. Most of the big Chinese horses on which they had left Kweilin had long since been lost, but Kublai Khan had issued them new horses from a seemingly endless supply. The steppe ponies could cover more ground, faster, than any horses in the world.

The sun was well above the horizon now. The samurai were in the vanguard of the left wing. Uriangkatai always put them in the vanguard. It was where they wanted to be. Yukio had *tuman-bashi* status even though he commanded far fewer than ten thousand men.

Of the original thousand samurai who had come with Yukio to China only about half were left. But there were over two

thousand men fighting under Yukio, the balance made up of
Chinese as well as Turks, Tartars, Tibetans, Koreans and
Arabs who had joined them in the last four years.

Jebu felt the hollow sensation in his stomach that always
preceded a battle. He took his position out in front of the first
rank of riders. Yukio rode up and down the line, saying
cheerful things, making everything sound easy. To Jebu's
right rode a standard-bearer holding up a square of gold silk
on which was painted a White Dragon.

The horns brayed, the saddle drums rumbled, and the
samurai began to move forward. Jebu tested his mount's
responsiveness to knee pressure as they trotted over the tall
grass, letting the reins dangle and making the pony veer to the
right, then the left as he drew his bow from his saddle case
and checked its tension, pulling lightly on the string.

He mounted a rise and drew in his breath sharply. A vast
carpet of white flowers with red centers filled the shallow
valley before him. In the morning sun the flowers were
dazzling. He had often wondered why a day of battle would
sometimes be so beautiful that it was hard to think of killing
or of facing your own death. Why was the world of men not
more often reflected in the world around them? Today would
then be a gloomy, foreboding day. Or contrariwise, why were
men rarely as beautiful as the world of sun and flowers?

His horse glided through the white field and up the other
side of the valley. There was the enemy. At first they were
only a dust cloud on the horizon, then a long black line of
horsemen brandishing lances. Rank after rank of mounted
men poured toward them over the rolling meadow. Jebu felt
his body bracing itself for the shock. These were heavy
cavalry, and they were not retreating.

The arrows began to fly. Jebu heard screams from behind
him. Some arrows whistled overhead from his side, but they
fell far short of the oncoming riders.

Somewhere in those mounted ranks coming toward him
was Arghun. Maybe they would meet today and settle what
was between them.

"Forward at the gallop," called Yukio, riding on Jebu's
right. The horns transmitted the order, and Jebu's pony and
all the others along the line picked up the pace. It was the
only way to get within range quickly.

But, inevitably, the attackers wheeled and began riding off in the opposite direction. In his frustration, Jebu wanted to try a shot, but he remembered the Zinja maxim, make every arrow count.

Now Arik Buka's heavy cavalrymen turned to their saddles and shot at the samurai over the rears of their horses. Men and ponies fell, screaming, all over the rolling grasslands. The devastating volley tore huge gaps in the samurai ranks.

An arrow thudded into his horse's chest. The animal fell to its knees, and Jebu flew over its head. He pulled himself into a ball in midair. He hit the ground on his shoulders, his armor rattling, and lay on his back for a moment, stunned. Then he rolled over on his stomach and raised his head cautiously, peering through the grass.

The enemy turned again and were coming back. Six horsemen were coming directly at him. He could feel the beat of their hooves through the soft earth under him. There was no place to hide. He decided to play dead, rolling on his side so he would be able to see.

He was surrounded by a rampart of tall gray-green grass. One of the white flowers hung directly over his head. It had no smell. They were upon him. Through half-closed eyes he saw one rider coming at him, lance lowered. To make sure he was dead.

Jebu grabbed the lance and jammed its point into the earth, hard and fast. The rider, still holding tight to the lance, was vaulted out of his saddle. He hit the ground with a crash of his steel breastplate, while his riderless horse ran on, following the others.

The man was lying on the ground, groaning. Jebu crawled over to him and smashed his windpipe with the edge of his hand. He muttered the Prayer to a Fallen Enemy while looking around wildly to see where the other horsemen were. They were wheeling around now to see what had happened. Crouching, Jebu ran to his dead horse and pulled his bow out of his saddle case. He fired an armor-piercing arrow at one rider, who took it through the breastplate and pitched out of the saddle. Another arrow caught a man in the right shoulder, making him drop his lance and ride off. Now the three remaining warriors had their heavy crossbows out and were shooting at him. He lay behind the body of his horse, using it as a shield.

A pair of riders galloped to either side of Jebu's dead horse. Mongols never jumped their horses. Two lance points stabbed at him. He rolled away from one, but the other caught him on the unprotected inner side of his arm and tore through his left bicep. Jebu grabbed the lance as he had before, but this rider brought his horse to an instant stop. He pushed the lance point deeper into Jebu's arm, tearing through muscle, trying to pin him to the dirt.

Jebu reached into his armor-robe. Luckily the blow gun was on the left side. One dart was already in place. Jebu flicked the plugs at either end away with his right thumb, put the tube to his lips, and sent a poisoned dart into his enemy's throat. The man clawed at the dart, letting go of his lance. He had barely pulled the dart out and thrown it to the ground when the poison began to take effect. He toppled out of his saddle and went into convulsions.

The dying man's pony danced nervously but did not run away. Jebu was in the saddle in two jumps and had the Mongol's bow out of its case, while his eyes searched the field for the two other cavalrymen. They came at him together, charging him with wild, warbling cries, sabers waving. His left arm was too badly hurt for him to draw the bow. He decided to try to outrun them.

He had no choice but to head in the least promising direction, north, toward the Gobi. A cold wind bit into his face, a strangely cold wind for midsummer. Round yellow and purple clouds towered above the horizon. Dust stung his eyes. He pulled his headcloth around to cover most of his face. The two horsemen pursuing him were gaining on him. The dust blowing in the air got thicker as he galloped northward. Soon it was all around him in a seething yellow cloud. He could no longer see. But his pursuers couldn't see him, either.

He turned his horse to the right, heading for where he thought the center of Kublai's army should be. He didn't want to come out of the storm in the middle of Arghun's wing. Riding with the wind blowing on his left side, he gritted his teeth against the searing pain in his arm. It hurt all the way from his fingertips to his shoulder. Blood was dripping from his hand. He slowed the pony down to a walk, ignoring the dust, and used his short sword to cut a strip from his gray cloak. He bound his arm with the strip of cloth. There would be a lot of sand in the wound, but he could wash it out later.

He turned to the right again, so that his back was to the wind. He wondered if the dust storm had brought the battle to an end. His eyes were sore, his teeth full of grit, his throat so dry it ached.

At last the wind died down, and he found himself on a stretch of steppe that looked just like the place he had been when the dust storm arose. A Mongol would know the difference, no doubt. Riderless horses grazed over the plain or ran about in frightened confusion. Half-hidden in the tall grass, bodies lay everywhere.

A flourish of trumpets, drums and gongs reached him. A tower, gold and white, was moving northward over the grassland. A dark host of mounted men topped a row of hills near Jebu. Mongol cavalry were advancing at a walk. He spotted Chinese war chariots, each drawn by four horses and carrying three men, and Arabs with scimitars on nervous, prancing stallions.

The moving tower came up over a ridge, revealing that it rested on a wooden platform which, in turn, was carried on the broad backs of four elephants. Jebu had seen the structure before, so it was no surprise to him. War elephants usually carried towers from which soldiers fought or commanders observed the course of battle. This one, like many things the Mongols did, was not really different, only bigger.

From a gilded chamber at the top of the tower Kublai Khan watched the progress of the battle. Jebu wondered how a man could stand atop a thing like that and not imagine he was a god. Perhaps Kublai did think he was a god. He seemed larger than human in his glittering helmet and armor, standing in the mist of his officers and a guard of archers.

Kublai passed on to the north. Jebu stopped an officer and asked the whereabouts of the left wing. The officer waved to the west. It was still on the left, where it would never be by this stage in most Mongol battles.

Jebu's arm no longer pained him. He had sent his mind to the wound and quenched the fire that burned there. But he needed treatment at once. He rode to find the samurai.

21

Most Mongol campaigns ended in a season, but this was a war between two veteran Mongol armies. It was now in its fourth year.

After proclaiming himself Great Khan in the Year of the Ape, Kublai had moved westward from Shangtu, taking his army through the rich, pleasant countryside south of the Great Wall. Yukio and his samurai were waiting for the Mongols at Lanchow, and Yukio presented himself to the *orkhon* Uriang-katai as Taitaro had suggested. Kublai Khan made it a policy to have contingents from many different nations in his army, and the samurai were welcomed and attached to the left wing.

Kublai and his brother circled each other around the edge of the Gobi Desert, like samurai dueling with swords, patiently, silently moving, poised to strike instantly at the right moment. Neither of these sons of the brilliant Tuli, grandsons of the immortal Genghis Khan, could outmaneuver the other. At last, with winter coming on, Arik Buka withdrew to a camp far to the north of Karakorum.

Kublai left a garrison to occupy Karakorum and moved the bulk of his army south into China for the winter. With the spring floods in the Year of the Rooster, Arik Buka fell upon Karakorum and took it back.

Kublai charged north to drive his brother out of the capital. The two armies clashed on the northern edge of the Gobi and Arik Buka fled. They met again ten days later and parted after a ferocious battle in which each side suffered heavy losses. They went back to their war of patience and maneuver.

In the Year of the Dog, Kublai returned to China. Arik Buka turned west, invading Central Asia, where he tried to

379

overthrow the local khans appointed by Kublai and replace them with his own men. During that year and the Year of the Pig, Kublai let his brother deplete his strength against the many enemies he made in Turkestan, Transoxiana and Kashgaria. When Arik Buka and his army returned to Mongolia in the Year of the Rat, Kublai began to move north again.

All through the battles around the Gobi, Jebu had thought of Taniko. He would find some way to spirit her out of China. They would be together at last. But during the years of the Mongol civil war there had been no way for Jebu to get near Taniko. "Kublai Khan does not take most of his women to war with him," he had told Taitaro sadly.

Taitaro had pieced together the story of how Taniko had fallen into Kublai Khan's hands, and he had told Jebu what had happened.

Jebu sat with his fists clenched, staring at the carpet of his yurt. "Horigawa and Sogamori," he said. "One killed my child and tried to destroy Taniko. The other killed my mother. I vow that when I return to the Sacred Islands both shall die by my hand."

"That is not the attitude of a Zinja," said Taitaro. "Spend more time with the Jewel. Have you noticed how much the designs in these Persian carpets resemble the Tree of Life?"

Even when there was no fighting, Jebu was nowhere near Taniko. For a time Kublai Khan stationed the samurai in Suchow, south of the Gobi. During the two years that followed, Jebu and Yukio and their men, along with various Mongol *tumans* and other auxiliary units, were shifted from city to city in the northwest marches of Kublai's territory, wherever Kublai thought his younger brother might strike next.

Taitaro traveled with the samurai, counseling them as individuals and in groups and helping them with their training. He took to meeting with teachers of other religions and engaging in long discussions with them. The Mongols had opened up vast territories to missionaries of all sects. No longer could a local ruler forbid preachers of a disapproved cult to enter his lands. The Mongols tolerated all religions and required their subjects to do the same. Taitaro enjoyed discussions with Moslems, Buddhists, Taoists, rabbis of the ancient Jewish community of Kaifeng, Nestorians and Roman Christians, as well as holy men of many other sects. Sometimes, as word of the religious arguments spread, they would attract large audiences.

Staging such debates was one of Kublai Khan's favorite amusements, and on one occasion the old Zinja was invited to Shangtu. The discussion held before Kublai and his entourage lasted several days, and representatives of various sects put forth their claims to possessing the only true religion. Taitaro took a position of absolute skepticism, rejecting the existence of all beings, dogmas and rules asserted by the other teachers, disproving the proofs his colleagues offered and pointing out the contradictions and absurdities in their mutually exclusive claims. His exasperated opponents frequently resorted to threatening him with a horrifying variety of painful fates in this life and the next.

One day an angry Nestorian challenged him. "You're not a priest, you're not a prophet, you're not a theologian. What the devil—and I use that word deliberately—are you?"

Taitaro spread his hands and said blandly, "I am a religious jester." Kublai Khan, present in the audience, laughed uproariously.

On occasion Taitaro met with other figures more mysterious and, to Jebu, more interesting than religious missionaries. But the old man had nothing to say about his meetings with Christian knights in black cloaks adorned with white crosses, Moslem sages who spoke in whispers and did no preaching, and red-robed Tibetan lamas.

"It is the business of the Order," he said.

"Who are they?"

"Knights Templar, Ismaelites, Tantric lamas. And others."

"Those names don't mean anything to me."

Taitaro laughed. "There is no reason why they should, Jebu-san."

When Jebu arrived at Taitaro's cart-mounted *yurt* at noon on the day of battle, there were wounded men crowded around it. The fame of the Zinja medicine and treatments, which Taitaro would dispense to any wounded man who came to him, had spread. Even Mongols, who would normally go to their own shamans with serious injuries, were among those clamoring for attention whenever Taitaro showed his face in the doorway. Jebu moved into the back of the crowd and waited his turn.

The men around him were talking about the battle. It was going badly. Arik Buka's left had attacked Kublai's center and scattered it. Thousands of men and six war elephants had been killed. The Great Khan himself had nearly been captured. Arik Buka's right wing, under Arghun Baghadur, had done even more damage to Kublai's left.

"It's foolishness to attack an enemy who's as strong and cunning as we are," an old Mongol said. "At best we'll come out of this with a third of our men gone, as we did three years ago. And how many men can we afford to lose before the Chinese revolt against us?"

A younger man said, "Genghis Khan subjugated the Chinese with a far smaller army than we have now."

"The Mongols of Genghis Khan's day were worth ten of today's breed." The old Mongol sniffed contemptuously.

When Taitaro finally went to work on Jebu he asked, "What happened to the man who gave you this?"

"I got him in the throat with a poisoned dart." Jebu looked around the tent. There were Tibetan and Arab doctors helping Taitaro and watching him work. The old Zinja commanded Jebu to cut off his wounded arm mentally from his body, a technique for controlling pain. Then he poured hot water from an iron kettle into the hole the lance point had driven into Jebu's bicep. He sprinkled a mixture of finely ground herbs into the wound, then bound it tightly with a linen bandage.

"Are you going out to fight again? You shouldn't. One wound like this is enough in a day."

"Excuse me, sensei, but it's insignificant. I have heard the battle is going badly."

Taitaro shrugged. "If you live, I must change the bandage tomorrow."

It was midafternoon by the time Jebu found the samurai position at the end of Uriangkatai's left wing. Jebu took a horse from his string of remounts and rode out to find Yukio. His left arm throbbed and dangled uselessly at his side, though the medications Taitaro had put into the wound eased the pain.

The samurai were formed in squares, the men standing or sitting by their horses. Yukio and his officers were gathered in a circle in front of the formation, in the shade of a cart. The dust floating in the air made Jebu's throat dry and his teeth gritty.

"I thought we'd seen the last of you," said Yukio sourly. "Why don't you stay back with your father and treat the wounded? You're no good to us if you can't pull a bow."

"After I got this wound I killed the man who gave it to me, without bow and arrow," said Jebu. "I may yet be of some use to you."

"The way this battle is going, we'll need every man we can get," said Yukio in a lower voice.

A messenger rode up. "Uriangkatai wants the samurai *tuman* ready for an immediate attack."

Another message came from Uriangkatai a moment later. "You are to move forward now toward the enemy's right wing. The direction of the battle has shifted. Arghun Baghadur is directly west of here, and the enemy center is to the northwest. Advance regardless of what happens and make no feigned retreats."

"Arghun was north of us," said Yukio. "Now he's west of us. They're trying to circle around us and sweep down on us. It's his turn to try a *tulughma.*"

The samurai surged forward in a tight line, horses shoulder to shoulder, at Yukio's command. Looking back and gauging the distance from one end of the line to the other, Jebu could see that the line was not as long as it would have been this morning. They must have lost at least a third of their men.

The grassland over which they rode was littered with the bodies of men and and horses, motionless and dust covered, as if they had been dead a long time. As they lay, dark lumps in the tall grass, it was impossible to tell whose side they had fought on.

They saw the enemy ahead, a black mass on the horizon, lances waving in the air like blades of grass. Jebu squinted. It hurt his eyes to look at the opposing line. They were riding into the sun now. That gave them an advantage. He readied himself for the killing rain of arrows that would come from the long-range, heavy bows of Arghun's cavalry. Yukio called an order to his own men to load and prepare to fire. The order was transmitted by horn signal down the samurai line.

How different is the way we fight now, Jebu thought. No

more individual samurai riding out to find somebody of good family on the other side to challenge to single combat. We maneuver in masses with all the precision of the Mongols themselves. We've learned from them—those of us who are still alive.

He kicked his horse into a fast trot. The distance between Arghun's line and their own had halved since they first saw the enemy. The arrows would start flying at any moment now. They were almost within bow shot.

The enemy horsemen wheeled and began riding away. Now would come the deadly flight of arrows fired while retreating. How many battles had these mounted archers won while seeming to run away? Unable to use a bow, Jebu drew his Zinja sword and waved it in the air above his head, yelling wordlessly, just to do something. The dust was so thick, his shout ended in a cough.

Still no arrows, except a few random, accidental ones that hit no one. The dark body of Arghun's riders had turned and were leading the samurai and the rest of the left wing—Jebu could see Uriangkatai's Banners stretched out over the plain to his left—to the north. Supposedly Arik Buka's center lay that way.

The grass thinned out and the dust grew thicker. The rolling plains turned into waves of dunes stretching toward the northern horizon. The horses' hooves slid in the sand. They were in the Gobi itself now.

There were more bodies than ever on the ground. This must have been where the fighting was heaviest this morning. Jebu had to whip his pony to keep it trotting straight ahead. It kept trying to change direction to avoid stepping on bodies. Step on them, Jebu thought. They won't feel it.

"This must be an ambush," he called, forcing his mount into a neck-and-neck gallop with Yukio's.

"Look at that," said Yukio. Jebu saw it a moment later, gleaming white and gold in the afternoon sun, looming above the undulating horizon. Kublai's elephant-borne tower. Before the tower came line after line of horsemen, sweeping over the desert, their ranks slightly curved like the saber blades.

"It's Arghun who's in a trap," Yukio cried. "Kublai's center is going to fall upon him."

But Kublai's horsemen did not attack Arghun's cavalry. Both groups formed into two wings and thundered together over the horizon.

Uriangkatai galloped up, followed by a wedge of guards. "I'm delivering this order personally to make sure you understand," the heavyset *orkhon* said. His face was flushed with excitement. "You are not to attack any of Arghun's units. Do you understand? No fighting with Arghun."

"What's happening?" asked Yukio.

"The Great Khan has won Arghun over to our side. They're attacking Arik Buka right now. We've won. Arik Buka is finished." He jerked his reins and started to ride off in the direction he had come from.

"What are we to do?" Yukio called after him. But Uriangkatai was too far away to hear or reply.

Jebu said, "We should join the rest of the Great Khan's forces and attack Arik Buka."

"But that means joining Arghun and his men," said Yukio. "We can't go near them."

Jebu shrugged. "It would be a shame if Arghun were in at the kill, and we, who have followed Kublai since he proclaimed himself Great Khan, were not."

Yukio nodded and gave the order to follow Arghun's Banners over the sand dunes. The standard-bearer drew abreast of Yukio and Jebu, and the samurai followed the White Dragon banner. Yukio summoned his hundred-commanders, and as they rode together he explained Arghun's defection from Arik Buka's army. He gave orders that none of Arghun's men, where they could be recognized, were to be attacked.

They crested a dune and Jebu was surprised at the sight spread below. He had expected to find butchery in progress in the valley beyond. Arghun's heavy cavalry and Kublai's center troops engaged with Arik Buka's center and left. Instead, there were only heaps of dead and wounded men and horses, with bands of foot soldiers going among them and sending some into the next world while aiding others. The battle had passed this way and moved on. Mongol warfare never stayed long in one place. Kublai's elephants and tower were already on the next hill, and as Jebu watched they sank below the horizon. The sun, too, was sinking.

A troop of riders came over the north side of the valley,

their horses at a walk, returning from the direction of the
battle. The riders were silent. More and more of them topped
the ridge. It was at least a whole *tuman*. From the look of the
steel armor of men and horses, it was one of Arghun's
Banners.

"Why aren't they going after Arik Buka?" said Yukio.

A leader rode out before the heavy *tuman* flanked by a small
group of officers. A standard-bearer held up a pole adorned
with yak horns and horsetails. The leader came on at a trot, as if
to parley. Yukio held up his hand to halt his own men.

The leader opposite them leaned forward in his saddle. The
men behind them had their bows out. A chill spread across
Jebu's back. He recognized the broad face with the long gray
moustache.

"It's Torluk," Jebu said to Yukio in a low voice. Even as
he spoke, Torluk raised his arm and brought it down in a
chopping motion. The archers behind him raised their bows
and fired.

22

There was no time to see how many samurai, all unpre-
pared, fell under that volley. Torluk drew his saber from
behind his back and with a wild bellow kicked his gray horse
into a gallop straight at Jebu. Jebu lowered his lance, bracing
it against his right side, steadying it with his nearly useless
left arm.

Torluk shifted in the saddle to avoid a straight-on impact
with the lance. The point slid off the curve of his steel
breastplate. Roaring, the Mongol *tuman-bashi* swung his saber
at Jebu's head. Jebu caught the blade on his lance pole. The
saber cut the lance in two but stopped short of hitting Jebu.

Jebu gripped the front half of the lance with his right hand. Like all Mongol lances, it had a hook just behind the point. He swung the hook and caught the armhole of Torluk's breastplate. Detached, Jebu's mind observed with wonder how well the Self defended him. Torluk went one way as his horse went the other. The Mongol crashed to the ground on his stomach. Jebu let go of the broken lance and let it fall with Torluk. He drew his sword.

Momentarily unthreatened, Jebu felt one with the pattern of battle that cast a network over the valley. Everywhere he looked, horsemen were locked in a single combat. The Mongols had abandoned their usual style of fighting in masses with bow and arrow from a distance, and had closed with the samurai. They're trying to wipe us out, he thought. Arghun had sent a whole *tuman*, ten thousand men, not just to kill Jebu, but to destroy all the samurai.

Still, he felt light, free from fear. He felt marvelous. He would act, he would fight. He didn't care whether he won or lost, lived or died. Even the pain in his arm did not bother him.

A huge warrior thundered down on him, swinging the iron ball of a mace at his head. Jebu had just time to bring up his sword. The handle of the mace cut itself in two against the edge of the Zinja sword. The heavy ball, undeflected, crashed against Jebu's helmet. He felt no pain.

Jebu felt much pain when he came to. His face was pressed into the sand, covered with dust, and more dust clogged his nostrils. Shafts of agony shot through his back and chest with every breath. He must have been trampled by horses. His Zinja training kept him motionless, barely breathing.

No light penetrated his closed eyelids. It must be night, he thought. He heard the clip-clop of hooves walking slowly, the crunching steps and low voices of men. He heard the sounds he always heard after a battle, mostly the cries and groans of the wounded. Bodies that had been young, strong and healthy a few hours ago, now ruined. The battle was either over or had moved to another part of the field.

He moved his consciousness slowly from one part of his body to another, starting with his toes and working upward over his legs, his torso, his arms and his head. An ability to diagnose one's own wounds was a basic Zinja skill. He let himself breathe a little more deeply. He could detect no bubbling sound in his chest. He was fairly certain there were ribs broken, but they had not pierced his lungs, the most dangerous possibility.

Nearby there were screams, shouts of rage, the thunk of a sword chopping through flesh and bone. The killer squads were going through the field executing wounded enemies. A voice crazed with pain babbled in the language of the Sunrise Land. Again the chopping sound and the voice was still.

They must be Torluk's men, doing the killing. They were coming closer. His hands were empty. He had to find a weapon. Every muscle in his body ached to move. Stop this, he told himself. Stop thinking, stop wanting. Rely on the Self. With armed enemies walking toward him it was difficult, but he made his mind a blank and kept still.

Then they were standing over him. "Recognize that gray robe over the armor? It's the monk, all right. The one the *tuman-bashi* wants."

"He looks dead," said another voice.

Fingertips felt Jebu's neck for a pulse. Instantly, still without thinking, he grabbed the hand touching him, heaved up with his back, and threw the man forward over his head. Only then did he realize he had used his wounded left arm. He grabbed for the sword arm, sprang to his feet, and stamped on the man's arm, breaking it and freeing the saber.

As he seized the saber and raised it to protect himself, he let out a cry somewhere between a scream and a groan. His sudden, enormous effort unleashed hideous agony throughout his body. It was as if a dozen red-hot lance points had been driven into him from every direction. He staggered a step, and then a veil of blackness fell over his eyes. He had barely time to see three of Torluk's men facing him, sabers poised, when he pitched forward into the desert sand.

A Zinja does not faint, he told himself. I'm a dead man now, for certain.

He woke to more pain. He was lying on his back, and a flexing of his tortured muscles told him his arms and legs were bound with ropes. He had been awakened by someone splashing water on his face. He opened his eyes, blinked

them against torchlight, and saw Torluk and Arghun looking
down at him.

"Is this the one?" Torluk said in Mongolian. His chest was
bare except for a thick swathing of cloth strips around his
middle. Perhaps he, too, had broken a few ribs when he fell
from his horse.

"It is," Arghun whispered. It was almost five years since
Jebu last saw Arghun Baghadur. The red of his moustache
was streaked with gray. The lines in his face and especially
around his slitted blue eyes were deeper. The eyes were as
empty of feeling as ever.

"Did you betray Arik Buka just to get at me?" Jebu asked
him.

Arghun shook his head. "I left Arik Buka's service for the
same reason I am going to kill you. Because I serve the spirit
of Genghis Khan. Roll him over."

Two men grasped Jebu's right side and lifted him. He
groaned in spite of himself.

"Don't cause him unnecessary pain," Arghun said. "He is
a brave man." They pushed him over and let him fall on his
stomach. "That's why I had you awakened, Jebu," Arghun
continued. "It is a bad death, to die unconscious and not
know the manner or reason of your dying. I want you to
know that it is I who am killing you, in obedience to the will
of Genghis Khan. I told you once before that I would avoid
shedding your blood." He turned to one of his men. "Give
me your bow."

"Let me get up to fight you, if you want me to die well,"
Jebu said.

Arghun laughed as he crouched over Jebu. "I'm many
years older than you are."

"I'm wounded. My left arm is useless. My ribs are broken.
It would be a fair fight." Why am I talking to him like this?
Why don't I just let him kill me and have done with it?
Something, the Self perhaps, wanted him to prolong his life
as much as possible. But a Zinja does not care whether he
lives or dies.

Arghun pressed one knee into Jebu's back and slipped the
double-curved, compound bow over his head. He pulled the
rawhide cord against Jebu's throat and turned the bow. The
string cut into Jebu's neck like the edge of a sword. The

tension of the bow pulled the string tight around his neck with a strength equal to that of two men pulling on each end of it. His lungs screamed for air. His windpipe was closed. Arghun gave the bow another turn. Jebu's head felt as if it were going to burst.

Through the dizziness and the ringing in his ears he heard voices. The bowstring tightened again, viciously. Consciousness faded—and returned in moments. The merciless rawhide cord was gone from his neck. Arghun's weight was off his back. Breath, never so sweet, whistled through his tortured throat.

Someone was kneeling beside him, cutting the ropes that held him. Yukio.

"We got to you. By the favor of Hachiman, we got to you in time."

A shout made Jebu turn his head. He gasped at the sudden pain in his throat and neck. The shout was Arghun's. He was standing face-to-face with Uriangkatai. Both big men had their fists clenched and their shoulders hunched.

"You will die. I swear by Eternal Heaven, you will die for striking me," Arghun roared.

"You are twice a traitor, Arghun," Uriangkatai replied in an even tone. "Once to your lord Arik Buka, and now to your lord Kublai Khan. You ordered a *tuman* of your division to attack our men from Ge-pen. By Eternal Heaven it is you who will pay for the needless deaths of hundreds of my warriors."

"They were foreigners," said Arghun contemptuously.

"They were soldiers of the Great Khan. They were under my command. You will answer to him and to me for the loss of their lives."

"Then I will answer for one more life as well," said Arghun, drawing his saber and turning toward Jebu. Yukio leaped to his feet and stood before Jebu's body, his samurai sword gripped in both hands, poised to strike.

Uriangkatai raised his hand. "Stop, Arghun. If I let my hand fall, the men with me will fill you with arrows." The desert ridge was lined with crossbowmen, their weapons pointed at Arghun.

The *tarkhan* exhaled slowly, relaxed, and put away his sword. It must be enough to drive him mad, Jebu thought, to come so close to killing me after all these years, and then to be stopped short.

Arghun turned back to Uriangkatai. Pointing to Jebu he said, "Understand, Uriangkatai, it is the will of Genghis Khan that this monk die. He is the son of Jamuga, the worst enemy of the Conqueror's youth. Do you think your father Subotai would have interfered with one carrying out the *yarligh* of Genghis Khan?"

"It is the will of Genghis Khan that fighting among the men of the *ordu* be punished to death. How much more are we obligated to kill a commander who starts a war among men on his own side. That is written in the *Yassa* of Genghis Khan."

"Uriangkatai, tens of thousands of men have fallen today. It is foolish for an *orkhon* and a *tarkhan* to quarrel over this one."

"If this one life is so insignificant, why did you order your men to attack my men, killing hundreds? Let the Great Khan judge the rights and wrongs of this." Uriangkatai pointed to two of the warriors with him. "Make a litter for the monk Jebu and take him to a wagon."

"Kill the monk," Arghun shouted, turning to Torluk and the men behind him. "Shoot him. Kill him now."

Uriangkatai turned to his own men and called, "Shoot any man who touches his bow."

Torluk and the men of his *tuman* remained motionless.

"Torluk, do you disobey me?" said Arghun wonderingly.

There were tears in Torluk's eyes. "I have followed you since we both were boys in the army of the Conqueror. But if we fire now and Uriangkatai's men fire back it will be war. We deserted Arik Buka and went over to Kublai Khan because this war must end, or everything Genghis Khan built will lie in ruins. Now you ask me to begin the war again." Torluk knelt. "Forgive me, *tarkhan*, for not obeying you. But the *orkhon* Uriangkatai is right. Take this question to Kublai Khan."

Arghun's eyes were those of a tiger at bay. "You give me no choice. We will go to Kublai Khan for judgment."

23

Two samurai lifted Jebu down from Taitaro's cart and carried him on a litter to join Uriangkatai's party before the Great Khan's tent. Taitaro walked beside the litter. Torches tied to tall poles illuminated the area around Kublai Khan's huge white *yurt*. The tent was surrounded by a hollow square of guards, one hundred men on a side and four deep. For two of the most prominent generals in the Great Khan's *ordu*, the guards immediately parted, but the message sent into the *yurt* brought no invitation to enter. Instead Kublai Khan's chief adviser, the Chinese scholar Yao Chow, came out waving his long, slender hands and shaking his head.

"A thousand pardons, son of Subotai," said Yao Chow bowing to Uriangkatai. "The Great Khan is holding council. He desires both you and Arghun Baghadur to be present, but not to bring a quarrel to him."

Uriangkatai said, "Yao Chow, tell the Great Khan war may break out again, here and now, if this matter between Arghun and me is not settled."

Yao Chow turned a worried eye on the groups of men that had come with the two leaders. "How many of you must enter? The Great Khan's *yurt* is already filled to overflowing."

Uriangkatai said, "For my part, the *tuman-bashi* Yukio, the monk Jebu and the older monk Taitaro to attend Jebu." He pointed to Jebu, who lay under blankets in a state of deep exhaustion, barely able to stay conscious. His crushed throat felt as if he had swallowed hot coals. Each breath, each heartbeat, was agony in his chest and back. Taitaro had treated him hastily on the wagon ride to Kublai Khan's headquarters, stripping off his armor, taping his chest and giving him a hot liquid infused with herbs for his throat. As a boy Jebu had been taught to hang by his hands for hours. The same sort of will now enabled him to cling to wakefulness.

Arghun said, "I need only the *tuman-bashi* Torluk."

Yao Chow nodded. "Those of you who are entering the Great Khan's tent, disarm yourselves and give your weapons to the guards. I will ask his permission again."

While they waited, Uriangkatai said to Arghun, "Look there, tarkhan. See where Arik Buka kneels in surrender. When we go into the Great Khan's *yurt* you must pass the lord you betrayed. Can you face him?"

The wooden door of Kublai Khan's *yurt* was open. Above it a flap which could be fastened across the door to seal it against wind and dust was raised on two poles to form a kind of canopy. Under this canopy a man knelt. Even kneeling, he was clearly tall. His head, shaved in the center, Mongol fashion, was a dark brown. The braids that hung down to his shoulders were black. His belt was draped over the back of his neck in token of submission. Guards with lances stood on either side of him.

Arghun glared back at Uriangkatai. "I have been obedient to the will of Eternal Heaven and the spirit of Genghis Khan. There is no man I cannot face."

Yao Chow returned with word that they were to enter the Great Khan's *yurt*. Uriangkatai went first, followed by Arghun. Arik Buka raised his eyes as Arghun approached.

"I kneel here thanks to your treachery," Arik Buka said reproachfully. "Of all my *tarkhans* you were the one I thought I could trust to the end."

Arghun answered coldly, "My loyalty is to the legacy your grandfather left the Mongols. I believed you were best suited to be Great Khan because you upheld the old ways. But I was wrong. You are a tiger, but Kublai is both tiger and fox. I should have remembered the words of the Ancestor: Kublai is the wisest of his seed. Now I have corrected my mistake." He turned away and strode through the doorway of the white *yurt*. Torluk followed Uriangkatai. Jebu, carried by Taitaro and Yukio, brought up the rear.

Kublai Khan, wearing a red satin robe embroidered with jeweled dragons, sat on a golden throne in the host's quarter of his tent, which was a mobile palace, four times the size of an ordinary *yurt*, walls and ceiling lined with cloth of gold. In chairs around Kublai sat his *orkhons* and *tarkhans*, the officers who had won the day for him. The rest of the *yurt* was packed with lesser officers, some sitting on benches or cushions, most standing. Slaves passed among them with trays of meat and vessels full of wine and *kumiss*. It was as much a victory feast as a council. The hum of conversation died as Uriangkatai and Arghun entered.

The men made a space near the center poles for Jebu's litter. They watched curiously as Taitaro and the other samurai set him down. The golden ceiling seemed to be rotating slowly around the center pole. Jebu blinked his eyes hard to make it stop.

Kublai's round face was flushed, his brilliant black eyes had a wild look. This was the closest Jebu had ever come to him. The family resemblance to Arik Buka was immediately apparent, but Kublai was older and had a good deal more flesh on his bones. He wore his beard and moustache long in the Chinese manner.

"What delayed you, Uriangkatai?" he said in a resonant voice that filled the silence. "And you, Arghun Baghadur? The battle has been over since sunset. I needed you here. And what's this about a dispute between you? Tonight of all nights I have no time for petty quarrels."

"This is not a petty dispute, my Khan," said Arghun in a voice as powerful as Kublai's. "It concerns a command of Genghis Khan himself."

"My Ancestor gave many commands," said Kublai. "Some were more important than others. He said a Mongol should get drunk no more than three times a month. That is a command every Mongol disobeys twenty times a month." He drained a golden goblet decorated with rubies and emeralds, and his officers laughed. "Do you recognize this throne, Arghun? It is the same throne on which my father, Tuli, Master of War, sat while he directed the siege of Merv. Were you at Merv, Arghun?"

"I was a boy in one of your father's Banners, my Khan."

"I found this throne in my brother's tent when we sacked his camp. What do you suppose he would have done with it, Arghun, if he had won this battle? Was he going to sit in it and watch while the vanquished were brought before him and executed?''

"Your brother loves tradition, my Khan." Some of the officers chuckled.

Arghun is getting the better of this whole discussion, Jebu thought. Why doesn't Uriangkatai speak up? If Kublai decides in Arghun's favor, Arghun will kill me, and no one can stop him. It's out of my hands now. The Self, working through these Mongols, will decide whether I live or die. Of course, that in me which is the Self will live forever in any case. I'm so tired. I don't care what they decide, as long as there is an end to this.

"Tomorrow I will sit on an open-air platform on this throne and my tradition-loving brother and his tradition-loving councillors and officers will be brought to me, and I will sentence them to death," Kublai went on. "Not my brother. Him I will keep beside me for the rest of his life as my—guest. But the rest of them, those who led my brother astray, will be suffocated under piles of felt. Think, Arghun Baghadur. That would have been your fate as well, had you not wisely chosen to give your allegiance to me."

"I think not, my Khan," Arghun, standing tall before Kublai and gazing bleakly at him. "If I had not come over to your side, you would not have won this battle." A shocked, resentful murmur rose among Kublai's men. Kublai himself only smiled and nodded.

"You will find, Arghun Baghadur, that I know how to remember a friend." He turned suddenly to the *orkhon* Uriangkatai. "Son of Subotai, only now do you give me a chance to thank you for your part in this day's victory. What is this dispute you bring to me for judgment?"

Uriangkatai drew himself up. He was as tall as Arghun, but much heavier. "My Khan, Arghun ordered one of his *tumans* under Torluk here to attack your left wing today after he had changed sides, while we fought the final battle with your brother. Hundreds of your men were killed. It was treachery, murder and an utter desecration of the *Yassa*."

Jebu could not imagine anyone talking to the Emperor in Heian Kyo the way Arghun and Uriangkatai talked to Kublai Khan. These generals were barely polite to their Great Khan. They argued with him, bantered with him, lectured him. And yet Kublai Khan ruled a territory thousands of times larger than the Sacred Islands.

Kublai turned to Torluk. "I remember you. You came to the *kuriltai* at Shangtu four years ago and warned me not to accept the title of Great Khan. What was your part in this?"

Arghun said, "My Khan, at my command he attacked the troops from the Land of the Dwarfs."

"I spoke to Torluk," Kublai said gently.

Torluk said, "My Khan, it is as my commander says. He ordered me to withdraw my *tuman* from the fighting against Arik Buka's center, turn back and attack the foreign dwarfs, who were following us. I was particularly to make certain that the monk, that man on the litter there, was killed."

Kublai looked thoughtfully at Jebu. "I have seen him before. He rides with the dwarfs, but he is no dwarf himself. He looks like one of us. Why did you send a *tuman* to kill him, Arghun?"

Arghun looked at Jebu, his fingers twitching as if he were about to leap on him and try to kill him then and there. "My Khan, this monk is the son of Jamuga the Cunning." He paused, as if this were all he needed to say. The assembled officers murmured among themselves.

"I thought Jamuga's family had long since been wiped out," said Kublai. "Monk, was Jamuga your father?"

"He was, my Khan," Jebu whispered. Kublai leaned forward on his golden throne, frowning.

Taitaro called out, "He was choked with a bowstring and finds it difficult to speak, my Khan. He admits that Jamuga was his father."

Kublai smiled. "You are the religious jester, are you not? What is your part in this quarrel?"

"I am from the Sunrise Land, may it please the Great Khan, and this monk is my foster son."

"Fascinating," said Kublai. He set his golden goblet down on the arm of his throne. "Arghun, did you order Torluk and his ten thousand to attack my warriors from the—the Sunrise Land—just to kill this son of Jamuga?"

"I did, my Khan. Three times before this I tried to kill him, and he escaped me. I had to make sure of him this time. I knew his countrymen would try to protect him. Only by attacking with overwhelming force could I make certain of carrying out your grandfather's command.''

Kublai raised his eyebrows and folded his hands across his imposing belly. ''Even that, it seems, was not enough. Arghun, my grandfather told me the story of Jamuga, but that was many years ago. There must be some here who never heard of him. You must refresh our memories. In what way did Jamuga offend my Ancestor?''

Arghun bowed. ''My Khan, Jamuga the Cunning was the worst enemy your Ancestor ever had. At first, he was one of his best friends. Indeed, he was your Ancestor's cousin. When your Ancestor was known as Temujin, Jamuga was his *anda*, his blood brother. He saved your grandfather's life many times. But in the end he betrayed him.

''Jamuga lived among the people who herded sheep and goats, the poor ones of our land. Temujin was of the Yakka Mongols, the horse herders who had always been the nobility among us. When Temujin fought against the other tribes and made all submit to him, Jamuga allied his followers with those of Temujin. But Jamuga told his people that after Temujin had united the tribes he would make a new nation in which all would be equal. The horse breeders would sit down with the goatherds and the shepherds, and all would live in peace with one another. The nations on our borders would leave us alone because we were strong and united.

''Temujin had a different vision. He did end the lordship of horse breeder over shepherd, but he replaced it with the rule of the Great Khan over all other khans, and the princes and generals over their tens of thousands and hundreds of thousands. He made war on the nations on our borders and took their wealth for us.''

''If we had followed the dream of Jamuga, all Mongols would be equal but poor,'' said Kublai with a smile. ''Because we followed the vision of my Ancestor, all Mongols are unequal but rich.'' There was a rumble of approval from the assembled officers.

Arghun continued. ''When Temujin held a *kuriltai* and was proclaimed Genghis Khan, Jamuga gathered the tribes who resented Temujim and had himself proclaimed *Gur-Khan*, Universal Ruler, of Mongolia. He raised a civil war against Genghis Khan and drew powerful enemies, the Merkits, the

Keraits and the Naiman, into war with our new nation. Temujin had not been in so much danger since the days when his father was poisoned and he himself forced to wear the wooden yoke of a slave.

"Genghis Khan and the forces brought together by Jamuga fought a great battle at Koyitan. The horde of Jamuga was destroyed, but he escaped. Genghis Khan sentenced Jamuga and all his family to death, down to the tiniest infant. Jamuga's wife and children were slain, his uncles and cousins, his brothers and their wives and children. The Khan decreed that all the men of Jamuga's tribe be slain, and all the male children higher than a cart wheel. All the women and smaller children were sold into slavery. That tribe ceased to exist.

"For years afterward Jamuga fled from nation to nation, doing what he could to turn them against Genghis Khan, warning them against the power of the Mongols, urging them to make war against his blood brother, fighting in their armies when they did. He went among the Kin of Northern China, the Black Cathayans, the Khwaresmians, the Hsi-Hsia, always hoping that at last he would find a power strong enough to defeat Genghis Khan. He never did. All those nations were conquered. Several times we learned that Jamuga had sired children in the lands to which he had fled. These were found and slain."

Taitaro knelt beside Jebu and whispered, "Now you know what sort of man your father was."

Jebu felt a lifting at the very core of his being. No one here thought well of his father, that was plain enough. But Jamuga the Cunning was indeed the sort of man Jebu could admire, one who believed that the shepherd was as good as the horse breeder and was willing to give his life to that belief. One who could not be crushed, but who tenaciously fought back against a power that seemed invincible. Were his body not so broken and exhausted, Jebu would have rejoiced.

His mind wandered with the pain and fatigue. He saw once again his initiation vision. Now, at least partly, he knew what it meant. He had seen this land of China, the Great Wall, the Mongol hordes sweeping over it. And he knew, now, who the giant was who had welcomed him as "little cousin." It was the one Jamuga had spent his life fighting, the one who had decreed death for both Jebu and Jamuga, the one Kublai Khan called his Ancestor—Genghis Khan.

Arghun went on. "After the conquest of northern China, Genghis Khan got word that Jamuga had fled to Korea. I was by this time a young man. I had served since boyhood in the armies of the Khan. I came to his attention for deeds in battle. In his generosity he honored me with the title *Baghadur*, Valiant. He laid the task on me, 'Slay Jamuga and all of his seed. Let none survive.' He sent me to Korea, where I searched for Jamuga and found he had sailed to the eastern island kingdom which we call the Land of the Dwarfs. I embarked for Kyushu, the southernmost of those islands, which is nearest to Korea. Disguised as a wandering Buddhist monk, I followed Jamuga's trail. He was not an easy man for people to forget. I caught up with him, fought him and slew him. But I found out that in the five years he had been living among the dwarfs he had taken a wife and fathered a son."

Arghun's words made Jebu think of Nyosan. In those days she had been known as the lovliest young woman in that part of Kyushu. Now she was dead, burned to death by the Takashi. A stab of anguish went through him and a sob almost escaped his lips. He rubbed his eyes with his right hand. His left arm was nearly paralyzed. He was so tired. If only this would end.

"Jamuga had put the son in a monastery of Zinja monks. I went there and that old man, the one standing beside the monk Jebu, had taken the infant under his protection. I was alone, and the warrior monks drove me off. I took Jamuga's head back to Genghis Khan.

"In the reign of the Great Khan Kuyuk, son of Ogodai, I went back to the eastern islands and tracked Jamuga's son, the monk called Jebu, to that same Zinja temple on the island of Kyushu, where he was staying with his foster father. We fought, but he escaped.

"The Great Khan Kuyuk died and I returned to the homeland. In his war with the Sung empire your brother, the Great Khan Mangu, made me *tarkhan* over the army in the south. I found the city of Kweilin defended by a contingent of the dwarf warriors, among them the monk Jebu. I believed that sooner or later the city must fall, and I would have my opportunity to kill him. Again Eternal Heaven decreed otherwise. Upon the death of the Great Khan Mangu the siege had to be ended.''

"Yes,'' said Kublai Khan dryly. "You were in great haste to march your army back to Karakorum to persuade my brother to declare himself Great Khan and deprive me of the title. This is an amazing story, Arghun. For over thirty years you have been trying to carry out this command of my grandfather's with no success. Lucky for you my Ancestor has gone to the next world. Imagine what he would do to an officer who took thirty years to carry out an order and still failed.''

All the officers laughed, including Uriangkatai, Yukio and Taitaro. Even Jebu painfully managed a smile. Arghun stood still, bearing the ridicule with set face.

Kublai turned to Uriangkatai. "Now that you know of my Ancestor's command to Arghun, do you feel he was justified in attacking your foreign troops?''

Uriangkatai held his hands out, palms up in appeal. "My Khan, my father, Subotai, was said to be Genghis Khan's greatest general. I rode at his side for many years. One rule he drilled into me was never to waste the lives of your men. If Genghis Khan thought a general was throwing men away needlessly, he would break him down to the ranks. Arghun claims he had the right to attack and kill hundreds of your warriors. Many of his own men died in that attack as well. He wasted Mongol lives as well as foreign ones.''

"Do you say that a *yarligh* of Genghis Khan may be neglected, Uriangkatai?'' Arghun roared.

Uriangkatai hesitated, frowning. "All commandments of the Conqueror must be honored. But the price we have paid today—'' He shook his head. "It is high. Too high.''

In a calmer tone Arghun said, "The price is almost paid.'' He turned to Kublai and held up a finger. "One more life. Let me kill the monk Jebu, and your Ancestor's spirit will be appeased.''

Jebu felt Yukio and Taitaro, standing above him, tense themselves. He himself had barely been able to follow the argument, but it seemed to him that Arghun had won his point. To the Mongols, what was one foreign life, more or less? Doubtless, to settle this dispute, Kublai would decree his death.

24

All eyes in the huge *yurt* were turned upon Kublai now. The big, dark man sat on his golden throne with his hands clasped across his belly, and smiled faintly. Except for his beard, he reminded Jebu of statues of the Buddha. After a long silence, he looked about him, raising his eyebrows.

"Has anyone anything further to say?" His voice was deep, pleasant. It rolled smoothly through the room like a great river.

Jebu wondered, did Taniko love this man? She had loved Kiyosi, and Kublai Khan had as many admirable qualities. I killed one man she loved, and now a man she may love is going to kill me. That is a kind of justice.

"Then hear my judgment," Kublai went on. "Arghun, there were many ways you could have carried out my Ancestor's commandment. You could simply have waited until this all-important battle was over, then come to me. Instead you chose a way that cost many lives. You ordered warriors of mine to attack other warriors of mine. This was an intolerable breach of the *Yassa*. It is obvious to me that you chose this surprise attack because you were not sure I would let you kill the monk Jebu. You did not trust me."

Arghun opened his mouth, and Kublai held up a hand. "Be silent. You are going to say that you acted in good faith to fulfill the commandment of Genghis Khan. Let me remind you that Genghis Khan has been dead for thirty-seven years." A surprised murmur arose in the room, and Kublai allowed it to die down before he continued.

"I ask you, Arghun—I ask all of you—are we to obey the last word Genghis Khan spoke on every subject? Might he not

say another word if he were alive? He was my grandfather. I
sat on his knee. I rode before him on his horse. I knew the
very smell of Genghis Khan. One thing I remember about
him, even if no one else does. It was impossible to guess
what he was going to do next. He was loyal to friends and he
never broke treaties. But he was never bound by his past
ideas. He was able to learn and change. Now that he is dead,
are we to stop learning? Is every man who says he has a word
straight from the lips of my grandfather to make himself my
master? My grandfather would have been the first to laugh at
such foolishness. If Genghis Khan were alive today I would
bow down before him and obey him. But he is not alive, and I
will not bow down before any man who tells me he knows
what Genghis Khan would have commanded. If I did that I
would be a fool and not worthy to be Great Khan. If he were
alive, would my grandfather think it good that hundreds of
men were killed today so that Arghun could take one life—or
try to? We do not know, so I must ask myself what I think
about it.

"My brother, Arik Buka, raised his standard against me
because he knew that if I were made Great Khan, many
things would change. Arghun, you were one of those who
encouraged Arik Buka to rebel against me, because you, too,
were against change. You brought your Banner over to me,
but you do not truly submit to me as Great Khan. You still
want me to do what you think my grandfather would have
done. I tell you, Arghun, that the Great Khan can take orders
from no one except the Great Khan.

"This is my judgment. It would be right for me to order
your death, Arghun, for causing warfare among my troops. If
you stood before any of the Great Khans who preceded me, I
am certain they would have had you taken out and strangled.
But I will not order your death because you are valuable to
me. You brought me a host, and you turned the tide of battle
today. I told you I know how to remember a friend."

Kublai turned to Uriangkatai. "You could, like Arghun,
have mistrusted my justice and sought redress for your grievances on the battlefield. If you had done that, we would have
lost everything we gained in today's victory. I uphold all your
accusations against Arghun. I give you the power of life and
death over him. The men he killed were under your com-

mand. You have the right of vengeance if you want it. You know that I do not wish to have Arghun killed. But I give you final say in the matter. Uriangkatai. Shall Arghun live or die?"

Uriangkatai was silent for a long moment before he replied. "I owe it to my men who were killed and to their families to have justice. I, too, believe Arghun deserves death. But the Great Khan's wisdom surpasses mine. If you wish Arghun to live, my Khan, so be it."

"You have acted wisely and well again and again today, Uriangkatai," said Kublai delightedly. "You are a worthy son of your illustrious father." He paused, and cheers rang through the *yurt*. Uriangkatai's broad face reddened, and Arghun stood solid, expressionless.

"Now we come to this monk," Kublai said. "He is the son of Jamuga, and Arghun says Genghis Khan decreed death for all Jamuga's seed. This monk is the son of Jamuga by blood, but he never knew Jamuga. His true father is the old monk who stands there with him, one who has lent his wisdom to my religious debates. For over four years this Jebu has served me faithfully and well along with the little band of his countrymen under the *tuman-bashi* Yukio. For that I owe him the same loyalty and protection any of my warriors deserves from me. Furthermore, he is a man of religion, and the *Yassa* forbids us to injure holy men of any faith.

"I decree that my grandfather's order condemning the family of Jamuga is rescinded. The monk Jebu is to live. Arghun, you are forbidden to harm him. I issue this command to show the world that I am Great Khan and take orders from no one, not even my most illustrious Ancestor, and certainly not from Arghun Baghadur."

Kublai Khan's assembled officers greeted his judgment with a mixture of murmurs of approval and mutterings of disagreement. Arghun stood silent, his head, adorned with graying red braids, held high, his shoulders back. Kublai fixed his penetrating black eyes on Arghun, waiting for the *tarkhan* to speak.

At last Arghun said, "I have done no wrong, my Khan. For more than thirty years I have kept faith with the Conqueror."

Yukio whispered to Taitaro, "He should cut his belly open. He has no other choice."

Taitaro shook his head. "They don't do that here."

Kublai said, "Let it be understood that your long and relentless pursuit of Jamuga's sole suriving offspring is altogether to your honor, Arghun."

Arghun said, "The spirit of Genghis Khan resides in the banner of the nine yak tails. Who will appease his spirit? He once said, 'My sons and their sons will clothe themselves in embroidered gold stuffs. They will eat sweet food and meats, and will ride splendid chargers. They will press in their arms young and beautiful women, and they will forget that they owe all these desirable things to us.' He spoke truly."

Kublai Khan shook his head. "You have understood nothing I said, Arghun Baghadur. The spirit of Genghis Khan that lives in the standard of our nation will be appeased because the Mongols have a living leader who does not submit to dead words. I wish I could trust you to serve me faithfully as you served my grandfather. But you turned on Arik Buka, and I know you will turn on me if I fall short of your expectations. Your only loyalty is to the empire itself, not to any man, but to a vision. In that way you are like Jamuga, the man you killed so long ago. That makes you a dangerous man. Perhaps I should have you killed, but I think that I may yet find a way to use you. For now, stop scolding me and get out of my sight."

Arghun turned, his eyes shining with a cold light, like the sun reflected on ice. He did not look at Jebu, but Yukio and Taitaro tensed themselves as he went by them.

"Bring the monk forward," Kublai Khan said. "I want to talk with this remarkable Jebu."

Yukio reached down to grasp the litter, but Jebu held his arm. Sick, exhausted, wounded as he was, Jebu had conceived a plan that pumped new life into his pain-wracked body. He would ask the Great Khan to release Taniko.

It might mean death for both of them. It was likely, at the very least, that Kublai would refuse. But Jebu would never have a better opportunity to get her away from the Great Khan than now.

"Help me up," he whispered to Yukio. He could not approach Kublai Khan as a weakling on a litter. He had to face him standing on his feet.

"You can't stand up," said Yukio. Jebu turned to Taitaro who looked back at Jebu and said nothing.

"Help me up, I said." He pushed against the litter, gritting his teeth against the pain in his broken ribs. Seeing that he was determined, Yukio crouched down, threw Jebu's right arm over his shoulder, and lifted him to his feet. Taitaro moved in quietly on Jebu's other side and put his arm around Jebu's waist. With the man in the middle towering over the other two, they moved forward together.

From the men around him Jebu could hear grunts of approval and words of praise. The Mongols admired strength and endurance.

Kublai Khan's face wavered in Jebu's sight. The glitter from the golden throne, lit by hanging lamps, hurt his eyes. To walk the few steps from the litter to stand before the Great Khan seemed as painful an ordeal in its way as Jebu's initiation into the Zinja, years ago. He started to bend to prostrate himself. Taitaro and Yukio thought he was fainting and caught him. Kublai looked into his eyes and held up his hand.

"No need for you to bow, monk. Come back when you have healed, and you can prostrate yourself nine times, as is our custom. You are a strong, brave warrior. I can well believe your father was a Mongol. If I could not tell it just by looking at you, I would know it from your deeds." The men around Kublai and Jebu rumbled their agreement.

"If I stand before you alive tonight it is the training of my Order I must thank, as well as my Mongol blood," said Jebu hoarsely.

"Your Order interests me," said Kublai. "We Mongols need better answers to the everlasting questions about life and the world and the gods better than our shamans can give us."

Jebu shrugged. "We Zinja do not worship, my Khan." The torn muscles of his left arm throbbed without respite.

"No gods at all? What a bleak existence. I wonder how you can be such fierce fighters without any gods. The most ferocious warriors we've encountered have been the believers in one god, like ourselves and the Moslems and the Christians. But we will discuss religion, perhaps, when you're better. Tonight I tell you I am sorry I've failed to render you full justice."

"In sparing my life you have been amply just to me, my

Khan," said Jebu. But Kublai Khan's words gave him hope
that the Khan would listen with favor to his petition. Jebu's
heart beat faster.

"Yukio," said Kublai Khan. "How many men did you
lose before Uriangkatai stopped the fighting between your
men and Torluk's?"

Yukio bowed. "Nearly three hundred, my Khan."

"You will be paid in gold from my treasury for each man.
And I shall place six hundred men from Torluk's *tuman* under
your command. You will train them in your way of fighting."

Torluk, who had been silent for the most part since he
entered the Great Khan's *yurt*, spoke up. "My Khan, with all
respect to your wishes, Mongols will be unwilling to serve
under a foreign officer."

Kublai turned his depthless black eyes on Torluk. "You
will pick the six hundred yourself. Some of your best had
better be among them. You will make it clear that any who
fail to serve loyally and obediently under the *tuman-bashi*
Yukio will have their left hands cut off and be cast out of the
ordu."

Torluk's eyes went blank. "Yes, my Khan."

"Now," said Kublai. "What of Jebu here? You do me
honor to stand before me, but I must not keep you on your
feet longer. You have suffered greatly at Arghun's hands."

"Arghun was simply obeying the laws of your people, my
Khan," Jebu rasped. "You owe me nothing. You have lifted
the condemnation of my family and me, and I am content."
He framed his words carefully, fighting down waves of dizziness and nausea that threatened to hurl him to the floor of the
yurt. To make no claim on justice, to appeal only to the Great
Khan's generosity seemed, in its nakedness, most in keeping
with the Zinja way. He knew that to want anything as badly
as he wanted to be reunited with Taniko was not the Zinja
way, and perhaps he was doomed to failure because of that.
But whether he succeeded or failed, he had to act.

"What your family has suffered and what you have suffered has been at the command of my Ancestor," said Kublai.
"I may change rulings of his, but I will never suggest that it
was wrong of him to rule as he did. Still, you have served me
well, and you have been badly hurt. I wish to reward you for
your courage and steadfastness."

Now the Great Khan had formulated the issue himself. With the same certainty with which he wielded his sword in battle, and guided by the Self, Jebu spoke.

"My Khan, there is a great favor you could grant me if you are so disposed."

Kublai looked surprised, as if he had not expected Jebu to offer any suggestions. Then he smiled and inclined his head.

"If I can, I will grant your request."

Jebu's heart was pounding and the blood roared in his ears. "It is a little thing to the Great Khan, but a large matter to me. There is in the Great Khan's household a woman, not one of the Great Khan's wives. She serves him, in some small way. She happens to be a countrywoman of mine. She was someone I knew in the Sunrise Land. I ask the Great Khan to give this woman to me."

There was a moment of surprised silence in the crowded *yurt*. Kublai stared at Jebu. Then there were whispers around the room and laughter. Kublai glared at those who had laughed, and the silence fell again. Kublai's face was dark and sour. I've failed, thought Jebu. I've only brought his wrath down on Taniko and me.

"What is this woman's name?"

Jebu tried to bow, sending pain blazing through his chest and back. "Her name is Taniko, my Khan. She is of the Shima family of Kamakura."

There was another long silence, while Kublai contemplated Jebu.

"You dare ask me for one of the women of my household?"

"The Great Khan has many," Jebu blurted. "I thought he would not miss one." This time there was laughter in spite of Kublai's black looks. Even though the brash reply seemed foolhardy, Jebu saw that the Self had guided him right. The Mongol officers now sympathized with him.

"You abuse my generosity," Kublai rumbled. "How do you know this woman is in my household? Has anything passed between you?"

Jebu shook his head. "No, my Khan. I happened to hear of her presence with you. I do not know if she remembers me at all."

"You had better not be prowling around my women, monk.

Eternal Heaven knows that monks are the most perverted, lecherous, degenerate creatures alive.'' Kublai looked pleased as this brought laughter from his generals.

"If the woman means so much to my Great Khan, I will withdraw my request," said Jebu boldly. Kublai looked thunderstruck.

"Ask him for a horse instead, monk," an officer behind him guffawed. "With four hundred women he doesn't have time to ride horses." The laughter and jests were quite out of control now.

Kublai reddened. "I forbid you to speak anymore to me of this woman. Go away now and tend to your wounds."

Uriangkatai spoke up. "A warrior has a right to ask one great favor of his lord, my Khan."

Kublai's dark eyes darted to Uriangkatai. "He has asked," he said with finality.

Amid laughter and friendly advice, Jebu was carried from the *yurt* by Taitaro and Yukio. "Pardon me for saying it when you're so badly hurt," said Yukio, "but you're a fool."

Sinking into exhaustion, Jebu said nothing. It was hopeless. He had tried to win Taniko away from Kublai Khan and only succeeded in infuriating the Mongol ruler. No one knew better than Jebu how vindictive the Mongols could be. Doubtless, he would feel Kublai Khan's wrath. Probably Taniko would, too.

Perhaps it would have been better if Arghun had managed to kill him.

25

From the pillow book of Shima Taniko:

I have not seen Elephant since he went away to fight Arik Buka three months ago. He had more time for his women during the war than he does now that he has won. No one has mentioned to me the troops from the Sunrise Land, who must have fought in the great battle against Arik Buka at the edge of the Gobi. I wish the kami would send that white-haired monk to me again with news of Jebu's safety. Or Jebu himself. I seem to have spent most of my life wondering if Jebu is alive or dead.

Kublai spends most of his time moving his armies about on his western frontier. He may have new wars to fight soon. His dream of a universal empire is fading. When his brother Mangu was Great Khan he ruled unchallenged from the China Sea all the way to Russia and Persia. But during the civil war between Kublai and his brother Arik Buka, the empire started to break up. A cousin named Kaidu, who rules a desert khanate northwest of here between the Tarbagatai mountains and Lake Balkash, refuses to acknowledge Kublai as Great Khan and is threatening war. Another cousin, Berkai, who is khan of a Mongol nation called the Golden Horde in faraway Russia, is making war on Kublai's brother Hulagu in Persia. Kublai cannot intervene in that war because he can't go through Kaidu's territory without fighting him. So now the Mongol empire is really four separate khanates.

Perhaps because of this, Kublai has abandoned Karakorum, Genghis Khan's old capital in Mongolia. He is building a new capital beside the ruins of Yenking, which was the capital of northern China under the Kin Tartars. He calls his new city Khan Baligh, City of the Khan. The idea of a city

built by Kublai himself has everyone bursting with anticipation. Nothing he does is dull.

—*Twelfth Month, seventh day*
YEAR OF THE RAT

Kublai was in a strange mood tonight, Taniko thought. "Are
you troubled, Your Majesty? Would you like me to play for
you?" During the years of the war with Arik Buka, Taniko
had learned to play the Chinese thirteen-stringed lute. She
always brought it with her when she visited Kublai.

"I am not troubled."

"I am happy to hear that, Your Majesty."

"You may play for me."

Taniko plucked out a tune called *The Fisher Boy Urashima*,
singing it in her own language, which Kublai did not understand but enjoyed hearing. This was the first time she had
seen him in months. They were in his bed chamber in the
Great Khan's palace in the new city, Khan Baligh. Kublai
had just moved his women down from Shangtu for the winter.
Taniko had been longing to see him and was delighted when
he sent for her, but since her arrival he had sat sipping golden
wine, staring at a painted screen and hardly speaking.

The song finished, she tried to make conversation. "Many
of your people are said to be shocked at your building a new
capital in China instead of reigning in Karakorum. As for me,
I am happy to be in a new palace in a new city. Is it true that
the buildings in Karakorum are made of mud?"

Kublai smiled faintly. "To a Mongol, a mud building is a
very solid and permanent thing."

Taniko shook her head. "I cannot imagine that the Emperor who dwells here would be pleased with a mud palace."
The room they were in was similar to his bedchamber at
Shangtu, but larger. Green silk draperies hid the walls and
made a tent of the ceiling. Most of the cushions on the bed
were green. And in one corner of the room there was a screen
as tall as Kublai depicting a range of golden mountains, one
behind the other, topped with clusters of dark green trees.

"I am sure the houses in your homeland are all quite
beautiful." He was forever teasing her about the supposed

superiority of things in the Sacred Islands. It always made her uneasy. Tonight she did not feel like parrying him.

"They are mostly of wood and paper, Your Majesty. But they are very beautiful, yes."

"Do you miss your homeland very much, Taniko?"

"Yes, Elephant, I do."

"I could send you back."

Her heart stopped. She stared at him, unable to speak. What was he hinting at? Did this have anything to do with his strange manner tonight? Or was he just toying with her?

"I don't think there is any place for me in the Sacred Islands," she said. "Horigawa brought me all this way to get rid of me, and my family is doubtless thoroughly ashamed of me. Has Your Majesty grown tired of me?"

"Far from it. But I find myself wondering how you feel toward me."

That was a surprise. How could a man like Kublai Khan ever concern himself with the feelings of just one of his hundreds of women? True, he had always been considerate. He had been careful in the beginning not to lie with her until he felt she would receive him with pleasure. She had enjoyed their occasional unions over the four years since then. She had even started to hope that she would conceive, knowing that under Mongol custom he would then make her a wife, improving her status among his women and guaranteeing her a secure place in Mongol society.

"If you talk about sending me away, it must be that I no longer please you, Elephant."

"I only pointed out that I could send you back to your homeland, if you wish. After all, you were brought here against your will."

"Why this sudden concern for my happiness?"

"Do you know a monk named Jebu?" He was leaning forward, his face thrust so close to hers that she could feel his breath hot against her forehead.

At first Jebu's name was a meaningless sound, it had been so long since she had heard it uttered. It sounded doubly strange on Kublai's Mongol tongue. Then it penetrated her consciousness. Jebu. He was asking about Jebu. Her body went cold from head to foot.

Kublai said, "It's hard to tell under that powder you wear, but I believe your face has gone white."

Her heart was hammering and her hands were trembling. It was not only fear of Kublai. Not only that. It was Jebu suddenly becoming real for her again, when for so long he had only existed in her imagination.

But it was fear of Kublai, too, that possessed her. The memory of her first sight of the Mongols rose in her mind. The maid raped and beheaded on the road to Wuchow. Kublai's talk of massacres. The children who would only starve to death if they hadn't been killed, too. A Mongol officer had tried to kill Jebu when he was only an infant.

She stared at the huge form beside her. Cruel, unpredictable, vengeful. She was in his power, and so was Jebu. Perhaps Jebu was dead already.

"It is startling to hear a name from one's distant past," she said, trying to sound noncommittal. "Yes, I knew the monk Jebu. He is a member of the Order of Zinja. About twenty years ago, when I was a very young girl, he escorted me from Kamakura to Heian Kyo for my wedding to Prince Horigawa."

All these years I have known he was somewhere in this land of China, she thought. To protect both of us, I have been careful to avoid seeing him or even trying to find out anything about him. And what good has it done? It has only brought us to this moment. We were probably both doomed from the moment his stepfather, Taitaro, spoke to me in front of Bourkina.

"The monk Jebu is partly of my race," said Kublai. "That accounts for his red hair and gray eyes. My grandfather, Genghis Khan, had the same hair and green eyes. I did not inherit them. Mongols who have that coloring are known as the *Borchikoun*, the gray-eyed men. Jebu's father, Jamuga, was a *Borchikoun*. He was Genghis Khan's cousin, his blood brother and his enemy."

Taniko nodded. "To while away the time on our journey to Heian Kyo, Jebu told me a tale of a Mongol warrior who came to our islands to pursue and slay his father. That warrior was red-haired and blue-eyed."

"Arghun Baghadur," said Kublai. "Owing to several odd turns of fortune, this Jebu is now part of my army. After our defeat of Arik Buka, Arghun tried to have Jebu killed, and there was very nearly a second battle. The matter was brought to me for judgment. Jebu had served me well, and I withdrew the condemnation of his family pronounced by my Ancestor. The monk then had the colossal effrontery to ask me to give you to him." He continued to watch her closely.

For the first time in many months Taniko whispered the invocation to Buddha. Kublai's account of Jebu's boldness delighted her. But it sounded more and more as if had brought disaster down on both of them.

"Were you even aware that he was in this part of the world?" Kublai asked her.

Doubtless Kublai knew everything that Bourkina knew, and the two of them had probably guessed at a good deal more. Nor was there any way of knowing what Jebu had told Kublai.

"The night you were elected Great Khan, I saw his stepfather, who told me that Jebu had been at Kweilin and was well. Elephant, Jebu means more to me than I have admitted to you. He was the father of one of my children, a girl. She was killed by Horigawa. Drowned."

Kublai nodded. "That was your husband's right." His voice dropped to an almost-gentle whisper. "Tell me, Taniko, do you wish to leave me and go with this monk?"

Her next words, she knew, might condemn both herself and Jebu to death. So hard did her heart pound that she could scarcely breathe. To deny the truth now would mean spending the rest of her life imprisoned in a lie. She had often wondered why she did not feel drawn to suicide, as so many samurai men and women were. Even now she could never put the dagger to her own throat. But if Kublai wanted to kill her for what she said now, she was ready to die.

Still, there was no need to be rudely blunt about it. She chose her words carefully.

"Elephant—Your Majesty—I have been truly happy with you. When I was brought to you I was terrified, in despair. For five years you have been kind to me. You have been gracious enough to spend hours with me. You have honored me among the women of your household. If I were to spend the rest of my life with you, I could be content. But, to be truthful, I long to see the monk Jebu more than I desire anything else in this life. If I were to be reunited with him, it would be like being reborn in the Western Paradise of Amida. I cannot imagine that such happiness could ever be mine."

She paused. Kublai sat looking at her, his dark eyes unreadable. He's going to kill us, I know it. But I must keep on talking to him anyway.

"I'm not as bold as Jebu, Your Majesty. I do not ask to be restored to him. I make only one request. You may wish to kill Jebu for daring to raise his eyes to a woman of the Great Khan's household. You may wish to kill me for the longing for Jebu that I cannot help. Let us see each other once before we die. It has been so many years since I saw him last. Grant me this one mercy, if I have ever given you pleasure."

Still Kublai remained silent. She waited for the death sentence, waited for him to call the guards to take her away. She was no longer frightened. Having spoken aloud her feelings for Jebu, she knew a vast belief and a soaring happiness. Let Kublai do what he wanted.

He reached out and took her small, pale hands in his huge brown ones. She sat beside him with her head bowed. At first he held her hands gently. Gradually the pressure increased until the pain was excruciating. She gasped. Immediately, he let go.

He crossed the room to a silver wine spout in the form of a snake's head. At his touch a pale stream gushed from the serpent's mouth into his golden goblet. He drank, walking to the screen.

"When I was eight my grandfather took me campaigning in China. For the first time I saw trees. They looked magical to me, like giants with their arms uplifted to Eternal Heaven. When I went back to the steppes they seemed so dry and empty that I vowed I would never live there. Or, if I had to, I would plant trees everywhere. My Ancestor had quite the opposite vision. He wanted to cut down all the trees in China and turn everything into grassland.

"I love mountains, too. The plains where I spent my childhood are so flat. They almost frighten me with their vast distances. Soon I'm going to build my own mountain here at Khan Baligh. I'll cover it with trees. I will have one of every kind of tree that grows anywhere in the world dug up carefully and transported to my green mountain to grow on it. At the top I will build a green palace for myself and those closest to me." He turned away from the screen and looked at her sadly.

"You will not see it."

She opened her mouth to speak, but he held up a hand to silence her, and she bowed her head in submission.

"My moments with you have given me great pleasure. They have been fewer than I would wish, but I must divide myself among many women. You, I gather, would be happiest if you could spend all your time with one man. I have sometimes wondered what it would be like to want one woman desperately, as the poets sometimes describe it. When a man has many women at his disposal, as I do, he cannot want one of them very much. At least, not for long. I have discovered a little of what it is like to want one woman all to myself, since I learned about you and the monk Jebu. Suddenly, you have become very necessary to me. It is that way with me. If I owned the entire earth except for one little patch of desert, I would not care about anything at all but that bit of land I didn't possess.

"Before this monk asked me to release you to him, you were even then one of the most interesting of my women." He paused and clenched his fists. "Now that someone else wants you, it seems impossible to let you go. Never to hear you play and sing your strangely beautiful songs for me. Never to hear your tales of the islands you call sacred. Never to enjoy your special ways of giving pleasure to a man. Never to discuss the business of governing an empire with a woman as wise and witty as you. Impossible to give these things up."

He came over and sat beside her on the bed, taking her hand gently. "I have tried, with my women, to do something like my green mountain. I want every kind of woman from every land on earth. If I let you leave me, my household will be incomplete."

Taniko felt all the exhilaration that had followed her admission of longing for Jebu drain out of her, leaving a hopelessness as barren as the steppes where Kublai was born. "I understand, Your Majesty," she whispered. In truth, she did understand, but she hated him for seeing her as an item to be collected, like a rare tree.

Kublai stood up and went back to the screen. "You may go back to the women's palace, then, Taniko."

She bowed low and withdrew from Kublai's green bed-chamber. He stood with his back to her, his hands clasped behind him, studying the trees on the gold mountains.

26

It was kind of the Great Khan, she thought, to let her ride. The wooded parks of Khan Baligh were lightly blanketed with snow, and the wind from Mongolia was piercing. Taniko, Bourkina and Seremeter all wore ermine cloaks and caps. Bourkina, thought Taniko, was along to guard her, of course.

She wouldn't try to escape. At least here in Khan Baligh she could hope that Jebu was somewhere nearby. She could hope that the Great Khan would grant her request and let her see Jebu once before the blow fell. This was where she wanted to be.

The women rode in silence. These dark, snow-dusted cypresses were very like the painted ones on Kublai's bed-chamber screen. They rode along a winding path that emerged at intervals from the trees and gave them a view of the new capital. A few months earlier the marshy plain around them had been uninhabited. Now the marshes had been drained and lakes formed. Walls were rising, encompassing an area three times the size of Heian Kyo. In the center, wagonloads of earth and boulders were being dumped to form Kublai's green mountain. Palaces had been built, and the foundations of more were laid. A stream of carts carried lumber and stone to the building sites. Even the war elephants were pressed into the work, pulling roughhewn stone columns for the grand facades.

North of the palace grounds a hastily built town had sprung up, crammed with officials, ambassadors, artisans, missionaries, merchants, courtesans, diviners, thieves and hangers-on. To the west, stretching endlessly over the undulating plain, were the rows of *yurts* that housed the army guarding the capital and the Great Khan.

"That way lie the ruins of Yenking," said Bourkina, pointing southward. Taniko did not answer. She remembered Kublai's description of the sack and burning of Yenking in the year of his birth. His were a cruel people. Right now Kublai and Bourkina were doubtless enjoying her suffering, while she wondered what would happen to her. And what had Kublai done to Jebu?

"There is an interesting new Tibetan lama temple up to the left," Bourkina said, "but I'm tired of temples. As a Buddhist, I'm sure you'll want to visit it, Taniko. We can part here. Seremeter can ride with me to see the view."

"Wouldn't you like to come with me, Seremeter?" said Taniko, a little catch of fear in her voice.

"Temples make me sad," said Seremeter. "They only remind me that there is no place here where I can pray to Ahura Mazda."

"Come, princess," said Bourkina, and they rode off without giving Taniko any more time to talk.

They're going to finish me now, she thought. That's why Bourkina brought me into the park. The executioners are waiting for me.

She hoped it would be a quick death, not some degrading fate such as being sold to a brothel keeper. There wasn't much chance of that, though. Such houses wanted girls barely out of childhood, not middle-aged women of thirty-three. It never ceased to amaze her that Kublai Khan had found her interesting, aging as she was. That was what made it hard to understand his need to possess her, his unwillingness to let her go to Jebu.

Above the trees ahead of her towered a circular white pagoda, roofed with a flat sheet of copper from which were suspended a thousand small bells. The bells transmuted the cruelty of the wind from the steppes into music. She could hear them even at this distance. Strange that Kublai would

choose this pleasant temple as the place where she would
suffer his jealous wrath.

Stranger still, as she thought about Kublai, that her years
with him had been happy. Not as happy as those with Kiyosi,
not even as happy as her childhood in Kamakura. She had
always been aware, with Kublai, of the taint of blood on
everything the Mongols did. Still, they had been fascinating
years, spent close to a powerful and sagacious man whose
decisions affected the rise and fall of kingdoms. She had
always known that this happiness hung on the slender thread
of Kublai's favor. That thread had finally snapped.

She rounded a bend in the path and saw a horseman
blocking her way. Her heart gave a little leap of fear. He was
a tall Mongol wearing a fur cap and a heavy gray cloak. His
red moustache drooped down on either side of his mouth,
giving him that look of sullen 'ferocity so many Mongols
wore. His eyes were as gray as his cloak.

He went on staring at her without a word. Was he her
executioner? Or just some officer to whom she was to be given
as a slave?

At last he said, "The waterfowl circles eternally, having
found no place to land."

The waterfowl? He had not spoken in Chinese or Mongol.
He had spoken in the language of the Sunrise Land. Words
she had not heard in years. She knew the voice. She looked
again at the face, and knew it, too.

She sat on her horse with her mouth hanging open foolishly
and began to cry.

"He was willing? He permits us to—"

"Yes," he said softly. "It really is so."

He gave his piebald pony a jolt with his knees, Mongol
fashion, and it leaped forward, bringing him to her side. With
easy power he lifted her out of her saddle and set her down in
front of him. He slapped her horse on the rump to send it
away, and then they were galloping down another of the paths
that wound through Kublai's park.

Her heart was pounding in time to the horse's hooves. But
it was also flying joyfully over Khan Baligh. She was still
speechless. She ought to say something to him. So far all she
had done was weep and babble incoherently. His words about

the waterfowl were so beautiful. But he had had time to prepare. He had known this was going to happen.

Suddenly she was angry at him. She tried to turn in the saddle and speak to him, but he held her too firmly, and she could not turn all the way around. The wind tore the words from her lips.

"Stop, stop." He heard her and gave the pony another nudge in the ribs. It came to an immediate stop, with the perfect responsiveness the steppe horses were famous for, if you knew how to ride them. Clearly, Jebu did.

"What is it?"

"You were waiting there for me. You knew long before I did. All the time I was dying over and over again for both of us, you knew." She struck her fist against his chest.

He smiled down at her. "Until just this morning, I, too, was dying again and again."

Now she was laughing, still turned in the saddle, her hands gripping his cloak, melting against him. "Jebu, I'm going mad, I'm so happy."

Jebu said, "In the Order we are taught that those who pursue happiness are pursuing an illusion. Those who think they have found it, have found an even greater illusion. Now I think the Order is wrong. For what I feel this moment I would gladly trade all of my life up to now and all that is to come."

Taniko was faint, dizzy with astonishment and joy as she felt his body—real, solid, there for her to lean against.

"You are no illusion."

She turned completely around to him. They held each other tightly, ignoring the slight, nervous dancing of the horse. He bent down and put his lips on hers. His mouth felt strange to her. She had not expected that. The bristles of his moustache scratched her lips. For all these years she had been living with a memory. This was a real man, a man in many ways completely new.

They were not the same people any more. It was hopeless. She had been deceiving herself. The Jebu who had lived in her heart all these years was no more real than the Buddha of Boundless Light.

But was not the Buddha a reality? Then she should not lose

faith so quickly in this man, whom she had found again after so long. She must not lose him again.

All these thoughts raced through her mind in the interval of the kiss. She drew away from him and looked up into his gray eyes. They had not changed.

"What will we do now?"

He smiled. "Whatever we like. i've had no time to plan. This morning the *orkhon* Uriangkatai sent for me and told me that the Great Khan had decided to grant my request."

"The Great Khan. He never even bade me farewell," said Taniko, feeling a strange disappointment in the midst of her happiness.

"I saw, when I asked him to reunite us, that it would not be easy for him to do it. Until this morning I didn't believe he would. We have much to talk about, you and I. We can't talk very well on the back of a horse."

"No." She nestled against him. He had not changed so very much after all. He was Jebu.

"If it pleases you, we can go to my *yurt*. It is in the army encampment."

"It pleases me," she said, squeezing his hand tightly.

They rode slowly down the path under the cypresses. Quail hiding in the underbrush darted away with a thrumming of wings. The trees were full of birds attracted to the woodlands because they were not hunted there. Deer and smaller animals whispered through the trees. Only the Great Khan and those he invited to accompany him were permitted to kill any animals here. He had not chosen to hunt since the park was enclosed, so the birds and animals felt safe.

They spoke no more as they rode out of the woods and down the road to the army camp. Thousands of horses grazed on the gentle, grassy hills.

Riding with Jebu along the rows of *yurts*, Taniko remembered her first entry into Kublai's camp five years ago. There was the same quiet, orderly buzz of activity. But the camp she entered today was a peacetime camp, and there were many women and children about. Taniko saw them staring at her. Some of the men greeted Jebu with a shout and a wave, eyeing her and turning away with small smiles.

It was hard to believe that he lived in a *yurt* like any

Mongol warrior, but he was opening the wooden door to his round gray felt tent.

"There will be others to greet you in a while," he said. "But I asked them to give us some time alone. Please honor my miserable tent, Lady Shima Taniko."

She smiled, walking daintily through the door. She did not have to stoop to enter a *yurt*, as most Mongols did. When she was inside she burst into tears again. He was beside her quickly, closing the door. Lamps were already lit.

He held her in his arms. "What is it?"

"It's just that it's been so long since anyone has spoken to me in our language, addressed me politely as we do at home. I never knew how much I missed it. I would not let myself know. And to think that of all people, the first one to speak to me in my own language after five years should be you, Jebu. It's too much of a blessing. I can't believe my good fortune. Help me to sit down. I feel dizzy."

Jebu took her arm to steady her as she dropped to her knees on the carpet. She looked down and saw that the design in the rug was as elaborate and colorful as any she had seen in Kublai's palaces.

"Let me make *ch'ai* for you," he said. He lit a charcoal fire and placed a cast-iron pot of water on a tripod over it. He brought a low black jade table out from the wall and set it before her. He sat across from her, waiting for the water to boil.

Taniko looked around the *yurt*. The floor was covered with layers of rugs as rich as the one on which she was sitting. Silk hangings divided the domed chamber into several small rooms. A statue of a Chinese goddess smiled benignly at her. It appeared to be made of solid gold and was decorated with jewels.

"You seem to have forgotten your austere Zinja ways," she said with a small laugh.

"I had also forgotten how beautiful your laughter sounds," he said, looking at her with shining eyes. "Yes, I've accumulated a great quantity of treasure. I do not plan to keep it. The Great Khan was most generous to his victorious troops. Especially to me."

"Do you want to keep me with you, Jebu?"

"My lady, that will be as you wish."

"You asked the Great Khan to give me to you."

"I phrased my request that way because it is the only sort of request he would understand. In his world, everyone belongs to someone else. What I wanted him to do was simply to release you from captivity."

Taniko made herself look at Jebu carefully to see how much he had changed. She had not wanted to do that, because seeing the changes in him would force her to admit the changes in herself.

His face was thin, with a hard mouth and hollow eyes that could have belonged either to a wild desert warrior or a mountain holy man. The chin was sharp, the cheekbones jutting. There were innumerable tiny creases radiating from the corners of his eyes, wrinkles put there by years of squinting into sun and wind. Thank Buddha, though, he was free of any horrible battle scars such as so many veteran warriors bore. Deep creases ran from the corners of his nose to his mouth, partially buried by the thick red moustache. The moustache itself and the hair on his head, which was shaved in the middle and gathered in plaits behind his ears, Mongol-style, were beginning to show streaks of gray.

He hadn't aged badly. But what about her? A woman of her age was good for nothing but raising a man's first children while he went out and got some more children on younger women. He had asked for her because he remembered her and felt sorry for her. It was an act of kindness, nothing more.

Jebu said, "Do you remember, ages ago, how we looked over Heian Kyo from Mount Higashi and I swore to you that I would be yours forever?"

"Yes," she whispered. She was crying again, but the tears were flowing gently, like a soft spring rain, not like the storms of weeping that had gone before.

"And you said to me that the lilac branch would always be there for the waterfowl," he went on.

"I remember that," said Taniko, thinking sadly how little difference those promises had made. He had not been there when she needed him. He had wandered all over the world seeking battle, after the way of his Order. And though she had not forgotten him, she had been there for other men as much as for him. There had been Kiyosi and Kublai Khan. Truly, compared with those two, with each of whom she had been intimate for years, what did this man who sat across the black jade table mean to her?

He, too, had loved a memory. He had risked all to win that memory from the Great Khan. And now, doubtless, seeing her in the timeworn flesh, he was bitterly disappointed.

"I've just been thinking," Jebu said, "how marvelous it is that we've managed to keep those promises in spite of everything."

"We have?" It was just then, conscious of the tears on her cheeks, that Taniko remembered she was nearly devoid of makeup. The facial paint suitable for a lady of Heian Kyo was just a nuisance on a morning ride. Not only was she aged and ugly, but he was seeing her without the protection makeup might have afforded.

Jebu said, "To think that so many years could have passed and you could be so far from the Sunrise Land, and yet I was able to find you and restore you to your people. To think that after all this time and over all this distance you still wanted to come to me." He paused and looked at her, troubled. The tea water was bubbling. He poured it into a glossy green bowl over a small heap of finely ground leaves. Setting the bowl on the table between them, he whipped the beverage into a lather with a bamboo whisk and offered it to Taniko. All this time he kept his eyes on her.

"I have wondered—there is something I have feared. I must speak of it to you and set my mind at rest. There was a sound of doubt in your voice when you spoke of how we've kept our promises to each other. The thing I fear is that you might have been happy with Kublai Khan, that you might not have wanted to come to me."

"Didn't you think that living among the Mongols was the worst thing that could happen to me? Horigawa did."

"Obviously, he assumed you would be treated as a slave. Did you truly want to go from the palace of the Great Khan to this warrior's *yurt*?"

"How can you doubt it, Jebu-san?" This was the first time she had called him by that affectionate term since that night at Daidoji.

Jebu shrugged. "I don't know what passed between you and Kublai Khan. He has many, many women. The day he triumphed over Arik Buka, Arghun came within a hair's breadth of killing me. The Great Khan in his triumphant mood wanted to show me some favor to compensate for my suffering. I asked for you. Perhaps he gave you no choice in the matter.''

She dabbed at her tearstained cheeks with the end of her sleeve. "He asked me what I wanted. I told him I wanted to go to you." She sobbed. A lady does not weep in front of a man, let her eyes puff up and her nose turn red. This was hideous.

Jebu poured and whisked more tea for her. She took the bowl from him gratefully.

"Why so much crying? Are you sure you don't wish you were still with him?''

"Perhaps it is you who wants that?''

"I don't understand.''

"Look at me, Jebu. Do I look anything like the woman you left at Daidoji? I was sixteen then. That was seventeen years ago. I've lived another whole lifetime. You wanted me back because you remembered what I was then. Look at me as I am now.''

Jebu frowned, a sadness coming into his eyes. "Are you trying to persuade me to send you back to him?''

"I don't want to go back to him,'' she said violently. "If only I could believe that you want me.''

He put his teacup down and took her hand. "Look into the core of your being and see the Self shining there, as I do when I look into your eyes.''

"You are deceiving yourself.''

"Am I? When Kublai Khan spoke to you of leaving him, did he seem eager to part with you?''

"He was so angry, I thought he was going to kill us both. Jebu, he asked me if I wanted to leave him for you, and I told him the truth. I told him that I had been happy with him. And I must tell you that, too, Jebu. I was happy with Kublai Khan. I did not submit to him unwillingly. But more than anything else in the world, I wanted to be with you. I told him that. He was angry. He sent me away.''

"He was just as angry when I spoke your name to him and asked him to let you come to me. Like you, I thought it might mean the end of our lives. Like you, I was overwhelmed when I discovered this morning that he was going to reunite

s. Kublai Khan was deeply unwilling to let you go. We may ever know why he decided to. Do you think he was deceiving himself?''

''What do you mean?''

''He saw something in you that he did not want to lose. You may think I'm just an impoverished monk whose mind is oftened by too much meditation and addled by too many battles, but is the Great Khan of the Mongols such a fool? He who has his pick of hundreds of women? Or is it just possible hat you are a lady to be desired?''

His words perplexed Taniko. Perhaps she was thinking like a petulant child. He was right. She did kindle desire in men. She felt a warm glow within, rising from that thought. But then another explanation for Kublai's attitude came to her, and the glow died away.

''He didn't want to let me go. He told me so himself. No matter how unimportant or undesirable a place or a thing is, if he doesn't have it, he wants it. He's like his grandfather. He wants the whole world and every person in it.'' She looked down at her tea and sipped it. She did not want to look at Jebu.

''There is only one way I can convince you.'' A smile was in his voice. He stood and moved around the table. He took her in his arms.

At first she didn't want him to see or touch her. She felt old. Her body was used, worn.

A coldness filled her. All right, let him have his way with me, she thought. It's as he said. Everyone belongs to someone. No, that is just how Kublai Khan saw it. I was his toy, his little creature.

Jebu doesn't want to possess me. He wants to show me that I am desirable. I am wise, I am witty, I am beautiful. That's what Jebu is trying to tell me with his hands and his body. But no, it can't be, not after seventeen years. It is not me he is doing this with. He does not see me as I am. There's a vision that only he can see. He wants to find his Búddha in me. Almost always, these things of the bed are things of the mind.

In spite of herself, she was gliding, like a ship that had slipped its moorings, like a horse given its head, like a falcon unleashed. Past and present swirled together until it seemed that she was with Jebu on the hill overlooking Heian Kyo, with Jebu in the murderous, pitch-black night at Daidoji, with Jebu in the tents of Kublai Khan, all at once. This was really happening. Why it was happening no longer mattered.

Joy filled her body and her mind. She was beyond asking any question. The delight of being with him, the only man in the world, was a happiness that consumed her entire being like fire. It was the boundless light she had so often called upon.

She heard voices, hers and his, mingling together, but could not tell what they were saying, if they were saying anything, or if they were just crying out without words. The light within her was dazzling. The *yurt* around her was plunged into blackness. Her body dissolved.

They lay side by side on the beautiful carpet, each listening to the other's breathing. She felt as if they were drifting across a lake on a dragon barge on a golden afternoon. She could not remember ever having known such peace, such completeness.

Then the doubts crept in again. He had proved to her with his body that he wanted her. But still he might have given himself over to illusion. She could never be sure that he wanted her as she really was.

There were scars, not on his face but on his body. He wore strips of cloth wrapped tightly around his chest. A scar, still red, completely encircled his neck. He had a hideous wound in his left arm. The skin was puckered and blackened around it, drawn together with some kind of stitching. Gingerly she touched the arm.

''What was this?''

He shrugged, looking deep into her eyes with his gray ones. Odd, that eyes of such a color could radiate such warmth.

''One of Arghun's riders gave it to me during the battle last month.''

''It was Arghun who killed your father. He was the Mongol warrior you told me about on the journey from Kamakura to Heian Kyo.''

''Yes, and not long after I left you at Daidoji, he came back and tried to kill me again.''

''You have so much to tell me, Jebu. So many years have

one by. I have no idea of the adventures you've had in the
ears we've been apart. You must tell me everything, from
he moment you left Daidoji. Take seventeen years to tell it,
' you like. We have the time.''

A strangely haunted look came into Jebu's eyes. "Yes. I
vill tell you everything. There is so much. It will take
while."

"What disturbs you, Jebu-san?" she smiled. "You need
ot tell me about the women you have known. I'm sure there
ave been many."

He did not smile back. "I must tell you everything. In
ime."

A shadow had fallen. She did not know what it was, but
here was something he did not want her to know. She could
ot imagine the Jebu she had known on the Tokaido Road
wanting to conceal anything. Much had happened to him. He
had changed. She had changed. Once we find out how much
each of us has changed, she thought, whatever was between
us before might be severed.

She was a happy woman, possibly happier than she had
ever been at any time in her life. Yet even this happiness was
shot through with veins of uneasiness, doubt, fear and sadness. She had not known that happiness would be like that.
She must write a poem about it.

27

From the pillow book of Shima Taniko:
I have known how the Great Khan lives. Now I am
finding out how the warriors of the Great Khan live. Jebu
has servants who cook and clean for him. Like the Mongols,
he drinks mostly milk and eats cheese. The Mongols eat

veal and mutton only on special occasions. Jebu says that cattle, goats, sheep and yaks are their wealth, so they prefer to live on the products of these animals, rather than butcher them.

All of us from the Sacred Islands have had to learn to eat meat, may the Buddha forgive us, but we eat a good deal less of it than the Mongols do, and we buy celery, onions, beets, beans and rice from the farms around Khan Baligh, so we can eat somewhat as we are used to.

I do not believe any woman of my country has had a chance to describe so many different places and ways of life as I have. Of course, this pillow book of mine can have no literary value. How could it, when it is written in the language of women?

This is a Mongol camp rich and at peace, located beside the capital of the empire. A very unusual state of affairs. I can see trouble for Kublai unless he embarks on a new war soon. The Mongols do nothing but hunt, gamble, chase women and get drunk. They seem to do more drinking than anything else.

I hear, though, that Kublai intends to make war once again on the Sung. That means that Jebu and Yukio and their samurai comrades will be fighting against those they formerly defended. Since the Sung courtiers betrayed them at Kweilin, I'm sure Yukio and his men have no qualms about aiding the Great Khan. Kublai has proved himself a good master to us all.

—*Second Month, second day*
YEAR OF THE OX

Taniko and Jebu spent their first three days alone together. Then he took her riding to the north, where the Great Wall crossed Nankow Pass. Even though it would soon be spring, the wind from Mongolia was bitter. They both wore fur caps, and Jebu protected himself in a heavy sheepskin coat, while Taniko wore the magnificent ermine cloak Kublai Khan had given her.

For two nights they slept and ate at a small Buddhist temple just south of the wall, where the monks knew Jebu. They spent three days riding or walking along the top of the ancient earth and stone rampart built a thousand years earlier

y the First Emperor, Ch'in Shih Huang-ti, to hold back the
arbarian horsemen to the north. No soldiers patrolled the
all now. China belonged to the barbarian horsemen.

"It was built to keep the Chinese in as much as to keep the
omads out," Jebu told her as he helped her over the broken
nd jumbled stones. "Poor farmers in northern China have a
endency to drift away from the Emperor's control. They
ither become nomads themselves or ally themselves with the
omads."

"Like you and Yukio," said Taniko.

Each day she felt more at ease with Jebu. They talked with
leasure and interest, but it was obvious to Taniko that Jebu
referred not to talk about what their lives had been like
uring the many years they were apart. Probably, she thought,
e wanted to avoid mentioning Kiyosi and Kublai Khan, to
ay nothing of Horigawa. A man doesn't like to think about
he men who have been before him with the woman he cares
or, men who may have been important to her.

She was just as happy that he kept talking about such
matters as the antiquity of Chinese civilization, Buddhism and
Taoism, the Great Wall, the Mongol conquests, what the
world was like far to the west, what might be happening now
in the Sacred Islands. These were things about which they
both had thought much, and had much to say. It was too soon
to tarnish the joy of their coming together by talking about
their own recent past.

As for their feelings about each other, their words and acts
when they were alone together said all that was needed.

After they returned from their excursion to the Great Wall,
Muratomo no Yukio came to visit them. On being introduced
to the young Muratomo, Taniko felt a momentary flash of
hatred for this short, pleasant young man, handsome except
for his bulging eyes and protruding front teeth. It was during
Yukio's escape from Hakata Bay that Kiyosi had met his
death. Even though Yukio doubtless had had nothing directly
to do with it, she could not forgive him the death of Kiyosi
and the loss of Atsue.

Yukio stood in the doorway of Jebu's *yurt* and bowed
deeply. Taniko placed her hands on the carpet before her and
returned the bow with a lower one of her own. He was, she
supposed, of better family than she. Again she thought how

pleasant it was to return to the formal manners of her peopl
after knowing nothing for so long but the simple ways of th
Mongols.

"Lord Yukio, I had the honor of knowing both your mothe
Lady Akimi, with whom I served at the Imperial Court, an
your distinguished father, Captain Domei. Also, I once ha
occasion to meet your older brother, Lord Hideyori."

Yukio's face lit up in a broad grin. "You are my angel."

"Excuse me, Lord Yukio? Angel?"

"My mother told me about you. It was you who helped m
mother meet Sogamori and persuade him not to kill m
brother and me. You are the lady who saved my life." Yuki
dropped to his knees and pressed his forehead against th
carpet.

Taniko sat demurely with her eyes cast down and her hand
folded in her lap. "I did not save your life, Lord Yukio. You
mother, Lady Akimi, saved your life at the greatest persona
sacrifice. She became the consort of a man she detested."

"I was a child at the time," Yukio said gravely. "My
mother made me swear that I would never fail in my gratitude
to the gracious Lady Shima Taniko."

"Sit down and have a bowl of *ch'ai*, Yukio-san," Jebu
said. "You have all afternoon to express your gratitude."

"The rest of my life would not be time enough," said
Yukio as he sat down with them at the black jade table.

Taniko remembered the morning eighteen years ago at
Daidoji when she had confronted Yukio's older brother,
Hideyori. She recalled the boyish charm of his wish to see her
behind her screen of state and his cold anger when she
mentioned this young man, his half-brother, Yukio. How sad
that Sogamori had commanded Hideyori's death.

"I'm sorry, Lord Yukio, but you owe me no gratitude,"
Taniko said as she poured boiling water into a cup with the
fine ground *ch'ai* leaves and whisked the green liquid into a
foam. "Please forgive me for saying so, but my family has
always been an enemy to yours. We are Takashi, after all."
And besides, because of Kiyosi she did not want his gratitude.

"Things aren't that simple, as you know well, Lady Taniko,"
Yukio said with a smile. "Not only did your intervention help
my mother to make her painful bargain with the vile Sogamori,

but your father, Lord Shima Bokuden, has sheltered my brother in Kamakura ever since my father's defeat and death.''

"Quite true," said Jebu. "I took Lord Hideyori to Lord Shima Bokuden myself.''

"Oh," said Taniko, looking down at her bowl of tea. She was tempted to remain silent, but she reminded herself that Yukio was a friend and ally of Jebu. She knew something of the utmost importance to Yukio, and it was her duty to speak.

"Please forgive me, Lord Yukio, but my father no longer shelters your esteemed brother.''

Yukio narrowed his eyes. "What do you mean?''

"When I tell you, it may give you such pain that you will forget all about gratitude and will hate the Shima family.''

"Please," said Yukio anxiously. "What has happened to my brother?''

"I do not know for certain," said Taniko. "Prince Horigawa kept me a prisoner before taking me to China. But I heard from a servant that Sogamori had ordered my father to execute your brother.''

Yukio's eyes, wild with shock and anger, transfixed Taniko. "Why? Why, after he let him live all those years, would he kill my brother?''

Taniko looked down at her hands and said softly, "Excuse me, please, for mentioning it, but Sogamori's eldest son, Takashi no Kiyosi, was killed in the fighting when you left Hakata Bay, Lord Yukio. Sogamori was quite maddened with rage and sorrow, and I was told he ordered the death of your brother as his only means of avenging himself on your family.''

Slowly Yukio turned his head and gave Jebu a long look. At last he said, "It should have been I. Better if I had died, rather than Hideyori. Now the clan has lost its chieftain.''

"Now you are the chieftain of the Muratomo," said Jebu.

Yukio looked at Jebu with an agonized wonder in his eyes, like a horse wounded in battle that must be killed to spare it pain. Jebu looked back with almost as much suffering.

Yukio stood up. "I must leave. I must be alone for a time." He bowed quickly, turned and hurried out of the *yurt*, his hand on his sword hilt.

Good, thought Taniko calmly. Suffer a little, Yukio, as I have suffered each day, remembering Kiyosi's death.

Jebu sat looking after Yukio, then turned to stare at Taniko.

There was such anguish on his hard, rawboned face tha Taniko reached out and took his hand. His hand lay in hers cold and lifeless.

"Don't reproach yourself for Hideyori's death. Sogamori i the one to blame. He gave the order to execute Hideyori Nothing you or Yukio did need have caused that."

A light came into Jebu's eyes. "Do you really think so?"

There was a knock at the door of the *yurt*. Jebu was stil staring at Taniko. She had been about to answer his question. but the knocking distracted her. It came again and this time Jebu heard it and called the visitor to enter.

It was Moko. Taniko had not seen him in the seventeen years since he fled Daidoji. Her heart leapt at the sight of the crossed eyes under a red Mongol cap with long ear flaps.

Moko threw himself full length to the floor and kissed the carpet in front of her. He was sobbing and wailing loudly. He looked up at her once, shook his head and then fell into a fresh paroxysm of weeping.

"Forgive me, my lady," he choked out at last.

"I would be weeping, too, Moko," said Taniko gently, "except that I've used up all my tears in the last few days."

"Oh, my lady, you have suffered so. But now you and the *shike* are together at last."

Taniko took Moko's hand and guided him to the place Yukio had just vacated. "So you're still with him, Moko. I wonder how a useful citizen like yourself could find employment wandering about with this monk who is little better than a bandit."

Moko laughed. "The *shike* has made my fortune for me, lady. The Great Khan has been most generous. We are all rich." His face fell suddenly. "Those of us who are left alive." He bowed his thanks as Taniko handed him a bowl of *ch'ai*, then turned to Jebu. "*Shike*, I saw the Lord Yukio come out of your *yurt* a moment ago with a face like the sky before a *tai-phun*. What's wrong?"

"Lord Yukio has learned that his elder brother is probably dead," said Jebu.

"It means he is the last of his line," said Taniko. "Think of it. Captain Domei had five sons. One would have supposed the future of the Muratomo to be quite secure. Now only Yukio is left. How quickly war can destroy a family."

How quickly war had destroyed her own family. Odd, that Yukio had said no word of sympathy to her about Kiyosi's death. He had known Kiyosi at the Rokuhara, and had known that she was Kiyosi's consort. Perhaps Yukio felt too ashamed to speak to her about it.

"It is difficult for me to feel sorry for Lord Yukio," Taniko said suddenly. She realized at once she had said more than she wished to. To explain the remark would mean telling Jebu just how much Kiyosi meant to her.

"He has just learned that his last living brother was killed," said Jebu.

Taniko thought quickly. "Yes, but I once met Muratomo no Hideyori. He made it quite clear to me that he felt no love at all for his younger brother. He was at pains to point out that he and Yukio did not have the same mother, and that Yukio's mother, my friend Lady Akimi, was not married to Captain Domei. Since Hideyori had so little liking for him, I'm surprised that what happened to Hideyori matters so much to Lord Yukio."

"However Hideyori may have felt about Yukio, Yukio always looked up to him," said Jebu. "He admired Hideyori, and always reminded us that Hideyori was the true chieftain of the Muratomo clan."

"My remark was foolish," said Taniko. "Forgive me." But she saw Jebu eyeing her closely. One day, Jebu, I shall tell you how much Kiyosi meant to me, she thought. How, in some ways, the loss of him was more painful than the loss of you. Because for ten years Kiyosi and I were nearly husband and wife. We had a son together, Jebu, a beautiful boy. Then one day an arrow flew and all was lost.

She must change the subject before Jebu asked her any more questions. She turned to Moko, and noticed something she hadn't seen before.

"Moko. Your teeth."

Moko smiled broadly. Where there had been dark, empty spaces in his grin, there were now white teeth that gleamed like peeled onions. Proud of his new smile, he held it for Taniko.

"Is this some sort of magic?" Taniko laughed.

"When one is part of a conquering army, my lady, rich with the spoils of war, one can purchase anything, even new teeth. These were made of ivory for me by a Chinese sculptor. I thought of having him carve me a set from black jade, but I decided that would be getting above my station.''

Taniko peered more closely at Moko's mouth. ''Ivory. Yes, I see now. They're a little too perfect to be real. Are they comfortable? Can you eat with them?''

''Better than I could without them. There are various minor problems, but on the whole I am a better man. The ladies who know me think so as well.''

Taniko smiled. ''So, Moko, you have followed Jebu to China, just as you once promised. Have you had much chance to exercise your skills as a carpenter?''

Moko nodded happily, pouring himself another cup of *ch'ai* and whipping it to a froth. ''Lady, I now know more about carpentry than any joiner on the Sacred Islands. Everywhere we have traveled I've studied buildings and talked to the members of the local carpenters' guild. I've even learned how they build their mud-brick palaces in Mongolia. And I don't just know about houses, my lady. I've studied junks and sampans from one end of China to the other. I believe I could build you anything from a Nan Chao dugout canoe to a Linan seagoing merchant vessel with sixteen masts.''

''Or a warship,'' Jebu remarked.

''Of course,'' said Moko. He looked uneasily at Taniko. ''But I have no desire to build warships. Useless things, except for destruction and killing.''

He's remembered that Kiyosi died aboard a warship, Taniko thought. A memory came to her. Long ago she had sent Moko to the Rokujo-ga-hara to see the executions of Domei and his followers. Moko had come back with a tale of having been seen by Kiyosi in a tree above the Emperor's head and having been spared by him. Yes, Moko, too, has reason to mourn Kiyosi, she thought.

''I've also performed many services for our samurai,'' Moko went on. ''I was in charge of food and supplies. I learned to bargain with Chinese traders and get the most and best for the least money. I also helped the shike's father, the holy man Taitaro, to treat our sick and wounded.''

Taniko said, ''Your honored father, Jebu, yes. Why have I not had a chance to pay my respects to him?''

Jebu shook his head. ''He's on another one of his mysterious journeys. He said he was meeting with members of the Chinese and Tibetan branches of the Order.''

"I owe much to the shike and to you, my lady," Moko said. "I'm going to do something for you now that will speak my gratitude in a small way."

"Moko," said Jebu softly, "you owe us no debt. Your companionship has been treasure enough."

"Yes, Moko-san," Taniko agreed. "You have saved my life many times over."

The little man waved his hands. "No, I'm going to build a house for you. I'll design it, I'll provide the materials. I'll hire the workers. It will be the most beautiful house in Khan Baligh. Not the biggest or the most costly, but I think that with what I know about building it will make the Great Khan himself envious."

Taniko was torn. She knew how much giving such a gift would mean to Moko. She could not refuse it. But it seemed to her too grand a gift to accept.

"You will shame us with such a gift," said Jebu.

"You will shame me if you do not take it," said Moko, his eyes glistening with tears.

"Excuse me, but I don't think there will be time for this gift. Perhaps, Moko, it would be best for you to plan to build this house in Heian Kyo." It was Yukio who spoke.

They turned and stared at him. He was standing in the doorway of Jebu's *yurt*, a grim smile on his face.

"Forgive me for entering without knocking," Yukio said. "I have been walking about, thinking, since I left you. I have accepted my karma. I am now clan chieftain of the Muratomo. I am the last of my line. If the Muratomo are to be avenged on Sogamouri, it must be through me. These wars in China have prepared me for the task. There are less than three hundred left of our countrymen who followed us here, but we have over two thousand warriors in all, and many of them will follow me for battle and for pay. I will not waste myself fighting the Sung, when I could be fighting my real enemy, Sogamori. When we return home, we'll find a whole new generation of samurai waiting for us. Those Muratomo who were boys when we left will be men now, and ready to follow the White Dragon. 'A man may not remain under the same heaven with the slayer of his father.' It is time to go back and settle accounts.''

"But how do we know this is the right time to launch a war in the Sacred Islands?" Jebu said.

Yukio waved a hand in dismissal. "There are many such questions still to be answered. We will talk long into the night for many nights to come. We will have to get permission from the Great Khan to leave at all. But our course is clear. Muratomo no Yukio and his samurai are returning to the Sunrise Land. From this moment the Takashi are doomed."

Jebu, Moko and Taniko stared at Yukio, overwhelmed by the announcement that had fallen among them with the impact of a Mongol fire bomb. Sadness and dread swept through Taniko. Must Jebu and I lose each other again as he goes off to another war? Her dread was not only for herself and for Jebu, but for the Sacred Islands. When she thought of the bloodshed and destruction that would follow Yukio's return, she wanted to weep. In a few months many women would have more cause to weep than she did now.

28

It was late afternoon. The distant ruins of Yenking and the new parks and palaces of Khan Baligh were enveloped alike in a golden haze. From this height in the Western Hills, Jebu and Taniko could see the entire plain on which three dynasties had built their capital cities.

"Khan Baligh is strange—elaborate and gaudy," said Jebu. "They don't have our sense of beauty."

Taniko smiled up at him and raised an eyebrow. "They, meaning the Mongols? Then you don't consider yourself a Mongol?"

Jebu shook his head. "By upbringing I am a man of the Sunrise Land."

"Now that I know something about the Mongols," said Taniko, "I know that you are a child of the sun goddess, the same as I." She rested her small hand on his as they leaned together over a low wall around one of the terraces of a half-ruined temple.

A cloud descended on Jebu's spirits when she mentioned her knowledge of the Mongols. Long before their reunion he had wondered what Kublai Khan meant to her. Now, except for oblique references like this, she had told him no more about the subject. She had voluntarily left Kublai Khan to be with him, of that he was sure. Why wasn't that enough for him?

Hand in hand they walked away from the wall and into the violet-shadowed inner chamber of the temple. This had been a temple to the Reclining Buddha, the soul of the Buddha sleeping in heaven before beginning his life on earth. Mongols had destroyed it fifty years earlier, when they first swept through the plain of Yenking under Genghis Khan. Kublai Khan was planning to rebuild it, along with all the other ruined temples in the area. At the moment it was still abandoned.

The central chamber of the temple was empty. The bronze statue of the Buddha that had lain there had long since been broken up and melted down. Dust-covered frescoes showing the Enlightened One at various stages in his life were unharmed. The destruction of the temple had been an act of war, not of desecration. The Mongols respected Buddhism, just as they respected all religions.

Jebu spread a blanket he had brought with him on the marble pedestal where the statue had lain. He took Taniko's hand and drew her down beside him. How beautiful you are, he thought. How beautiful my life is, that it brings you to me.

"You're not thinking of lying with me here, Jebu-san? This is a holy place."

"That's precisely why I chose it. The union of bodies is the height of holiness. I see that I still have not fully explained the teachings of our Order to you." He reached around behind her to undo the obi at her waist.

She put her hands inside his robe, caressing his chest. "Explain later."

When they returned from the Western Hills a few days later, they found that Taitaro had come back. He was waiting for them in Jebu's *yurt*.

"Of all the pleasant sights I've seen in my life, I can think of none that brings me more delight than the two of you together."

Taniko looked down at the intricately patterned carpet of the *yurt*. Jebu said, "One day we will ask you to bless our wedding."

"But not yet," said Taniko. "Unfortunately I have another husband still living."

"I promise you I will attend to that when we return to the Sunrise Land," Jebu said.

"A Zinja is not vindictive," Taitaro warned.

"I know," said Jebu. "You're going to tell me to spend more time with the Jewel."

"What is the Jewel?" Taniko asked.

"One of the thousand all-important things I haven't yet told you about," Jebu said. "Have you heard of Yukio's plan, sensei?"

"Yes, and I've come here to take you to Yukio's *yurt*. He says he has something important to discuss with us. You'll recall I was granted the vision of Yukio returning to the Sacred Islands in glory."

"Then you approve of our going back?"

"We must drink the happiness of each moment, not mixing it with the unhappiness of the future."

Jebu was about to say that he didn't understand when Taniko spoke up. "I live in horror of the day Yukio sets foot on the Sacred Islands, Taitaro-sensei. The war he will bring upon our land will make the battles the Takashi and the Muratomo fought before look like children's games."

"I agree with you, daughter," said Taitaro. "For hundreds of years my Order had hoped gradually to put an end to the bloodshed in our land and other parts of the world. Now that I've seen the wars of the Mongols—the kind of war Yukio will fight when he goes home—I think that was a vain dream."

* * *

The thousands of hammers at work in Khan Baligh rang incessantly through the warm spring air. The building of the new capital began at dawn and continued until sunset every day, and some of the laborers worked on into the night by torchlight.

Nearer at hand, smoke rose from the center hole cooking fires of the long, disciplined lines of gray *yurts*. Children ran up and down the streets playing games. A band of older boys on ponies galloped down the center of the street with wild whoops, forcing Jebu and Taitaro to jump to one side. Herds of the shaggy steppe ponies, the mounts of the Khan Baligh garrison, grazed without fence or tether in the nearby hills.

All these sights have become so familiar to me, Jebu thought, that the land where I was born will seem strange when I first set foot on it. There are no prairies for grazing there, no warriors in felt tents. How small our islands seem in comparison to the vast spaces of China and Mongolia.

Taitaro broke in on his thoughts. "It pleases me to think I might become a grandfather."

Jebu sighed. He decided that Taitaro was the one person to whom he might confide his problem. He unfolded what he knew of the story of Taniko and Kiyosi and then told how he had killed Kiyosi in the battle of Hakata Bay.

"How much did this Takashi heir mean to her, do you think?" Taitaro asked him.

"I can't be sure, sensei, but she probably cared for him greatly. When her life must have seemed over to her, he brought her a whole new life. She does not know that it was my arrow that killed Kiyosi. How can I tell her?"

"You must eventually come to it," said Taitaro.

"Only Yukio, Moko and I know that I killed him," said Jebu. "Taniko need never know."

"Quite true," said Taitaro. "But if she never knows, what is between you and her will be a lie. Remember that both you and she are manifestations of the Self. The joining of male and female in body and mind is one of the most effective ways of breaking through the illusion of separateness. If there are barriers of deception or concealment between mind and mind, the union will fail. Illusion will be kept alive. You will be depriving her, as well as yourself, of the highest joy of which human beings are capable.''

Jebu watched two young men wrestling on the ground in front of a *yurt* while a crowd cheered them on. ''Perhaps it is not necessary to achieve such supreme joy.''

Taitaro stopped walking, turned to Jebu and smiled, his long white beard fluttering in the breeze from the northern steppes. ''You have the right to make that decision for yourself. Do you wish to make it for her as well?''

Yukio's *yurt* was twice as large as most of those in the encampment. The entrance faced south and was covered over with a canopy. An honor guard of two samurai stood before it, and the White Dragon of Muratomo fluttered above it. He has always been a great commander, Jebu thought. Now he is beginning to assume the trappings of one, as well.

Recognizing Jebu and Taitaro, the guards ushered them in. Jebu stopped inside the door to give his eyes a moment to adjust to the lamplight. Yukio sat on cushions in the host's quarter of the *yurt*. A large, hunched figure sat on a bench facing him. Both men turned.

The man with Yukio was Arghun Baghadur.

Arghun rose to his feet and bowed to Jebu and Taitaro. Jebu stood still, speechless with surprise. Yukio broke the silence.

''The Great Khan's decree has ended the enmity between Arghun and Jebu, and therefore between Arghun and the rest of us.''

''I hope this is true for you as it is for me,'' said Arghun, fixing his blue eyes on Jebu.

Jebu's head spun. How could Arghun dare visit Yukio's *yurt*, decree or no decree? How could Yukio bring himself to receive him? He was certain Arghun's eyes held no friendship. They were, Jebu was convinced, incapable of expressing anything but cold ferocity.

Finally he said to Yukio, ''The Great Khan rescinded the order of his Ancestor which obliged Arghun Baghadur to hunt me down and kill me. I do not recall that the Great Khan required me to forgive Arghun for killing my father or for trying again and again to kill me, to trust Arghun or to sit in friendship with him. Not long ago you yourself were saying, Yukio-san, that a man may not live under the same heaven with the slayer of his father. Even if I do not seek vengeance on Arghun, since we're under the Great Khan's law, how can I sit in the same *yurt* with him?''

"What if I ask you to?" said Yukio quietly. His eyes were watchful.

Jebu could not believe what was happening. "Can you forget that this man caused the slaughter of hundreds of our samurai? Can you forget how he treacherously sent ten thousand men against us under the pretense of being on our side?''

"I have not forgotten that the *tarkhan* Arghun has been a dedicated, tenacious and nearly invincible foe. Nor have I forgotten that it is the duty of a general to listen to all points of view. I ask you and your wise father to listen to what Arghun has to say. Please do me that courtesy.''

"Of course," said Jebu through tight lips.

"Please sit down."

Jebu drew over an ebony stool inlaid with mother-of-pearl horses. Taitaro sank to a cross-legged position on the floor.

Arghun said, "Some years ago you and your men found yourselves unable to live as samurai on your islands. You decided to go abroad and offer your services as fighting men to the Emperor of China. You will understand, then, the position I am in. It has become impossible for me to continue as a warrior in the army of the Great Khan. Therefore, I am doing what you did. I offer my services and those of my followers to Lord Yukio."

Jebu was stunned. "You have the audacity to offer to ally yourself with us after you tried to kill all of us?''

Arghun looked at Jebu gravely. "It happens quite often that leaders in war ally themselves with those they previously were trying to kill.''

"As for audacity, it is a very valuable quality in a military leader," Yukio said with a smile.

Taitaro said, "It will show a great deal of audacity on your part, Lord Yukio, if you accept this offer."

"Why would a *tarkhan* who commanded a whole Banner now stoop to taking orders from the leader of a people he has always despised?" asked Jebu.

Arghun held up a broad hand. "I have always admired

your people, shike Jebu. I greatly enjoyed my stay among them."

"Yes," said Taitaro dryly. "During which you served the Takashi."

Arghun shrugged. "It was necessary for me to serve the Takashi. I was hunting Jebu, who served the Muratomo. Tell me, old monk. Your Order hires out its members to fight for various masters. Does a Zinja always go through life serving on one side of a conflict? Or does he change sides as his Order commands him?"

Taitaro nodded. "He may well change sides many times. But I still do not understand why you wish to change from Kublai Khan to Lord Yukio, when you enjoy rank, wealth and power as it is."

Arghun's seamed face darkened. "You do not understand my position. The Great Khan publicly disgraced me. I devoted much of my life to trying to carry out a command of Genghis Khan, and his grandson mocked me for it. I do not wish to go to war against the Sung as an outcast. When I heard that Muratomo no Yukio had received the Great Khan's permission to take his contingent of foreign troops back to the Sunrise Land, to renew his war against the Takashi, I decided that I wanted to join him. I helped Kublai Khan become Great Khan, but I no longer wish to serve him." He lowered his voice. "I do not respect him. I would sooner fight in a foreign land and even die there than watch our empire turn into something I loathe."

"Jebu, if I were to take Arghun into our ranks, could you set aside your enmity toward him?" Yukio said.

"Forgive me, Lord Yukio," said Jebu, "but you would be mad to accept this man's service."

Arghun shrugged his wide shoulders and stood up. "I have said what I came to say. Lord Yukio, I leave my future to you. Consult with your friends and advisers. I will wait to hear from you."

Jebu was relieved. Perhaps now he and Taitaro could talk some sense into Yukio.

"One last thing," said Arghun. "Your force consists now of about two thousand fighting men. If you accept me, I will not come to you empty-handed. There are many Mongols who are personally loyal to me. There are many who fought for Arik Buka and who do not want to fight for Kublai Khan. You could return to your homeland with considerably more than two thousand men.''

There was a light in Yukio's eyes. ''How many more?''

''An entire *tuman*,'' said Arghun with a faint smile. He bowed and was gone.

The three men in Yukio's *yurt* were silent. Jebu studied Yukio in the flickering lamplight. His eyes burned with dreams of victory and vengeance. He would be impossible to convince, but Jebu had to try. He waited for Yukio to speak first.

''Ten thousand cavalrymen.'' Yukio breathed.

''You should have asked.'' Jebu said slowly, ''whether they will be the same ten thousand who tried to slaughter us at the edge of the Gobi.''

Yukio leaped to his feet and stood over Jebu, his fists clenched. ''Would you deprive me of victory? With ten thousand Mongols fighting for me, Sogamori won't have a chance.''

''What makes you think your samurai will fight alongside the Mongols who only recently tried to kill them?''

''My samurai have fought side by side with Mongols for the last four years.'' Yukio sat down beside Jebu on the bench and put his hand on Jebu's shoulder. ''I know how you feel. This goes back to your father. But I didn't know your father. You yourself never knew him. Look at the gift Arghun brings us. Can't you put this old enmity away?''

Jebu turned and stared into Yukio's eyes. ''As easily as you could ally yourself with Sogamori.''

Yukio was silent, breathing heavily. At last he stood, paced a bit over the thick Chinese carpets, and said, ''Sogamori is the enemy of the realm, not merely my enemy. I fight him, not for my personal revenge, but to save the Sacred Islands from misrule.''

''If you embark with a *tuman* of Mongols under Arghun, you will be leading a Mongol invasion of our Sacred Islands. Arghun's men will so outnumber yours that you will have no control over what they do.''

Yukio sat down again. ''Jebu, people were wretched under the Takashi when we left. Now they've had five more years of misery. The moment I land and raise the White Dragon, samurai will flock to me from every province. Soon Arghun's *tuman* will be only a part of my forces. I will use ten thousand to deliver the first blow, a devastating blow from which the Takashi will never recover.'' Yukio stood once more, walked to the center of the *yurt* and turned to Taitaro.

"Sensei, you have not spoken. I know that to their skill in the arts of combat the Zinja add sagacity. Do you see what I can accomplish with Arghun and his troops? Or do you share your son's blind hatred of Arghun?''

Taitaro smiled. "As we say in go, I have the advantage of the onlooker and can see things that are not apparent to the contestants. Though I have, on occasion, fought Arghun, I bear him no ill will. Even so, Lord Yukio, I believe you would be mistaken to accept Arghun's services. He is one of the most dangerous men I have ever seen. I have been the channel for a vision of your triumphant return to the Sacred Islands. But believe that your victory will be marred by sorrow and defeat unless you act with purity.''

Yukio frowned. "Purity? Do you mean I must land on the Sacred Islands without any foreign warriors?''

Taitaro folded his hands in his lap and looked down at them. "You have over two thousand warriors whom you have gathered yourself, trained yourself, led yourself. They are loyal to you. Most of them are foreign, but they are still a fighting force that is purely yours. They have had samurai training and samurai leadership. Arghun's ten thousand, on the other hand, are a borrowed, foreign power. They are not truly your men, and you will not be able to control them. Unleashing a horde of barbarians on the people of the Sacred Islands can only bring you infamy.''

Yukio shook his head. "You think as your son does.''

"On the contrary.'' Taitaro stood; walked over to Jebu, and looked down at him. "Jebu-san, I heard the hatred and vengefulness in your voice when you spoke to Arghun tonight. You have made no progress in your feelings about him in the eighteen years since you fought him at the Waterfowl Temple.''

"Your counsels are impossible, sensei.''

"They would be worth nothing if they were easy.'' Taitaro turned back to Yukio. "I know that you, too, find my advice hard to act upon. But if you do not follow it, all will end in ruin for you.''

Yukio shrugged. "I told you years ago that a military

commander who puts his stock in omens and visions is likely to lose. I'm sorry, sensei, but nothing you say has changed my mind. I will make the bargain with Arghun, and you two will learn to live with it, if you want to stay with me.''

Jebu's heart sank. ''Yukio, would you choose Arghun over me?''

Yukio turned his back. ''Yes,'' he whispered. ''Because he brings me ten thousand warriors.'' He whirled on Jebu and Taitaro. ''Again and again you two monks have tried to do my thinking for me. It's time you learned there can be only one commander in an army.''

''When you land on the Sacred Islands with your *tuman*, be sure that you, and not Arghun, are that one commander,'' said Jebu.

''I want to be alone now,'' Yukio said hoarsely.

Taitaro and Jebu bowed and said good night.

As they walked under the stars Jebu said, ''This is a calamity. I was hoping you could persuade him, sensei.''

''I knew I wouldn't,'' Taitaro said. ''My vision at the *Ch'in-cha* temple in Szechwan already warned me that I would fail. There will be a dark side to Yukio's triumph, and nothing can prevent it.''

29

Twenty seagoing junks lined the riverfront of the city of Haitsin on the north China coast, two days' ride from Khan Baligh. Each ship was capable of carrying two hundred soldiers and as many horses. There were not enough ships available on the coast to transport Yukio's entire force at once, so the warriors had been divided into five groups that would leave different ports on different days. The first ships were to leave Haitsin on the fifth day of the Third Month.

The night before the sailing, Yukio gave a banquet for his officers at the largest and best inn in the city.

"Tell him I've gone to burn incense at the temple of Niang niang for a successful voyage," Taitaro said. "I've had quite enough of Mongol feasts." Niang niang was a local goddess who had originated as a sea-captain's daughter. The sailors of Haitsin brought models of their ships to her every spring.

The inn was a three-story building fronting on Haitsin's largest marketplace. Two Mongol officers were fighting on a second-floor balcony as Jebu approached. One pushed the other over the railing and he fell into a crowd of gaping onlookers below. One who may not make it to the ships tomorrow, thought Jebu.

The junior officers were dining and drinking on the lower floors. One of Yukio's men led Jebu to the top story, where those of the rank of hundred-commander and above were gathered. Jebu stepped through a gilded doorway and nearly choked on the smell of roasting meat. A roar of shouts and songs hammered at his ears.

Yukio's officers were seated on benches at long tables already awash with wine. Courtesans danced through the crowd, a few of them altogether naked. The warriors reached after them, pawed them and roared with laughter.

Jebu saw Yukio at a table set on a platform at the far end of the room. Yukio was dressed as the Mongols were, in a robe of embroidered Chinese satin. On the wall behind him hung a White Dragon banner. Shameful to display the Muratomo family insignia at a brawl like this, Jebu thought. In the Sunrise Land the room would have been quiet with, perhaps, music in the background. His host would have risen and politely escorted him to a place. Above all, there would be no stink of burnt flesh. Had Yukio forgotten all that? Was this what he wanted to unleash on his people? Jebu pushed his way through the crowd toward Yukio, and Yukio waved to him.

Just as he got to the table, two men sitting near Yukio looked up. One was Arghun Baghadur. The other was the *tuman-bashi* Torluk. Jebu felt his face grow hot. He expected to see Arghun here, but he hadn't known that Torluk was also part of Yukio's Mongol contingent. All he could think of was the memory of Torluk seated on his pony in front of his silent *tuman*, giving the signal to fire on the samurai.

"Jebu, sit by me," Yukio called.

It was past bearing. Jebu turned and began to push his way out of the room.

As he crossed the market square, he sensed that he was being followed. Port cities like this were infested with thieves. Also, there were secret societies of Chinese rebels that still harassed the Mongols. Jebu stepped into a side street and a hand seized his sword arm. Thinking he was about to be attacked, Jebu whirled with his hand raised to strike a killing blow.

The man holding his arm was Yukio. His brown eyes were furious.

"You embarrass me in public with your rude behavior," Yukio growled.

"Is it possible to be rude at a riot like that?"

"You are determined to destroy everything I am doing. Nothing means more to you than your hatred of Arghun."

"You mean more to me, Yukio," Jebu said sadly. "I still think you're making a mistake allying yourself with Arghun."

Yukio spoke more calmly. "I realize it is worry for me as much as anything that makes you act as you do. If it reassures you, I know Arghun and his Mongols are dangerous. It's just that there is a certain kind of risk a military man must take, if he wants to win wars."

They began to walk, side by side, down to the riverfront docks. Only the red and green lanterns on the masts of the junks lit their way. Jebu walked warily, keeping his hand near his sword hilt.

"Perhaps you're too concerned with winning and losing," Jebu said.

"That's one part of the Zinja philosophy I've never been able to accept fully," said Yukio. "What is the point of fighting if you do not try to win?"

"We fight because we choose to fight. We hope to achieve a state of insight which unites us with the Self."

"Is that better than winning?"

Jebu laughed. "It's something you can get whether you win or lose. That can be very convenient, sometimes."

Yukio laughed with him. "You realize, Jebu-san, you've

made me look like a fool, running after you when I should be with my guests?'' Yukio walked over to the river's edge and sat down, looking out at the water. "You are very important to me. You are so important I seriously considered giving up ten thousand fighting men, just to please you."

"You didn't consider it for a moment."

"Jebu, I've known you for fifteen years. The night I escaped from the Rokuhara, I probably wouldn't have reached the first farmhouse outside Heian Kyo without your help. You swore that night to serve me. You held out your sword to me. Ever since, you've kept me alive. You've given me strength when I was convinced the Muratomo were finished and was ready to cut open my belly. You sustained me through these years of exile. You've taught me your skills, given me good counsel, been my friend. I put all that in one scale and Arghun's *tuman* in the other, and you, by yourself, nearly outweigh the ten thousand men."

Jebu sat silently beside Yukio at the river's edge. He felt his eyes grow moist. The bright lanterns reflected in the river blurred. Mooring ropes creaked, and Chinese sailors called to one another.

"If you think so highly of me, why won't you listen to me?"

"Because in the most crucial moments of my life I can listen only to myself."

"Perhaps that's your way of achieving union with the Self."

Yukio turned to Jebu with appeal in his eyes. "You say a man does what he thinks he must do, and the desire to succeed must take second place. That is all I am doing. I may lose this war with Sogamori if I bring in Arghun and his men. But bringing in Arghun and Torluk and their ten thousand warriors is what I must do. It is an opportunity I cannot turn away from. The Mongols may betray me, but not until after we have conquered Sogamori. Then I will be invincible. Jebu-san, if you believe I am going into danger, come with me. In the name of all that has happened between us, do not force us to break with each other. I need you now more than ever. I am on the verge of winning. My whole life has been leading up to this moment. Stay with me now."

Ever since Yukio had announced that Arghun was going with them, Jebu had been thinking about the fact that he was well past thirty years old; in fact, he was closer to forty. Zinja generally retired from the field and often married after the age of thirty. He had found Taniko again. If they could overcome the obstacle of Kiyosi's death, why couldn't he and Taniko go to a Zinja temple somewhere and live as Nyosan and Taitaro had? Except that he would never leave Taniko as Taitaro had left Nyosan.

Jebu contemplated his dream. He looked into Yukio's wide eyes, saw the call for help in his face. He reached out and took Yukio's hand.

"When I first met you, I swore to serve you and offered you my sword. I will never take back either, the promise or the sword."

The next morning the samurai were out earliest of all. No one had suggested it, but by some unspoken agreement they all came down to the wharves to watch the sunrise. A fresh, sea-scented breeze blew up the river from the coast, gently rocking the anchored junks.

Yukio stood in the stern turret of the junk nearest the sea, the one that would be first to sail. It was an awesome ship, with seven raked masts. Flat-bottomed so it could navigate both rivers and ocean, it was unpainted and undecorated, as was customary among the northern Chinese.

Jebu stood beside Yukio and looked down at the samurai, less than three hundred of them, who had survived the years of China. Most of them had long since adopted the dress of Chinese or Mongol warriors, but on this day they were all wearing the battle dress of the Sacred Islands. They must have scoured their belongings to find every helmet, every breast and shoulder plate, every gauntlet and skirt they still had.

Yukio addressed them. Later he would be talking to all the warriors under his command, but he wanted to begin the day with a special word for the samurai. Gripping the railing, he leaned toward them.

"We fled the Sacred Islands five years ago, impoverished and defeated. Since then we have won victory after victory. We stopped a Mongol army at Kweilin. We helped Kublai Khan triumph over Arik Buka. We have learned new ways of fighting and the use of new weapons. We have been handsomely rewarded by the Great Khan of the Mongols, and the wealth we bring back with us will buy us power.

"We leave behind the ashes of many mighty warriors in this foreign land. Sakamoto Michihiko . . . Imai . . . Kiyowara . . . Tajima . . . Jomyo . . . Oba . . . Saito . . . so many others I cannot name them all. All their names are inscribed on the scroll of honor which accompanies us on our return to the Sacred Islands.

"During these years we have fought not just for ourselves but for the house of Muratomo. We now return to the Sacred Islands to overthrow Sogamori and his family, and we will call upon the brave men in all provinces to lend their efforts to the cause. We will rid the realm of Takashi tyranny. We will restore the holy institutions that have been abused or destroyed by the Takashi. We will win even greater glory for ourselves and our ancestors than we already have won by our deeds here in China. Today we sail into history."

He lifted his arms over his head, and the samurai shouted, "Muratomo!" three times in unison.

While Yukio was speaking, the rest of the warriors were gathering on the docks. Yukio came down from the ship, mounted his horse, and joined Arghun and Torluk in overseeing the assembly of their troops. Seated on the ponies that would sail with them in the holds of the junks, the Mongols formed a great half circle facing the ships. In front of each unit of a thousand men stood an officer bearing a standard on a long pole. The samurai took their position in the circle, the White Dragon banner of the Muratomo fluttering before them. To one side waited the noncombatants who would be sailing with Yukio's warriors, among them Moko and Taitaro, and, modestly hidden in a sedan chair, Taniko.

Horns sounded. An officer tied a long strip of white cloth to each standard. He brought the other ends of the strips together in the center of the half circle. Yukio, Arghun and Torluk dismounted and stood on the ends of the cloth strips. A shaman added another ribbon to those under the feet of the leaders. He tied the other end to the thigh bone of an ox and, gesturing with the bone, began a series of incantations in Mongol.

At this moment the ceremony was interrupted. A band of riders in black sable cloaks came thundering down the street that led from the outskirts of Haitsin to the docks. Arghun, surprised, reached for his saber as the riders swept down on them.

"Prepare! The Great Khan comes!" shouted one of the riders, an officer wearing a gold tablet.

Jebu expected to see Kublai Khan's elephant-borne tower. Instead a small group of men on horseback approached at a trot. He recognized Kublai Khan immediately, the man in the center of the group who was taller and darker than the rest. He had never before seen the Great Khan on horseback, but like all Mongols he rode as one born in the saddle.

Kublai Khan rode directly into the center of the assembly. He wore a long white satin riding coat and sat astride an unblemished white horse. One Mongol tribe of famed breeders supplied him with a thousand head of these horses each year.

Yukio, Arghun and Torluk immediately fell to their knees. In silence all the warriors dismounted. They knelt and stood nine times, paying homage in the Mongol fashion.

It made Jebu uneasy to see Yukio kneeling to the Great Khan at this moment. True, Yukio was still in the Khan's service, but he was about to become a new person by crossing the sea. No longer one of the Great Khan's warriors, but chieftain of the Muratomo clan.

Kublai Khan spoke in a voice that carried along the waterfront. "My hunting led me in this direction, and I remembered that my fierce warriors from the Sunrise Land were about to depart. I came to add my blessing to the shaman's. Let me not interrupt these ceremonies. Muratomo no Yukio, may Eternal Heaven grant you success in your war across the sea. May you crush your enemies, may you see them fall at your feet. May you know the great happiness of a conqueror."

Yukio was a tiny figure looking up at the Great Khan on his white horse. Jebu could see that his face was flushed with excitement. Bowls of mare's milk were brought to Kublai Khan and the three leaders of the expedition. They dipped their fingers in the milk and sprinkled it toward the standards. Trumpets shrilled and drums thundered. Three times the warriors—Mongols, samurai and others from many lands—

raised their war shout, shaking the walls of the warehouses nearby.

Kublai Khan waved a hand in farewell and rode his horse slowly across the open space before the assembled horsemen. He smiled and nodded as he passed Jebu, as he did to other men he recognized.

He passed close to the sedan chair in which Taniko waited. Jebu felt his heart lose the rhythm of its beat. He heard the Great Khan ask a low-voiced question of a kneeling attendant. The man answered, and Kublai nudged his horse over to the chair, reached down and swept the curtain aside. In our land that would be an offense deserving death, Jebu thought. In a cold sweat he heard Kublai exchange a few words with Taniko. Then the Great Khan let the curtain fall.

In a moment Kublai and his escort were gone. Now the warriors climbed down from their horses and left them to servants, to be led down wide gangplanks into the bellies of the junks. The men formed files and began to board the ships.

Yukio stood again beside Jebu on the deck of the junk. "The Great Khan spoke of happiness. It was a happy day when we escaped safely from the Takashi fleet at Hakata. But this is surely the happiest moment of my life, to be going home again."

Although Yukio's men boarded with Mongol efficiency, the sun was at the zenith by the time the fleet was ready to cast off. Yukio's ship was the first to push away from the wharf. The pilot shouted commands, a drummer on deck struck up a steady beat, and oarsmen strained. Slowly the junk swung into midstream, where tide and wind could carry it out to sea. Crewmen hauled on ropes, and sails rattled into place on the seven masts.

Later, Jebu stood alone in the bow of the junk. Yukio, restless as ever, had taken a small boat to visit and inspect the other ships in his fleet. There was a strong salt smell in the air, and seabirds glided alongside the junk. Jebu felt a presence close at hand, and turned. Taniko was beside him.

"Home," she said, her eyes sparkling. "I thought I would never taste the food of the Sunrise Land again."

"What did he say to you?" Jebu cut in.

Her eyes clouded over. "I do not like to remember what he said, Jebu." She stared, not back at Haitsin, now only a gray blur on the riverbank behind them, but ahead at the blue horizon. "He said, 'Do not forget me, little one. Tell the people of your small country what you know of me and my empire. I shall see you again.' Jebu, perhaps it is wrong for us to go back. We are carrying a flame with us. When Yukio steps on shore, he will set our homeland ablaze from end to end. We do not know whether the Takashi will destroy us or whether we will defeat them. But all the warriors in the Sunrise Land, Muratomo and Takashi together, would not make one wing in the army of the Great Khan."

He knew she was right at least in one thing: They were going from one war to another. But he took her hand and said, "We must act as our insight tells us, Taniko. We cannot avoid choice. And every action has its shining side and its shadow side."

"But, Jebu—" Beneath his hand, her own trembled. "He said he would see me again."

To be concluded in
LAST OF THE ZINJA
Book Two of SHIKE